The Sand Prince

The Demon Door Book One

Kim Alexander

Gaby -
Enjoy your trip
through the
Door -
K

The Sand Prince/ Kim Alexander

Dedication

For my parents.

Prologue

"Let us begin," said the Duke. "Talk to me of this wench. Is she fair? And if she is not, is her father a wealthy man?"
"The family has much land, and the girl is….young."
The Duke smiled, his teeth straight and white in a face darkened by many long rides on his great horse, Mammoth. "You may send for them."

-The Claiming of the Duke, pg 5
Malloy Dos Capeheart, Little Gorda Press (out of print)

Mistra City
Greenleaf Gate, va'Everly Residence

The Great Gorda River swung south out of the mountains and, having expended its energy on the downhill trip, turned itself into the Flat Gorda. Despite its new name it was actually at its widest, exchanging the cold peaks for the calmer midlands. With the great walls of the Guardhouse high above, you would need a good boat and the better part of an afternoon to cross the Flat Gorda, and hopefully a pole or a net, because the fish were fat and the water clean. After passing through farms and fields, the river turned east and changed its name again, this time to the Little Gorda. At this point you could exchange your boat for a pair of boots, because even at its outskirts, Mistra's builders had loved their bridges. Once inside Mistra City proper, it branched out in every direction, mostly little brother and sister canals seeking to rejoin each other on the road to the sea, but a few finally gave up, either too shallow or too narrow to find their way. If you kept your boots, you'd need them to follow the track of one such nameless canal past the Greenleaf Gate. If you were looking for a leaf or something green you'd best look elsewhere because there was nothing to see but the damp backs of buildings, slimy retaining walls, aged cobbles and one huge wrought iron gate. The lights from the house it protected were dim and distant at the top of a winding path.

At the bottom of the path and much closer to the canal than she would have liked, Lelet va'Everley—Lelly to her friends—was having what those friends referred to as a "High Snit."

On a normal evening, her driver gathered her at the front door, which, if she wasn't wrong, was the exact purpose of a front door. So why, she asked herself again, had she been rerouted to the Greenleaf Gate? She couldn't even remember the last time she'd come this way. Certainly the maid had been supremely apologetic in relaying his last minute change of plans, but Per would have to answer for this. The smell, for one thing. And there was mud on her shoes—her *white* shoes. She held her wrap up out of the dirt—that would be all she needed, stains and who knows what on silk, she'd have to ask Father for a new one. Maybe she'd do that anyway….

She thought she heard the moaning gasp of water brakes some distance away in the damp darkness. 'Crying brakes are happy brakes', she'd heard Per say that often enough, along with a million other little sayings—'A horse can tell,' for instance. *Tell what?* she'd always wondered. That she was going to be late and with dirty shoes and the smell of canal rot in her hair? *And* she was almost out of cigarettes—less than half a stack left. She abhorred the habit of twisting off the lit end and saving the rest for later but it was better than running out. She tucked the stub end neatly into the shiny little metal pocket.

She definitely heard a horse snort. It sounded annoyed.

"Finally." She continued composing her little outraged speech, and plucked up the hem of her white silk dress. "How many of us will have mud on our gowns tonight, Per? Is that what is done now, *Per*?" Spattered with mud wasn't festive but she was hoping it might turn out to be funny, particularly if Per tried to argue with her. Everyone would be wearing white tonight for the Quarter Moons party, but she imagined she'd be the only one with muddy satin slippers, white, black, and brown.

The trap had stopped well out of sight. She hissed between her teeth. "By the Veil, Per, you'll have to carry me on your back." She peered through the murk. Outside the half circle of smudgy torchlight at the back gate, it was quite dark. She took a step. Something breathed quietly in the darkness. Was that the horse? She took another step, two more, and walked into a wall. The wall moved, and before she could scream she found herself looking at her own feet, as she had been swung over a shoulder. One of her shoes lay shining and dainty on the muddy stones.

"Don't scream, wench. It will go worse for you."

Instantly she screamed long and loud, echoing between the leaning brick walls.

Did he just call me a wench?

She heard the wall? Person? Kidnapper? mutter something she couldn't understand—something about a Duke? He began to half-run into the dark alleyway, bouncing her head off his back. Her screams attracted the attention only of the rats.

My shoe! Someone will find it. She kicked off the other and tore at her dress, shredding the stiff little white satin roses from the fragile bodice. She could see them like stars on the black path, receding into the darkness.

She smelled the horse before she saw it, and struggled to twist around and face her captor.

"Please," she said quietly. "My family has money. You must know that. Whatever you've been paid, they will pay more. Just set me down and I'll walk away. No one will know. Let me go."

In response, the dark figure lifted her over the side of a cart. She felt herself falling as if from a great height. *He is tall.* She thought. *He won't let me go.*

Her head struck the side of the cart as she landed and then it got very dark and quiet.

Chapter 1

Eriis City
20 years earlier, Eriisai calendar
100 years earlier, Mistran calendar
Dzhura Square

"An orange? But what do you do with it?" Yaanda held the huge dimpled globe between her hands and looked at her mistress curiously. Hellne, the princess of the kingdom-city of Eriis, had only recently tasted the fruit for the first time, and took it from her maid.

"First," she instructed, "one peels off the skin. Then you may eat it. That's what it's for." She handed it off to their chaperone, a sour faced older woman called Beete, whose black robe stood in contrast to Hellne's sapphire and silver silks and her maid's floral headpiece. "It's a bit messy, though. Beete, would you mind?"

The woman glowered at them but began to work on the thick skin, juggling the orange and her shopping basket, full of whatever caught the princess's eye. Hellne was used to her sour face and ignored her.

"Madam, if you'll allow me, I'll have it done for the ladies." Beete gave it up with a scowl to a young man, the fourth of their party. He took the fruit and began dismantling it quickly and neatly. As he was the only human present, he had the advantage of experience.

"Malloy, you continue to astonish," said Yaanda. Hellne smiled sweetly at her maid and reminded herself to talk to the girl about familiarity when they had a moment alone. As it was, the market square was not the place for correction, since, as Hellne had intended, they were the center of attention. She knew she was overdressed for a day of shopping, but the jewels that held the veil to her hair caught the light in such a pretty way, who could blame her? And the glittering gems she'd fastened to her wings, she knew by the end of the week the girls who watched her through lowered lids and half glances would be flaunting bits of glass and shiny stones on their own leathery wings.

No, she thought, it was her obligation to draw as many eyes as possible when she ventured out into the Quarter. And today she offered a gift: not only did the residents get to see their princess and her retinue, but on this day the demons at the market square got to look at a human, and that was rare indeed. And if you had to look at a human, this was a fine one—young, and as pretty as they came. Of course, ‘pretty’ for a human was grotesquely ugly for a demon. Still Hellne had gotten used to Malloy’s looks, even to appreciate them. She smiled to herself. If her father or his counselor knew how much she appreciated them, there wouldn’t be enough of him left to sweep up. It was terribly exciting.

The woman who had presented her with the oranges was talking with Malloy—something about climate? And how it agreed with the trees. Trees? *Ah,* Hellne thought*, so that’s where the oranges come from.*

"The air," the woman was saying, "it moves all night, and the trees like that."

Hellne pouted. Just because he drew all eyes shouldn’t mean he was allowed to let his own eye drift away from her.

"Malloy, we’ll be late for dinner, I need to get ready." He nodded at the older woman and the party continued through the market. "I know, let’s make the orange a gift for Daddy. He loves things from Mistra." They all knew her father the King did not love things from Mistra, and did not care for the young assistant to the ambassador, most particularly. The human gave him no specific cause for complaint, though. Malloy was scrupulous in his behavior in public. This was not his first assignment.

"Yaanda, it needs to be the sage and gold for dinner, would you pull it down? I think it’s in the back closet. It may need a pressing." Yaanda was about to answer when Beete stepped in front of the group with her hand out. A bright, hot flame danced above her palm.

"Light, Wind, and Rain, Beete, whatever’s gotten into you?" Hellne looked around for an unseen assailant.

"This one," Beete nodded at Malloy, "was about to lay hands upon Her Grace’s person."

Malloy went pale, and with good reason. This was a serious offense.

"Pardons, Your Grace. And apologies for troubling you, Beete. I was offering Her Grace some of this fruit. I regret my hand came too close to her. I am in the wrong and stand corrected."

Beete frowned but then shrugged and flicked her wrist, putting out the flame. "Accepted, on behalf of Her Grace."

Hellne stared at Malloy’s near-panicked expression, and despite herself, she burst out laughing. Yaanda waited until she was sure it was safe and no one would be incinerated, and joined in. Malloy laughed with them, a good deal more weakly. Hellne, meeting Malloy’s eye, gave him a private smile. They had plans to meet that night, and he would do a good deal more than lay his hand upon her person. He tossed the half peeled orange into Beete's basket and they continued towards the palace.

Chapter 2

Eriis City
20 years earlier, Eriisai calendar
100 years earlier, Mistran calendar
Palace, diplomatic residence

After enduring a late dinner with the King, his Chief Counselor, the Princess, her brother Araan, and a collection of those currently favored by the High Seat, Malloy returned to his temporary quarters in a part of the palace far removed from the royal family itself. The king, unsurprisingly, had sampled a slice of the orange and pronounced it 'delightful' before pushing it aside. If it was up to the king, it was said, The Door, the mystical portal between Mistra and Eriis would be shut, locked, and boarded over. As the ambassador's assistant, it was Malloy's job to make sure that the king did not have his way, and part of that meant entertaining Hellne, because as much as the old demon disliked humans, he doted on his daughter, the princess. Malloy's father would have said the king let that girl run wild, a fact for which Malloy was grateful. He hadn't seen or spoken to his father in many years, a fact for which he was also grateful.

He wondered what his friends would say if he showed up with the demon princess on his arm back at the Guardhouse in Mistra. They were already asking a lot of questions—"Can they really shoot fire from their hands? Are they all red-eyed? Have you ever seen her wings? You've got to be twice her size! No wonder she likes you!"

He wished he could answer his friends with the truth of what it took to be the Princess' lover. She was so tiny, so delicate and perfect looking, he assumed he'd have to take great pains not to hurt her.

He was mistaken.

He found out for himself months earlier and shortly after his arrival. It was after one of the countless ceremonies, rituals, events, and parties that filled the days and nights of the royal family, and which he was expected to attend. In this case it was The Ceremony of Fire and Wings—the Viewing of the Moons (it had some longer, more complicated name in the old Eriisai tongue, but later he found he couldn't recall what it was). She'd allowed him to reach under the long brocaded sleeve of her black and scarlet gown and touch her fingertips with his own. That was when he knew she was his for the taking—on Eriis; one did not touch the hand of a casual acquaintance. Malloy figured it was because the hand was their primary place of power—their fire came from their hands (he spent a sleepless night trying to figure out how to use that in his writing, finally making his hero, the Duke, into an ex-bare knuckle brawler. It wasn't the same, but still). She looked over at him with that blank mask they all affected, and then gave him the barest suggestion of a smile. If she'd been offended, one of her father's guards would have escorted him back through The Door in disgrace if he was lucky, or to someplace called the Crosswinds, if he were not. From what he heard, there was no coming back from the Crosswinds, except in a dustpan.

The twin moons reached their zenith, one just below the other, and lit the rocky valley below the castle walls in stark, dramatic black and white. The demons and their few human guests murmured their approval. Everyone drank a glass of *sarave*, a sort of sweet wine, and then the King rose first and everyone followed him back into the castle to the receiving courtyard for the after-viewing party.

The courtyard was an open atrium at the heart of the palace, surrounded by many stories of private rooms, audience chambers, kitchens, and lecture halls. Directly behind the courtyard was The High Seat, the place of power, the seat of the king. Malloy got the impression you had to pass under the eyes of Light, Wind, and Rain (their local elemental deities) before you got to see the king. The whole structure formed a huge T. To reach the courtyard it was a straight shot down the main boulevard of the city itself, then through the Royal Arch, on into the palace and down the Great Hall. The Arch was carved into the wall separating the palace grounds from the city proper. Part of the inside face of the wall was left unworked. The demons loved that section of bald rock, decorating the space around it with statuary and ceremonial viewing stations. There was even a statue of the king himself, decked out like a warrior. The demons had gotten that idea from the humans, finding the thought of armor, plate, and helmets amusing. The king's statue was already old when Malloy arrived on Eriis, and there was much talk recently of Araan and a new king, and more negotiations. It was said that the king kept his wits only with the help of the Mages. These Mages, the native magicians, lived somewhere close by, under the ground, but he had never seen one.

Malloy knew there was some unspoken understanding of who got to live where on Eriis. It seemed to him that it was largely the whim of the royal family that moved their friends and followers from the Old City through the Royal Arch and into coveted palace quarters, and, if you didn't please your benefactor, that same whim could toss you back to the common folk just as quickly. He'd made the mistake of asking after a familiar, now absent face at dinner, and was answered with polite, blank smiles. There was no reply because to the demons, he had never spoken. *Here on Eriis,* he thought, *there really are no stupid questions.*

Hellne had bid her father a pleasant evening after only a few minutes at the party, and to Malloy's surprise, she'd vanished. He gave a mental shrug, he'd been wrong before, or maybe she was playing a little game. A tug on his sleeve and a slip of paper in his pocket proved him wrong. He didn't see who had delivered her note, but the invitation was in her hand, although of course unsigned.

He followed her directions, feeling very large and clumsy passing the elegant, slight men and women who actually lived there and knew where they were going. None of them quite looked at him—although that was just one more thing about them, they never stared. Still, it wouldn't do to look like he was lost.

Following her directions, he turned from the main hallway to a narrower one he recognized as mainly being used by her servants, and stepped out of the dim tunnel onto a nearly hidden, side entrance to her balcony. Her room was on a high floor and faced the Arch and wall and the city. If she wanted to, she could step off the edge and fly to the market on her little wings, but he knew she never would; that was considered vulgar. He'd been there before, usually with Araan or her father or maids and friends in attendance, but never at night, and certainly never alone. She'd lit the bowls of glowing stones they used instead of lanterns or candles, and he thought she'd never looked so pretty. In the soft light, her golden skin and red, tilted eyes glowed, and with her silky, black hair down, she looked almost human.

She greeted him with a smile—a real one—and they shared their first kiss.

She bit him.

"Explain to me again what you mean by 'hurt'," she demanded as he held a cloth to his wounded lip. And then, "No, I don't feel that at all. What are you even doing?" when he was recovered enough to demonstrate a human style kiss. To his relief, he found a human-like body with perfect breasts (a bit small for his taste, but he'd expected that) and slender legs (although not a single strand of hair) under her heavy silk gown. She allowed him to remove the garment and gently stroke her thighs to the part between her legs, and said that was called her *ama* and was to be treated with absolute respect. But when she reached for him with her hands full of a lovely blue flame, he screamed. That made her laugh.

"Do you want to scorch my cock off my body?" he asked, backing away.

"Cock." She tried out the word, then wrinkled her dainty nose. "That's unattractive. No proper person would say something like that. I believe you mean *yala*?" She extinguished her flame and he let her look at it—his *yala* now, he guessed—more closely. "It's fluffy," she observed. She looked up at him and down again, her brilliant red cat eyes reflecting the glowing rocks. He had a sudden fear she might bite him again, only in a more tender place.

Finally she shrugged. "I suppose the size will have to make up for your lack of flame. Are you absolutely certain you have no fire?"

Being her lover was like getting in bed with a gorgeous, potentially lethal animal. He craved her but he was also a little afraid of her. He had no idea how she felt about him, except that the invitation remained open. When she forgot herself and left him with a bruise or burn, he told himself it was her way of expressing passion.

That had been six months ago, and through innumerable viewing parties, performances that he could neither understand nor properly describe, dinners, bottles and bottles of *sarave,* and too many injuries to count, he understood her no better. But he didn't care. He looked at her delicate, lethal perfection and he thought he might be in love. And tonight he was going to prove it.

He'd finally finished his book: *The Claiming of the Duke*. It was everything he dreamed and the very best he could do: exciting, action packed, lots of drama, with complex, interesting characters that spoke with true and original voices—in other words, the book that would make his name and bring him the life he wanted. All that was left was to wait for the glowing reviews to come rolling in. In no time, he'd be out of the Guardhouse and living in a big house in the center of Mistra, giving lectures and writing his next book. He thought perhaps a thinly fictionalized version of his own experiences with the demons might make a strong follow up (in his mind, the main character was not a lowly assistant, but the ambassador himself, and the Princess was less violent and more ardent).

Until that day, though, Malloy toiled as assistant to the ambassador. It wasn't a glamorous position, but it gave him access to things. Interesting and important things. Some of the things were secrets. It didn't hurt to jot down a few notes, just in case. He'd give her the fruit of his best work today: his novel and his secrets. He hoped it would ease the sting of bad news: he was recalled back to Mistra, he would be leaving that very evening. He knew she'd be annoyed, he hoped she'd be overcome with grief.

Following the now-familiar secret passage to Hellne's balcony, he found her as he usually did, hair down and with the stone bowls softly glowing.

After joining (as they called it on Eriis) and taking a moment to make sure nothing was bruised or burned that couldn't be hidden, he said, "I have good news and bad news."

She folded her hands and waited, her face, as ever, unreadable.

"The bad news is I'm leaving."

He got a reaction, that was something—even a slight frown or a twitched brow was a victory.

"How dull," she frowned. "How long?"

"Not long. There's something going on back home and they need me there. But I'm leaving right away."

She gave a tiny sigh, reflecting a world of displeasure. "Hmm. You mentioned good news?"

"Ah! Of course." He handed her a small, flat package wrapped in bright silk. "I made this for you. It's the key to our being together. It's yours, now."

She held the package up and beamed at him, or more likely elected to let him see her approval. "I'll treasure it forever."

He silently cursed. He'd been so excited about giving her something so special, he'd forgotten her people had no tradition of wrapping gifts. At first she thought the pretty paper or fabric *was* the gift. But, as she explained to him, when someone handed you something secret, what then? Open it in front of them and risk a disappointed face? That would be unforgivably rude not only on her part, but on the part of the giver who had forced her reaction. He had to admit it made sense.

And sure enough, she slipped the unopened gift into the slashed pocket of her heavy gown. She'd changed out of the elaborate outfit she'd worn for their trip to the market earlier that day, a narrowly cut blue dress and some sort of see-through silvery veil. He could see a handful of discarded fabric on the floor peeking out from under the bed, where it would sit until Hellne's maid collected it. She'd left the jewels in her hair, even though the white and blue clashed with the brocaded sage and gold of her ceremonial gown. She fancied the stones and left them in place, barely holding together the coif of soft coils. The gown she wore, he knew, was her seventh best, reserved for the sort of state dinner they had just attended, notable only because it was delayed to wait for the return of the recently appointed Eriisai ambassador, a young fellow named Preeve, through The Door. Oddly, he hadn't appeared. That she had a seventh best gown—and a fifth, and a tenth—chafed, because the forest green cleric's robe and dark hose were all he owned. That they were in good repair and flattered his frame hardly helped. These people had a way of sizing you up without ever appearing to notice you, but he had no doubt that they noticed. The only balm was the way she'd undone the lacing—or rather, her maid had undone it—which left her exposed from the nape of her neck to the middle of her back, where her wings were tucked out of sight (he preferred them hidden, reminding him a little too much of the wings of a bat). The collar, layer upon layer of tissue thin fabric carefully arranged like flower petals—silk, he supposed—had come apart but still framed her face.

Even though they'd had this conversation before, about unwrapping gifts, she wasn't going to look at the book. She might be a beauty and certainly charming in her own strange way, but it was a good thing her father was in charge and her brother a capable heir. He tried to imagine her leading a negotiating session and laughed to himself. *Next time I'm here, I'll show her how it works. She'll have read my book by then, and seen what I wrote for her on the back page. Another gift—a little insurance in case idiots take over and they actually shut The Door.*

He pushed the thought of closing The Door for good from his mind. No one in the Order wanted to be responsible for letting the demons slip through their hands—not while there was still a chance to learn how they did their astonishing magic. In Mistra, at the Guardhouse, magic was something that took a lifetime to master, at the cost of literal sweat and blood. Of course, the demons smiled politely when the humans called it 'magic', to them it was like walking or breathing—just something you did. Fire, for instance, they all had that to one degree or another, and they used it both in sport and in bed (as he had come to learn, to his regret), and he'd begged Hellne to show him what was called her True Face, turning herself into a living, flaming weapon, but she acted embarrassed and changed the subject. Well, he'd be back soon enough and he'd show her what the book, his key, meant. Maybe as a reward she'd show him what she looked like, transformed. He thought that change, showing her True Face (and confessing her true love) might make a good climactic moment for his next book. *The Princess Revealed*, how was that for a title?

Would it be madness to think his affair with this lovely young lady would help to bridge the gap and bring real magic—magic that flowed from your hands, not dusty old books—into Mistra. Why shouldn't he be the one to bring that kind of power to the human world?

Aim high, he thought, or not at all.

He rose to his feet and stood next to her. The top of her head came up to the middle of his chest.

"I don't want you to worry. I'll be back as soon as I can. Look for me at dinner soon, as usual," he promised her. "These talks back at the Guardhouse can't last that long. They'll send me back very soon."

Was she worried? The Eriisai made the best card players he'd ever encountered: you simply could not tell what they were feeling. He found he was actually concerned—the Eriisai ambassador's absence and his sudden recall back through The Door to Mistra were probably coincidence, but it felt… off.

"I'll miss you." She affected a pout so he could see it. "It's boring without you. Just go and tell those silly old men what to do and come back to me."

They kissed.

"I'll see you soon, Hellne. This will all be over and we'll be together. I promise."

Neither of them could guess how long that would take.

Chapter 3

Eriis City
Three hours later
Under the palace

"Rushta!" Hellne swore. The stair was dark and she'd caught the heel of her sandal on the hem of her sage and gold brocaded gown. She held the small, glowing chunk of crystal, the only light in the stairwell, higher up, but all it revealed were more stairs cut from dark tan stone, circling down and out of sight. It would have been so much easier, so much more convenient to shimmer to her destination—just think about where you'd like to be, and off you went. But where she was going, one did not simply appear, with or without an appointment. So she lifted her hem a little higher and continued down, down, far beneath the light filled palace she called home. Tonight she had a meeting with the Mage—the Zaalmage, as the chief of their mysterious order was called—and she wanted to make a good impression.

Generally, she didn't care what sort of impression she made. Hellne was the princess of Eriis, the youngest child, her father's jewel, and it was everyone else's job to favorably impress her.

Malloy had impressed her. And now he was gone.

She took a calming breath and gathered herself at the great stone doorway to the Raasth. It appeared to be part of the walls around it, with neither hinges nor handles. She squinted at the door and moved the lighted stone back and forth, looking for a way in. She'd never visited the Mages in their lair before, why would she? They worked their magic in the dark; there were whispers and rumors about their favored ingredients, their unnatural practices. And they only accepted boy demons as students to the Peermage—even the humans on the other side of The Door took girls as novices in their Order, and everyone knew humans were a primitive race.

Malloy hadn't seemed primitive, though.

As she prepared her best, most placid face, the stone door to the Raasth blew away like smoke, and the Zaal—for who else would be receiving her?—waved her inside. It was dark but she could see a circular room lined with bookshelves rising into the gloom and out of sight, and rows of well-used wooden tables and benches. She thought she saw robed and hooded figures peering out from other doorways on the other side, but it was dark and they were quickly gone. She wouldn't begrudge them; the brothers of the Raasth never came out into the daylight, and who knew when they'd last seen a woman, much less a princess? Let them look, she knew they, at least, wouldn't talk.

As she stood before the Zaal, she was somewhat disappointed to see a rather ordinary looking old demon, more white hair than black, and the typical tilted red eyes in a lined face. He looked like her father, if her father never went outside. She didn't know what she'd been expecting; something more exotic; horns, or strange round eyes like a human. He bade her sit across from him, and waited for her to arrange her gown around her feet before sitting himself. At least he had some idea of how to behave. And as if to prove he wasn't a manner-less peasant from the hills, he handed her a silver cup of water, and she took the required three sips before handing it back. Now they could talk.

"Quite a surprise, when you asked to speak with me, Princess. I don't believe we've had the pleasure of a breath of wind such as yourself here in our humble Raasth before."

Hellne did not consider herself to be unusually clever—the realm had her older brother for that—but any woman in possession of her own wits could tell when she was being patronized. It was only due to his age and station as Zaal that she made no remark on his speaking first. And she needed his help, she reminded herself. And there was no injunction on shimmering out of this nasty, dark place once she was done. She sniffed. It smelled like dust, and age, and blood.

"Yes. I thank you for agreeing to see me, Zaal. I know the hour is late." She wondered if she could just get to it or if he would want to hear gossip from the world above.

"Princess, I am inclined to think this is not a social call, what with the hour. How may the Peermage be of assistance?"

She gave an inward sigh of relief. "I would ask your help. Something you can do. The Mages can do. I want—I would like you to protect someone. He is very important to me."

"Well," said the Mage, "if he is important to you, he must be vital to the safety and security of all of Eriis. What is the High Seat without its Princess?"

"It's well tended by my father, and will be occupied next by my brother Araan. As you know." She was an ornament, she knew it, and she suspected he knew it. "This individual is important to me in a way that requires discretion. I can count on the Raasth for that, I trust?"

"Since my brothers have sacrificed their voices for the study of the power of the Word, I think you may rest assured against gossip." He paused and sipped his water. "Who is the lucky boy?" He paused and smirked. "I jump ahead. We do speak of a young man? You did say 'he.' It's not mine to make assumptions..." She gritted her teeth and nodded politely. He continued, "I assume your father doesn't know you've taken a… companion." She colored and he added, "Or perhaps he does know, and that's why the fellow needs protection." He frowned. "Protection against the High Seat. This may prove to be costly, Madam."

She shook her head. "My father—and my brother—they don't have anything to do with this. My… friend… has been called away from Eriis. I want to insure he is safe until I see him again."

"You're having an affair with the ambassador? I didn't think Preeve had it in him."

She drew back in her seat. "You assume much, Zaal." She was about to correct him, then thought better of it. "I would prefer not to use names unless it's required by the Powers." She hoped Light, Wind, and Rain would not require her to confess the identity of her lover to this old man, but could instead read his name in her heart. "Can you help me? Can you keep him safe?"

The Zaal cocked his head and rubbed his ear. "Safe is one thing. Alive is another. I can guarantee your friend will remain alive. I can't promise what condition you'll find him in." She shrugged. Malloy was young and strong. As long as he lived, she knew he'd find his way back to her side. "I'll need something your friend has had in his hand."

She reached into the pocket of her gown and drew out a small, flat package wrapped in silk, which she handed over. The Zaal laid back the fabric, revealing a book, bound in heavy paper and with a brightly colored painting of a pair of humans on the cover. It read, in ornate script, *The Claiming of the Duke* by Malloy Dos Capeheart.

"He gave this to me, just this evening," she said.

The Zaal sniffed the bright scrap of silk, and then the book itself, and made a face. "Your friend got this from one of the humans of Mistra, then? And he's not here in Eriis?" He sniffed at the book again. "Human-made, it stinks of human. Even if it wasn't in the Mistran tongue, the smell… well, you wouldn't notice that." He shook his head. "Preeve aims high." Then he fixed a curious eye on her. "Though you did not actually name the ambassador, did you?"

Hellne drew herself up. "Who he is does not matter. Can you insure his life until I see him again? With this?" She indicated the book. She hoped he'd give it back, not that she intended to read it. She'd read enough of the earlier drafts and doubted it had somehow improved. She loved him well enough to encourage his hobby, but that didn't mean she had to participate in it. But it was Malloy's gift to her, and the wrapping was pretty, so she wanted it.

"Yes," said the Zaal. "We can guarantee his life. I remind you, only his life. Do you understand?"

Hellne was heartily sick of men telling her what she did or did not understand. So he might take an injury, so what? If trouble should come between the humans of Mistra and the demon kingdom of Eriis, the important thing would be Malloy's life when the trouble blew away.

She nodded. "I understand. I assume you require a price?"

Here the Zaal laughed, or attempted not to laugh, since that would have been unforgivably rude even if the lady he laughed at wasn't a princess. He quickly passed his hand over his face. She frowned but let it go.

"Yes, Madam, a price. You are correctly informed. Tonight, all I require is something you will hardly miss. The price will be named in due course. I don't know what will be charged against you. I don't know when it will come due. But it will. We do magic, and magic always claims its price."

Malloy, alive and with me, she thought. *Worth it.* "Please do not attempt to scare me, Zaal. I understand I will eventually have to give up something of value, more than likely at the most inconvenient time."

He nodded, suddenly brisk and businesslike. He led her to the largest thing in the dimly lit room, a circular table marked and scored with grooves and indented here and there with narrow holes. It was ugly. She was glad for the low light, because it was stained and he apparently wanted her to put her hand on it.

The table bit her. She jumped back, surprised, and looked at her hand. The third finger of her right hand, nipped open, just exactly as if by sharp teeth. As she watched, the little mark faded and vanished.

"You are recorded, Princess." He handed her back the book and its wrapper. "Payment will be due."

"But he'll be safe?"

"Allow me to repeat myself. He'll be alive. This I say without hesitation. How he comports himself is up to him, safe or damaged, it's all the same to the charm we just worked."

Hellne had never been so glad to shimmer, using her gift to take her back to her own chambers in one-two-three heartbeats. Her rooms were dark and Yaanda, her Prime maid had long since gone to her own bed, leaving one small stone lit on the bedside table, a slim silver pitcher of fresh water, and Hellne's feather light silk quilt turned down. Feeling restless and not ready to retire, Hellne went out onto her terrace, taking a moment to trail her hand through a potted lavender plant, crushing the tiny flowers between her fingers. The scent, sweet and fragile, reminded her of Malloy. Malloy, who was now safe.

She went to the low rail and looked out over her city. It was quite dark, both moons had set, and most households had put out their stones. Gazing at the far distant line of mountains, she noticed a smudge on the horizon, dark on dark. It wasn't the season for rain, but she supposed there was a storm coming in. She sighed and stepped back into her room, throwing her heavy gown on the floor, but then she picked it back up and retrieved her book from the slashed pocket.

Alive, I made sure of it. You'll be fine and whatever happens, I'll see you again. She tenderly kissed the silk wrapped book and hid it in the back of her desk, behind an overflowing dish of necklaces and a jumble of pens, paper, and corked bottles of ink, and went to bed comforted that Malloy would soon be back at her side.

When the storm came, it was made of magic, not rain, and when it had passed, the life and the city Hellne knew were changed forever. Her father was dead. Her brother, like so many others, vanished. The Zaal and all the senior Mages, her father's council and court, gone. Yaanda, her friends, clan brothers and sisters, gone. More than half the city was rubble and smoke. Her garden was gone, all the gardens were gone. The humans had struck with no warning and left no escape—The Door between the worlds was locked. The surviving demons would live or die as best they could in the sand and ash left behind.

The charm, however, held fast.

Chapter 4

The Duke rubbed one hand against the other as if his wrist was aching him.

It was an old injury, Cybelle knew, from the days when he'd fought, stripped to the waist and gleaming, in the basements and cellars of Mistra. It was after the War, and she thought he fought against his own memories as much as his unlucky opponents. He never lost. Had he conquered those terrible visions as surely as his opponents? She thought perhaps not.

-The Claiming of the Duke, pg 35
Malloy Dos Capeheart, Little Gorda Press (out of print)

Mistra
1 day after the War of the Door, Mistran calendar
Hours later, Eriisai calendar
The Guardhouse

"Nice work my lad." Malloy's friend David slapped him hard on the back, knocking him forward a step. "They said you weren't good for anything but scribbling love poems in your room, but I knew you had some meat in you." The young man paused on the stair leading to the great common room and added, "I hear she didn't suspect a thing. Ha! Classic Malloy."

Malloy followed his friend and the rest of the yawning, joking group of apprentices and novices. He rubbed his head, trying to figure out what David meant. Suspect what thing? And why did everyone think he wrote love poems? He'd told them it was an adventure story often enough.

Still grumbling, he took his seat on one of the benches in the long, dark room. The masters and clerics and tradesmen that came and went took their meals in pleasant rooms with light and air, but their errand boys sat and ate on rough wooden benches in a hall lit by greasy torches. The huge kettle of oatmeal hanging over the grate sent up a nutty smell that made his stomach rumble, despite the throbbing in his temple. He'd had a little too much wine to celebrate the rare night off; he was paying for it now. He'd fallen asleep early and awakened late, but at least he was on time for breakfast.

His master, and the other ambassadors and clerics, were gathered at the front of the big room looking even worse than he felt, but there was an air of celebration. He wondered what they'd been up to; they usually didn't join their lessers this early in the day. Then he remembered his worry. What happened last night? He'd gone to attend his master the ambassador only to be turned away at the door. He thought he'd seen a glimpse of the Eriisai ambassador, and he thought he'd seen knives. But he must have been mistaken. He and a red-haired serving girl exchanged looks, and she handed him the wine she would not be serving his master, before disappearing down the hall.

The head cleric stood up to address the roomful of rowdy young men, and they settled into silence at once.

"This is a great day for Mistra." He paused and looked to the men beside him and grinned—actually grinned. Malloy felt his balls shrink up into his stomach. "This is a day we've been working for, all of us, some in great roles—" and here he indicated the Mistran ambassador, "and some in positions that were more, shall we say, discreet." And to Malloy's astonishment, the cleric pointed right at him. "Stand up, Malloy. It is partly due to your hard work that we were successful in our endeavors."

Malloy stood and looked around. Everyone was applauding, and those nearby reached out to whap him on the shoulder. He sat as soon as it seemed appropriate. The cleric continued.

"The charm we've been working on all these months was deployed through The Door before first light. It was completely effective." More cheering. "The threat from Eriis is over. Those who survived are unable to retaliate with their own weapons, because The Door is now sealed with the blood of humans, and as we well know, there are no longer any humans on Eriis." The group of them triumphantly raised their arms to show off their matching knife marks—they had been the donors. The ambassador from Eriis had been helpful as well, providing a great deal of his own blood, along with several internal organs. He was not present that morning, his remains having been stuffed into a barrel and buried in the Guardhouse's dump.

By the Veil, by the Veil, by the Veil, Malloy tried to focus. It couldn't be true. He was just there yesterday. And they'd done one better than just closing The Door, they'd done some grotesque blood magic and burnt the city down. He thought of Hellne and managed to vomit sour wine on the floor between his feet, rather than on the table.

"To commemorate this astonishing victory, the Quarter Moons party will—from this day forward—celebrate our safety and freedom behind The Door. The demon enemy is vanquished. We will have much more to say and great plans for the future, but for now let us consider these to be days of rest. Our work begins again the day after the Quarter Moons party. Until then, enjoy your well-earned liberty."

The young men wasted no time gulping down their gruel and tea and coffee and bread, and filing out to their own pursuits. Malloy made to follow them, his head spinning, but the head cleric and his master waved him over.

He followed them to the cleric's personal study, a low ceilinged room with a huge fireplace dominating one end and an equally huge desk, a great slab of blackened oak at the other. Between them were sagging, overfilled bookshelves. Twin round windows of wavy glass showed the green world outside.

Malloy sat on a stool in front of the desk and waited. He wasn't sure what he'd done to be singled out, but only hoped he hadn't somehow helped them destroy Eriis. The taste of vomit lingered in his throat and nose and his head throbbed.

"We are in your debt, young man," said the cleric. "Without you, we never would have caught the demons unaware."

"Thank you, sir," he said slowly. "I was only doing as I was instructed."

His master the ambassador laughed and slapped him on the back again and said, "We only told you to watch her, we didn't tell you to make her follow you around like a puppy dog. You had that little demon bitch right where you wanted her! And more than once, I'll wager. Kept her away from her kin and away from their plans and plots. She was supposed to be watching us!"

"I'm sorry, sir, I don't understand. I kept her entertained, as you said. We... grew close. But, she didn't know anything about any plans."

"Hmm?" The cleric leaned forward in his chair behind the he desk. "Certainly she did. That's why they had her in such close proximity with us; she was supposed to report back to her father and brother. You came between her and her little job. Very well done."

"No," Malloy said, "I don't think so. I don't think there was any plot at all. I never heard anything about them preparing any weapon. And you've blasted them with something? And sealed The Door? Why? They were trying to teach us." He knew he was crying but couldn't stop his tears or his mouth. "I loved Hellne, she was beautiful. They didn't want to harm us. Why would you do this?"

The cleric and the ambassador looked over Malloy's head at each other. The ambassador said, "You're saying you had affection for that creature? You didn't seduce her to gather information?"

"Well, it started out that way. You said to keep her entertained! But I didn't have to pretend to want to be with her." *Oh,*

Hellne, I'm so sorry. He thought of her rare smiles, her perfect breasts, her sharp teeth, and covered his face with his hands.

The cleric said, "And it never occurred to you why we might want to keep the princess occupied?" He folded his arms and sneered, "Did you imagine it was all for fun?"

"Perhaps we misjudged this one," the ambassador said. "He only seems clever. I think we just got lucky. He would have been catting around with that demon girl whether we told him to or not." He sighed, disappointed.

"No, this is wrong," Malloy looked up at them. "You've done something terrible. We must open The Door and help the survivors."

"The others mustn't hear this nonsense," said the cleric. "Lock him in his cell until he's sorted out his 'feelings'."

"Often there is a sort of delusion that comes when working in the field, as our Malloy has done. Some time alone will mend him. And if that doesn't work, there's always the lash. I've seen it change many a mind."

***

"Malloy, wake up, now. I know it's been a few weeks, but we thought a nice visit today would be just the thing. Your master and I would like to talk about the demons, and Eriis, and how they were our enemy. Do you feel up to that?"

"Throwing things at us is not going to bring that girl back, young man. Now you've lost your water cup, you'll have to drink out of the bowl. Hmm. Well, we'll be back in a few weeks to see how you are progressing."

***

"He's not talking to us at all, Ambassador. He sits on the floor and writes in the dust with his spoon. He has not repented. I think we've wasted enough time on sorting out his feelings. Let's leave this to others with more time on their hands…."

***

WHAP

"It's all wrong, you're wrong. I taught her how to kiss. We were in love. They wouldn't hurt us."

WHAP

"She loved to go to the theater. She had pretty hair."

WHAP

"I made her laugh. I carried her around her room."

WHAP

"I… think she told her brother what we talked about. But, no…."

WHAP

"She burned my skin many times. She wasn't human."

whap

whap

"The demons meant to destroy us all. She was a lying bitch and a spy."

tap….

"Malloy, would you like a glass of water? And perhaps a bath?"

"Please, may I stay here and help to keep The Door shut?"

"But what about your book? We understand it has developed quite a following among ladies of a certain age and intellect."

"I only wish to serve the Order."

After six months, he got his wish.

Chapter 5

Eriis City
1 year after the War of the Door, Eriisai calendar
5 years later, Mistran calendar
Under the Palace

One day, Hellne's Mages requested her presence.

This in itself was a surprise, since the Weapon, even the new Zaal was rarely seen above ground. Always reclusive, they had become even more secretive. Even in the terrible days following the Weapon, as her father crossed over from life to the place beyond the Veil, the Zaal had not come to offer respect. The guidance she was expecting, even from this unwelcome source, was never offered. She suspected their air of mystery was a cover for their guilt—for had they not failed in every fundamental way? They had failed to see the threat from the human world. They had failed to safeguard the city. And they had failed to protect even their own ranks—the entirety of the Peermage, the keepers of that vast repository of knowledge, had fallen that first day.

She'd hoped the deal she'd made had died with the old Zaal, but why else would they want to see her?

"Can I leave you alone for an hour?" She sighed. "That's not very motherly, is it?"

The baby just gazed at her, as usual. She hadn't gotten used to another presence in her chambers, and although she was used to all eyes following her, this one made her uneasy with the directness of its stare. At least the child was quiet. She lifted him—he was heavy—and put him in a woven basket, covering him with a blanket. Hopefully people would think she was carrying a load of sand. Wrestling an entire population away from starvation and despair had been easy compared to how this small creature had taken over her life. Everyone wanted to see him. Everyone cooed over him—she couldn't understand the fuss, it was just a baby. 'What's his name?' they all asked. She said she hadn't decided. She could barely stand to look at him, much less call him by a name.

She thanked Light and Wind (but not Rain, not anymore) that at least it had the appearance of a normal child. Babies had tiny little features and this one had inherited most of the proper ones. If he had been born with light hair or brown eyes, she'd decided she'd take a quiet trip to the Crosswinds and come back alone. But the little thing had the correct black hair and red eyes, although she could see by their shape that those eyes would one day be a problem. Well, that was for the future. Right now, she kept the baby alive, and at least it didn't scream all night.

She didn't relish taking him downstairs to the Raasth, though. That dark place felt unwholesome, and what if the baby caught something—a chill? Was that something humans caught? Or half-humans?

"Nearly there," she said, half to herself, half to the baby, as she crossed the square and passed through the old statue garden. It made a strange contrast, the garden—now a broken jumble, of course—hard up against a grim looking hole in the city wall. She nodded at the statue of her father, which had survived with the loss of only a hand and part of his face, took a deep breath, hoisted the basket, and readied herself for an unpleasant meeting.

But when she finally arrived at the entrance to their series of chambers, down and down what felt like miles of stairs under the oldest part of the city, it seemed they'd anticipated her unease. They'd turned the lights up, for one thing. The soft glow came from all around—she couldn't quite pinpoint the source, but they'd made it bright enough to see all the little ceremonial items tucked into nooks along the walls. She'd heard that to enter the Conclave, one must give up something personal, something of great value to the future Mage. The elders would somehow look inside the item to see inside their potential brother. And now it was bright enough for Hellne to see what she hadn't noticed, a year earlier. Dolls with delicately painted faces, little toy animals, a well-used *chlystron*, books, bundles of letters, all stacked towards the ceiling and out of sight. Some were so old they were little more than heaps of dust. But other than these untouched relics, there was no other dust to be found. The doors were open, the floor swept, and there was a clean pitcher of cold water waiting for her. The grubby worktables had been covered with fresh paper and the dirty old work books had been carefully wiped clean. Nothing could completely mask the smell of blood and dust, and there was no way to hide the enormous ceremonial platform that dominated the space, but this was a noticeable improvement.

"Madam," they said, "Your Grace, you honor us. Let us take your burden and come and sit and talk. Share our water." One of them, the newly appointed Zaalmage, reached for her basket. There were four, but only the Zaalmage would speak, as was proper. The others in their sooty robes remained just out of the circle of candlelight, watching. The one who spoke, spoke for all.

Do they even have tongues? she wondered.

"Thank you, Zaalmage, but I will keep this by my side." She put the basket between her feet, adjusting the blanket. She was seized by the desire to keep the baby away from their eyes. "I will gladly share your water." She sipped the three sips, and the Zaalmage did the same. She sat back and waited.

"Madam," he said after a moment, "We have found something. We think." He glanced back at his fellows. "As Your Grace knows, our masters are no longer with us. The loss of the combined knowledge of the Peermage was incalculable. It is as if The Weapon knew who of us to take, leaving only us worthless apprentices and novices. We had much to do to even trace their footprints, much less follow them."

"Yes," she agreed mildly, "it seems to have left behind only the most useless."

The Zaalmage blanched. The others shifted uncomfortably. "Not at all Madam, what I was implying, no, everyone knows without your guiding—"

She put up a slim hand. "Why am I here, Zaalmage?"

"We think the Peermage was developing a weapon. A Weapon, like theirs."

She held her face still. "We had a Weapon to use against the humans?" she asked.

It was not surprising she hadn't known. Her father, in his wisdom, had told her nothing of his plans, explained nothing of statecraft, taught nothing she might ever need to fall back on—should the unthinkable happen.

Thank you, Daddy, for sending me to all those lovely parties, she thought.

"We… yes. That is what it appears to be. We have the translations of substance and translations of word. We have the records of small tests. It is transformative in nature rather than destructive, but it would be a very powerful weapon indeed."

She sat and considered this for a moment. "It *would* be? Does it exist or not?"

The mages shared another glance. One nodded and the Zaalmage continued. "It is not complete. There are certain ingredients we no longer have… access to."

"Such as?" she asked.

"Blood, Madam."

She snorted a laugh. "Certainly we have plenty of that, right here among us."

Another glance. More shifting about. "Human blood, Madam. We can almost smell it."

She nodded. *Don't move, baby, don't make a noise.* With her heel, she pushed the basket further under her chair, suddenly sure what the price of her magic was going to be. "I can see where that might present a problem," she said. "If one were to come across such a luxury item, what then?"

The Zaalmage brightened. "Well, it's very interesting, the way it’s written. We think they were still experimenting. A little blood, now, that might work if the Door was already open. We already know that even a small amount of human blood, a drop or two, along with the right words, might create a crack wide enough for a person to slip through. Well, we have neither the blood nor the words, but the Peermage did write of such a thing. But, it appears that if one could somehow procure a whole human person's worth of blood, well, that'll blow the Door apart and leave the path swept clear to transform everything on the other side into whatever we wish. We would be free to remake that world. Or unmake it. If we could only find a source for even a small amount, we could continue their experiments and eventually this weapon would be ours to use. That is to say, yours to use."

Hellne rose to her feet. "Zaalmage, the city thanks you for your work. No one knows better than I how it feels to have the weight of expectations on your shoulders. And I personally thank you for telling me about this fascinating discovery."

She let the Zaalmage bask in the glow for a moment.

"But," she said, "we have greater needs than a theoretical weapon we have no way to deploy or even complete. Set it aside." The Zaalmage looked genuinely shocked. His colleagues rustled. She could hear the agitation in their whistling breaths. "We rely on you for so much, please do not exhaust yourselves in the pursuit of something that can no longer help us. I bid you instead, concentrate on the creation of daily needs and wants, to make life in Eriis more like it was. Think how grateful we were to learn how to cool ourselves. Perhaps you can cool the air as well."

"But, Your Grace…"

"As to this other… project… my mind is set. Please do call on me again soon, Zaalmage, I find your work so very interesting."

She picked up the basket, and made her way towards the open doorway.

The Zaalmage followed after her, sniffing, a strange expression on his face. He shook his head as if to clear it and said, "Madam, please give our matter further thought. For the sake of our departed Peermage and the King, if nothing else."

She turned, holding the edge of the blanket down with her free hand.

"Yes, my father and the Peermages are gone, as you remind us. You might recall that I was there when my father left us. The second worst day of my life and a tragedy for the realm, so close on the heels of the greatest tragedy of our lives. So I thank you for bringing it up."

The Zaalmage looked properly mortified, but wasn't ready to drop his case. She cut him off before he could apologize again.

"Now let me remind you that there is a city full of people who are eating and drinking sand. I have heard some of them are catching jumpmice in the fields and cooking them with the very heat of their hands. Sand and rats, gentlemen. Think about that and tell me what you think you ought to be doing down here. I wish to hear nothing further about your imaginary weapon. If I change my mind I will certainly consult you. Good day."

The Zaalmage and his colleagues slunk back to console each other, and she was out the door and heading back to the light of the city above.

After a climb that seemingly went on for a day, she turned a corner and rested for a moment in the stairwell. She drew a breath, weak with relief. Her debt, it seemed, had not come due. Perhaps it had died with its maker.

The baby's tiny fist stuck out from beneath the blanket, and she let it grab her finger.

They must never, ever know the truth about you.

***

Back in her own quarters, Hellne set the basket in the corner and lit the glowing stone lamps. She opened the heavy silk drapery—the night air tended to be clearer of the ever present dust—and tossed the daytime quilt, along with its drift of grit, onto the floor. With the clean, evening sheets exposed, she set the baby in the center of her bed. (It had already rolled off the edge once, and she prided herself in her rapidly improving maternal skills.) She walked back and forth around her room, pulling the pins from her hair, thinking, thinking.

What had Malloy said? *This is the key. I've made it for you. This is the key.*

Of course, he might have been lying, that was one of the human's favorite pastimes after all. He might have been laughing at her all along. But if there was even a chance he was telling the truth, well, what had that filthy Mage said? A bit of blood and the right words? She hadn't known that either, and he'd said it as if it were common knowledge. There was so much she didn't know.

But one thing she did understand was the value of putting a little something aside for the future.

She took a needle from her sewing kit (one couldn't simply transform old clothes into new ones, it claimed too much energy, and besides, new clothing—really any newly transformed thing—was now considered quite vulgar. Bright colors, new things, all were part of the past) and set it aside. Next, she went to her desk and pulled the bottom drawer all the way out. It fell to the floor and she pushed it aside. She reached inside and felt around the bottom of the next drawer up. That was where she'd hidden Malloy's book.

She unwrapped it and put it on the bed next to the baby. Then she took her needle in one hand and one of the child's tiny fingers in the other.

"I won't take much and you won't miss it," she told him. "I promise I'll take a lot less than those hooded freaks downstairs. Ugh, I can't believe I brought you there. Hellne, get yourself a maid."

For his part, the baby laughed and tried to grab her hair.

She stabbed his finger. His face was a picture of surprise, and then it screwed itself up into a howl.

She looked at him curiously. "You felt that?"

She hadn't expected that, but perhaps she should have. His father, she recalled, was as delicate as a new flower. She looked at his tiny hand, at the bead of blood welling, and frowned—it was just a little needle, after all. She stabbed her own finger and felt nothing more than a slight warmth. Well, maybe the child was just startled.

Do babies startle?

She held the little finger over the back page of the book, where Malloy had made some sort of human looking scrawl. Blood made the ink run for just a second, and then it righted itself, unsmearing before her eyes. More human magic, they were just so fond of their words.

She held the book at arm's length. Would a crack in The Door open here in her room?

She waited. Nothing.

"Well, not today, then. Still, I imagine this might be useful later. Maybe one day you'll figure this out and go visit your father. Won't that be exciting?"

She set the book aside and blotted the baby's finger.

"See? You're fine."

The baby had stopped crying and was back to gazing at her with its big, red, and round eyes. It was unnerving, the way it watched her. Normal babies had tilted eyes and a subtle gaze, never resting on anything for very long, a habit that carried them into adulthood. This child was so direct, the only one who had ever stared at her like that, she suddenly recalled, was a hunting hawk she'd had as a girl. A gift from her father from the human world. The bird's eyes were amber, not red, but perfectly round, and it held her gaze just this way. Watching her, taking the measure of her, silent and constant.

"Rhuun," she said, remembering. "My hawk's name was Rhuun. He was my weapon. He would fly so far I couldn't even see him at all, but he always came back to me."

The baby looked up at her as if he were listening.

"Will you be my weapon, Rhuun?"

The child gurgled and tried to catch her finger again, his tears forgotten.

"You have quite a good grip for someone so small," she told him. "Perhaps we'll have a little Naming party for you after all. Let all those gossips get a good look at you. 'Eriis is his father', I'll tell them. 'He belongs to the city and to me.'"

She picked him up, a bit awkwardly. He grabbed a handful of her long, black hair and stuffed it in his mouth. She laughed.

For the first time, she could look at him and see something other than Malloy's face looking back at her.

"I made you," she said, "and you'll always come back to me."

She sat back on her bed and watched the low clouds whip past her window and held him until long after he'd fallen asleep.

Chapter 6

Gwenyth ran her fingers over the silken gowns.
"Your hands had best be clean," the Duke said sharply. Why must he ruin everything? she wondered.
"And you won't be wearing any of that lot unless I'm showing you off at dinner." He slammed the cabinet shut. "Cotton and wool, that's good enough for you. That fancy stuff is only for ladies."

-The Claiming of the Duke, pg 70
Malloy Dos Capeheart, Little Gorda Press (out of print)

Mistra
9 months after the War of the Door, Mistran calendar
Almost 2 months later, Eriisai calendar
The Guardhouse

If Brother Blue had been an indifferent assistant he was a model novice. *New name*, he told himself, *clean new life*. He'd even overheard his old master, the ambassador, admit to his new master, the head cleric, *a few months in the dark and a few sessions with the lash had turned him around.* He never spoke of his so-called writing career anymore, and was only interested in studying the history of the Order and perfecting the charms that kept The Door shut. He'd always been good with words, he, as the demons might have said, manifested towards the word. It was even hoped that one day he might go on to teach the next generation of Fifths the vital mission they were entrusted with.

"After all," concluded the ambassador, "he is clever, even if he's easily swayed. Keep a close eye, he should be fine. We all make mistakes."

They had given Blue a choice, the cleric and the ambassador: serve the head cleric and take the vows of a novice, or go back to his father and the farm and get behind a plow. He'd taken his vows immediately and ceded the money he'd earned from his book to the upkeep of the Guardhouse. He didn't need money. He only needed to keep The Door shut, because if it opened, something terrible would happen. He saw it in his dreams, The Door opened, and blood and death came for him wearing her face. Those were bad nights.

Blue had been handed from the ambassador to the head cleric, and the transition, once Blue applied himself to his new task, was a smooth one. He was serving the cleric his tea and biscuits as he did every morning, just as the light came in through the twin round windows. He'd been serving the cleric for three months, and was grateful for the quiet in his mind. The dreams still came, but not as often. Sometimes only once a night, now.

The cleric was entertaining a merchant from the city that day, who was neither quiet nor grateful. A silk merchant, who'd done tremendous trade with Eriis, and had not been informed about recent events.

As he set the tea service aside and began to clean, Blue tried not to listen. Angry voices made him tense, but whatever it was, it surely had nothing to do with him. *Concentrate on your broom, and the floor under your broom.*

va'Everly raged, "Do you have any idea what this is going to cost me? And not just this season? How could you fools do something so… so… foolish?" His fair skin was blotched and he'd pushed his dark blond hair all over his head. He got up and paced around. "What am I supposed to do with the warehouse full of orders already filled? I've paid the workers and dyers and weavers—I've even paid the damn couriers! Now the red eyes can't pay me for the goods!"

The cleric templed his fingers. "First of all, I am sorry for our little miscommunication. But just because the Guardhouse made a convenient port does not make it your property. We were not beholden to share our plans with you." va'Everly looked like he was about to strangle the cleric with his hands, when the older man said, "Insurance."

"I beg your pardon?" va'Everly stopped his pacing.

"I assume you have insurance when you send a ship full of your lovely silks to the Southern Provinces?"

"Well, certainly. Only a fool trusts the weather. Or a ship captain. What's your point?"

The cleric smiled. "We are prepared to pay out the insured cost of this year's loss to your family's company. As if the ship, as it were, had gone down."

va'Everly considered this. "We insure heavily," he said. "Our products are not crates of pigs or tables and chairs. Luxury items, you know. Delicate. Expensive."

The cleric shrugged. "Details. We have insurance of our own, of course. And all we ask in return is that you keep the details of this transaction private." This wasn't the first time the cleric had to console a merchant. Blue had been present for similar recent conversations regarding boxes of pigs, tables and chairs, along with wood, linen, silver, household wares, and every kind of food and drink under the moons. This silk seller was just one more. The cleric was an excellent book keeper and made sure his premiums were up to date. He knew a day like this would come, he'd told Blue. It was expensive, but what was that against saving Mistra? He'd just raise the endowments for the next generation of Fifths.

Blue didn't mind hearing about money, but he hated when his master talked about the other place.

va'Everly laughed. "I keep all my transactions private. So that takes the sting out of this season. But those nasty little creatures over there were good customers. What else have you got in mind?"

"We thought you might be interested in an experiment," the cleric said. "I know the va'Everlys have not been blessed with a Fifth in quite a long time. However, I understand you have a Third at home."

A Fifth, thought Blue, was the very best thing you could be. A child born fifth was always promised to the Order, while he, a Fourth, only arrived here after a long trip through the dark.

"A Third, yes, a spare" agreed va'Everly, who had calmed considerably. He sat back down across from the cleric, smoothing his gorgeous peacock-blue silk tie. The shade was famous, it was called Ever Blue. "My First is already sitting in on meetings, a shame she missed this one."

"Why not send your Third here to serve as a Fifth?" The merchant frowned, not wanting to appear too eager. "There's more." The cleric reached under his desk.

"I'm listening."

So was Blue, who forced himself to continue to sweep the hearth. Hearing about the other place made his heart race, but he couldn't turn away.

"Before we sealed The Door against those villains, we procured some very special toys. Well, they were toys to the demons, they aren't to us." The cleric pulled up a leather strapped metal box and opened it, revealing what appeared to be baby socks tied with ribbons. "These are called *chlystrons*," the cleric said, "and they are used by demon children to bring along their evil gifts. We are hoping they'll do something similar here, bringing good gifts to good human children." He paused, frowning. "We haven't had much luck with adults. It does something to the mind. The brave volunteers will receive excellent care." He brightened. "We've had interesting results with children though. The *things* they have in their minds. We haven't had one break through to transformative magic, but we feel it is only a matter of time. How would you like your Third to be the one that has magic? A va'Everly, gifted with the power of the hand. Think about that. Oh, and we'll waive the fees, of course." Blue wondered why the cleric neglected to mention that the things the children had in their minds usually were alive, and had teeth. There had been several unfortunate incidents.

va'Everly poked one. "What are they, full of sand or something? What do you do with them?"

"Hold them in your hand and thus manifest." The cleric and the merchant looked over at Blue, who stared at the *chlystrons* with wide, blank eyes. "My Princess had her own, given to her by the King himself, in a special box on her mantle."

The cleric rose to his feet, ringing for assistance.

***

Blue spent another few weeks in his cell before his mind was quiet again. The *chlystrons* produced nothing but monsters and madness, and within a few months all the children had either been buried or sent home, and the experiment was deemed a failure. It was decided the minds of the demons were so depraved a proper human brain couldn't conceive or control their dark gifts. All efforts to learn or acquire the power of the hand were halted. Instead, the Guardhouse turned its attention to a different kind of magic—the kind that erases an entire race of people from the history books. Demons moved onto the pages of the same volumes that held dragons and unicorns—mythology and fairy tales. It was surprisingly easy. Only a few humans had ever seen a demon in person, and after a few seasons, Eriis and the demons became a metaphor for the worst of human behavior, and The Door, the gateway to Hell. And with the passage of time, the Guardhouse remained, the Order remained, but as to what was behind The Door they held shut? No one remembered.

The little demon toys were locked safely away.

Chapter 7

Eriis City
5 years after the War of the Door, Eriisai calendar
25 years later, Mistran calendar
Royal Quarters

The child was a disaster.

He listened to everything, repeated everything, and understood nothing.

"You must never say anything like that ever again," Hellne snapped at him. She paced back and forth—it was only the work of three or four steps to cover distance in the boy's room. And the window veiled night and day with heavy dark silk to keep the dust out of his unusually delicate eyes.

The child's huge red eyes were at the moment full of tears and he rubbed his face where she'd slapped him.

"But I just said what you told me, I'm different and special," he wailed.

"Stop that noise, and if you cry it'll be the last thing you do with your eyes. And stop acting as if I hurt you, it's ridiculous."

She was furious with the boy for simply not understanding it was in his own best interest to remain unheard by her court and the less they saw of him, well, why borrow trouble? And she was even angrier at herself for losing her temper with the child—again. But she reminded herself that what little grief she caused him now would pay off when he managed to survive to adulthood without his secret—their secret—coming to light. She couldn't think of that morning with the Zaalmage without being gripped by nausea.

She sighed and kneeled down to catch him in a rare embrace.

"Rhuun, when I tell you about being different and about being special, that is for your ears only. That is for you to put away in a little book in your head that no one else gets to see. Other people don't understand like we do."

He leaned against her shoulder, his sobs trailing off against her neck. She stroked his soft hair. At least that was normal—not coarse and shaggy like his father's. But when she patted his back to soothe him, she felt only the sharp bones of his shoulder blades. No knobbed ridges where his wings ought to have been. Nothing there at all.

"Couns'ler Yuenne says I'm ugly. He saw me looking at him when he said it. You told me never say an'thing bad about someone when they can see you. That's why I said about special."

Rushta! she thought, *Damn Yuenne. If only he'd do what he was supposed to do and leave and never come back.*

Hellne recalled the week leading up to Rhuun's Naming Party. Yuenne had come to call, bringing a gift—a bottle of *sarave*—and found her at her desk, working on the speech she was expected to give. The baby was in his basket at the far end of the room, away from the windows and covered by a sheer muslin blanket to keep the dust out. Yuenne headed straight for it. Diia rose to her feet and blocked his approach.

"Leave him be, Yuenne. I've just gotten him to sleep. If a jumpmouse in the Quarter twitches its tail, he wakes up. You'll see him at the party, along with everyone else."

He nodded pleasantly at Diia, who folded her arms and remained standing, and went back to lounge in the seat across the desk from Hellne.

"Have you decided on a name?" he asked.

"Yes," she replied, "I have a few things in mind."

He looked surprised. "I would have thought you'd name him for your father. Am I mistaken?"

She set down her pen and looked up at him. *He is lying,* she thought. *He didn't think that at all.* And with absolute certainty, *As long as I am Queen, everyone will lie to me.* She felt a wave of dizziness, and very alone. She folded her hands on the desk to hide a tremor. "My father. Remind me, Yu, since I think you know your histories better than I. How many kings called Fadeer were there? Including my father, I can think of only two."

He tapped his chin. "Well, your father, of course. And the big one, Fadeer who ruled when the city wall was designed. And I believe there was a third, very early in the regency, before the humans came."

"Three then. I think that's sufficient. Three, including Father. Rest him now." He didn't reply—she knew he often let people shovel sand into their own mouths by simply not replying. "After all, he failed to see the threat the humans posed. And after the Weapon, he made up for his failure by successfully turning his face to the wall. Three Fadeers are enough."

He nodded, his precise smile never budging. "Then the little heir will have a new name. And, I am pleased to tell you, possibly a playmate in a few months."

"You and Siia? I am delighted to hear it." She was. She liked Siia. Everyone knew Yuenne had done well for himself by marrying into her clan. Although of course, now it didn't matter, as most of her clan was gone. "They won't be alone. Did you know, they are calling it the Ash Born, there are so many babies on the way?"

"Do you know what they call it outside the Arch?" She shook her head. "They're calling them Dust Bunnies."

She laughed. "I like that. I should try and use it in this speech." She leafed through the pages on her desk. "People could use a smile. I'll have to talk about the attack first, and how the humans tricked us, I'm not looking forward—"

"Oh, but you mustn't." She thought he looked genuinely concerned. "No, they didn't trick us." He templed his fingers. "Think, Hellne. Would you rather be the leader of a clutch of ragged victims, or the Queen of a proud race, vanquished only by treachery after a vicious battle?"

She cocked her head. "I'm not sure I follow. The human people attacked us unawares."

"Let me ask you a question. What colors do we wear?"

"Somber colors," she replied. "The colors of Eriis; ash, smoke, dust, sand. As you know, you helped me craft the law…."

"Indulge me," he said. "Why do we wear only these colors? And what would happen if you made yourself a new gown of, say, blue and green?"

"I would be breaking my own law," she said. "And it would be extremely vulgar." She could scarcely remember those terrible weeks after the Weapon, at the time she'd signed the law because bright things, new things, seemed an added insult to those who were lost.

"But you could do it," he said, warming to his topic. "Because inside the Arch, we have our food and drink transformed by others. We have the spare energy to create whatever we like. But we don't, because we must set an example. If a transform farmer decided to stop working and make his wife a pretty dress, before long we'd have a city full of starving people in bright clothes."

"What has this to do with—"

Yuenne shook his head. "We were never tricked by those hairy beasts. They don't have the capacity. It was…. it was a secret battle. Fought out of sight by the Mages. Who ultimately were defeated."

Hellne raised a brow. "Let the Mages take the blame?"

He shrugged. "I rather doubt they'll raise any objections, since they're all dead. The old ones, anyway. The new ones? Time will reveal their worth."

"A war," Hellne mused. "The War of the Door?"

He smiled his cool little smile. "Well done. Control the message, Hellne." He tapped the desk. "Or it will control you."

She'd finished the speech, and prepared to introduce the young prince to his remaining people.

On the occasion of the Naming Party, everyone who survived the Weapon (who was of the right clan, of course) was invited to share *sarave*, water, and bread. As a treat she'd even had the Mage's work for three days and nights to put meat, and greens, and even bites of sweet ices on the tables. That nothing tasted quite like it used to, well, things were different now. And the story of how Hellne had sent a complaining courtier to the Crosswinds was making the rounds as well. It was said the young man had remarked over a small state dinner that the bread tasted like sand, and the cheese tasted like a different flavor of sand. Everyone around him at the dinner table had laughed, but Hellne hadn't smiled. She had called one of her family guards over, whispered something in his ear, and the guard had escorted the apologizing man away. His increasingly hysterical sobs echoed down the corridor behind him and no one had seen him since. No one said anything unflattering about the royal table now, not even in private. The food they ate, it was generally and loudly agreed, was superior in every way to whatever had gone before. There were quicker and less embarrassing ways to dispatch oneself than to insult the Queen.

The Great Hall of the Royal Quarters was decked with her family colors—black and cream (the old colors, black and scarlet, had been retired after the Weapon). Not like the old days, when the crowds on a Naming Day would fill the Hall and spill onto the grounds outside, and there would be as many gifts handed out as received, and everyone tried to outdo their fellows in the fineness of their silks and the brightness of their decorations. The parties would last for days, with food and drink sometimes brought over from the human world—marvels like ice cream and something called beer. She wondered if her unnatural proclivity for the humans had begun with a taste of their food. No need to worry about that anymore, at least.

Well, it may not outshine the sun, but it's a start, she thought. *And these people need something to look at that isn't covered with dust*. There were even black and white flowers, her own design, materialized by the Zaalmage himself. Hellne had to force herself to visit the Raasth, but understood the value of keeping an eye on one's tools. Helping to design the flowers had been a good excuse to see what they were all doing down there. As far as she could tell, it was all scribbling in books and experimenting—on sand, on jumpmice, on each other for all she knew. They'd created a flying mouse, and a small flock of the little winged creatures had been debuted at this party. In the new prince's honor, they'd been dubbed Rhuumice. Of course, the Mages had never seen her son, nor would they. It was far too dangerous.

At the moment the Rhuumice were grazing on the flowers. She'd have to dispatch a maid to shoo them away.

She eyed the crowd, a nicely balanced mix of old families who'd survived the Weapon and the rising families who'd abandoned their now-dead fields to live in Eriis City. It looked to her like a river of sand, a moving field of grey, brown, and ashy colored silks. She'd written the colors into law with Yuenne's assistance but thought she needn't have bothered. Whatever she wore was copied at Court and in town. Many of the ladies wore black and cream hair ornaments, and some of the men affected scarves in the same colors.

They look so fine, they smile so politely, but they're just here to see if the rumors about you are true, she thought, looking down at her child. He, as usual, looked back up at her with a steady and somewhat suspicious gaze. *Well, let's get on with it.*

She'd stood up—hoping she looked like a proud new mother and not terrified and alone—and let them all see the baby, who despite his odd shaped eyes was the image of his mother and of his grandfather. She tackled the unanswered question before anyone could whisper it behind a hand. She gathered herself and took a deep breath.

"This child was born a year ago," she told them. "A time we all remember too well. This child belongs to the ones we lost—the men in the fields, the women at their tables, the Mages at their books. This child comes to us from the brave and the proud and the vanished. We will never forget those who went before, but we thank Light and Wind for the gift of this day, and of this child. He is the son of Eriis, and Eriis is his father. His name is Rhuun, Prince of Eriis and Heir to the High Seat. Thank you for helping to make him welcome here today."

She sank into her seat and pressed her forehead against Rhuun's. There was a generous and genuine round of applause and even some cheering.

There, that ought to hold them. For now.

"He really does resemble your father, rest him now." Counselor Yuenne leaned over her shoulder to examine the child more closely. "And I must say, Your Grace, it's almost an act of what those human friends of yours used to call 'magic,' the way you produced this child, at a time when your people need it most. How very clever of you." He smiled thinly.

"Yuenne, you've known me nearly my whole life. Please dispense with Your Grace." Yuenne had been one of her father's most trusted advisors. It had been the sheerest luck he and his wife had been spared by The Weapon.

"Funny thing, though. I believe it was our very last conversation, your dear father and mine, when he was telling me he was concerned for you. Spending so much time with those people. The ambassador's boy he disliked in particular. Well, you wouldn't know that. Your father never wanted to trouble your mind. But the humans, he never really trusted them—and for good reason, as we all know to our own grief. The eyes, you know. He never got used to the shape of their eyes." He lifted his *sarave* in a toast and called to the assembled:

"To our queen and to Prince Rhuun, given to us, it seems, as if by magic."

The roomful of party goers echoed his words. Her throat had gone dry and she was glad for the sip of *sarave* to gather her thoughts.

He knows. Any fool could see it and Yuenne is no fool. What now?

She rose to her feet.

"Counselor Yuenne, everyone in this room knows your name and how my father (*rest him now*, murmured the crowd)—how my father relied on your bravery. Well, I say the time for bravery is not past. It is one year since the Weapon was unleashed on us. And look! We live. We thrive. We increase our numbers." She indicated the baby in her arms, the families with children, and the handful of women who would soon join her ranks. "We know we will live, but we don't know about the world beyond the mountains. Where are our brothers and sisters? Are they gone? Is Eriis alone? Counselor Yuenne, I call on you to lead an expedition into the Vastness. Seek our people, or at least find the footsteps of their passing. Counselor Yuenne, will you take up this quest?"

Yuenne wasn't smiling anymore.

He lifted his glass again.

"I shall leave at once. It is my honor to do your bidding, as I did your father's. I will travel to the Vastness," he paused. "And I will come back, Your Grace. That's a promise."

The cheers and applause were heartfelt.

Hellne clutched the child to her chest. *I made this boy, and whether he's an embarrassment or a weapon or takes my seat one day, he is mine to use, Yuenne. Think on that as you head into the Vastness.*

Infuriatingly, Yuenne had returned from that journey and made a hero of himself. Hellne noted the only thing worth celebrating from his trip was the fact that he survived it. He found nothing.

"Only sand, I'm afraid, and plenty of it," he told her in private. "Hard to imagine there was ever anything there."

The Zaalmage's pet hypothesis was that the cities had been moved somewhere else, and they and their people were trapped just out of sight. It gave off a scent of hope, and had many proponents who referred to it as The Hidden Kingdom Theory. The popularity of their notions gave the Mages renewed enthusiasm.

"Human blood, Your Grace, even a small amount, and we could begin to turn our theories into proper experiments." The Mages had a mania for blood, human blood from which she couldn't seem to distract them. And the debt, unpaid, always at the back of her mind. But if the Zaalmage knew what she'd done, surely he would have come to claim what was owed. The Zaal was not subtle, not like advisors at her court.

When Hellne spotted Yuenne having a serious discussion with a then two-year-old Rhuun, crouching down to talk with him eye to eye, she did her best not to panic.

"And what are my gentlemen and heroes of the court talking about today?" she asked brightly.

"Wings, Mama," Rhuun told her. "When do I get mine?"

"Yes," said Yuenne with his little smile, "It shouldn't be long before this young man fledges. How old is he? Only two? He's as big as a child twice his age. I imagine he'll manifest in all sorts of interesting ways."

Hellne sent him back on his second grand expedition to the Vastness shortly thereafter, feeling only a moment's hesitation that she might be making Yuenne's wife a widow and leaving his young daughter fatherless. Then she thought about Yuenne smiling, smiling and having an interesting conversation with the Zaalmage, and sent him on his way.

And now Rhuun was five and already more than a head taller than his playmates. And what would happen when there was no fledging? (For she had all but given up on that idea.) And worse yet, what if he never manifested fire? She'd had a *chlystron* made for him, tied with a ribbon in her family's color, and it just sat in his little hand. He looked confused and then threw it on the ground, saying it burned him, and he couldn't be persuaded to try again.

One part of her wanted to hide him, stuff the basket under a chair, throw a blanket over him and never let him come to harm. But this was foolish and weak, and she put it aside in favor of the part that remembered how she'd grown from a silly girl to a queen practically overnight. She had made him, and the making would continue. She resolved to let him grow without her hand holding him up. It might be unpleasant but it would give him the strength that didn't come from fire or flight.

Ugly, on the other hand, well, no one called her child ugly.

Back to the Vastness with you, Counselor. Maybe this time you'll find some manners out there in all that sand.

Chapter 8

Eriis City
8 years after the War of the Door, Eriisai calendar
40 years later, Mistran calendar
Royal Library

Rhuun spent much of his time in the royal library, finding it both quiet and safe. It wasn't much of a collection of books, the Queen wasn't a big reader, but it seemed to her to be a thing one ought to do. It was mostly an under-lit collection of half-desiccated texts and cast-off furniture in a largely undamaged series of connected rooms. The boy didn't read the books, and he didn't know a silk cushioned, wood framed couch imported from Mistra from a cheap Old City imitation, but he liked the way the room smelled. And it was dark and even a little cooler. The constant baking heat made him feel a little faint sometimes. No one knew that, not even his mother.

He was in the library hiding—no, he told himself—he was sitting and *thinking* after lessons one afternoon when his mother found him. She had a small girl demon in front of her, and gently pushed the child forward.

"Look, Rhuun," she said. "This is Aelle. She is the clan daughter of our friend Counselor Yuenne. You like him."

The boy looked suspiciously at the pair. Like all of his kind, they looked quite similar, slender and poised— one just a larger version of the other. The girl had silky black hair loose around her shoulders, his mother's was tightly coiled and dressed with sparkling black and white beads, as was proper. He knew Counselor Yuenne. He smiled all the time. Rhuun had seen him kick another boy down a flight of stairs for walking in front of him too slowly. And this was his daughter. She wasn't smiling, at least.

"Aelle will be taking lessons with us for a while."

"My father is traveling. I am to stay here," the girl said. She looked indifferently around the library. "Can we go outside? I want to practice." The Queen crouched down so she was eye level with the child.

"Rhuun prefers to stay in here. Perhaps you can convince him to go outside with you. Now, have a nice afternoon."

She turned and vanished, leaving a bright spot in the air. That was one of her favorite abilities, she'd told him, one of the nicest things she could do. Be in one place and then suddenly be in another. You never knew who you'd surprise, and that was great fun. And if anyone ever said anything you didn't like, well, you could just leave. Then they'd have to think about what they'd said and why. He'd understand when his own abilities manifested. There was plenty of time, she said.

The boy imagined she would reappear—poof!—sitting on her High Seat at Court, startling and surprising her councilors. She was very important, his mother. It was easy to understand why Counselor Yuenne handed his child off to her. But what was he supposed to do with the girl?

Aelle had crawled into a once-handsome wing back chair which someone had pushed up against his favorite couch. Her feet stuck out in front of her. The chair might have been designed for a giant or a human, she nearly vanished into it. She scooted herself forward and looked around at the rows and stacks of books. They were mostly historical documents, along with some memoirs of those who had survived the War of the Door. In other words, boring.

"Can you talk?" she asked. "I heard you were simple in your wits."

"Of course I can talk," he answered testily.

She reached out and poked him in the arm. A tiny jet of flame shot from her finger. He yanked his arm away.

"Don't do that."

"So you can talk, but you are simple." She nodded as if that explained everything.

He scowled. "Where's your father?" he asked. "I bet he's dead. I bet he got sucked up by the Crosswinds. That's why Mother is being nice to you."

Aelle looked furious. Tears stood in her eyes. He would learn Aelle never cried unless she was angry.

She said, "He is not dead. At least I have a father."

He immediately felt sorry for her. Why was he so stupid? "I'm sorry. Don't cry. He's not dead."

She rubbed her nose and got up, wandering around the dark room. "Let's go out. It's boring in here."

"I don't like it out there. I can't fly. I can't do fire. And Niico is there."

The first time he'd been scorched, he figured he'd been no more than 5 or 6. He'd been burned across the backs of his legs by Niico, who had recently fledged and was showing off his new little wings. He'd stumbled home to tell his mother, who'd taken a look at him and said, "Can you walk?" He nodded, trying not to cry. (She hated when he cried.) "Then you will heal."

She turned her attention back to her maid, and continued planning the evening meal. It wasn't the last time Niico had gotten a strike on him, but it was the last time he'd cried to his mother.

Aelle nodded. She'd been a target as well, as they all had at one time or another.

"They get you. The bigger ones. They used to get me too, until I fledged." She brightened. "And I got my fire last year, so I can blast some, too. But Niico is the fastest. He's the best."

"He's the worst." There was a pause. "Mother says I'll get my fire soon. I don't think that's right, though. I don't think I'll ever get it." He had never told anyone this, although he was certain it was true. He wasn't simple, far from it, but he was different. And here, that was worse.

He wasn't sure why he was telling Aelle. Maybe because she had cried in front of him?

Aelle took his arm, taking care to avoid grabbing a still healing burn. "Come on. Let's go out."

"But I can't—"

"But I can."

The bigger ones didn't get him that day. Aelle was around a lot after that.

***

She *was* around a lot, but she wasn't always, and besides, it would have made him feel like a baby to have someone standing in front of him all the time. So, after lessons about heroes from before the Weapon, the geography of cities that no longer existed, and the names of the mountains that no one could see anymore (they were still there, of course, hiding behind a sky full of dust), there were still days when the bigger ones caught him.

This particular day, he'd done his best to avoid ruining another tunic, but still ended up with a tear on one knee. At least the leggings were black, that way no one could see the bloodstain. *It was because I got mad,* he told himself. *That's why they came after me. If I was invisible, they'd leave me alone.* But he had yelled after them in a rage, and they'd left off picking on some other pre-fledged victim and come at him.

He ran for it.

He headed for the Streets of the Pearl Suspended in *Sarave* (which in the ornate, old language of Eriis referred to the Pearl Moon adrift in the *sarave* of the night sky, but these days everyone just called the Quarter) where the buildings were close together and there wasn't room to fly, and sure enough, after several twisting alleys, they got bored or lost him, because he was alone.

His mother told him to stay out of this part of the Old City, but like so many other things she said, there was never an explanation. He hated it when he didn't understand something, and finally, he decided he'd obey his mother *if* he could figure out why she gave the order. So far, the Quarter was just little kids playing in the dust, shops, people hurrying and talking and laughing, and (sometimes) loud voices. No one bothered him, and while there were just as many furtive stares, there were far fewer whispers.

Usually he had time to stop and say hello to the old Master who sorted sand from chunky grit to stuff so fine you couldn't feel it even if you stuck your hand in the basket. And the Mother who made sweet ice always had a new flavor to sample. (He was partial to the brown kind.) He always nodded at the group of kids, some fledged, some not, who hung around the doorway of their own school. It was smaller by far than the school the royals and the clans sent their own children to, but he wished it was his school. It had no play yard, for one thing, just a dusty side street and marks on the walls where generations of fireballs had struck. They acknowledged each other but had never exchanged a word.

Today he passed it all by, blind to everything but his own anger. The children watched him pass, noting his fierce scowl and ripped leggings. They nodded to each other as if to say, "You see? He may be the prince but he comes here to escape his problems."

Rhuun finally ran out of steam and came to a stop, looking around curiously. It was quiet and a little dim on this side street. He didn't think he'd been this way before. Then he remembered the sting of the gravel when he'd fallen, the laughter of the bigger kids, and the white pain of the fire that caught him on the arm. He got angry all over again.

"*Scorp*," he muttered, examining his leggings. "*Scorping scorp.*" It was the worst word he knew. It had something to do with joining, but he only had a vague idea of what that meant, either. He just knew that when he said it, his mother nearly took his head off.

"Is it as bad as all that?" a gentle voice asked. There was humor, but it didn't seem to be directed at him. He looked up from his torn leggings to see a woman sitting just inside the doorway of a crumbly stone building. He rubbed away some angry tears and stood to face her.

"Sorry Mother," he said politely, addressing her as he had been taught to call all older women who were not part of his mother's retinue. "I've got a big hole, see?" She didn't lean forward to look. "My mother will be angry. But sorry."

"I know you," she said. "You're the Queen's boy." Now she did rise from her stool, and leaning heavily on a carved stick, came out into the alley. She was tiny—at eight Rhuun was already nearly her height and her thin hair, cropped close to her scalp as was the prerogative of widows, was more grey than black. Her mouth was heavily bracketed by lines, but the skin around her eyes was smooth as a girl's.

She can't see, so she doesn't squint, he thought, *so she doesn't have lines.*

"I am called Mother Jaa, and I was there when you were born, young Prince." He knew he was easy to spot, a tall boy with strange eyes was a well-known sight in the Old City, but how would *she* know who he was? If she was one of his mother's ladies, why wasn't she at Court? She didn't look like any of the ladies he'd ever seen, that was sure. For one thing, none of his mother's ladies were blind.

"Come inside and I'll make you some cold water. You seem a bit overheated." He hesitated, but the thought of learning something, maybe a secret thing, about his life was irresistible, so he followed her in. The house had no door, just a white curtain covering the doorway. She had it tied to one side so she could sit on her stool and take the breeze. If it was a house, it was the smallest he'd ever seen. The room where his mother kept her robes and silks was bigger. He looked at the table and chairs, the cot in a curtained off corner, the vase and bowl.

"Where's the rest of your house?" He didn't see a door leading to a courtyard, or a corridor, or even a dryroom where she might refresh herself.

She laughed and handed him a cup of cool water. "This is all I need. Now, there was some trouble with your leggings, I understand?"

"I fell," he said, and left it there. She nodded and went to a cabinet in the corner and retrieved a needle and thread. He watched, amazed, as she threaded the needle on the first try. "How did you do that?"

"I know where things go," she told him. "Now let me see," and she took his knee in her small, warm hands, and joined the ripped edges of the fabric, "My clan sister's eldest daughter is your mother's Lady of All Work—Diia. And when you came into this world, I was there to greet you. What a set of lungs! We thought you'd call the *daeeva* down from the mountains!" She smiled at the memory. "Your mother was very brave—no screaming or crying from that one. She was very happy to see you."

Rhuun wondered if, because she was blind, Mother Jaa was thinking of a different woman and a different baby. The *daeeva*, now, that was superstitious nonsense, as his mother called it, the spirits of the dead which came around if a child misbehaved or made too much noise. Diia had threatened him with the *daeeva* more than once, until the Queen had taken her aside and reminded her they lived in a royal city, not in a hut with the pigs. There weren't pigs, not anymore, but he'd never heard about the *daeeva* again—until now.

"There." His leggings were perhaps not as good as new, but good enough to avoid his having to offer an explanation. "Now, what about this?" She laid a crooked finger on the fresh burn on his arm. He couldn't recall anyone outside of his mother touching him as much as this old woman had in just the few moments since he'd come inside her house.

"It's nothing. It'll go away." In fact, it made him see bright lights behind his eyes with even her barest touch.

She nodded. "Of course. I find if something troubles me, I look for a good place to put it. Until this goes away, perhaps we should find a place for it?"

He had no idea what she meant.

"I told you, young man, I know where things go. Useful, very useful to tuck things away. You never know when you might need them. And look, you can put things in their place as well." This time she placed her finger on his forehead. "Close your eyes, do you see? There's a place for things like pain. You see it, don't you?"

And for a second—just one second—he did.

"Fly now, Young Prince, but do come and see me again. I think we can find a place for many things. It would be my honor to have your assistance."

***

It became Rhuun's custom, after that, to divide his time between the safety of the library and the adventure of a trip to the Old City. He started a game with himself of finding shortcuts to Mother Jaa's house, knowing that even if he got lost in the maze of alleys and courtyards, someone could point him in the right direction. Everyone knew her, and, after all, everyone knew him. Despite his mother's concern, he was looked after far better than if he'd spent his afternoons at the play yard. None of the people in the Old City wanted to be the one to damage a prince.

Aelle asked him where he disappeared to, and he said he went for walks in the oldest part of the city. She was beginning to study form shifting, which had recently come off the proscribed list of talents and abilities (along with skills in the arts and certain luxury items like simple flowers and body ornaments) and didn't have time to wander around.

"I don't understand," he'd said to Mother Jaa one hot afternoon, sweeping the dust from her doorway. "If you can just make the dust go outside, why bother with the broom?" It was considered quite rude to ask a person what their abilities were, since not everyone could do everything equally well, but he'd seen her do marvels and felt it was a fair question.

She was raising and lowering the temperature of a cup of water in her funny white mug. It looked broken to him, but she let him touch it and he found that the cracks were only on the very surface. As he watched, rising steam was replaced by a rapid crawl of ice crystals. He thought sometimes she did things just so he could see that they could be done.

"The dust gives the broom something to do, and the broom gives you something to do." That explanation seemed to satisfy her. She nodded and went back to her cup.

He leaned on the broom, looking skeptical, which he knew she could feel, if not see. "Very well," she said finally. "I find a simple task clears the mind. The dust goes outside, the floor is clean, the broom has done its job, your hands have done their job—so many things accomplished and you aren't even thinking of them." She leaned forward. "That's how we found the place for pain. That's how you'll be able to find it again, anytime you need to use it."

He surprised her by saying, "I found it. Just like you said."

***

Two nights earlier, his mother had noticed his leggings had been repaired by a hand other than her own. He told her he'd done it himself, silently cursing himself for not simply wadding up the torn, stained garment and shoving it in the back of his big wooden dresser, as he'd done in the past.

"Don't lie to me," she snapped, "I know you didn't do this." He was as stubborn as she was irritated, but he felt if she knew about his visits to Mother Jaa, she'd have something worse to say about it, and maybe Mother Jaa would be in trouble as well. He stared at the floor and stuck to his story, even after she lost her patience and finished the argument with a sharp slap. He didn't see it coming (he usually did) and instead of grabbing onto the sting and holding on to his anger, he let it slide past. It was gone, like a mouse into its hole, like water into sand.

Now he did look up at his mother, looked her in the eye and said, "I did it myself. I'm not a baby, you know."

She raised a brow and smiled slightly. "Very well. Repairs are your job, then."

***

Rhuun continued, "Two nights ago Mother ... was cross with me, and I found it, the place you showed me. I put it away. It's still there, I think. Um, can you teach me to sew a seam? And thread a needle?"

The old woman looked a bit surprised. "Well done, and a fast mind. Sewing lessons, yes, I think we can do that as well." She reached out her hand and gently laid it on his shoulder. "I am sorry you will have so many opportunities to practice, *shan*." He knew she didn't mean sewing.

Then she smiled again and pointed at the doorway. "You missed a spot."

Chapter 9

Eriis City
8 years after the War of the Door, Eriisai calendar
40 years later, Mistran calendar
The Quarter

After sending Rhuun home after his first needle-threading lesson, Mother Jaa sat for a while with her favorite white mug. It was porcelain, and it came from the other place. Hellne had gone through her things in a frenzy after her baby was born, giving the young maid Diia many of the gifts and trinkets from her "special human friend." Diia had passed many of them to her family, and Jaa had gotten this thickly glazed white cup. She'd been told it was made of melted glass, and was almost unbreakable. Her hands told her it bore a network of fine shatter marks, but that made it unique and to her, far more beautiful than if it had been perfect.

Jaa thought about the look on the boy's face when she talked about his mother. She didn't need eyes to see how he longed to know how he came to be… *different.* She recalled the day Hellne's travail began. One of her household guard found the young queen laying half in and half out of her dryroom, unable to even get to her bed. She had no women to assist her, she'd sent her few surviving maids and ladies back to their homes. Diia told her it was because Hellne didn't like the eyes people cast at her ever growing belly, even though the story put about talked of the sacrifice Her Grace was making, allowing those women to work alongside their own families instead of serving hers.

Even though she was growing old there was nothing wrong with her memory, thank Light and Wind. *And Rain,* she added to herself with a sour chuckle. Since the day in her own long-gone youth when she'd traded one sort of sight for another, she'd been expecting the call to come: the Queen needs her young maid after all. Diia, the girl with back-country folk must come at once; the Queen is in distress, you must come and bring the women who can help bring a child into the world. Bring those who can stand guard along the way and insure that the child—or the mother for that matter—do not wander off the path of life, into the Veil. Bring the one who knows how to deal with pain. That last one was Jaa herself, who held Hellne's head and helped her find a place to put her agony. The infant was among the largest they'd ever seen born alive, and Hellne was, typical of her race, a small woman. It was understood that the idea of her ever bearing another child was extremely unlikely, and so this one must survive. Once it was clear both mother and child were going to live, Hellne insisted they hold it up and show her—eyes, hands, feet, a cap of dark hair. Jaa wondered what Hellne hoped to see, and what she feared. In any event, the Queen found the baby's appearance satisfactory, and nodded, then lay back exhausted. They laid the child on her breast. Mother Jaa was correct in telling Rhuun that Hellne was happy to see her child—see it finally outside her body.

Once she could complete her *toilette* unaided, she dismissed them all. Diia would be ultimately hired back when Rhuun was about six months old, and she never left again. Jaa returned to her little house here in the Quarter, and began to wait.

And now the boy was growing, and he seemed to have a talent for putting things in their place, even if he was completely without other gifts. She wasn't so sure that was true either, despite what they said about him behind their hands at Court. For someone who claimed to look down on gossips, Diia usually had a lot to say.

"I know you think he makes it rain, Jaa, but there's something… well, he's different. Hellne says it was from The Weapon, while he was still floating inside her. That's what she says, anyways. Nice enough boy, polite, but…."

Jaa sipped her water and traced the cracks in the porcelain with her fingertips.

Lots of things coming and going from that other place in those days, before the Weapon, thought Jaa. *I think I had better talk to Diia. I think idle talk, rumor, and speculation had best be laid to rest, lest someone takes that kind of talk seriously. The kind of someone who lives underground, for instance. Dangerous talk. Blood talk.*

She dipped the tip of her crooked old finger into the cup, and savored the resulting chips and slivers of ice.

Chapter 10

Eriis City
9 years after the War of the Door, Eriisai calendar
45 years later, Mistran calendar
The Quarter

In the end, it turned out to be a matter of telling people what they wanted to hear.

Old Master Vee, the sand sorter, was too busy keeping his three daughters from burning each other to cinders to worry about something that might or might not have happened during the war.

"It was a terrible time," Diia said to Master Vee. "And my Hellne, well, she took some awful risks even bringing that child to birth. Worked herself to a shadow in those days. Before I started making sure the poor thing ate and slept, that is. Well, I don't need to tell you how difficult it can be, even with healthy children. The Weapon, you know, it didn't just change the landscape. Oh, she sends these hair beads—three sets, you have three girls, don't you? With her compliments. Your sand is always first choice in her kitchens."

Diia led her elderly clan-aunt out into the street, and looked for Jaa's review. She nodded approvingly. Diia could be counted on to repeat any story, as long as she was featured in it.

Mistress Kaaya, the pretty young kite maker, had an appraising eye and sharp tongue. Jaa knew she'd need a delicate kind of convincing.

"Her boy," Kaaya told Mother Jaa over water one afternoon, "Now, he'll be tall. Some women like that. And he seems polite enough. Whatever the queen did before the war, at least she's raising a respectful child. The Weapon, you say? Well, I suppose it makes sense, it changed so many things. And yet I recall there was some talk…."

Jaa placed her gnarled old hand over Kaaya's slender, ink stained one. "There is always talk. There was talk about a young soldier, if I recall. Wasn't he secretly wed?"

Kaaya blushed crimson. Jaa couldn't see the younger woman's face but she could feel the rising heat. "Quite right, Mother. Idle talk is just that—fit only for those who don't have anything better to do. The Weapon, of course. It's just a shame, he'd be a handsome boy, sort of, if it wasn't for those eyes. Well, not handsome exactly, but… oh well.

And please, let me pay you for the mending. You do the finest work, I can barely see the stitches."

Sometimes, they'd do the work for you, if you were patient.

Diia and Jaa stopped for cups of sweet ice and sat together in Dzhura Square. This, the oldest part of the city was built around squares and plazas, connected by a twisting maze of alleys, side streets, and the occasional named boulevard. Before the war, it had been lined with trees and bright with flower boxes. Now it was twice as crowded and the air was almost as full of dust, kicked up by sandals and wheeled carts, as the plains beyond the city wall. It was still not uncommon to see people coming and going with their traveling scarves thrown over their faces.

"True," said Diia, rather loudly, "but as anyone can see, the air definitely improves. Well, you know who we have to thank for that." She nibbled at her ice. "And don't tell me the Mages—Light and Wind alone knows what they'd get up to if our Queen hadn't set them straight."

"Not quite natural, I think, for a person to live underground," commented Jaa.

With a little prompting, the residents of the Old City reminded each other that things were finally improving. The years of hunger and fear were behind them. One could see all the way across the city from the Tower of the Moons straight to the City Wall, most days (if only briefly), and who was to thank? Who came to the Quarter in those first days to make sure everyone had at least a cup of water and a place to sleep? Not the Mages—they hid safe underground through the whole thing. *When they make the rain come back to Eriis*, they told each other, *then we can talk about the Mages. Maybe the boy, the Queen's strange son, maybe there was more to him than one could see....*

***

"Ow!" Rhuun had stabbed himself with the needle again. "My fingers are too fat." His sewing lesson had stalled out at 'threading.' Jaa, having listened carefully to the wind that blew down her street, was starting to think the boy himself was his own best advocate. Diia wasn't so sure.

She spends her days by Hellne's side, thought Jaa, *and she sees the way our Queen looks at her son. And these days, Diia doesn't piss without the Queen's blessing. But our people, here in Quarter, are perhaps not so... close to the situation. They will get used to him. People can get used to anything, if they have water and bread.*

Rhuun set his needle down and kicked his heels under the stool. "Tell me about the old times, Mother Jaa. Before the war. Did you ever go to the other place?"

"I did not, in fact I don't think I've been out of the Old City since before you were born. But!" she said, with a smile, "I know someone who went over, and came back to tell." She didn't need conventional sight to see the boy's wide eyes. "Your mother's lady, Diia, is one of my grand nieces, as I've told you, and her father's cousin— so some relation—in my clan anyway, his best friend was a man named Teeuh, and that man was the ambassador's assistant. He went twice before the war. He told us all about it; we didn't believe half of it! Water from sky to sky, can you imagine? And people travel on the water in boats." She pronounced it boh-hats.

He sat back, disappointed. "That can't be true. There's not enough water, you wouldn't get anywhere."

"Well, I suppose you know best…" She waited, knowing his curiosity would defeat his pride. He quickly apologized and she nodded and continued. "There are flowers of every color, and birds in the trees—he told us one might think they were mice with wings."

"Like Rhuumice?"

She'd heard many times from him about the magical Rhuumice, although she knew the boy had never actually seen one.

"Something like that, yes. Well of course we had many of these things before the war—not birds, though—but they have something we never had. It gets cold. Very cold, so that the ice, like this—" she held out her cup, now frosted over, "it fell from the sky."

"From the sky? I don't…" Since he didn't want to risk offense, she let him change the subject. "What are the human persons like? Did he tell you?" he asked.

"Now, the humans, they're an interesting lot." *Walk carefully, Jaa,* she thought. "They are clever, very clever, and while they can be foolish and destructive in their anger, they have much capacity for kindness and generosity. Teeuh told us most of them don't even know we exist. Isn't that strange? A whole world right next to them, and they don't know a thing about us."

"Maybe I'll go there one day, and tell them who we are," said Rhuun.

Jaa sipped her water thoughtfully. "You might be exactly the right person to do so, *shan*. Now, it is still light, am I correct?"

"Mother Jaa, you are always correct."

"Let us thread a needle, lest your garments fall to rags and we have to start transforming my table and chairs into a shirt for you. Have you doubled in size since last week?"

"What happened to the ambassador? And to Teeuh?"

Jaa didn't answer for a while.

"I'm sorry, Mother. It was rude of me to ask."

"No, not rude. I was just remembering them. Teeuh vanished the first day, I think the Weapon took him. The ambassador… he went to the other side and never came back. Humans can be dangerous, Rhuun. Most of them may not know we exist, but there are those who watch the Door, I think, and wait for us to knock."

"Look! I did it!" He held up the needle and thread, the human world, for the moment, forgotten.

Chapter 11

Eriis City

10 years after the War of the Door, Eriisai calendar

50 years later, Mistran calendar

The Palace

Hellne, as she grew older, discovered she disliked dining alone. The only thing she was less fond of, was trying to have a meal with squalling brats roving around the room. So when she asked Yuenne to join her for dinner, it was understood that his wife Siia and their two young children would not be in attendance. But since this was a casual dinner 'to catch up with my dear friend' as she put it, and not a formal meal, Rhuun was expected to join them. At least, she thought, he knows how to comport himself at the table. She'd made certain of that.

She, if she was honest, preferred a formal dinner. There was always something to do or say or pass, and less opportunity for chatty talk. The rooms looked nicer too, lit for formal occasions with great glowing stones in black and cream—casting their soft yellow light—and matching black and cream silk hangings. Tonight was simple. The far wall, which once had opened onto a view of the valley and mountains beyond, now revealed the burning plains. At this time of evening, the wind and ever present dust were at their lowest ebb, so the silk sheers were drawn back. Low bowls of glowing stones cast a wavering yellow light which slowly grew stronger as the sun set behind its curtain of grey and yellow clouds. The long table was set with bread and meat—today shaped into neat squares, stacked on silver dishes. She and Yuenne had already taken their seats and sipped their water when Rhuun skidded into the room at a full run and slid into the chair next to his mother.

"I don't ask that you report your activities to me moment by moment, Rhuun. I do ask one thing, though." Hellne was only slightly annoyed. The boy was such a cloudhead, she was surprised he wasn't late more often. At least he was clean and his clothing didn't smell like smoke. She frowned at him. He was too tall for the chair, his knees hit the bottom of the table.

"Sorry, Mother," he muttered. "Lost track of time. Won't happen again." He poured her a splash of water before helping himself to a cup. *He tries*, she thought with a sigh. She watched him fiddle with his utensils, which looked child sized in his long fingers. *He looks more like his father all the time.* She tore her eyes away from him.

"As I was saying, Hellne, this time I'd like to go further out into the Vastness, and perhaps stay through a season." Counselor Yuenne spoke to the Queen, but his eyes drifted to her son. "Maybe one day you'll go with me, Rhuun. Wouldn't that be an adventure?"

Rhuun looked up and said, "I'm going through The Door one day. I'm going to see the humans."

Hellne dropped her fork and began to cough. Instantly Diia was at her side with water and a fresh *serviette.* When she had recovered, she said, "Please do forgive me, a speck of untranslated sand." With a bright smile, she turned to Rhuun. "What a funny thing to say! Now, Yuenne, a whole season—"

"What do you know about humans, Rhuun?" Yuenne asked. "I don't think they're very nice, do you?"

"Oh, I know all about humans," the boy told them. "They can be nice or nasty, and they're very clever. They have birds and ice." He turned back to his dinner, the topic depleted.

Hellne looked helplessly at her son. She couldn't fill his mouth with sand to stop his talking, but she could find out where he'd come up with birds and ice and ideas about the humans.

The evening continued with plans made for Yuenne to depart for the Vastness. That was one problem, at least, out of her hair. *Someone's been chatty,* she thought. *Someone has my son's ear. I'll have to have a talk with Diia. She can send one of the kitchen boys out after Rhuun and find out where he goes and who he sees. And who sees him.*

Chapter 12

Eriis City
10 years after the War of the Door, Eriisai calendar
50 years later, Mistran calendar
The Quarter

A week later, Rhuun was surprised to find a door, a real ashboard door in place of Mother Jaa's old white curtain. He pulled the latch, and finding it unlocked, pushed it open.

"I like your door, Mother!" He was surprised to find a young couple with a child of about two (which took one look at him and began to howl).

He backed out, more confused than anything else. Had he forgotten which was her house? Was he on the wrong street?

One of her neighbors stuck her head out the door at the commotion.

"Where's Mother Jaa?" he asked.

The woman shrugged sadly. "She's gone."

"What do you mean, gone? She can't be gone. This is her house!"

"Not anymore." The father of the screaming child joined Rhuun on the street. His accent was heavy—they must have just recently moved to the Old City from the outskirts of the Vastness, the in-between place people were now calling the Edge. "This is ours, now. Mother, she's gone."

She was old, thought Rhuun, *but I didn't know her time was close. I didn't even get to say goodbye!*

"I'm sorry I just walked in on you," he told the man. "And that I scared your baby." The child was still wailing. "Mother Jaa was my friend. I didn't know she was gone."

The man said, "You're the one. Tall boy. Stay right here." He ducked back through the door, emerging a moment later with a small parcel wrapped in paper. "She left this for you."

Rhuun thanked the man and made his way home. *Gone? How could she be gone?* For once he didn't notice the eyes on him, or respond to the smiles. He always ignored the frowns and dark looks anyway.

Once in his room, he opened the paper. It was her sewing kit, a neat cream colored ashboard box with a Rhuumice carved into the lid.

He smiled at it, but felt a stone in his throat. He took the pain and put it away, just as she had shown him.

Chapter 13

Eriis City
10 years after the War of the Door, Eriisai calendar
50 years later, Mistran calendar
Queen Hellne's receiving room

"Is it done?"

In response to Diia's question, the young man pulled a flat, paper-wrapped parcel from his coat and handed it over.

Diia thanked him, passed him his payment, and closed the door to the Queen's receiving room behind him. She laid the package on the desk.

Hellne tore away the ash-paper wrapper to reveal a dingy old piece of fabric. It had once been a cheerful white curtain, but years of dust and countless hands pulling it aside had rendered it light tan. The bottom was in tatters.

"Mother Jaa was kind to me. I don't know that I would have managed Rhuun's arrival without her." Hellne tried to recall his birth, but it was a jumbled blur of pain. It was the first and only time in her life she understood what Malloy had been talking about. She also distinctly remembered Jaa's cool hands on her brow. Other than that, it was mostly light and sound. The sounds, she'd been told later, were her own screams. Two maids had fainted dead away from all the blood, it was a marvel she and the boy had both survived.

"You did the right thing," said Diia. "Jaa always had something to say. Maybe too much."

Hellne folded the curtain, stroking the ripped edge flat. "It's just that I need to be the one to tell him… talk to him…" *Tell him what?* she asked herself. *That his father's hand was on the Weapon that made him a cripple?* She'd told the story so often, the effects of the destructive magic of the Weapon on her unborn child, she sometimes wondered if it might be true after all. Maybe if his father had been a proper Eriisai, he'd have turned out the same way. She sighed and shook her head. He had his father's face, and to imagine otherwise, was admitting she was simple in her wits.

Diia gently removed the curtain from Hellne's hand and folded it small. She rewrapped it in the paper and put it in a cabinet, out of sight. "There is talk, Madam."

Hellne looked up. "Talk?" She chuckled. "How unusual." There was an old saying about the wind stopping when all the Eriisai held their tongues at the same time. "Some water, if you please. That rag brought dust in with it."

Diia busied herself with wiping a silver cup clean. She held it up, it had a thick lip and kept the water cold. She laid a tray with the cup, bowl of ice, and a slim pitcher of water. "Talk in town. About your son."

"That he hasn't manifested, that there's something wrong with him." She waved her hand. "I know this, Diia."

Diia used a pair of etched ebony tongs to carefully set a sliver of ice in the cup and set it in front of Hellne. "Not exactly. I mean, not completely."

Anyone else would have been escorted out already. Hellne did not welcome conversation about her child. The Weapon had an unfortunate result; what more needed to be said? On the other hand, Diia did sometimes carry back useful gossip from town. She had clan relations who had come in after the Weapon, from the dead fields and hills to the Quarter. Those people were rumored to still manifest gifts that city dwellers, in their lives of idleness and indulgence, no longer possessed; gifts of premonition, gifts of speech with the dead. It was Hellne's belief that there were no such gifts. That they told those stories to make themselves feel superior to their betters inside the Arch, and lessen the sting of their lost homes in what was now called the Vastness. But if anyone spoke to the *daeeve*, it would be someone from the hills. And if anyone were to perceive that her son was something beyond crippled, it would be one of them as well.

"You might as well tell me," she said. It was bound to be some superstitious nonsense, but it might come in handy one day.

"Madam," Diia looked Hellne in the eye for the briefest instant, then at the floor. "They say he will bring back the rain."

Hellne laughed bitterly. "The rain? Really. Do they think he can turn the calendar backwards? Or do they say he'll suddenly manifest as a great Mage? Will he make the flowers bloom again? Will he tear The Door down while he's at it?" She glared at Diia, angry at herself for allowing her futile anger and frustration to surface. "Did you and Jaa have a hand in this?" At the time, she had agreed a little word dropped here and there by a friendly voice would do no harm, and possibly some good. This was far beyond 'a little word.'

Diia blanched. "No, Madam, to all of it. I am merely repeating what I've heard in town. Jaa and I, as you agreed, made sure his name and yours were honored. We spoke of your hard work and love for all your citizens." She cleared her throat. "The other, they've been saying all on their own."

"Well then they will be disappointed. I mean, obviously no such thing will ever happen. At least, not because of anything that boy does." Hellne took a sip of water. *Bring back the rain. The poor thing can barely manage a fork.*

Diia swallowed nervously. "Shall I try and put a stop to it?"

"Of course," she began, and then paused. If the people in the Quarter painted Rhuun to be some sort of potential hero, well, the key word was *potential*. That could mean anything, and there was no expiration date. If they believed in him, they would, naturally, want to protect his beloved mother against anyone who might think to cause her harm. She thought again of Yuenne, and his little smile. And the Mages. They'd been quiet lately but they were always there, literally underfoot. "No." Diia looked confused. "No, let them talk. Better they should tell themselves he's different and special. After all, he doesn't appear to be simple, and he'll one day have some sort of place at my Court, Light and Wind alone knows what would be appropriate."

Malloy, though, she thought. *He wasn't simple. He was clever. He was cleverer than I was. He tricked me into taking his spark, and that's a long step past clever. Malloy, are you still alive? I've got a weapon of my own now, and I still have your little book. Remember? It's the key to our being together.*

She smiled and helped herself to another sliver of ice. "Let them talk, Diia. He may not bring back the rain, but that doesn't mean he won't bring us something important, one day."

Chapter 14

Eriis City
14 years after the War of the Door, Eriisai calendar
70 years later, Mistran calendar
Royal Library

"Rhuun, I know you're in here. Where are you?"

He heard Aelle calling from the door of the library. He was leaning against a far wall, the big slabs of yellow stone had somehow retained some coolness. He was reading a biography of a general named Kaata. General Kaata had died during the War, and he had heard a rumor that one of his mother's generals had been his father.

Rhuun had become quite a collector of rumors. His transformative ability had never manifested in any meaningful way, but he had a little reactive trick he could always count on, a way of blending into the background. It didn't make him invisible as much as unnoticeable. It was a mean sort of gift, but it worked very well for him. He found he enjoyed eavesdropping. It was so much more satisfying to hear people call you 'simple' and 'a shame, really' and ‘a cripple’ and 'something to do with The Weapon, it must have been' when they didn’t know you were listening rather than hearing it whispered behind your back. Right now he was examining the book more than actually reading it—it was slow going indeed for a supposed man of action—and looking for clues. So far his mother hadn't appeared, it was just a list of battles and how he'd provisioned his troops for them. Lots of grain and sheep. The most interesting part were the things that no longer existed. Grain and sheep. He was close to putting it aside, and when he heard Aelle call for him he was glad for the distraction.

"Back here," he called out. "Come and look at this. I took it from the kitchen."

She appeared around a corner. He held up a dark brown bottle. "You took *sarave*? Is it good?"

"No, it’s awful," he acknowledged cheerfully. "Try it."

She shot a thunderous scowl at something in the corridor behind her, then reached for the bottle.

"Give me that." She took a long drink, making a horrible face. "Not good." She took another drink, then motioned sharply for someone to join them.

A young male demon stepped from behind a bookcase. He looked to be a slightly smaller version of Aelle, and very attractive—even by their look-alike standards—with eyes that leaned towards the darkest garnet. Aelle's were much lighter, her eyes were touched with pale rose, like her mother. The boy's appearance was somewhat diminished by a freshly burned cheek—so fresh it had barely started healing. The boy stepped forward with a smile.

"I'm Ilaan. You must be The Beast." Aelle gasped and Rhuun rose to his feet, the book tumbling to the floor. The boy raised an appraising brow and made a show of craning his neck.

"Aelle, you were not even kidding." He looked from one to the other, seemingly surprised that Aelle looked like she wanted The Weapon to vanish her, and that Rhuun was about to commit some sort of uncategorized violence. "Oh, sit down. She just says that because you're so tall. She thinks you're the rain, why else would she drag herself down here all the time? For the books? Aelle, do you even know how to read?"

She had gone a funny color.

"Aelle," said Rhuun, "who is this?" *She thinks I'm the rain? Really?*

"This," she said with all the adolescent distaste she could muster, "is my brother Ilaan. I'm to look after him. For obvious reasons."

"Can I have some of that *sarave*?" asked Ilaan.

"No!" they said in unison.

"What happened? To your face?" asked Rhuun.

"Niico," the boy answered. Rhuun passed him the bottle.

"He's got a thing for Niico," said Aelle, with an impressive eye roll.

"I appreciate perfection," said Ilaan. "He hasn't come around to my way of seeing things." He took a tentative sip of the *sarave*. "This is disgusting."

"Ilaan hasn't come around to keeping his mouth shut," Aelle added. "So Father said he should spend more time with me to learn how to behave. Also, to keep him from being dismembered."

"Next time I'll get you *sarave* that tastes like something, not that your Dirt Brew here isn't a fine choice," Ilaan told them. They both looked at the boy.

"What? The cook likes me. She won't tell anyone if a bottle here and there vanishes. And who would she tell? Your mother? Doubt it. That's a conversation no one wants to have. Although, she *is* pretty amazing. Your mother, I mean, not the cook."

"How has he not already been dismembered?" asked Rhuun.

Ilaan grinned and pointed at the ceiling. Instantly a very narrow band of focused fire leapt from his hand and a tiny hole to the sky opened. It was no wider than a finger. The thin shaft of light pierced over three feet of rock and made a pinpoint circle at their feet. He said, "For some reason no one wants to practice with me. Niico only did this," pointing at the quickly fading burn, "because I was distracted. He actually spoke to me."

"Big day in Boy Town," said Aelle. "I am sorry, Rhuun, but I'm stuck with him."

"I hear you can't do much of anything at all. Tough luck on that, Beast." They ignored him.

"Doesn't your father think I'm a bad influence, what with my 'tough luck' and all?" Rhuun had often wondered about that, and since they'd already brought up the subject of their father, he figured he could ask.

"Oh, no," said Ilaan before Aelle could speak. "No, just the opposite. I mean, if you were the child of some poor peasant or soldier or something, you'd be even bigger target practice than you are now—no offense."

"Too late," murmured Rhuun.

"Aelle wouldn't have come within a hundred miles of you. Your mother, being your mother—now that makes you the very best kind of friend for Aelle to have—according to Father. It was his idea. Got big plans, does our dear father. High seat shaped plans."

Aelle threw her hands up and a sheet of fire blasted towards the boy's face. He waved his hand at it and it vanished.

"That," gritted Aelle, "is the only reason he's still alive."

Rhuun sat back down against the wall, watching the two of them argue. He felt as if he were watching a performance at Court, except he could follow what was going on and no one was looking at him or whispering behind their hands. He understood that Aelle's friendship hadn't been completely her idea—she was too pretty and too conventional to seek him out. It was just luck that she'd decided to keep coming back. *And she thinks I'm the rain? No, that can't be true.*

And her brother? There was something about Ilaan that said he'd stick around, if only to be the center of a gossip whirlwind when they'd appear anywhere together.

"So," said the boy, bored with arguing with his sister, "What's good to read down here in the Book Mausoleum?"

He picked up the fallen biography. "General Kaata? Really? I'd rather take my chances out there," he nodded in the direction of the practice yard. Rhuun said nothing. "I see," Ilaan said. He noticed the scars Rhuun had already collected up and down his arms. "Aelle, why don't you and I go see the cook and I'll get us something without quite so much dust in it. Beast, don't move. We'll be right back."

Beast, thought Rhuun. *I guess it could be worse.*

He leaned back against the wall, the General forgotten, and waited for his friends.

Chapter 15

Eriis City
14 years after the War of the Door, Eriisai calendar
70 years later, Mistran calendar
Inside the Arch

As Aelle and Ilaan walked arm in arm through the royal wing, arguments momentarily set aside, Ilaan said, "I like him. Strange but deep, I think. Doesn't say much, though, does he?"

"*Please* do not call him Beast," Aelle asked, although she was pretty sure the sand was out of the bottle. She was mentally burning off her hair for ever letting Ilaan hear her say it.

"Are you joking? He liked it."

She laughed, her face a perfect mask, and nodded at an acquaintance of their fathers. Lady something or other. She had two maids in tow, all richly dressed in shades of sand and grey. Since they had learned to control their internal temperatures, the fashion had returned to pre-war embroidered and brocaded robes and gowns. Both maids carried baskets; one of flowers and the other of bread. Neither had any fragrance whatsoever, but that was what you got when you transformed sand. Flowers were a huge luxury, she must be having a party. The bread—Aelle suspected—was for the poor. That was how it worked—wealth with one hand, charity with the other.

Aelle's smile vanished as soon as the woman was out of sight. "Liked it? When you called him a beast I thought he was going to pull your arms off."

"Unlikely! Anyway, if we called him Tiny or Lumpy or Slim or something, that would be insulting. Beast, though. That's a proper name to strike fear in an enemy's heart."

She hesitated, then said, "Father will be pleased that you like him."

"Father will be pleased when you take the High Seat."

She pulled him to a halt. "Don't say that," she hissed. "Someone might hear you. That Lady or one of her maids might have heard you. Maybe *you* want an audience with the queen…."

"She *is* amazing."

"*Rushta*!" she swore, "Shut up! This is just what Father is talking about."

"You know it, I know it, Father invented it, your big friend back in the books certainly knows it. Does he think you're spending all your time with him because he's so pretty? He may be a beast but he's hardly stupid. What do you think he tells himself? '*Oh, Aelle, she can't resist me'*...."

Aelle opened and shut her mouth a few times. Finally she looked at the ground and said, "I like him. *Really*. A lot." She fixed her brother with a burning look. "If you say something clever you're dead where you stand."

He crossed his arms and put his chin in his hand. "Just tell me how I can help."

She let out a huge sigh of relief. "Thank you for turning down your...'you-ness' for me."

"You really *do* think he's the rain! Oh no, how embarrassing for you!"

"And it's back."

The boy laughed and took her arm as they continued towards the kitchens. "Just because it's what Father wants doesn't mean we can't make it into something for ourselves. Let's get some *sarave* that won't kill us all and go read some books."

Chapter 16

"All these dresses and no one to wear them—honestly, darling, people are starting to talk. One mad woman shouldn't put you off an entire gender." Cybelle dos Shaddoch popped a chocolate in her mouth and shut the wardrobe.
The Duke glared at her from the doorway. "When I want your opinion... never mind," he said. "It'll never happen."
She laughed. "You depend on me and you know it. And I'm of the opinion you need someone other than your horse to talk to."

-The Claiming of the Duke, pg 12
Malloy Dos Capeheart, Little Gorda Press (out of print)

Mistra
80 years after the War of the Door, Mistran Calendar
16 years later, Eriisai calendar
Va'Everly Residence

"... and they got red eyes, see?" The little girl looked up from the floor and held out the book she'd been drawing in for her older sister's inspection.

"What? Who has red eyes?" Lelet va'Everly was more interested in rooting through their oldest sister May's jewelry box than what Scilla was working on. She found a pearl earring and held it up. "Wonder where the other one is."

"Lelly! Look. I drew this for you. It's demons." Scilla pushed the book in front of her sister's face.

"What are you doing with my journal? Are you writing in it?" Lelet snatched it out of her sister's hands. "Oh, Scil. You drew all over it. Did you go in my room?"

"Rane gave it to me, he said you'd like it," said the girl. "He made me." She paused. "Am I in trouble?"

Lelet slammed the little notebook shut, remembering not to swear in front of her sister. A child of seven should be spared the kind of language she wanted to use, and as she was frequently reminded, she was a lady of thirteen and might consider acting like one. She took a deep breath. "Rane is not allowed in my room. And you are not allowed to draw all over my journal! Scil, you should know better, you're not a baby." She opened the book again to assess the damage. A long, narrow face dominated by glowing red eyes and sharp teeth looked back at her. "Is this supposed to be me?" she asked.

"No, it's demons," answered Scilla. "I know all about 'em."

Lelet pushed a hairband decorated with dainty pink silk roses aside and found the matching pearl. She put the pair in the pocket of her dress. "Are you going to have nightmares now?" She picked up the rose band and held it up to her hair—which she wore cut just below her chin and dyed pale blue. She thought the pink roses suited her and they joined the earrings in her pocket.

"I don't have nightmares," said Scilla indignantly. She picked up her red pen and began to draw eyes on her hand. "Red eyes and they can make themselves turn into fire."

Lelet shoved May's bureau shut and turned to see what her sister was doing. "Quit drawing on yourself, May will have a fit."

"I wish I could turn myself into fire," Scilla added.

Lelet sighed and shook her head. Her little sister was always going on about something bizarre. Fire, demons; where did she come up with these things? She supposed it was for the best that in just a few years Scilla would leave for her new school, The Guardhouse, out near the coast. From what Lelet could tell, all they did was sit around all day and talk about things that didn't even exist. Scil and her new classmates would probably get along famously.

May, the owner of the bureau, earrings, hairband, and room, walked in and found them in their usual positions: Scilla sitting on the floor gazing at Lelet, who was ignoring her in favor of whatever May left unlocked. She stood behind Lelet at her dresser.

"Hand it over," she said.

Lelet rolled her eyes and fished the earrings out of her pocket.

"And what else?" May asked.

"She took your hairband with the pink roses," Scilla said.

Lelet glared at the girl and tossed the headband on the dresser. "Rane was snooping in my room. He *stole* my journal." She folded her arms. "And Scilla's talking like a crazy person again. Honestly, I am the only normal one in this family." She picked the band back up and began to fasten it in her short hair. "Can I borrow this? I'm going to dinner at Althee's."

"Can I come?" asked Scilla.

"No," replied Lelet. "Only normal people allowed."

"Take that back at once," said May. "Scilla, I know it's a considerable step down from dining with Miss Lelly, but please consider having dinner with Rane and me. We can talk about how boring it is to be so normal." She made a dreadful face behind Lelet's back and Scilla giggled.

"Fine, sorry I said you weren't normal." She picked up her journal and opened it so May could see Scilla's artwork. "All little girls draw things like this."

May glanced at the drawing and said, "Good use of negative space, Scil. Would you make me one?"

"Ugh!" Lelet headed for the door. "I won't be out late."

She left her sisters and headed out the door and down the drive towards the boulevard. It was a cool late spring evening and the walk to her friend's house would give her time to rewrite the scene, making Scilla even more strange and May more calming and motherly. All the blame of course would fall on her evil, depraved, wicked brother Rane. (She didn't know exactly what 'depraved' meant but it sounded dramatic.) How one family could produce someone as perfect and kind as May and as hideous as Rane—plus a big freak like Scilla—well, it didn't bear contemplation. Of course there was the eldest, Pol, but he was already a grownup and hardly ever around, he didn't count.

Lelet's private worry was that she was going to turn out like her little sister, or worse, her mother. She could hardly remember her face, but what she could recall wasn't good, or kind, or motherly at all. No, remaining normal, that was the most important thing.

By the time she got to Althee's, the story had grown into a saga of theft, injustice, and destruction. "Red eyes," she told her friend. "Red eyes and fire! Where does she come up with this stuff?"

Chapter 17

Eriis City
15 years after the War of the Door, Eriisai calendar
75 years later, Mistran calendar
Royal Library

"If I'm going to teach you how to fight back," said Ilaan, "we need a place to practice. I gather that going out onto the play field is not on the table?"

Rhuun had at first been deeply offended by the offer. He'd never asked for help, nor did he want it. Mother Jaa had given him everything he needed. He was just fine. And anyway, Ilaan was barely fledged! He threw his scarf over his head and stormed out. But after a long walk through the fine, grey grit outside the city wall, he finally had to admit that Ilaan was not only unusually gifted, he was also the only one who was willing to show Rhuun how to defend himself, rather than simply use him as a target.

"Anyway," Ilaan had said. "You'll be doing me a favor. Because when you pull Niico out of the sky, and you will, who'll be there to nurse him back to health?" Aelle and Rhuun shared an eye roll. "I always have a plan, Beast, remember that."

They moved the battered couch, the sprung, shedding armchairs, and a few near empty bookcases away from the center of the back room in the library. Rhuun said it had to be the back room—he had insisted, and he rarely insisted on anything—that it was the only room he would consider as a practice area. He didn't tell Aelle or Ilaan he was afraid someone might wander in and see his efforts, which in his mind were already comical. But he paid attention, and despite his lack of flame or flight, he began to be able to do more than merely crouch into a ball and protect his head.

Standing up straight was proving to be the biggest challenge. Ilaan had instituted a system by which every time he caught Rhuun crouching, slouching or hunching his shoulders, he had to take one walk unescorted across the play yard. That served as an excellent motivator.

The inside stuff wasn't so bad, though. Once Rhuun realized he could move pretty quickly and even with some grace, the rest started to follow more easily. And there were weapons other than flame, and attacks other than from above.

And if everything really turned to sand he could show his True Face, although that would be like setting your house on fire because your chair was broken. Anyway, the only benefit changing his form to his True Face would gain him, was disabling his opponents through their falling down laughing.

He could do it, despite his inability to do practically everything else. He'd practiced in front of his mirror turning from one ugly thing into another. One second, his normal face—smooth golden skin, along with a few faint scars here and there, and those unfortunately shaped red-amber eyes—the next, an unrecognizable charcoal colored thing roiling with smoke and ash. Only the eyes were the same. When first manifesting, the children dared each other to show their True Faces, and he'd seen a few of them himself. They became slender flames that had only the barest resemblance to their normal forms—a suggestion of arms and hands, graceful sweeping flares for legs. They'd all wanted to see his True Face but he'd lied and said he couldn't change, maybe one day. He was so distressed by the sight of his own True Face that he vowed to never show anyone, ever.

Thinking about that day was when he'd agreed to allow Ilaan 'show him a few things,' as the younger boy put it.

Momentum, now that was an interesting thing. And fulcrums.

Ilaan, for all his practiced boredom, had spent some time studying the books in the library. He showed Rhuun a particular human move called punching. "Something like this might be useful to you, if you can get close enough."

"It looks like it hurts," he observed, squinting at the line drawing in the old book.

"I believe that is the general idea of punching."

"Can I try it now?" Rhuun made his version of a fist, but Ilaan had vanished and reappeared in one heartbeat behind him.

"You can try," he laughed, "but I think you'll have better luck punching the wall, or a chair. Now, we were talking about defense…."

***

Ilaan took what was clearly a perverse pleasure in knocking Rhuun's feet out from under him.

"Your feet are very far away from the rest of you," he'd observed. "One might say unnaturally. That's what I'd aim at, if it were me."

"It *is* you," Rhuun muttered. He'd tripped and fallen hard against a remaining bookcase, and made it worse by angrily kicking it as hard as he could.

"Instead of beating it to death," drawled Ilaan, "you could move it out of the way."

Being the only one of them really suited for physical labor, the siblings stood and watched as he shoved the heavy case out of the way. The last few books, softened by age, fell out and onto the floor. Something landed on his foot. It was a bright fabric package. The three of them spent a moment just taking in the reds and blues of the fabric. It was so bright!

Rhuun opened the silk bag and inside was a little paper-bound book. As he looked at the cover, he had the strangest feeling he'd seen it before, although he knew that couldn't be the case.

Aelle and Ilaan leaned over his shoulder to see what he was looking at.

"Humans," said Aelle with distaste.

"How interesting!" said Ilaan. "It must be really old."

The cover was a painting of a man and woman, that much was clear. But they were unlike any Rhuun had ever seen. The woman's skin was very white, and her hair was bright red. Even though she appeared to be an adult, her hair was worn loose. And if that wasn't strange enough, her eyes were green. At least the man had proper black hair, although he wore it tied back, almost like a woman. His eyes appeared to be dark. Also, the way he loomed over the lady, he looked to be some sort of giant.

Ilaan asked, "What's he doing to her?"

The woman in the picture had a hand up as if to defend herself but also had her head tipped back and her lips parted. Her other hand was pulling on the lace drawstring of her gown. The man had a billowy white shirt half-open and was reaching for her with a very determined look.

"I think he wants to kiss her," said Rhuun, "but there also seems to be an element of battle."

"Well, she'd better raise a flame if she intends to ward him off," said Aelle.

"Humans can't do that," said Ilaan, "as you would know if you paid attention in class. And I don't think she's trying all that hard."

"*The Claiming of the Duke*," read Rhuun, "by Malloy Dos Capeheart. Funny name. But it looks like a real antique. What's it doing down here?" He leafed through the fragile, yellow pages. "And look, some of it is missing. And there's writing all over the back cover. It's all stained. Maybe I ought to give this to Mother to let her Mages take a look."

"No," said Ilaan quickly. "Then you'd never see it again. They'll only cut it apart and set it on fire or something. Read it first, you're always going on about humans this and the other side that. Have you ever seen a real book from over there? This could be your only chance. Look at it and then if you still think you should, you can give it over."

Rhuun nodded slowly.

"Would you mind if we quit early?" The meeting with the edge of the bookcase had made his whole arm go numb, but he'd learned a good lesson about avoiding a blow. "And I want to look at this."

Aelle shrugged. Ilaan said, "See you tomorrow?"

Rhuun, who was already absorbed in his reading, did not answer.

***

The Duke was a brave man, as it turned out, and also clever, although not particularly kind. He was some sort of ruler of his kingdom, although there were other characters like Princes and Counts and Lords and Ladies that also seemed to hold a lot of influence. There was even a Queen, whom everyone spoke of with great reverence and a little fear even though she never made an appearance.

Queens must be the same all over, Rhuun thought.

The Duke had two problems: the first one was solving a murder and the second was in the form of a young lady named Gwenyth (although sometimes it was spelled Gwyneth. Were there two of them? He thought not). *Was the Duke supposed to marry her? He treated her very poorly*, thought Rhuun, *although she seemed to respond to his rudeness with increasing affection.* He gathered that was how a male human behaved towards a lady he was fond of. And how could he not be fond of her? She was curious, capable, sweet, she never had a cross word for anyone, and best of all, she never used two words when one would do. Rhuun appreciated that.

He also couldn't help but read and reread the passages that involved her bosoms, which were frequently described as 'creamy', 'alabaster', and 'heaving.' Sadly, and in part due to missing pages, he couldn't find any references to anyone joining (although he certainly looked) so her bosoms would have to suffice.

He found he thought about Gwenyth a lot.

He also found himself wondering more and more about the human world.

Rivers, what were they like? He pictured the endless plains of sand outside the Old City replaced by something else, but it was very hard to mentally stretch the contents of a water glass across a valley.

And just as interesting, smells. Food, for instance. The coffee was rich, the apples were sweet (he knew what sweet tasted like, but how could a smell be sweet?) and there was something called chocolate that seemed to have a strange, almost magical effect on the women.

And the women! He understood sweet Gwyneth's behavior—she was just trying to figure out how to get the Duke to be kind to her—but some of the others, like poor murdered Lady Cybelle, they carried secret weapons, they spoke in riddles, and they were absolutely obsessed with their own clothing (and that of their friends). And yet they all lived in fear of the men, who were also their greatest prize.

And this human world was packed full of creatures—not just men and women but things like birds and dogs and fish. (Fish remained a cipher. How could you live in water? Could you breathe it?)

The only things that had survived the Weapon were his own people, flying insects, and a variety of little jumping rats. It turned out making meat from meat was much easier than making meat from sand, so rat farming was big business. In fact, his mother had not only a huge ranch but a whole species of jumpmice named for her. Hellne Gold's, the Queen's Own Finest. At one time, he'd been told, there were Rhuumice, flying mice made especially for his Naming Party. They proved to be voracious eaters and finicky breeders, and they quickly died out. He was embarrassed at the idea of something having his name on it (or near enough to his name), but he thought the idea of flying mice was charming. He wished he could see one. He'd asked his mother, many years before, if he could visit the Mages in their Raasth to have them make him one, and she'd nearly torn his head off. Something about never coming back once he went down those stairs, strictly forbidden, I'll kill you with my own hands if they don't do it first—the point had been made in abundance. His mother had actually looked frightened, something he rarely saw.

He never asked again. Even when walking in the statue garden, he gave the entrance to the Raasth a wide berth. The sudden dark gap in the wall filled him with unease. Unlike his adventures in the Old City, he felt sure there really was something down there… something hungry.

But a flying mouse, now that would be a fine thing. Of course, something made just for show would be a huge luxury. He'd heard stories about the days right after the Weapon, when people were so hungry they didn't bother transforming anything at all. Everyone knew what their food and drink were transformed from, but now no one talked about it at the dinner table. It was better that way.

In his book there was some sort of transformation regarding birds and fish as well. It all went to the kitchens and to Cook—that he understood—but when it came back out it was under another name. Almandine. En Croute. Coq Au Vin. Sandwiches. It just wasn't clear.

Then there were horses.

If the Duke himself was a wonderful teacher of human behavior, and if Gwyneth was his private, perfect *shani*, then horses were something like a personal miracle. The Duke was always riding off on his horse, Mammoth, and Rhuun searched the other old books until he found a line drawing of the human people riding into battle. Horses, it seemed, could take you anywhere, they were huge and did your bidding without your even having to tell them where to go—now, that was magical. You wouldn't even need to fly, if you had a horse. It was better. It would defend you and protect you. It could be your friend.

He began talking to Mammoth in his head or under his breath, as if the great beast had replaced his own feet.

Aelle caught him mumbling.

"Who are you talking to? Who's Moth?" she asked.

He made sure to set that habit aside. It was bad enough being crippled without also being the Queen's Mad Son.

Also less than successful, was his attempt to copy the way the Duke looked on the cover of the book. (For who else could it be?) His hair was the proper length and color, so he tried tying it back with a piece of heavy string. He was very pleased with the style, but Ilaan took one look and laughed until he had to sit down and couldn't speak for a full five minutes.

"Please tell me," he finally could gasp, "that you didn't go outside like that."

Rhuun threw the ribbon out the window.

Chapter 18

"McVeigh, I'd be lost without you," said the Duke.
"Yes, sir," replied the older man. McVeigh had been his valet, butler, and occasional sparring partner since the Duke had been in short pants. McVeigh fastened the black pearl, big as a blueberry, on the Duke's cravat.
"Care to attend this ridiculous circus in my place? All you have to do is dance with a few empty headed girls, laugh at their father's jokes, and not get so drunk that you vomit on the pool table."
McVeigh nodded and handed the Duke his coat. "That was unfortunate, sir. Who knew felt would be so expensive?"

-The Claiming of the Duke, pg 22
Malloy Dos Capeheart, Little Gorda Press (out of print)

Mistra
100 years after the War of the Door, Mistran calendar
20 years later, Eriisai calendar
va'Everly residence

"Up? Or down?" Lelet sat at her mirror and pushed her hair around on her head.

May lounged on Lelet's bed and glanced up from her novel, "Up, I think. Not that there's much to work with."

Lelet shrugged. "I like it short. When it's long it's not nice and curly like yours, it just hangs there."

"I hear the boys prefer long hair on a lady," her sister replied.

"Ugh, boys. Billah doesn't care one way or the other." She carefully twisted and pinned sections of her bright pink hair above her ears. "He likes it this color, though."

"I shouldn't say that's a mark in his favor," May said with a smile. She wasn't overly fond of Lelet's latest beau or hair color. "You're seeing him this evening?"

"Yeah, there's a party." She placed the last pin, admired the enameled cornflower against her bright hair, and sat back. "I kind of don't want to go, though."

May set the book down and sat up. "Something wrong?"

"It's just…" Lelet stood abruptly and crossed the room to open her balcony doors. The tall glass panes shivered as she banged them open. Cool, rose scented air drifted in from the beds planted below. "Did you ever count the number of parties you went to?" She leaned against the doorframe and began to gnaw on a fingernail. She was trying to quit smoking and her hands were paying the price.

"Don't slam and don't bite your fingers," May said, more out of reflex than hope of correction. "Since when do you not want to go out?" Lelet had made a career of escaping from the family's home, as if it were on fire, at every opportunity, starting with climbing down the trellis from her balcony when she was barely old enough to reach the railing.

Lelet held her hands out with a grimace. "Sorry. Maybe if I got them painted I wouldn't chew on them. I do want to go, I'd rather not hang around the house all night, and Althee will be there, at least." May took some comfort in the news. Althee was famously sensible, even if May thought she dressed like a lunatic—redheads should not wear red. At least Lelet looked like a proper young lady. (Except for her fingernails, of course, and the unfortunate hair color.)

"Maybe you should date Althee," May said.

Lelet laughed. "Probably I'd have a better time. I think it might be Billah, though. He's the problem. I mean, there's nothing wrong with him. Exactly."

"Is there anything right with him?" May found the young man overly familiar and too fond of his own voice. But he had a handsome face, and that was all that mattered to Lelet—at least, it appeared, until now.

"After a few drinks, he's perfect." She sat next to May. "Did I tell you what he said about that bottle of wine I brought over for dinner the other night? He said it was," and here she put on a low yet somewhat nasal voice, "'woody, yet aromatic, with notes of ocean and juniper.' He takes one class, and he's an expert! Honestly, who talks like that?"

"Well," said May, "was it woody yet oceanic?"

"No. Maybe. I don't know, it was just wine." She flopped onto her back, dislodging a few hairpins. "Everything is just everything," she muttered.

May decided she'd had enough of Billah for the time being. "You know, Scilla will be here next week. She can't wait to see you." It was the first time their youngest sister would make the trip home for a visit since joining that relic of the past, the Order of the Door and The Veil. May had argued with their father but tradition would not be denied. It was a great honor to have a Fifth join the Order, and off

Scilla had gone. "I'm planning a special dinner. You'll be there, of course."

"Hmm? Oh, right. Good. Next week, I'll see what's going on." Lelet sat back up and May rearranged her hair. "She likes that place? The Guardhouse?"

"She says she does. But she misses you," May said. In fact, Scilla asked about nothing else—would Lelet be there? And what would she wear to dinner, and would they have time to go for a ride, and what color was her hair? "I think that—"

"Another thing that Billah does, is I think he spends more on clothes than I do."

"That's saying something," remarked May. "It sounds like you're a little tired of him. You know, you are allowed to break things off. You aren't married, after all. Perhaps it's time?" May couldn't fathom why Lelet trailed around after the boy when there were so many other things she could be doing. She knew her sister was looking for something. May hoped she found it soon.

"I guess," Lelet bounced off the bed and began to rummage in her closet for shoes. "But I hate to think about finding someone else. Ugh, it's so boring. Well, you know that. You and Stelle are up to your ears in eligibles." May smiled and looked out the open doors at the darkening sky. "Any movement there? Or are you two ready to give up and marry each other?"

May blushed and said, "We are still looking at the Family Registers. It's a big decision." Both May and her friend Stelle were Seconds, and the Seconds carried the family name forward. Neither had the luxury of gathering relationships like Lelet did, picking them up and putting them down as her whim dictated. Lelet was a Fourth, and Thirds and Fourths were unofficially referred to as 'spares.'

Having settled on low-heeled eggshell kid boots, Lelet headed down the stairs and out the front door, grabbing a charcoal-grey velvet coat hanging on a brass coat stand near the front door. "I can borrow this, right?" Without waiting for an answer, Lelet swung May's coat over her arm. May watched as she got in the cab. "Don't wait up," Lelet called over her shoulder.

"Don't spill anything on it. And don't stink it up with smoke! And dinner. Your sister, next week. Don't forget and don't make plans," May called after her. She sighed. "She's going to forget," said May.

"Who is going to forget what?" asked her younger brother Rane as he passed her on his own errand out the gate. As he pulled his long, fair hair back into a horsetail, May noted he was wearing a very nice pearl earring, and she hoped he'd return it, finding a mate would be a nuisance.

"Lel is going to forget about the dinner with Scilla," she told him.

"'Course she is, she's an idiot. Next week, right?" He kissed her on the cheek. "I won't forget. Don't wait up." Rane was a Third and like Lelet, his life was his own. He seemed to have devoted it to things May was glad she didn't know about. At least he'd stopped talking to people who weren't there. Or at least stopped doing it in front of those who really were there. While she was frustrated with Lel, she was constantly worried about Rane. Their mother had talked to her invisible Gentleman her whole life, until finally she acknowledged no one else.

***

Four hours later, Lelet had a glass of sparkling red wine in one hand and a cigarette in the other. Althee had declared the party a disaster and fled the scene. Lelet didn't blame her. She wanted to leave, but Billah said he wasn't ready. Althee lived alone in a small, charmingly decorated flat in a part of Mistra that attracted artists, cafes, and shops. Not like Lelet's house which was in a fashionable, but rather staid neighborhood. Sometimes she wondered how Althee could stand being on her own so much, and other times she wished for nothing else.

Lelet looked around the room at her friends and then up at Billah. He had an arm flung heavily across her shoulder and was orating about something, some play he'd seen that he found to be very deep. He looked the part, she thought; tall and quick with a funny remark, good looking, and well dressed—of course well dressed. His Ever Blue jacket came from her own family's silk works, although the va'Everlys only made the fabric. The day would never come where they'd do something so crass as to own a shop, so she didn't know where he'd bought it. The vivid shade made her own pale blue gown look washed out by comparison, although she knew the grade of silk on her back was much finer.

That's not a reason to break up with a man, she told herself. *He tells you constantly how he adores you. You've got no cause to be unhappy.* She took another drag on her cigarette and then stubbed it out. She thought about getting another drink but decided the risk of acting foolish and starting an argument with Billah wasn't worth it.

Maybe I should quit smoking. Maybe I should color my hair. Maybe I'll start riding again. Maybe I'll run away.

Chapter 19

Eriis City
17 years after the War of the Door, Eriisai calendar
85 years later, Mistran calendar
Royal Library

Rhuun and Aelle were joining by now. He found it both inevitable and inconceivable.

That first day, the day she showed him what to do, the changeless heavy grey clouds were a little lower than usual and there was a fine, powdery grit in the air, making it hard to see and difficult to draw breath. Even the gifted ones like Ilaan felt lazy and unmotivated.

Rhuun, wiping his eyes for the millionth time, hurried across the play yard, having been caught in a slouch. He had checked and no one was around. Not a surprise, who would want to practice or play on a day like this?

He thought he was in the clear when a familiar voice said, "I see a great Beast lumbering across the plains!" There was a chorus of giggles. His nickname no longer felt like an insult in the mouths of his friends, but coming from Niico, it burned. He hunched his shoulders even more and continued without turning. *Stand up straight*! he could hear Ilaan saying. *Use that height for something.*

The first blow, when it came, fell across the back of his calves. They were aiming low. Now he had to turn, if only to see how many he'd have to face. Three. Niico, of course, on point with Daala behind him. A blowing wave of ash blinded him for a second and he instinctively began to crouch to protect his head. A jet of flame grazed his cheek as it went by. Putting the pain away was an instinct by now, and in a moment he was ready to move. He tried to figure out if he could make a run for the safety of the library, but it was too far. He could see Aelle in the doorway, she seemed to be fighting with Ilaan, who was holding her by the arm.

"Where are your little friends, Beast?" called Niico. "No girls to protect you today? No one to hold your hand?" His friends were holding each other up laughing, and sending short, sharp blasts at his legs. Niico took a great leap into the air, instantly sprung his wings and hovered directly above Rhuun. His hands were cupped, no doubt preparing a bolt. "Hey, look up here! I'm talking to you!"

Niico, rather than using his flame, dumped a double handful of ash on Rhuun's head. For a long moment he could neither see nor breathe. But he could hear them laughing.

"Freak! Beast!" they shouted.

Do it now, said Ilaan's voice in his head. *Or do it never.*

He stood. He reached up. He reached all the way up and caught the tip of Niico's wing as he swung past. Instead of a graceful arc carrying him up and away, Niico's momentum carried him face first into the dirt. Momentum was just as interesting as Rhuun hoped.

Rhuun realized he was still holding the first flange of Niico's wing, now dislocated and twisted completely behind his back. He stretched it out and brought his foot down on it, crushing the fragile bones and delicate membrane under his heel. A leathery shred came off in his hand. Niico screamed like a new fledged girl and lay still. His friends had vanished.

It was the most intensely pleasurable moment of Rhuun's life.

Aelle and Ilaan joined him in the blowing smoke of the play field.

Ilaan said, "You've made an enemy for life. About time." Then he helped a sobbing Niico to his feet, saying, "Oh, I know, it looks bad now, but I'll have you back in the air in no time…."

Aelle merely looked at him. Finally she said, "I'll see you later," and left without another word.

***

Later that evening she would introduce him to another kind of pleasure. It came with a price, but as he watched her slip out the door and turned his attention to his new collection of scorches and bruises, he decided it was worth it.

"I am yours," she told him before leaving. And, not taking any chances, she added, "and you are mine."

***

What if I could go there?

The thought just appeared in his head as if it had been waiting for him to catch up.

What if I could really go there?

The idea took on some urgency when he realized the last few pages of his book were missing. There was going to be a wedding—Sir Edward had been killed—once on the dueling field (he was just faking it that time) and again from the Duke flinging him out a window into the rocky crags of the sea below. (It was all very dramatic.) The murder was solved, the jewels had been found, even Cook and old Mrs. Beedle had agreed that sweet Gwenyth would make a perfect bride. But the Duke hadn't appeared at the chapel (what was a chapel? It had been one of his complete failures of translation.) and Gwyneth in her white gown (the color was extremely significant, and since the color white on Eriis indicated victory won without battle, it made a sort of sense) was in tears at something called an altar. And then—nothing!

"You ought to go, then," said Ilaan one particularly hot afternoon as they lounged in the library. Aelle gave him a death glare, which had lost a great deal of potency as they grew up.

They were halfway through a bottle of *sarave,* being by this time old enough to not have to steal it, and Ilaan was in an expansive mood. "You should sneak through the Door and find the person who wrote it and ask what happened to your girlfriend. Beast, you'd be a legend."

"She's not my girlfriend," said Rhuun uncomfortably.

At the same time Aelle said, "I wish you'd never found that stupid book."

The human world, and all the nasty, vulgar creatures in it, was the only competition Aelle hadn't managed to drive away.

"Did you ever figure out what all that scribble was? On the back page?" asked Ilaan.

"No," answered Rhuun. "I can't make it out. Plus it's got some nasty brown stains all over it."

"Time to throw it away," muttered Aelle.

"Can I see it again?" asked Ilaan. "I've been studying pre-War language and it would be a perfect project. I'd get all sorts of credit. Did I tell you, the Mages contacted Father? They're interested in me."

Rhuun was not surprised to hear it. "Are you interested in them? I mean, they know everything about everything, no one gets to look at their books, but don't you have to live down there?" He paused. "And Niico…" He'd never told Ilaan how Niico had caught him out early one morning, coming home from Aelle's house, and how, to his own amazement, a 'punch' had settled things between the two of them. While Niico had merely been stunned and knocked to the dirt, he'd broken two bones in his hand. He felt it was a small price to pay. But Ilaan thought Niico was the rain itself, and wasn't the sort to set his prizes free.

"Father has some ideas about where I do my training. We're going down to see them soon, I'll let you know if it's too hideous to bear. So can I see it?"

"I suppose," said Rhuun, "as long as you don't plan on setting it on fire or something."

"Bring it tomorrow and maybe we can start to translate it. Who knows," he added with a wide-eyed whisper, "it may open The Door."

Aelle stood up. "I'm glad you think this is so interesting, but I don't think it's funny at all. The law is in place for a reason, as you both very well know." She marched off.

"She's really angry. Maybe we shouldn't do this," said Rhuun without much conviction.

"Her friends at Court don't like you anyway, this will give her something to complain about," said Ilaan with a grin. Then he sobered and said, "This is all thanks to my father, I'm afraid. Aelle would never say she wants the High Seat—that sounds a little too… head-chop-offy? Shall we say?" Rhuun had to admit she'd never put it that way. "She will say, she does want you to follow your mother. That's the Natural Order of Things According to Aelle. But also she wants you where she can keep an eye on you. If you set off on a grand adventure, so do her plans—and I'm afraid Father's plans have become her plans. Not that she doesn't care for you, you know she does. But maybe we ought to keep this between us."

Rhuun thought, *A grand adventure which leaves her behind. Just like her father's been doing her whole life. But if I really could....*

"If I could really go there…" Rhuun was no longer thinking of Aelle, or her plans at all. "I'll bring you the book tomorrow."

Chapter 20

Eriis City
20 years after the War of the Door, Eriisai calendar
100 years later, Mistran calendar
Yuenne's family residence

It was when Aelle watched him pour himself a second glass of *sarave* without comment, that was when he knew she wanted something. It turned out to be as bad as he feared.

"Why can't we just stay home by ourselves tonight? You just had a party." She had, not a week past, and he'd even stayed through most of it. Surely that was enough.

"It's not a party," she countered. "It's just some friends coming over."

Technically, she was correct, although he was already planning his escape. He let her have her way almost all the time, but on the subject of socializing, he made her earn it. It was a grim thought, he realized. He'd rather face his mother than his friends. He did like Rhoosa, though. And at least Ilaan would be there, although he and Niico were in a phase where they couldn't bear to be physically parted for more than twenty seconds. There was a good deal of under-the-table hand holding and it made him uncomfortable. At least Aelle didn't insist he hang all over her.

"Well," he said, "I just wished you'd mentioned it." She smiled and kissed him, accepting his concession.

"It's just that my parents are both out this evening, and we have the place to ourselves. It'll be fun." Her parents, he knew, were dining with his mother, and she had practically a wing of the big house to herself as it was.

He slid his hand under the hem of her dress and then pulled her down into his lap. "Wouldn't this be more fun?" She seemed to hesitate—this tactic had worked before—but then got to her feet and flapped her hands at him.

"After. Right now go change your face, you're dusty. And put on the new jacket—with the braid trim on the collar. It looks good on you." As he didn't leap to his feet, she put her hands on her hips and looked down at him menacingly. "What else?"

He shrugged and got up. "You're pretty when you're bossy, that's all." That made her laugh, but when he reached for her again she pushed his hand away.

"They'll get here at second moonrise." She squinted out the window. "Be here before that or I'll show you bossy."

By the time he returned, he was already late—he'd overslept, and in a rush to leave, he'd put on the wrong coat and had to go home and find the one she preferred. Her friends were already gathered around the table in her visiting room. She'd set the glowing stones out in pretty black and white bowls, and everyone had a glass at their elbow. They were playing Galiina's Bluff, and it looked like Niico was ahead on points.

Aelle glanced at him with a look that informed him there would be no 'after' that evening. He helped himself to a glass of *sarave* and headed for a low couch facing the players. Then he thought better of it and took the bottle with him.

"Stone and bowl, thrice," said Daala to Rhoosa, but as soon as the words were out of her mouth she winced. "Twice, I mean. Can I change it?"

"That's not how it works, obviously," said Rhoosa. The other girl groaned.

Niico laughed. "Let's see it, Rho."

Rhoosa set the card that she'd been playing face up. "Quince," she said, "so it wouldn't have mattered." She pursed her lips and pointed to Daala's hand. "That one." She'd picked the third card from the top. Daala sighed dramatically and held it up. Rhoosa pointed at it and it vanished in a quick burst of flame. "Yes! Victory trip, hands up, everyone." They all laid their hands on the table, fingertips touching. "Ready? Let's go." They vanished.

Rhuun refilled his glass and waited for them to return. He wondered where Rhoosa had taken them—he'd heard she favored a ruined viewing terrace a short walk from the city wall. He didn't mind that they'd forgotten him, but he wished Rhoosa would shimmer with him, just so he could see what it was like. Of course, Aelle would have his head if he asked her to do something so intimate.

The group reappeared, laughing and breathless.

"You really have to show me how you do that," Ilaan said to Rhoosa.

She shrugged. "I've tried. You're just not special enough." While anyone (except Rhuun, of course) could shimmer from place to place, and you might even transport an unfledged child this way (although there were many who considered this lazy and undignified), Rhoosa was unique in her ability to shimmer multiple people at once. The palace had its eye on her, but she made no promises. "Remind me to tell you my new idea, though." She handed the deck to Aelle to deal the next round and leaned forward, lowering her voice. "It's to do with *color*."

Rhuun looked up. "Ought I to leave the room?"

Rhoosa flushed—she'd forgotten he was there. "Of course not. I mean, you wouldn't… you won't…."

Aelle smiled. "I think it's me and Ilaan that ought to step out. He won't say anything, will you, *shani*?" Rhuun shook his head. Reporting back to his mother on one of the few people who treated him decently was not likely to happen. "But," continued Aelle, "my father would have a fit. He says decisions should start at the top."

"By 'the top' he means himself," said Ilaan.

Niico and Rhoosa shared a look, and she said, "Oh, did you hear? I'm an aunt. Kaaya had a girl." They all lifted their glasses. "No bigger than a button. Kaaya's going to call her Thayree. The naming party is soon, you all should come." She smiled at Aelle. "Perhaps you can convince our friend over there to come as well."

Before Aelle answered, Rhuun held up his own glass. "Of course I'll come to her party. I'm sure my mother will send a gift along with me."

It always amazed Rhuun how Aelle could smile and frown at the same time.

The game continued, and Niico flared nearly Daala's entire hand. She pushed back from the table. "You're all just better liars than me," she told them, and sat on the couch next to Rhuun. "Look at this mess," she said. Niico's last flare had left her with nothing but half a suite of fractured rock, not even a clan card. There was no way she could win.

"Me again!" Niico declared. "Rho, I insist you shimmer us somewhere interesting. Not that old pile of rocks again. Surprise me." She gladly agreed, and with hands together, they all vanished.

Rhuun and Daala looked at each other for a moment. She looked as if she was waiting for him to say something. Or do something. He cleared his throat and stood, reaching for the nearly empty bottle. "Going to get some water and clear my head," he said. "Be right back."

At first it seemed like he'd escaped successfully. He sat on the stone tiled floor of Aelle's courtyard, and leaned back against the wall. There was enough *sarave* left in the bottle for another swallow, and he closed his eyes. Even the wind had dropped, it was perfectly quiet.

Suddenly: hands on his chest, and a swath of fabric across his legs. Lips on his mouth. And it wasn't Aelle. But he didn't open his eyes and he didn't push her away. He imagined for a second that it was Rhoosa, kissing him. Then it was Gwenyth. Then he hesitated. He could hardly believe one woman wanted to kiss him, and now here was a second one. It might never happen again. But finally he pulled away and murmured, "Daala. What are you doing?"

"You know," she answered.

"They'll be back any second." She reached for him again, and he gently pushed her off his lap. "Go back inside."

"She doesn't have to know," Daala said.

Many months later, he would have time to consider which was the worse mistake: hesitating for that long moment, or laughing at her.

"Why are you laughing?" she hissed. "What's so funny?"

"Well, of course she'd know, I'd tell her. But I won't if you go back inside. We'll forget about this."

She got up and smoothed her tan tunic. Her face was crimson. "She's only with you because of your mother. You think she loves you? She feels sorry for you." She turned and raced back into the house.

He rapped the back of his head against the wall, wishing he was far more drunk. Or somewhere else, somewhere far away. Or both. "That's not true," he said, although she had already gone. *Is it?*

Chapter 21

The girl traced a finger down the leather binding of an ancient looking tome.
"Are all of these yours, my Lord? Have you read them all?"
He scowled at her. "Come away from there. It doesn't become a woman to be overly interested in books."

-The Claiming of the Duke, pg 62
Malloy Dos Capeheart, Little Gorda Press (out of print)

Mistra
100 years after the War of the Door, Mistran calendar
20 years later, Eriisai calendar
The Guardhouse

Even before the war, the Order of the Veil and the Door had no love for demons. And now that the narrative was up to the Order, the books were written accordingly.

Brother Blue helped to write them.

It took many years for the dreams to stop and his mind to truly be quiet, but it only took months to make himself invaluable to his new master, the head cleric. The more depraved he made his demonic history, the better his meals, the softer his bed. And the cleric had a tincture to put in his wine that sometimes let him sleep without dreams. He was proud of himself; a writer after all. And when the head cleric became too feeble to lead the novices and brothers, Blue found himself appointed to the task. Write and teach, and keep The Door shut. His life was perfect. His long life—for he had already celebrated his century year, and certainly not too many people could claim that! He privately suspected 'she' (even in his mind, he couldn't speak her name) had cast a long-life charm on him, wanting to keep him her slave for as long as possible. And for the most part, he kept control of his wits and bowels, so he counted himself lucky. This was a life that as a poor farmer's son he could never have. If he hadn't been lucky enough to be a Fifth, he supposed his life would have turned out very differently.

He didn't like to think about the Princess. It gave him a pain in his chest that left him weak and short of breath.

Today, though, he felt as well as an old man could. No dreams and a strong stream in the morning. Sometimes that added up to a very good day.

Today he was lecturing his class on a topic he had practically invented: demonic mythology. "The Sealing of the Door? We don't really know what happened. In a way, yes, they attacked us," he told his wide eyed novices, "in that we are surrounded and attacked by evil every day. And they *are* evil—if they even still exist. Still, we must not take any chances, we must keep The Door shut. And if—The Light Preserve Us—if one of them breaks through our defenses and arrives here, We Cast Them Back. Now. What do we say is beyond the Veil?"

Scilla's hand was up, as usual. Brother Blue had already taken note of this clever new girl. A va'Everly, well, they hadn't seen one of those in many a year. Hopefully this one would remain undamaged. But she seemed eager enough, she could turn out well. He nodded at her.

"Beyond the Veil is cold and dark. Beyond the Door is heat and noise."

"That's correct, that's what we say. But what does it mean? How can the unseen world be both cold and hot?" he asked.

Scilla chewed her pencil. "Is it a metaphor? For discomfort? Noisy is also unpleasant. Dark isn't so bad, though."

"If there was never anything but dark you might feel otherwise. Of course, here there is no correct answer. And none incorrect, either. While we know what it used to be like, it's been many years since anyone passed through the Veil and Door and returned." *Many years and gone*, thought Brother Blue. *If they only knew, these children. Well, done is done for another year, and we remain protected.*

"From this side, you mean, Brother?" Scilla said, obviously feeling as if she'd scored a point.

Blue was used to children like Scilla. A clever little girl with impertinent questions. A child who wouldn't be missed, only fondly recalled. She was just the most recent in a long line of clever children who'd spend their lives throwing their minds, and will, at The Door. That's all it was, now—children and old men.

"Of course that's what I meant." He looked around the classroom. "That's the point, isn't it? Keeping The Door shut and the Veil down? Many generations of the Families have sacrificed much for it to remain closed."

A girl near the window stuck up her hand. "Isn't it true they sometimes come over? I heard it from my granny. She said they sneak through and steal babies."

Out of the corner of his eye, Blue noticed Scilla rolling her eyes, and hid a laugh.

"It is true that generations ago there were those few human people who could travel back and forth. But the Sealing of the Door was the end of that. As far as stealing babies, I think your Gran might have been trying to get you to behave, possibly, Maire? Now, on the subject of demons. What do we know? Very little for sure. From the records we have from before The Door was sealed, we know they were capable of unending wickedness. They were an undersized, stunted race, unable to tell each other apart. They spat flame and tore each other to pieces for sport. One can understand the temptation to escape their polluted world, whether for revenge or perversity, who is to say? We thankfully do not know their minds." *I thought I knew her mind*, mused Blue, *but I could not have been more wrong*. He could still clearly recall her face, and wondered how he could have been taken in by her lies. He had not spoken her name aloud for nearly a hundred years.

Brother Blue sighed and looked out the window, seemingly lost in thought. The children faded away as once again he was young, strong, and walking down a tree-lined boulevard with the most beautiful woman in any world by his side. The low murmur of the smiling, elegant demon folk around him increased in volume and he blinked and realized the children were staring and whispering nervously. He knew he had a tendency to wander off. At his great age it was expected, and no one knew the history of the Order better, so it was forgiven. He swung back around and continued at a somewhat higher volume.

"But what if one of them was tempted to come here? One of the Red Eyes? Perhaps they are curious. Certainly they are dangerous. From what we know about their side now, what with the dark and the heat and the noise, I'd want to leave it myself. It is my great hope and our mission that none of you will ever meet one in person." He rummaged briefly through the books on his desk, until he found the right one and held the painting on the page up for the class to see. The students leaned forward, studying the horrific vision, the flames, and the burning eyes. "Those who travel from the other side, we do not have conversations with them."

A wide eyed boy behind Scilla whispered, "Demons."

"And what do we do if we are unfortunate enough to encounter a visitor?"

The class answered in unison.

"We cast them back."

Scilla answered along with the rest of the class, but her little notebook was now a heretical document. She wrote: "*Ask about dark*."

On the other side of The Door, a pen was lifted in response. An answer was prepared. Finally, someone on the human side was ready to talk.

Chapter 22

Eriis City
20 years after the War of the Door, Eriisai calendar
100 years later, Mistran calendar
Royal Quarters

Aelle sat at the edge of the bed and gingerly flexed her wrists.

"I think you actually broke this one!" She excitedly showed him the odd angle, the swelling. "That's excellent, *shani.* You'll be leaving me behind soon."

Rhuun laughed. "Like you'd allow that." He stretched, hearing the little bones in his back creak, and glanced down at the livid bruises and burns on his stomach and legs. They were healing—not as quickly as her wrist, but he could see them already fading. They would join all the others as pale silvery marks, one more thing he had that made him different. He eyed Aelle's flawless dark golden skin and the swirl of tattoos marking a second, inked-on pair of wings that stretched from shoulder to shoulder and nearly to the cleft of her pretty, dimpled bottom. When she turned to face him, his eye was drawn to her *ama* and her elegant gold and jet piercings. She was perfect. Already, not a mark on her. And her hand looked nearly normal.

"Aelle…" She plucked her pale grey dress off the back of a chair and rearranged it on her slim form, turning it this way and that. Aelle had matured into a small boned woman with delicately drawn features. Her dark, arched brows over pale, rose-red eyes drew stares wherever she went. He towered over her. He towered over everyone. She was well bred enough not to mention it.

"Hmm?"

"Do you feel like this is enough? For you?" She glanced around his rather spare room, the same one he'd had his whole life. The only decorations were three framed relics, antiques from the other side taken during the war. One was a fragment of what once might have been a plate. It was blue and white and held an image of a girl and an animal of some kind. The second was a palm sized scrap of silk. The third was a ribbon of silver mesh which had been part of some long dead human's armor. The silk was by far the brightest thing in the room, and probably the whole palace.

She sat again and poked a bruise on his thigh. He winced and tried not to wince.

"I assume you're not asking me to redecorate. You know very well what I want. The line remains unbroken, what's more important than that? And if I get to help you—well… One day you may have your mother's seat at Court. For now you are at her right hand, no? And I am at your right hand. Everyone in their place." She nodded, it was settled.

"Aelle, we've been through this. I will never have her seat."

She smiled a private sort of smile. "We'll see."

"Anyway," he continued, "all the politics. All that posturing. The only one who likes all that is Ilaan. It drives me wild with boredom. I only attend so Mother won't—"

"Won't what? Throw you out of the royal quarters? Give you the silent treatment? Make you have dinner with her three times a week instead of two?"

"Bite your tongue." She had already bitten his.

"Well," she said, trying to be reasonable, "we'll just have to make sure you are sufficiently entertained. Maybe I'll learn to divide. It's difficult but I'm certain I could do it."

He thought of joining with two of her and didn't know whether to laugh or cry—he seriously doubted he'd survive the experience.

"Or maybe you'd prefer this?" She flickered, and he blinked. Standing in front of him was a double image of himself. He looked away.

"Ugh, really Aelle. It's bad enough one of us has to look at that. I don't know how you stand it."

She changed back into her own form.

"One becomes acclimated," she said.

"Being entertained is different from being happy," he said. "Would that life make you happy?"

"Why are you asking these things? You know it's what I want. What we want. We will be together at Court. And one day we will share the spark—no, don't get that face. They'll look like you or they'll look like me and it'll be fine. What more is there?" She was starting to get that little line between her eyes. He hated it when she mentioned the spark; she knew full well he would never consent to passing his deformities on to another generation. But he wasn't the only one who was lately tempted to provoke.

"That's not what I meant by 'more'…" he said.

"I know exactly what you meant. That stupid book again."

"It's not—"

"It is exceptionally stupid. Little human persons doing human person things. It's not real. It doesn't exist." Her skin was starting to steam.

"Of course it does. The other world—don't you wonder? Wouldn't you like to see it?"

She placed her palm on the center of his chest. Curls of smoke immediately started to rise.

"This is real. We exist. That other world—what do I care? The war ended and they sealed the Door and left us to die in our own filth. Well, guess what, humans? We didn't. We are here. We are alive. This is what we have and we'd all better learn to live in it. If I ever saw a human I would kill it on the spot, and you should feel the same way. I will never understand your obsession with those creatures. So yes, I do want more and that road runs through you." She frowned and looked confused for a moment. "I didn't mean it that way. I only want us to be together in the best world we can make for ourselves." She took a deep breath and smiled. He could see her centering herself. "We will do so well together at Court. Look how well we do here."

She stood up and gave the fingers of her hand a little shake. "There. Good as new. Next time perhaps we can get a flame going. I love a good singe." She leaned over and kissed his cheek. "See you at dinner. Remember to dress for the performance after. Your mother expects us at first moonrise." She chuckled. "Isn't it funny how we say that? When was the last time anyone saw the moons?"

After she had gone, he leaned back on his too-short bed with a glass of *sarave* and encouraged his skin to knit, letting the pain slide off and go where he directed it. He regarded his chest, which was still a smoking ruin.

I shouldn't feel this at all. Or maybe it should feel like something other than pain. And for the millionth time, *What is wrong with me?*

As he watched, it began to mend.

He stood to dress, and consulted his reflection to make sure he was acceptably in one piece. The top of his head was cut off; after the third time, he'd gotten tired of re-hanging the mirror. Nothing new there, oval eyes just plopped onto his face, and a long straight nose, a permanent dark mark near his hairline on his left temple from whacking his head on doorframes and windows. But hardly anyone stared or whispered anymore, as Aelle had pointed out, they were more or less acclimated. Now he was met with a sliding away of the gaze a sort of invisibility that suited him very nicely.

He leaned down and examined his face more closely. He ran his hand over his chin—yes, it was time. He didn't know why his face felt like sand every week or so, or why if he did nothing it turned into hair, he only knew it was different from everyone else and so it had to go. There was only one way to change his skin, and long ago he'd discovered that showing his True Face burned the stubble to cinders. This time he watched. Sometimes he didn't. When he was younger, he'd shut his eyes tight and count to ten—that was enough. But now it seemed like too much effort. He bent down and leaned on his elbows, leaving another scorch mark on the old wooden dresser, one of many dozens. He turned, saw the seething monster in the mirror, counted, and turned again. Done.

Done or not, it would never be enough for Aelle, who wanted all eyes on her all the time. And with her face and bearing, it was proper she should be admired. He had learned long ago that what she felt, she was completely confident that everyone felt. It simply did not occur to her that someone might not like to be stared at or talked about.

Aelle treated him as if he were normal, and thus to her he *was* normal. She knew just when to allow him to not attend yet another party, and she certainly didn't hold back on his behalf during their joining—which he thought perhaps, would have been worse. The only thing that aggravated Aelle was his study of the humans and his interest in the book. And if that was the only thing they had to argue about, well, he was grateful. He was lucky, wasn't he? She was beautiful, accomplished, clever, and her company was certainly more entertaining than dodging fireballs in the play yard. But in his heart he knew she'd never be satisfied until he replaced his mother at Court. And she still believed he'd take his mother's seat, when everyone from the head cook to the sand workers to the Mages in their dark Raasth, knew that would never come to pass.

Even if that was his dream and not just hers, he'd never rule this place.

Just as he'd never 'get a flame going.'

And he'd never stop thinking about the other world.

And his book wasn't stupid at all.

He was getting tired of feeling grateful. He'd have to do something about Aelle.

***

That evening, exactly as she had predicted, he sat to his mother's right, and Aelle sat to his. The theater, Cloud Forest in the Mountain, was recently restored and its second season of new and classic works was doing excellent business. People were anxious, after all this time, to see and be seen, and the performances gave everyone a reason to dress and go out.

This was the opening night of Yridaane's *Fire and Desire: A New Perspective.* Rhuun shifted uncomfortably in the too-small seat, keenly aware that the unlucky theater-goers behind him were also shifting and grumbling, because he was in their way. He told his mother and Aelle he wanted to sit in the back, and they looked at each other and smiled. The Queen and her entourage always sat front and center. It had been so before The Weapon, and so it must be the case now. It would have been a grave insult to the actors and playwright to do otherwise.

"Yridaane would fill his mouth with sand! You know how he is," said his mother. "As for them," she glanced dismissively at the audience, "let them crane their necks. They can tell each other what an honor it was to have their view blocked by the prince." And that was the end of it.

The performers, all gifted in sharing sense-memory, led the audience through the four stages of passion, from the first look to the touching of the hand, through fire to ash. Those in attendance were intended to feel the emotions and intentions of the actors, and add their own back into the action in a neat synchronistic loop. It was an unusual skill, and one that nearly died out for lack of use after the Weapon. Rhuun found it dull, until they got to the fire part, and then he found it painful. But everyone else, including Aelle, had a rapturous look on their face. Again, they felt something he didn't. Ash represented the end of passion, because according to Yridaane, consummation was the same as destruction. Rhuun hoped that wasn't true.

***

"Pretentious," his mother said afterwards, as they sipped *sarave* in the Great Courtyard. It was custom for her to host a party after any performance she attended, and the audience members, even those who couldn't see half the action on stage, were delighted to attend. "But one cannot say one was not entertained," she smiled. "Personally, I preferred the old perspective."

"I liked it, mostly," said Aelle. "But I didn't like the end. What a sad outlook, that once a flame is lit, the romance is over."

"You thought this performance was about romance?" said Hellne. "That's sweet."

Aelle flushed and was about to reply, but her father appeared at her elbow and quickly added, "She has the innocent heart of the young." He looked at Rhuun. "And she's never been disappointed."

"Father…" she had gone bright pink. "Please."

Rhuun knew he ought to say something nice to Aelle, but what? "I thought it was about romance, also." He did not. "And I didn't much care for the end, either." It had been his favorite part, because it meant he could get out of that tiny chair and get a drink. He wanted to tell Yuenne he hoped he'd never disappoint Aelle, but that would be such a grotesque lie, it didn't even bear repeating.

"Ah! The great Yridaane himself!" said the Queen. "Congratulations, another triumph." They all gave a polite round of applause as the playwright joined them. He had two thin braids at his right temple, held at the ends by a black and a white bead, and his black tunic was lined in cream (in what Rhuun thought was an over-the-top attempt to copy his own family's colors). He mentally rolled his eyes. *Artists.* Yridaane also had a dark smudge on his cheek, perhaps from the pretty young actress who had performed the role of Ash, and who stood close by his side. Again, Rhuun allowed himself to feel superior—Ash being represented by someone covered in soot didn't seem like much of a stretch. But maybe he just didn't get what the artist was trying to say. Maybe Aelle would explain it to him later.

Yridaane bowed deeply. "I go where the pen takes me," he said. "I can only hope my audience is willing to follow." He looked from face to face expectantly.

"I thought it was beautiful," said Aelle.

"Moving," added Yuenne. "Especially the end." He dipped his head at Ash, who smiled and blushed.

"Um, it was interesting?" said Rhuun. "I liked how they put their, um, hands and feet?"

"I see," said Yridaane. "Hands and feet. Well, everyone takes something different away, or else I haven't done my job. I suppose."

"Hands and feet are very important," said the actress. "I think you're very perceptive." She smiled at Rhuun in a way that made him both uncomfortable and a bit warm. He could feel Aelle stiffen as she moved closer to him.

"He doesn't think much of theater," Aelle told the actress. "He prefers books."

The girl's eyes widened and she leaned forward. "You are a writer?" Now Yridaane got a bit of a look on his face. Rhuun wanted to say he was, just to see what would happen.

"No, I'm more of a reader. But I did like the play." He found he was smiling back at the girl. Aelle placed her hand on his arm. He could feel the heat through his sleeve. *I'll pay for this later*, he thought. But he kept smiling at the actress.

"Sometimes the best drama happens off the stage," said Yuenne. "Your Grace, may I fetch you another glass?"

"That would be lovely," said Hellne. "We don't want to keep you two all to ourselves," she told Yridaane and the actress. "I know there are many here who wish to compliment you both." The playwright looked grateful, but the girl could barely conceal a frown as he led her away.

Hellne turned to Rhuun. "Hands and feet? Really?"

He shrugged. "Should I have said I didn't understand it? He'd have thrown himself into the Crosswinds."

She shook her head. "I did nothing but expose you to the correct influences, I don't know why I even bothered." She stalked off after Yuenne, stopping every few feet to acknowledge her guests, her face a composed mask.

"I'm sorry about that," said Rhuun.

Aelle looked away. "About what?"

He leaned down so she could hear him without raising his voice, the courtyard had become crowded. "What my mother said to you. She didn't mean anything by it."

"So you aren't sorry about practically *scorping* with that little actress right here in front of me?" She had removed her hand from his sleeve but he could still feel the heat boiling off of her.

"You see things that aren't there, Aelle. You take offense where none is given."

She looked up at him, the blank expression on her face at odds with her words. "So now I'm seeing things? The way she looked at you…."

"I can't control other people's eyes. And her job is to please the Court. I am the Court, as you like to remind me." He looked at the crowd, and his heart sank. People were glancing—discreetly of course—in their direction. "I didn't want to come to this thing at all."

"Well maybe next time you should stay home," she said, still smiling pleasantly.

"Maybe I will."

They stopped and looked at each other, realizing how foolish they sounded, and she sighed. "Go home, then. Go have a drink."

"I do not want a drink," he said.

She raised a brow and opened her mouth to speak, then changed her mind. She said, "Do what you like. I'm feeling a bit tired, I think I'm going to go home as well."

"I'll see you tomorrow?"

She shrugged without turning back to him as she walked away.

He thought he might like that drink, after all.

Chapter 23

Eriis City
20 years after the War of the Door, Eriisai calendar
100 years later, Mistran calendar
Inside the Arch

"Of course it's good for you, but I wouldn't be proud of the way you went about it."

Aelle picked at her lunch, only looking up to glower at her brother. She nodded at the server, who poured her more water.

The cafe was busy this afternoon, and the streets were unusually full of people walking or even flying about, as the habitual grey dust had started to draw back beyond the boundary of the city walls. It was widely cheered as a tangible improvement in what Hellne had dubbed Returning Eriis to Comfort. All her efforts—that is to say, the efforts of her Mages—had been turned towards simple improvements. And not having a mouthful of grit along with your meal? That counted as an improvement. And with the improving visibility, a display like taking wing in public was no longer considered vulgar.

Aelle and Ilaan had fallen out of the habit of dining together, he had to convince her to see him and that was after she changed her mind and canceled three times. Like most of their conversations lately, this one had fallen to furious whispers and fixed smiles.

"But I *am* proud, and it's good for the family. Doesn't Father agree?" He felt Aelle was so deeply into the habit of disapproval in her own life that now it was extending to him.

"Yes," she conceded, "but that's only because he sees you, the youngest ever to be admitted to the Mage Conclave. He doesn't see what you're doing to Rhuun. This is bad for him, and that makes it just as bad for me. Or am I not a part of this family anymore?"

"How is it bad for Beast—" he began, but she cut him off.

"Don't call him that ridiculous name anymore! It was cruel and undignified when we were children and it's worse now. He might still take his mother's seat, and how would it look?" Out of habit, she lowered her voice and looked from side to side before mentioning the High Seat.

Now it was his turn to look disgusted.

"Is that what this is all about, again? Still?" He sat back and folded his arms. "Father has really turned your head around. You still see yourself on the High Seat, don't you? Talk about ridiculous. You know perfectly well that is never going to happen." Ilaan didn't bother to look around.

"Why not?" she hissed. "He is her son. He is her *only* son. And we are…."

"Let's count how many things are wrong with that statement. Hellne," here he did lower his voice, "is young, and she could still marry and have another child. *Any* child would be better suited to take the seat, and you know I love Rhuun, but it's true. He'd rather stare out the window or read a book than talk to anyone—he hates being looked at, and what is power but the drawing of all eyes? And you and he are… what? Wedded? Betrothed? More than friends? Passing notes in the classroom?"

"It's your fault for encouraging this stupid book business."

"Ah, it always comes back to that, doesn't it? You share your life with him and you're jealous of a few dusty pages of text."

"That is not it!" She was near tears of frustration. "Why must you always make me out to be stupid? You know that's not it. He thinks about the human world all the time, he can't let it go. Like he'll get there someday, and he's always… rehearsing for it. You encourage him. If he focused for one minute on the world he lives in, he'd be a lot happier."

"Happier with you? Happier to follow your plan for his life, yours and Father's?"

She stood.

"Aelle, no. I'm sorry. I talk too much. Please, sit down. I didn't beg you to come out to lunch with me to fight with you."

She sat slowly.

"I miss you," he continued. "I miss seeing both of you at once, not just Bea—Rhuun during the day. Remember the time we set Lady Yiil's flowers on fire?"

She smiled despite herself. "We got in a storm's worth of trouble for that one. We had to spend the next two weeks turning sand into flowers for her."

"And Beast of course couldn't do anything but haul buckets of sand for us…" he laughed.

"And he dumped that one haul onto your head for making him carry a dozen extra. You were soooo mad!"

"I had sand in my ears! For days!" he laughed.

They smiled across the table. Then she sobered and said, "We aren't like that anymore, Ilaan. He's her son. And I am with him, and we—you and I both—have a responsibility to him, and to Eriis."

He laughed again, this time in disbelief.

"Seriously? You're somehow making this fantasy world you've created into an act of nobility?" She began to answer but he put up his hand. "It seems we've had this argument every time we've seen each other for the last 10 years. Maybe it's not the book that's bad for Rhuun. Maybe Rhuun is bad for us."

She had no answer for that one.

"I'm having a party to announce the Conclave thing," he told her. "It would mean a lot to me if you were there."

She seemed relieved to have a topic other than her own life to dissect.

"The Mages are certainly lucky to have you," she said, "but won't you miss working up in the light and air? This is a big decision, your life will change a great deal. Have you really thought about it? And what about Niico? Not to mention me and your… why do you have that look?"

He sat back with a satisfied smile. She hadn't heard the best part yet.

"They made a few concessions on my behalf. I get to come and go as needed between my study up here and their workspaces down below. I have no intention of locking my glorious self away in a smelly dungeon. And give up Niico? That represents literally years of hard work! Oh, and I think you'll agree robes and hoods don't exactly cut the cloth, so that was off the table. And can you imagine a world without my voice in it? And then I told them that while their space down there is certainly atmospheric, I have many books and things up in my study that I intend to keep working with. They thought about it, and they agreed with everything."

Her look of skepticism fought it out with her awe. "They gave you everything you asked for. Just like that." He smiled sweetly. "And your good friend the Prince and your other confidant our Queen had nothing to do with it?"

"It's a new day on Eriis," he shrugged. "It's in two nights. Say you'll come. Everyone will be there. Niico will be there." Of course he would be there, even though Aelle tiptoed around him, and Rhuun avoided him whenever possible, nothing would keep his *shani* from sharing his night.

"Do you really think that boy loves you?" she asked.

He narrowed his eyes and leaned forward.

"How many times have you asked yourself that same question?"

She stood again.

"Well, this was fun. I'll think about your party. Thanks for lunch." She tossed her *serviette* on the table and strode off.

***

Ilaan went directly from lunch with Aelle to the Royal Quarters.

We have to figure out how to stop fighting, he thought. *She's my sister and I do love her dearly, but just because she wants something doesn't make it so.*

He wished he'd been a better advocate for her when they were small. Yuenne's fingerprints were all over her plans for herself and Rhuun. If he'd taken her on one of his endless adventures to the Vastness, maybe she'd be interested in something more than a royal match for herself, but for Aelle, it all came down to taking the High Seat, as if that was the only thing she could do to make Yuenne proud. The tragedy of it was, she was probably right. He wasn't even sure if Rhuun had a place at her side in her fantasy, or if her affair was with the seat itself. He knew it was never going to happen, not only because his friend would flee in terror from the idea of ruling, but because he—Ilaan—had had a little breakthrough in translation.

Rhuun might get to go on his own adventure after all.

The book was in danger of disintegrating after so many years of handling and inspection, but he knew the ink was charmed to never run or fade. He knew because Hellne told him, the day she handed him the little book and made him her spy. At one point he'd asked Rhuun if he could tear off the back page so Rhuun could have his book and he could have his inscription. They had oh-so-carefully separated the back cover from the rest of the book. Now he had the spell all the time, and the book, which was still useful for translations, during the day.

The spell itself wasn't written in any language he knew, although the demons and humans spoke a largely common tongue. But five years of studying dead languages—demon and human —had paid off. He'd been able to pin down roots and variants here and there. And they had long since assumed the brown stain was the blood of the human author. And now he had an update for Hellne.

After running the gauntlet of her social secretary, her three ladies of attendance, and her personal guard, he came to the most terrifying off all—Diia, the Lady of All Service. This woman had been with the Queen since the war and the Weapon, since the time she was practically a child herself, and she took her job very seriously. Her job, as she explained it to him, was to keep her beloved Hellne apart from the constant invasion of noise and trouble her subjects brought to her door. If you got on Diaa's bad side, you'd sit in the corridor until dust dunes rose around your ankles.

Diia was very fond of Ilaan. He knew she saw him like the queen's little pet, he'd been coming around for years, running this or that errand for Her Grace. He wondered if she knew how much he really did for Hellne. Whether she did or not, unlike her own child, Ilaan made the Queen smile, and that was good enough for Diia.

Ilaan set a piece of fruit on her little desk, and she tut-tutted him for wasting sand on an old thing like her.

"Now Diia, if you were any younger your wings would vanish." He leaned down for a peck on the cheek. "May I visit with Her Grace this afternoon?"

"I'll announce you."

The eight or ten petitioners in the corridor heaved a collective sigh.

***

"I heard about your little bidding war with the Conclave" Hellne said after they'd sipped their water. "Very clever. It certainly would be a shame to hide you away in the dark, Ilaan."

After all these years, he still found her an unending source of fascination. While his sister wanted her seat, Ilaan wanted her life.

"I think they want me to… ah… serve as a go-between."

"You mean they want you to spy on me. That's fine, I expect the same service. So, how many are in the Conclave these days?"

"I believe ten, Your Grace, although I haven't met them all."

She laughed. "Well, you only really need to meet one, am I right? Sorry, that was disrespectful towards your new brothers."

"You know perfectly well that no matter where I am, I am always and foremost at your service."

"My goodness, you certainly can talk!" She paused and had another sip of water. "How is your sister? Still measuring my room for her furniture?"

He paled but she had her sly smile on so he didn't panic.

"She… ah… continues to…."

"I fear Rhuun is going to disappoint that girl. But it isn't like the signs in the sand weren't there in front of her. Too bad you weren't born a female."

"I often remark upon that myself," he agreed. She toyed with her long necklace of jet and cream beads. Jewelry was another affectation that had recently come to the fore. While it was considered vulgar—and in truth, could easily cross the line of law to never display colors other than the eternal black, grey, white, and brown—there was a world of variety in the style of ornaments you could make. And what you did to adorn yourself under your clothing, well, that was not the business of the boulevard.

"Ilaan, you have the Conclave in an interesting position. They need your gifts. We both know you are talented in both the hand and the word. That's unusual. And they know we are great friends, and believe me, you're the first Mage, excuse me, Mage-to-be that's ever shared my water! But just because they are lucky to have you, and you probably cost the Zaalmage a few nights sleep with your requirements, don't underestimate them. We need them, but that doesn't mean I trust them."

He looked concerned.

"Do they plot against you? Do they think to seat someone else?"

"No." She frowned. "No, I am fairly certain they do not. But they are always busy at their own little projects. Watch them for me, Ilaan, can you do that? I'll even gift you with little bits of information you can bring back down to their Raasth. Oh, and you must be sure of one thing. Never take Rhuun down there with you. There can be no exceptions."

"May I ask why?"

She fixed him with a stare. "Let us say the air is bad for him, that far down. Promise me. He does not go down to the Raasth."

"Certainly, there is no question. Your Grace, I wanted to tell you about our project. I have something."

She lifted a brow. "After all these years and all your studying, I should hope so. I didn't give that book to you thinking it would just sit there forever."

You didn't give it to me at all, he thought, recalling a day years ago, and how scared he'd been; in the library by himself, looking for just the right spot in just the right bookcase. *If you had, we could be having lunch on the other side of The Door by now. I've had to pry it away from your son, piece by piece.*

"While talking with the Zaalmage, I noticed some volumes that appeared to be in a form of our book's script. I intend to finish the translation as soon as I can look at them more closely. I'm very close as it is." He took a sip of water to hide his nerves over the next question.

"What happens when I've finished? Do we really intend to let Rhuun go to the other side?"

"Do you think you could stop him?"

Ilaan agreed it would be pointless to try.

"I have a job for him. I think it best that you deliver the particulars." They both knew that if Hellne told her son there was water in a cup, he'd flip it over. "I know you feel as if you're deceiving him, but hasn't it made him happier to have the book in his life? Everything you and I have done together is for his benefit."

Ilaan thought about Aelle and simply wasn't sure.

"I'm sending him on a mission he'll be particularly interested in. I want him to find the author of his little book, and if possible, bring that person back to us on Eriis for a visit. You've told me the Door should open—even just that tiny crack—close to where the author is now, and we know the author of the book is the author of the spell. It should be the work of only a few days, and he'll be home. I want to talk to the person who wrote the book, Rhuun gets a look at the other side, everyone is happy." She looked past Ilaan for a moment, "He will fly, but he will come back."

Ilaan said slowly, "I could tell him the author, Dos Capeheart, left a beacon of some sort, waiting for someone to come over and find him." He shook his head. "I'm just lying to him now."

"Hardly! Our author left us that inscription intending for it to be used in just this way. How is that not a beacon?"

He shook his head again and began to shred the cuff of his tunic.

"Look at it this way, Ilaan. Rhuun wants to meet this person, does he not? I would also like to see the author. The author, not coincidentally, left us a way to reach him. Let us do as he intended. Use the inscription to bring him here to visit us. It all works perfectly."

"Madam, I have a request."

She looked interested. He rarely asked her for anything. "You may ask, Ilaan, and if it's in my power, I'll be happy to help you."

"I am having a party. Two nights from tonight. A celebration at my father's house to announce my accepting the Conclave's offer. I would be deeply honored if you would consider attending."

She looked amused.

"I'd enjoy seeing your family. Barring disaster, you may expect me. Leave the particulars with Diia."

***

On his way back home, feeling as if she'd done him the greatest favor in the world, he wondered again how the Queen could so effortlessly change his mind for him in any way she desired. He was still pondering this when he was surprised to find Aelle sitting with her back propped against the door to his study.

"I didn't want to just barge in," she said. "I…."

He took her hand and pulled her to her feet. "This is your house as much as mine, you didn't have to sit in the hall like a petitioner, Aelle. You look terrible. Has something happened?"

She went to her favorite seat, the one at the window. "You know how you think one thing is true, and you're really sure, and… like, what if we suddenly found out the air was made of stone?"

He didn't reply, only waited for her to circle around to her point.

"You'll be joining the Conclave soon, and you have Niico, and Father's so proud of you. And I… Well, that question you asked me at lunch." She looked up at him, dry-eyed as always. "I'm not ready for it not to be true, Ilaan. I'm just not."

"Let me ask you something. If Rhuun vanished, if he never existed, what would you be?"

She frowned. "You're trying to be clever."

"That's not an answer."

"I would… probably still find myself at Court somehow. That's what Father raised me for, isn't it? And if Father never existed, and you were gone, and there was no Court, well, I guess I'd just fly through The Door and be a different person." She rubbed her forehead. "But all those people haven't disappeared." She gave him a tiny smile. "And you know I can barely fly across the street." Her smile faded and she looked at the floor. "I do love him. But sometimes I can't stand to be around him. I know I should be kinder, but half the time I feel like I'm the one who has vanished."

For once, Ilaan didn't know what to say. Aelle took a deep breath.

"That's for us—for me to figure out. Isn't it? I know how this ends. But I'm just not ready. Can you give me more time? Please?"

"It's not my time to give, but I'll never fly away. And you don't even have to knock. Well, maybe you should, actually."

She laughed. "Definitely." She looked curiously around Ilaan's study. "What's all this?" He had apparently taken down everything he'd ever owned and strewn it all over the room.

"Conclave stuff. The Mages are very big on ceremony, and I don't want to put a wrong foot forward." He pointed to a large and heavily embroidered bag sitting open on his desk. It had an odd radiance that seemed to come from inside, although when she looked in, it was empty. "This is for my object."

"For those of us without an invitation, care to explain?"

"They have this thing before they let you join, it's called the Naa Kansima. It means Lifting Up the Glass to Reflect Upon What Lies Within."

"Lifting Up… That is very fancy!" she laughed.

"The Mages don't believe in short names. It's the last thing I have to do, and mine is in two days, the day of my party."

She raised an eyebrow. "You must be pretty certain they'll let you in!"

"Yeah, it would be a crap party otherwise, I guess. They told me it's more for me than for them, although with those old dry farts, it's hard to tell what they're talking about half the time."

"So you have to—what? Pick something in here?" She scanned the room with renewed interest.

"It involves giving up something of great personal value. It can be anything from a piece of jewelry to an old toy. But they examine it somehow and look inside the potential Mage. For character flaws, maybe."

"So, what's your backup career choice?" She grinned.

"Oh, it's funny when it's about me. Nice. No, I think they go looking for untapped ability, that sort of thing."

She spotted the little book sitting on his desk, and made a lunge for it. "A perfect opportunity to get rid of this thing!" She tossed it in the bag, which slid across the desk and onto the floor.

"Show some respect!" He snatched the bag off the floor and put the book back on his desk. "First of all, it's not mine—as you know—and second, being jealous of inanimate objects gives you wrinkles."

He picked up a boy's tunic, brown and cream and quite faded. "I'm thinking of this. I wore it on several important occasions. Or this," an old string of stuffed winged mice, some missing eyes and others chewed by real mice, "I loved these. Or this!" An empty bottle of *sarave*. "Niico and I finished it off just a few days ago, and we created some fond memories." She giggled and "eeeeewwwed" at the same time. "Listen, don't move. And don't touch anything; I will know where your grubby mitts have been. I'll go fetch a new bottle and you can help me pick."

He shimmered out of the room and spent no more than a few heartbeats in the storeroom before returning empty handed.

"You put it back in there, didn't you?" he asked.

"Maybe," she shrugged. "It's almost like you don't trust me."

He made a great show of carefully placing the by-now rather tattered book on the top of his tallest bookshelf. "I will know," he warned her, and shimmered away again.

He reappeared a few moments later to find her curled in the window seat with a sweetly bland smile on her face. He set down the new bottle of *sarave*, and immediately took the book back out of the bag.

"Oh, come on!" she cried at his wounded expression. "You'd have been shocked and disappointed if I didn't!"

He poured them both a glass. "Moving on! Now," he held up a framed map of the Vastness, a gift from their father. "But is it personal enough?" He put it aside, picking up the tunic again. He thought about the boy he'd been that day, the first time he met the queen, and his trip to the library. "I think this will be perfect."

She nodded. "I suppose. It would have been my second choice." She sipped her drink. "I'm really glad you'll be going back and forth. Don't disappear into the darkness with those people."

"I have plans," he told her, his eyes bright. "Things are changing, and I'm going to make sure the Mages change with them. You'll see. You'll get your time, both of you. Just be patient."

Chapter 24

Gwenyth put her hand upon the latch. If the Duke came upon her now, there would be terrible trouble. She thought of his threats, that he'd spank her, as she deserved, and blushed furiously. He had told her more than once there were places she must not go, but after what she'd seen, what could be worse?

-The Claiming of the Duke, pg 103
Malloy Dos Capeheart, Little Gorda Press (out of print)

Mistra
100 years after the War of the Door, Mistran calendar
20 years later, Eriisai calendar
The Guardhouse

Scilla—now Little Sister Scilla of the Order of the Veil and the Door—opened her eyes as the sun rose, and looked at her cell. *Call it that, because that's what it is,* she told herself. No new furniture had been added since she moved in, nor was there room for much more than the desk, the little fire grate, and bookcase. New paint had not freshened the walls, and the rag rug had not suddenly gained thickness or plushness. The Children of the Order were famous for their austerity, claiming it sharpened the mind and held The Door shut.

Scilla had other plans.

Her little notebook had begun speaking when spoken to.

She'd thought she'd followed her brother Rane off to the land of birds and bats when she'd seen it. And she had good reason to, what with his insistence on talking to things that weren't there. And she wasn't deaf, she'd heard enough whispers about her mother, who had died bringing her into this world.

Scilla had written:

Ask About Dark

There had appeared:

It is not always dark. However, we find it quite peaceful.

Who are you? she scribbled instantly.

Someone with answers.

Are you beyond the Door?

You already know the answer to that one... try another.

Can I go where you are?

It has always been my fondest wish to see one of you join us.

She slammed the book shut and threw it on her bed, retreating to the far side of her cell. It wasn't a long trip. She held a hand in front of her face, watching it bounce and shudder—from fear or from excitement? She should bring the notebook to Brother Blue. She should tell the elders that one of the dreaded demon race had made contact with her from beyond the Door. She should thank her stars above she was in a protected place and safeguarded from corruption.

The Voice, as Scilla started calling it, was polite, witty, and very helpful.

Scilla began to even think perhaps she'd finally found a friend. She feared bothering it, writing to it too much, seeming too eager. But she was very eager. She thought about it all the time, wondering where it was and what it was doing by day, and sometimes even dreaming about the Voice at night. She could never see it in her dreams, only sometimes a hand would be reaching out for hers through a dark haze. It was very important that she clasp the hand. She hadn't yet, but she was certain one night she would.

This Order, as you say—you'll be there for life? Is that what you want? You are so very clever, it's hard to believe you should be shut away.

She sometimes wondered if it was male or female, or neither (both?) but it seemed too large, too important for petty things like that. The very idea bordered on demeaning, like the way coloring your hair like a clown was demeaning. Like how ignoring your sister for the sake of parties and boys was demeaning. That sort of behavior, along with certain feelings, left you weak and vulnerable. She had a low opinion of those who flirted and drank and smoked and played little games.

Here on Eriis, we walk side by side under a glowing sky of gold and green. We read long into dusky evenings, we talk about our plans and hopes and dreams. We don't fritter our time away on idle pursuits, or ignore those who love us. This sister of yours, tell me what she's done now.

So the Voice was ageless and sexless, always interested in whatever Scilla had to say, ready to advise her, if that's what she needed, or just listen as she poured out her grievances against her family and the Order. The Voice agreed that Lelet didn't deserve the life she'd been handed. It wasn't jealousy, it was just good common sense. And when she confessed how she sometimes dreamed of making her sister pay, the Voice didn't tell her to grow up and stop being foolish. The Voice, as in all things, was on her side. The Voice was the only one who seemed to understand that Scilla was more than just a Fifth, and deserved a better fate than being just another brick holding the Door shut.

Do you study the Door very much? How it's held shut?

Ah, The Door. The Voice was very interested in anything she had to say about that. And wasn't it a shame, the way they were being kept apart? And wasn't it sad that even the idea of these two great lands coming together again, was enough to get a novice punishment duty? (Scilla had only endured the week of pre-dawn floor scrubbing and late-night pot washing once, before learning to keep her opinions to herself. Well, herself and the Voice.) Her classes had taken on a new luster, now that she knew the truth. She kept her mouth shut more and her ears wide open, listening for the truth behind the parade of lies her elders taught. When she thought she'd caught them in an untruth, the Voice was there to tell her what really happened.

Do they really tell you we tear at each other? What a thing to say!

She stopped thinking of them as demons, although the Voice confirmed that was what they called themselves. To Scilla, they were now 'the people', or 'the others.' As far as their being depraved little fire monsters, well, that was a lie beneath contempt. Who was kinder or more civilized than her companion the Voice? And was there a more beautiful name for a place than Eriis? She said it to herself all the time, loving the shape it made in her mouth.

Sometimes the Voice had little notes or messages waiting for her when she opened her notebook, like:

It's very fine here today. I'm planning on taking a lovely walk outside the city gates. If only you were beside me, my friend— what sights I could show you! The Towers of the Moons! The River of Glass! Truly, Eriis is a place of wonders. But once again I am filled with sadness at how the truth of our existence keeps us apart.

Any messages at all from the Voice made Scilla's heart pound, but here it was calling her 'friend.' Her desire to take that friend's hand was matched only by her passion for seeing Eriis for herself. Sometimes she couldn't bear the close stone rooms with their low ceilings and smell of age, and had to leave her brothers and sisters in their meditation to walk out under the sky. *The same sky as the Voice walks under right now*, she would think with a sort of awe.

She would take the winding stone stair from her cell early in the morning, and follow the path from the Low Gate into the forest— the very edge of the Great Forest. About a half metre from the Guardhouse a circle of trees had fallen victim to a lightning strike, so long ago that their shattered stumps were now plush with moss. Some were as high as her head (the tall ones still looked a bit like snagged teeth) while others were nearly as flat as the ground. She didn't know how it was possible for lightning to strike in a circle, but that's what it looked like to her, and she wasn't about to share her secret, favorite place with anyone who might know the answer. Two great old trees had come down, and their remains made perfect seats, as they just slightly bowed towards each other. Scilla liked to think they were having a conversation that lasted decades. In her mind, they were reminiscing about the time before, when Eriis and Mistra were neighbors in fact as well as in proximity.

***

One day, Scilla had an idea. It struck her with such force that the pen leapt out of her hand, leaving a blob of ink on her verses and a stain on her brown dress. She told the elder she had a stomach ache and asked to be excused.

She raced back to her little room, down the stone stairs, past the candle master who was busy in the east tower replacing tapers (who told her not to run), past an unlucky novice who had mid-morning floor scrubbing duty (who told her not to step in the wet bits), finally arriving at her own wooden door. She touched the ancient grain, now slick as glass. It would be the door to her room for the rest of her life, unless….

Scilla opened her notebook. There was nothing new from her friend but she knew as soon as it heard her idea, it would answer her—it would be so proud. She wrote:

What if we could figure it out, together? You and me—what if we could open The Door?

With her heart in her mouth, she waited for an answer. It came quickly.

No, Scilla! It's far too dangerous!

There are books in the library from before the War. I could just look. It wouldn't be dangerous at all.

No, there is no way I could allow you to do something like this. You are clever, of course, but if you got caught—I couldn't bear it. The books you'd need to find are so rare, they'd be hidden carefully. You'd never be able to take them back to your cell.

But if I found the right books, and brought them back here without being seen, what then?

Well, of course under the right circumstances—and your safety is my only concern—it would be my honor to take this journey with you, my sister.

Scilla's eyes filled with tears. The Voice was her true sister, brother, parent—her friend and only companion. She'd find the books, and she and the Voice would open the Door. They'd walk along the Gilten Mile together, and everyone in Eriis and Mistra would know their names.

That very day, Scilla asked to speak with Brother Blue.

"I wish to volunteer to help clean and sort the library."

He looked less surprised than she'd anticipated. "You have a mind for old things, my dear. As an old thing myself I find that quite agreeable. I used to be something of a scribbler myself, back in the old—the very old days. We'll be glad for a young face and a strong back. You do have a strong back, I trust?"

"Yes Brother." She was only half listening, she could already smell the ancient volumes. Her search had begun.

Chapter 25

Eriis City
20 years after the War of the Door, Eriisai calendar
100 years later, Mistran calendar
Yuenne's family residence

Aelle liked to tell people she simply wasn't very efficient at shimmering from place to place, but the truth was closer to feeling like she couldn't breathe. If she didn't intimately know the destination, all she could picture was reappearing inside a wall. But in the case of a short hop to her room she felt confident enough to do it. And it was much more satisfying than simply clomping on her own feet from her brother's room, who never walked when he could help it. He'd say he didn't look down on those not as talented, but she felt judged anyway.

She reappeared—not inside a wall—and took a calming breath. Unlike her brother who enjoyed his lofty perch, her suite of rooms opened onto a walled courtyard. She'd lined it with shallow bowls of stones which cast a fine golden glow at night, and had a small reflecting pool installed in the center. Of course, it was only filled with the inch or so of water it held when she had guests, but on those occasions it made a dramatic centerpiece. Other times, she kept it dusted.

She tossed a handful of long scarves from the chair at her dresser onto the floor, and sat and looked at herself in the mirror. She closed her eyes, and looked inside to find the pathways and cut-throughs, the ropes to climb and the ledges to leap off, and when she looked up at herself again, a different face looked back, narrower through the jaw and with darker eyes. A fuller lower lip. Quite pretty, really. It was easier to create a new face than copy an existing one, but she could do that, as well. She smiled. *Good at something, after all.* She slowly rotated through her friend's faces, fixing flaws, changing hairstyles, until she got to Rhuun, and here she stopped. Her smile faded. She fixed the shape of his eyes and nose and erased his scars, but that made it worse, because it wasn't him anymore. She changed him back.

"Why won't you be happy?" she asked the reflection.

As usual, the reflection only looked worried and a little sad.

With a sigh she changed back to her own face and went to the cabinet in the room they didn't quite share. Her bed wasn't long enough, he'd told her, and anyway, Yuenne looked at him like he was a new species of jumpmouse. He rarely spent the night. The only time she stayed the night with him, she'd encountered the queen early the next day, and seen pity in the older woman's eyes. From then on, she told Rhuun his room wasn't big enough for one, much less two, and he'd better get used to the walk home.

The bottle of *sarave* in the cabinet was empty, and she was certain it hadn't been the last time she'd looked. She put the bottle with the others in the bin in the corner and threw her own dress on the bed. Stepping into the dryroom, safely away from the fine fabrics, she turned.

Catching a glimpse of her True Face in the mirror—a flick of flame, a snap of sparks—made her feel better. And as usual when she changed back she felt refreshed and cleansed. Her doubts were burned away along with the pile of ash at her feet. She transformed the ash into a flat square and tossed it in the bin along with the bottles, ready to be re-translated into something useful.

She shook out her long hair, enjoying the freedom from the tight coils, before pinning it back up. A fresh tunic, this time a pale grey silk over white leggings, and she was ready for the evening.

I'll just suggest Rhuun talks to Hellne, she decided. *Telling him to do anything is like shouting at the wind, but if he thinks it's his idea, it might happen. She can't go on pretending time isn't going by, and neither can he. They just need a little push to get them working together.* She sighed, this time with frustration. *He's so clever, as smart as Ilaan in his own way, and if he let people, they would love him. I'll talk to him while we're at Ilaan's party, he'll be in a good mood—it is Ilaan's party, after all, and he thinks Ilaan makes it rain. He'll be certain to listen to me. Yes. Everything will work out. It's got to.*

***

"Aren't you curious?" she asked him the first time she'd been invited to the Night Cafe. "It's supposed to be amazing. Come with me, it'll be fun!"

He'd looked at her over the top of whatever he was reading and said, "Define fun."

He was lounging in her largest chair (she'd had it made for him) with his feet propped on her windowsill. Looking at his long, long legs, she almost changed her mind and said she'd stay home, but that would be giving in. As they got older, she hoped she'd get some sort of control over her feelings, but it was no use. Despite his appearance (or perhaps because of it) she wanted him, all the time. More than he wanted her, she suspected. More than he deserved.

"Rhoosa will be there." She knew he liked Rhoosa. And he did look up again.

"And who else?" She didn't need to answer. He chuckled and shook his head. "Right."

"I won't be very late." She hesitated. "Will you be here when I get home?"

He looked up at her again. "Do you want me here?" He knew very well she did.

"Do what you like," she snapped, "it's up to you." She threw her scarf over her head and stormed out.

He was gone when she returned. After that she stopped asking, and he never questioned where she went.

No, she decided, no point in going all the way over there and chancing a run-in with Hellne only to be rebuffed.

If only he'd give it a chance, if only he'd let himself have fun, if only he acted like he wanted to be with me... She was beginning to find her own company tiresome. The Night Café would be a welcome distraction. *No,* she decided, *no trip to the Palace and no him.*

Instead, she ran into her father.

"A bit late for an evening out. Are you meeting Rhuun?" he asked.

She gritted her teeth. So close to a smooth exit! She turned and said, "No, Father. I'm going to meet with some friends from school. Please don't wait up."

"I hope you don't intend to go outside the city wall. Things are improved, but I wouldn't call it safe."

She frowned. "Why do you..." then touched the scarf at her throat. "Oh. No. This is. It's. No, it's sort of come back into fashion. You know, like you say, Father—fashion is mostly useless things."

He nodded slowly. "Fashion. I see."

She waited to see if he'd let her go or call her back for more questions. You never knew with her father.

"Well, don't keep your friends waiting, then." He shook his head and with a little laugh headed back to his own room. "Fashion. Of course."

She took a breath and calmed herself. Then she threw the scarf over her head, and thus rendered anonymous, headed towards the Old City.

***

The twists of alleys and courtyards looked even dirtier and more dangerous at night, and she was glad of the little glowing hand stones to show her the way. She felt like a *daeeva* lurking about in the dark, it was positively thrilling. The destination was an ashboard door like every other she'd passed, but with a black mark in the upper corner. She walked right by it the first time. Next time, the night cafe would be in a different place.

The door was charmed and since she was invited, it opened to let her in. She threw back her scarf. The space was surprisingly cavernous on the inside, and noisy with young people chattering and laughing and drinking. The special here was a beverage the barkeep insisted was a direct copy of one from the other side, something called *birr*. It was bitter and an ugly tan color, but it cooled the throat.

The party had started and she found a place along the wall. The first few times she'd attended she'd only watched, amazed, until she finally was brave enough to try it herself. Now she made a point of visiting the night cafe as often as she could get away. She spared a moment for Rhuun—he'd love this. Too bad.

Rhoosa bounded through the dark room, shimmering from doorway to back wall, shouting for quiet, and stood on a stool so everyone could see her. She clapped her hands.

"Time! It's time! If you're in, get ready." The demons formed a large, loose circle, leaving a space in the center of the room.

"I'm first," she said, and stepped off the stool. She stood in the circle, threw her arms out and tipped back her head. It got very quiet.

Her long white tunic turned bright pink.

A cheer went up.

"A new color!" she exclaimed. "I've never done that one before! Who's next?"

Aelle recognized a young man from her class—Hollen. He wore grey and in his turn in the circle made it turn to light green. Then, just when everyone thought he was done, he turned it dark green. It was tremendous.

Now it was her turn. She gulped the rest of her *birr* and took her place in the circle.

Stripes! Red and black. People gasped. When it was over she fell back against the bar, flushed and exhilarated. Shifting her face was easy, that was how she'd manifested, but transforming inorganics took a lot out of her.

Hollen handed her a fresh *birr*. "That was something—you've been practicing!"

"I have, but it isn't easy," she told him. "If my father caught me he'd send me to the Crosswinds. I have to lock myself in the dryroom. Nice colors on you, too."

He smiled. "I couldn't decide between green and blue. Hey, let's both do blue next time."

She nodded, "Like a team!"

A voice at her ear said, "Aelle! Nice job. Where's your man? He's too big to hide."

"Daala," she said to the woman beside her. "Hello."

Hollen headed towards the other side of the room, calling "Blue! Don't forget!" over his shoulder as he went.

"Daala, Rhuun never comes to these things, you know he hates a crowd." They watched as another young man made his tunic ripple rapidly in white and black. An unusual choice, but allowable on the strength of the pattern. "Are you going tonight?" she asked.

"No," Daala replied, "I can't beat what's already gone. I'm saving it 'til next time. Have another." She passed Aelle another cup of *birr*. Aelle paused, then shrugged. No harm. And it did quench the thirst, despite the taste.

"I think Hollen's taking it this time," she said.

Daala smiled. "Taking what, 'Elle? I saw how he looked at you." Daala saw lechery everywhere.

"Bet he can raise a hot flame, too." Aelle set the glass down. How much had she drunk? "Not that it's the most important thing…."

Daala leaned closer. "You know what they say, the taller the flame…" Aelle knew they were no longer talking about Hollen. Of all the friends he didn't like, Rhuun didn't like Daala the most. She never failed to ask about him, though.

"No flame. Nope. But like I said, it doesn't even matter." *I think I'd better stop talking, now.*

They watched another demon take the circle, turning her garment into a rich amber red. *Ah, nicer than mine, even though it's only one color. I'll try again next time* she thought. *A beautiful shade. Not quite red, not quite gold. Like his eyes. Wherever he is right now.*

"He doesn't need to raise a flame for me," she said angrily.

Daala raised her brow and said nothing.

"He does other things. I don't want to talk about him anymore."

Daala handed her another *birr*. "I think maybe this ought to be your last, 'Elle. I'll get Hollen to see you home."

The winner, by applause, was the startling black and white patterned tunic, although it was hardly unanimous. Wasn't color the whole point? Rhoosa jumped back onto her stool.

"No sad faces, and get those sour words out of your mouths! You'll have another chance next time. One more for each of you and then off into the night you go."

She left ahead of the crowd, politely declining an escort. She had to remember on nights where she took a turn, not so much *birr*! But a cup of cold water set her right, and she even enjoyed the walk back home.

***

To her surprise, Rhuun was waiting for her. Well, he was asleep, but he was there. She stood at the side of the bed and looked down at the length of him, the dip and curve at the small of his back. Was that the most beautiful part of him? The only beautiful part? She could see the tracery of his scars even though she knew she couldn't feel them. In the faint light of the nightstones it looked as if he had a ragged silver net thrown over him. The coverlet teasingly hid the rest of him, and she wanted to pull the blanket off and wake him with fire.

She looked up at the mirror and smiled at her reflection: long red hair, green eyes, and white, white skin. She was saving it as a special gift for him. She looked down at him again. If he woke up now his heart would burst in his chest, that wouldn't be much of a gift! She changed back to herself, and just in time. He stretched and rolled onto his back, pushing the hair out of his face. He looked up at her for a moment with those strange red-amber eyes, and then reached out and ran his hand along the inside of her leg. He stopped at her *ama* and gently rubbed the jet and gold piercing with his thumb.

She threw the coverlet on the floor and, putting her questions aside, sank into his arms, her hands already glowing with a dim blue flame.

Chapter 26

Eriis City
20 years after the War of the Door, Eriisai calendar
100 years later, Mistran calendar
Yuenne's family residence

Ilaan felt a change coming, and it wasn't just that the dust was rolling back by mid-morning instead of lunchtime.

He'd been going over the last few words of the inscription (which he privately referred to as 'that *scorping* book', or 'the damned thing' or 'I wish Hellne had given Beast a new pair of sandals like a normal mother').

He was so close he could smell it, and it smelled like blood most of the time. The writing appeared to be a poem, and a fairly simple one at that; just a call to another person on another shore, tearing down the barriers between them, walking under the same sun, that sort of romantic nonsense.

He'd long since decided the writer of the spell (and the donator of the bloodstains) was the same person who wrote the text. The poem was sentimental, and that fit with the absolute rubbish between the covers. Was any race of people ever this willfully obtuse, unpleasant, and rude? A race of lumbering, murdering, ignorant giants!

"You can't judge them by our more sophisticated cultural standards," Rhuun had argued in his typically stiff necked way. He would defend that ridiculous thing to the very end. "They're not like us, and it would be a lie on the author's part not to reflect the prevailing norms of their behavior. Anyway, I like it."

There was no accounting for taste.

Ilaan preferred military history. There was always a clear winner, and he paid close attention to who won and why.

He stood and stretched. He was so close to having it completely worked out. Right now it looked like there was enough blood—and the blood was the catalyst that got things moving, that much he knew—there was enough blood for one trip to Mistra, another back to Eriis, and that was it. Hopefully, if Rhuun was able to track down dos Capeheart and bring him back, their human guest would be willing to part with a little more—he'd have to if he wanted to be sent back home. They'd have to keep him away from the Mages, though. He understood better now why Hellne was doing this without their knowledge. At first, it was a secret he held with the Queen, and that was all he needed to know. But she herself had written into law, shortly after the devastation of the Weapon, that the Mages get the first and the finest, whatever they needed to complete their work. If a real human didn't count as first and finest, he didn't know what did. A whiff of fresh human blood might be enough to make the Zaalmage leave his Raasth and see the daylight. The Zaalmage talked about human blood the way an old man talked about the beautiful women he'd joined with in his youth—frequently and in glowing terms. No, Hellne had been quite right to keep this quiet, as, he thought, she was right about so many things.

He glanced out the window—shadows had started to fall on the far side of the War Tower. His *Naa Kansima*, his ceremony of the object, would begin shortly, and he hardly wanted to be late. He didn't know what to expect, exactly, except some phrases he was to repeat, but he was quite sure it was nothing he couldn't handle. He turned back to the inscription. Was he close enough to test it? He decided to try it out quietly first, and then, if it went well, he and Rhuun would talk about the timing of opening The Door. Before the end of the year, maybe it would be time to try it for real.

Things in their order. First, the Conclave. Then, The Door. He began the walk down to the ruined sculpture garden, and then on into the Raasth.

***

His father had been at his side on the day of his first interview. He was at once proud of his youngest child's accomplishments and at the same time (surely only his son would notice) barely contemptuous of a life devoted to study. Even down in the dark corridors below the city, Yuenne had the air of man who was on his way to somewhere windy, somewhere involving a tough hike, somewhere that might be dangerous.

"Remember what we discussed, boy," Yuenne said quietly. They stood outside the tall stone doors of the Raasth. "They need you. They know you have the Queen's ear and the Prince's, and they certainly know about your talents of the hand. They may act otherwise, but you are in a stronger position."

Ilaan nodded impatiently. They'd been through this. "Be polite," he repeated to his father. "But be firm. My value is great and so my conditions should be accepted without question."

The Zaalmage received father and son with the expected sips of water, made icy cold for the occasion. Ilaan didn't care for cold water but he sipped it anyway.

They sat on either side of the long wooden table, the biggest piece of real wood he'd ever seen. He ran his fingers back and forth across the silky grain until he caught a sharp look from Yuenne. He returned his hands to his side.

The Zaalmage pushed back his hood. To Ilaan's disappointment, he looked perfectly ordinary—no exotic scars or disfigurements of any kind. He was just a rather pale man in his middle years.

"We are pleased you've come to see us today," the Zaalmage began. "We are few in numbers—of course, not as few as those years after the Weapon—Counselor, you remember."

There was a short pause. When it became apparent that Yuenne was not about to reminisce about his old friends the Mages, the Zaalmage cleared his throat and continued. Ilaan smiled to himself, recognizing one of his father's favorite negotiating tactics. The Mage didn't even know they'd begun.

"It may seem a sacrifice for one so young to join us here in our Raasth," the Mage continued, "but the service he gives to our city and the knowledge he will gain are far greater in value than a walk through the market. He may sometimes miss his voice, but what he loses there he gains in the massed chorus of learning. He may think of his old friends and his old life, but he will rest knowing he is keeping them safe and well provided."

Ilaan stole a glance at his father, who nodded, a faint smile on his face.

"As to that which is lost and that which is gained," said Ilaan. "We—that is, I have some thoughts on those very things."

At first, the Zaalmage rejected his proposals outright. Ilaan shrugged. "I suppose I can continue to perfect the study of the hand on my own. And these," he indicated the shelves, "are not the only books in Eriis. I spend a great deal of time in the Queen's library, for instance. She insists I have whatever resources I might need. We speak of it often, the Queen and myself. And my voice may be a poor thing but I believe our Queen would feel its absence. So my voice, I think, stays where it is, and so do I. Naturally, should I elect to accept the Conclave's offer, my days shall be spent for the most part here in the Raasth. But if the Mages feel as if their traditions are more important than increasing their numbers….."

Baring his teeth in an unhappy grin, the Zaalmage bade the boy to sit back down. He gulped the rest of his water, an obvious gesture of anger.

"Counselor, I would have thought you raised your son to respect traditions. The Mages do not comport themselves as we do for our own pleasure. This is a disappointment."

"Please do not address my son through me," said Yuenne. He sounded bored. "If he is fit to join you, certainly he is fit to speak for himself."

Ilaan rose to his feet, and nodded at his father to join him. "There are classes I am interested in attending at the lecture halls. They start soon and I wish to make a place for myself. Please let me know if instead of a little study here and there, I can enter the Conclave, join the brotherhood, and work at your side. I look forward to speaking with you again, Zaalmage."

As they climbed the stairs back up into the light, his father looked at him in a way he couldn't quite understand.

"Did I do wrong?" he asked Yuenne. "I think he might say no after all."

Yuenne laughed. "That hooded old freak never saw it coming. You were very fine indeed. Well played." Ilaan felt strange, almost lightheaded. It wasn't unpleasant.

"They will accept our terms," assured Yuenne. "Anyone with an eye can see your value."

That lightheadedness again.

Ultimately, the Mages had agreed to all his conditions.

***

And now the day had arrived, and he went down those stairs by himself.

When he arrived—finally—at the Raasth, the scene was much the same as his last visit. Dim light was coming from everywhere at once, and many generations of well-loved objects, each in their own nook, stretching towards a ceiling he couldn't make out. He nodded at the bodiless head of a doll, which stared back at him with empty eyes.

At the center of the great room stood a round stone platform, dark with ancient stains. It was almost exactly as far across as he was tall. Perhaps a bit wider.

Unlike his last visit, today he noticed that other hooded figures darted in and out of the shadowed doorways of many other rooms. He'd only ever been in this, the main library. Set around the platform, there were five long wooden worktables. Each were gouged and scarred, marked by pens and fingers, and burned by years of experiments. They seemed as old as time —real wood was an incredibly precious and scarce commodity. The walls were lined from about shoulder height down with bookcases (made of cheap and plentiful ashboard). Unlike Rhuun's library, these were filled with proper, neatly maintained volumes. Many—like the human/Eriisai book he'd noticed—were quite old, but some were contemporary and had been written by the Mages themselves. Just because they had sacrificed their voices in the service of the Conclave, did not mean that they had nothing to say. Also unlike Rhuun's library, even the oldest books had been charmed to remain intact. Above the books, lay the objects. His would join them today.

The smell of dust and age, paper and—faintly—blood, were all around him.

The Zaalmage had his nose nearly touching the page of a book he was translating from High to Mid Eriisai. He'd told Ilaan at their last meeting, that he hoped it would one day allow them to lower the daytime air temperature by two degrees.

"That's a worthy ambition," Ilaan had said politely. He was quite sincere—well, almost completely sincere. But that day, the Mage gave him a withering look and turned back to his work.

Now, the Mage shut his book and looked up. "We are ready. Are you?"

Chapter 27

Eriis City
20 years after the War of the Door, Eriisai calendar
100 years later, Mistran calendar
Yuenne's family residence

"You really think you're that close?" asked Rhuun, not for the first time. He knew Ilaan's ceremony of the thing was the next day, and he was afraid it would conflict with their project. "What happens, do you think, when I get there? What should I be wearing? I don't intend to scare people and I want to see as much as I can. Maybe I should just stick to the shadows and stay out of sight?"

Rhuun had gotten very good at not being seen. Of course, it didn't work that well on Ilaan, who almost never got caught by reactive powers. He said, without a hint of hubris, that he just reacted first and faster. Hand and word. There were not many who could catch his friend unawares. "You may show up over there as bare as a sand hill." He laughed. "Can you imagine?"

Rhuun glared at him. "No."

"Forget about scaring people, they'll be lining up to see that!" Ilaan laughed. "Lining up…. the idea…" his laugh died away. "No, that's horrible."

Rhuun looked at him blankly. "I'm afraid I don't follow."

"You are not going to get me to explain my jokes, so quit trying," said Ilaan.

"Oh, that was a joke! Very funny. You should perform before the Court. There's a hat with mirrors on it I think would fit you very nicely."

Rhuun resumed his pacing around Ilaan's study. He'd worn a scuff into the polished floor from the grit he'd tracked back and forth. He paused and, ducking slightly, looked out the window. Ilaan had taken over the turret shaped study at the top of his father's villa and had a lovely view of the Market District, the Quarter, the War and the Moons Towers, and the grey and endless plains beyond. He'd gotten use of the place by telling Yuenne he liked being able to watch for his father when he returned from one of his adventures to the Vastness. "I'm glad the Mages are going to let you stay up here. I didn't much care for the idea of going down there whenever I wanted to see you."

"Have you ever been down there?" asked Ilaan.

"No," he answered. "When I was small, Mother told me the Mages ate little boys."

"She's a basket of laughs, your mother." Ilaan laughed uneasily.

Rhuun thought perhaps his friend had an eye for only one woman, and bizarrely, it was his mother the queen. He was always so strange about her. He nodded and said, "Just one of the many, many entries in The Queen's Big Book of Scaring the *Rushta* out of her Child. It's a long book. A really long book."

"Did she tell you girls were stuffed with sand and teeth?"

"Light and Wind, Ilaan! No! But I guess someone told you that!"

"No, I sort of came up with that one on my own." His eyes widened. "Wait. Is it not true?"

"You'd better sit down, friend, this may cause you to revisit some important life choices," Rhuun said with a laugh. "Really though, it would be awful if you lived down there. I'm glad you'll be allowed to go back and forth. Now, what's the first thing I should say? A simple greeting? What if they run away?"

"No, it's only demon girls who run away." That earned him a pencil chucked at his head. He plucked it out of the air.

"No one is going to run away from you, Beast. You'll be fine. Just, you know, don't try and tell a joke."

Rhuun threw up his hands and said, "Are you going to help me at all in any way? Or should I ask the jumpmice in the corner for advice?"

"You already know more than anyone about the humans. You study that book like it's etched on a mountainside. You'll be ready." Ilaan nodded firmly, willing it to be true. "You'll be there tomorrow night?"

Rhuun sighed dramatically and rolled his eyes. He'd been hearing about Ilaan's Conclave party nonstop for weeks. "Did you invite me? Did I say yes? Will there be *sarave* and plenty of it?"

"Well, yes, to all of those things, but you should know…."

Rhuun looked alarmed. "You did not."

"I did. I invited your mother. Oh, don't have that face. She's always been very kind to me."

"Yes," snipped Rhuun. "The daughter she never had."

"Oh look! The Beast rises up onto its hind legs and makes little jokes! Where's that mirrored cap?"

"Just seat me between my mother and your boyfriend, my night will be complete."

Ilaan looked crestfallen. "I thought you and Niico had… ah… come to terms. He's doing so well in his matches. He's been in very good spirits."

"Excellent. He won't try to tear my arms off."

"He just acts that way around you because you're the only one who ever got the better of him at the practice yard. Now he wins every match. I still think he's not sure how you pulled it off, not that I take any more credit than I am due, which is to say most of it."

"Twice," said Rhuun. Ilaan looked puzzled. "I tagged him twice. Ask him about the second time I put him in the dust. I hit him. With my hand. Remember that thing you taught me, a punch? It works. But I think he was more surprised than really knocked down. That was the last time he started anything with me."

Ilaan chewed his lip for a moment. He finally said, "He did tell me about that. He didn't expect to see anyone out that early and reacted badly."

"See anyone? Where was he coming from?"

"He was with me, of course." Ilaan continued, "He told me about it and I told him he'd have to leave you alone or it was over between us. You're right, he was pretty shocked that you hit him. No, it didn't hurt him." Another, longer pause. "I imagine it hurt you, though. Your hand. And where he scorched you."

Rhuun felt something moving in his chest, pushing and stretching. For a moment he was horrified to think he might weep. He stood and went to the window. *Breathe. Again. Again. We can talk about this. I can trust Ilaan with this. Everyone doesn't know. Everyone is not looking at me.*

It had been optimistic at best to hope that no one would ever notice, particularly since as a child he hadn't known he was the only one who had the experience of pain. It had been his mother who'd figured it out. *Why do you cry?* she'd asked angrily. *Don't tell me you can feel that.* And later, *Don't tell anyone you can feel that.*

He never had. And since Mother Jaa, he'd never had to.

"How long have you known?"

Ilaan said, "For a while. I suspected, but you never say anything. Is it bad?"

"Not always," Rhuun answered. "Sometimes I barely feel it. But it used to be worse. I guess I got used to it." For some reason, he didn't want to tell Ilaan about those long-ago days in the Quarter, sweeping out the dust and walling up the pain. He hadn't thought of Jaa in years, even though he used the skills she taught him nearly every day. And he could sew a seam straight as a pin.

Ilaan was making tiny piles of sand on his desk, moving them from one little cluster to the other. "During our practice, did I… I must have. I'm—"

Rhuun shook his head, saying, "If this turns into an apology, I'm heading straight for the Crosswinds. Please. Do not."

Ilaan looked up, sweeping the grit off his desk in one move. "Does—oh, *rushta*, does Aelle know?"

"No," Rhuun spun back from the window. "No, and you can't tell her. Swear you won't tell her."

"Rhuun, how can she not know? And why don't you tell her to not—"

"Not what? Be normal? Please allow me to keep what little I have." Rhuun thought he could bear anything but the look on Aelle's face. Not having a flame was bad enough, but not wanting to receive one? Even she would have to admit there was something wrong with him. He tensed, wanting to be gone.

Ilaan could see it. "I won't say a word. If you like, I'll even tell Niico he can start trying to set you on fire again."

It worked. The moment passed and Rhuun relaxed back into his chair. They sat silently for a moment.

"Niico was with you the whole time, huh? Talk about keeping things quiet. You know, I thought he was following me. I spent the next year looking over my shoulder." First Aelle, now Ilaan. He wished there was a battle he could win on his own. "Thank you, though. He could have left you. He really, really enjoyed trying to kill me." Ilaan smiled at that one. "I'm glad you and he are happy. And if I must I'll sit next to him."

Ilaan shook his head. "Just show up, you don't have to stay until the morning dust rises."

"Aelle says she'll go, she asked me to tell you. You know she can't resist a party, even if she wants to set both of us on fire half the time."

"Me in the Conclave, you and Aelle and the Queen and Niico. It'll be perfect—I can't wait," said Ilaan.

"Me neither," said Rhuun.

One of them meant it.

Chapter 28

Eriis City
20 years after the War of the Door, Eriisai calendar
100 years later, Mistran calendar
The Raasth

"We are ready," the Zaalmage said. "Are you?"

Ilaan found his throat dry, so he simply nodded. He held out the heavy embroidered bag.

The ceremony of *Naa Kansima* took place around the broad stone table. Ilaan was placed at what he thought of as the foot, pointing away from the door, and the Mages took positions all around. The Zaalmage stood to his right and the bag lay on the table between them. The glowing library lights were nearly extinguished. He could barely see across the table.

"You are clever with the hand. We are all clever with the hand. You are drawn to the word. We are all thus. You wish to learn, but we fear you believe you already know more than we can offer. *Naa Kansima*… We call out the object to see what you are."

The Mages all raised their hands and tossed ash onto the table. A grey flame rose from the ash, smelling like burnt blood and casting no shadow. As he had been instructed, Ilaan took his old brown and cream tunic out of the bag and handed it to the Zaalmage.

"A piece of your life, given over to us."

"No less," said Ilaan, trying to keep his voice level. "No less than a piece of my life."

The tunic passed from hand to hand, each in turn sniffing and listening to the old garment. The only sound was the hiss and pop of the grey flame. Finally, the tunic was passed back to the Zaalmage.

"You think you are a new thing," the Mage said. "You think you fly above our heads."

Ilaan swallowed, he could hear a 'click.' "You think you'll bring old and new together. You think the past is a waste and the future is your tool and your toy."

"No," Ilaan stammered, "no, I…."

The Zaalmage threw the tunic into the grey, leaping flame.

The Queen was there, in the flame. She looked no bigger than his hand but the image was vivid and sharp. She was talking to someone in the darkness behind him. She was saying, "Sweet boy, and he'll be of use one day…" she was gone, replaced by an equally sharp image of his father speaking to his mother, "All that cleverness, and what does he do all day? He's not Zaalmage yet, he'll do as I tell him…" the Queen again, "No, Diia, not the whole family. They make me tired. The girl's a little fool, poor thing, and the boy? Well, I know he thinks he's being clever…" His father again, talking to someone in the dark that he couldn't see, "Then we have a deal—one for one." He saw himself in the library with Rhuun, watched as the fireball he launched smacked him square in the chest, and the look of pain on his friend's face, there for anyone to see who bothered to look. And then Niico, and they were children, and Niico sneered and spat fire at him, and he didn't care. And then, dimly, his own hand putting something small and bright on a bookshelf.

The flame flickered out. The images faded as rank smoke rose. The garment lay unmarked on the stone table.

"What did we see, Brothers? Who is this boy? He thinks many things, but he has so many masters." The Zaalmage turned to Ilaan. "Are you ready to have a new master? Will you set the others aside?"

"Yes," said Ilaan in a dry whisper, seeing again his friend's anguish, the Queen's disregard. He felt as ill as if he had a belly full of ice. "I am ready."

"We believe you are. Welcome and join us, Mage."

The Zaalmage handed around cups of cool water, which Ilaan gratefully accepted.

"What else did you bring us?" Ilaan didn't follow. Had he forgotten to bring something else? "In the bag. There is something else. I can smell it."

"No, Zaalmage, I was told to pick one object, and I did. There's nothing else, see?" He tipped the bag over, giving it a shake. A slender curl of yellowed paper fell out and fluttered to the stone table. "What… How did that…?" For a moment Ilaan had no idea. Then, *Oh. That shouldn't be here.* He wasn't sure why, but he wanted to grab the scrap of paper back and shimmer away.

The Zaalmage had already snatched it up. Frowning, he examined it closely.

"Interesting. A word or two in the human tongue, I see. Given its age and the relative flimsiness of the paper, I would judge it to be torn from pre-Weapon popular entertainment from the other side." His frown deepened and he held the paper close to his face, and sniffed deeply. "There is something very strange about it, though. Where did it come from? How did it get here?"

"No idea, really, other than it's from a book from the Queen's library," Ilaan lied. "I'm not sure how it got in the bag, it's not even my book…."

The Zaalmage looked about to speak. Instead, he held the scrap to his face. He sniffed it again. Then his tongue darted out and touched the paper.

"Brothers," he said. "Brothers, attend."

The shifting, rustling robes moved as one around the table.

Ilaan reminded himself that the little novel was safely locked away upstairs. He could hear his heart in his ears. What was this about?

"Brothers, before I speak, smell. Before I speak, touch. Taste. Carefully and quickly."

The hooded figures passed the curl of paper reverently from hand to hand, each taking a deep sniff and a tiny taste, until finally it reached the Zaalmage, who turned to Ilaan.

"This belongs to a human."

"Oh, well, yes—it did." A wash of relief passed over him. They'd just gotten a stray whiff of old Dos Capeheart. He wondered if the ceremony was over. "It belonged to a human who gave it to someone here on Eriis. It's been in the library here for a very long time. That old human—probably dead by now—that's what you are…er…sensing."

"No," said the Zaalmage. "This was in a human's hand today."

"But that's impossible," said Ilaan. "This is Rhuun's. I mean, this book belongs to Prince Rhuun."

All at once the mages froze in their places, their sighing and shifting ceased. The Zaalmage took a deep, shuddering breath which seemed to release them.

The Zaalmage turned back to Ilaan, looking for a moment a bit disoriented. But he quickly regained his composure and said, "We will talk again soon, my young brother Mage."

"The Conclave… the *Naa Kansima,*" began Ilaan, who was feeling as if he'd missed something important.

"Ah, yes, the Conclave, of course. You'll hear from us. Oh, yes you will. Sooner rather than later. Now if you'll excuse us…" The Zaalmage turned his back on Ilaan and nearly galloped into one of the darkened corridors, followed by his robed, hooded, hissing, and sighing brothers.

Ilaan was suddenly alone in the big round room.

Well, that was a lot to take in, he thought. He wanted to think more carefully about what the flames had shown him, but that could wait. Based on how young everyone looked, most of that stuff was from a long time ago anyway. He pushed it aside. The little display with the paper, well, he didn't quite know what to make of that. But at least it was over and it appeared that no harm had been done. He had a party to toss in only a few hours and he had to get ready.

"Now, the food changers should already be there, and the servers ready to pour. Do I have enough glasses…?" Since no one was around to take offense, he shimmered himself out of their dark Raasth and back into the brightness of his own comfortable quarters.

***

In a low ceilinged stone room, in total darkness, the Zaalmage raised his hands to calm his restless, twitching brothers. In fact, he could barely contain himself. As he spoke, light, grey and dim, streamed from his palms.

"What is the law?" There was a collective moaning gasp.

"The law makes him ours. The law gives him over to our hand. The Queen's own law brings him to us. Our long wait is over! We shall take him this very night!" He leaned towards them, "Are we bold enough to tread the steps? Are we brave enough to face the sky and take what is ours?"

A triumphant hiss.

"Brothers, we may proceed!"

They had only a few hours, noted the Zaalmage, and there was much to do.

Preparations to make.

Knives to sharpen.

Chapter 29

"Don't you know why you're here, girl?"
Gwenyth dashed away her tears. She had been told that the Duke was very impatient with emotional women.
"My Father said... I am to..."
"That's enough, wench. Get you gone or I'll send you to sleep in the stables!" The Duke pointed towards the back stairs and the girl fled to the comfort of the kitchens. Damned if she wasn't a beauty! He reminded himself of how that had gone for him in the past.

-The Claiming of the Duke, pg 40
Malloy Dos Capeheart, Little Gorda Press (out of print)

Mistra City
100 years after the War of the Door, Mistran Calendar
20 years later, Eriisai calendar
Barton Grove High Street

"Oh, these are nice. And they go with my black dress… but I really shouldn't." Lelet spent another moment admiring her hand in the black lace glove, set with tiny red stones and with a row of black pearl buttons at the wrist, before stripping it off and setting it back on the table with its mate. "Father sent down a missive from the mountain. It involved my budget."

"How awful for you," smiled Althee, who had no budget for gloves or anything else she fancied. "Gloveless, and at a time like this." She tried on a red velvet cloche hat with a spray of blue and green feathers. The feathers curved around under her chin. "What do you think?"

Lelet tucked her chin into her hand. "Even for you, that's a bit much. Maybe without the feathers? In a different color? And if it wasn't a hat?"

Althee laughed and put the offending hat back on its form. "I know. Redheads"—and here they spoke together—"should not wear red." She nodded at Lelet's own hair. "What's off the table with that shade? Does it have a name, incidentally?"

Lelet smoothed her hair and looked offended. "The bottle claimed it was Living Pink. Are you saying it's less than fabulous?"

"I'm saying I hope you saved the receipt." She looked around the shop. "Anything else you can't live without? Because I'm desperate for lunch." She scooped the black lace gloves off the rack and handed them to the hovering clerk. "Ah, why not? I'll take the red velvet also. On my account, thank you."

"Oh, Al, no. I couldn't possibly."

Althee shrugged. "That dress you're wearing tonight needs gloves. You look like a disembodied pair of arms without them. I can't do anything about the hair but I like to help where I can." She took the parcels from the clerk and they stepped out of the dim coolness of the shop into the bright day. It was just before noon, and the boulevard was crowded with the idle children of the Fifty Families—mostly Thirds and Fourths—spending their family's money, and being seen.

"Did you hear? Suelee snagged herself a Second. She's moving to Upper Garden," said Lelet, who hadn't sorted out if she was envious or contemptuous.

Althee shrugged. "Good for her, I guess."

Lelet nodded sagely. "I know, the inherent unfairness in the system prevents the… ah…."

"Prevents the natural progression of the superior intellect," Althee reminded her.

"Intellect! Of course. I knew it was superior something. That was the part where I dozed off," Lelet admitted. She was not over fond of lectures, and she'd been dragged to this particular one by Althee. "Something about hindering flowering? Or was that the orchid one?"

"All right," replied Althee. "I won't make you come to any more talks." They strolled on in silence for a few minutes. Lelet lit a cigarette and Althee opened her mouth to comment before changing her mind.

"That man was right, though," said Lelet. "The one about the system."

Althee looked up, surprised. "I thought you were asleep."

"I was, but before that. The bit I heard was right. I mean, obviously you should be in charge of your family's business. Like, why did you have to go back to the house last night?"

"To do the books. Cecille is hopeless with figures."

"But she's the First. And you're a Fourth. She'd rather be out shopping, but she can't. Maybe it is wrong," Lelet laughed. "Didn't mean to get radical. Should we have lunch here?" They'd stopped in front of a busy café. Lelet tossed the butt of her smoke in the street. "This is the place with the cute waiters."

Once they'd been seated and had coffee in front of them, Althee said, "See, that's a nice thing about being a Fourth. If you want to enjoy a waiter, no one will look at you cross-eyed. If May started hanging around with the staff, your father would… ah…."

"He'd be less than pleased," Lelet said quickly. She knew Althee had been about to say 'kill himself' and wanted to save her friend the embarrassment. No one said that phrase in front of the va'Everly children. "Not that anyone seems excited about Billah…."

"So is tonight to be the night? Did we just fix you up with Dumping Gloves?"

Lelet sighed, "I don't know. I'd just have to find someone else, and that's so boring."

Althee grinned. "I could set you up with my spider guy. He still asks after you." The Seshelle family made their fortune in import-export, and had a spider wrangler on full time retainer to mind the goods. The rate of theft in their warehouses was so low as to be legendary.

"The fact that you have a spider guy just makes me love you more. How is Ranette, by the way?"

Ranette was Althee's pride and joy, her pet Alsatian Rugosa, an arachnid as big as her palm, with silky, auburn spider-fur. She'd adopted the creature after it had been deemed too small to put on guard duty. She let it walk around on her desk while she was working. It kept interruptions to a minimum. "He is fat and fine, and taking after his namesake by stealing my hatpins."

"You know it's slightly disgusting that you named it after my brother. Who is also slightly disgusting."She couldn't fathom her friend's affection for her repulsive older brother.

"I think he's delicious." Althee sipped her coffee and scanned her menu. "Don't tell him I said that, I'd never hear the end of it." She glanced up at the waiter—young and handsome— and smiled. "Salad with the dressing on the side, and the fish, thank you."

"The breaded cutlet, pasta side, and should we get half a bottle of the white?"

Once the waiter had left, Lelet continued. "Don't worry. I don't tell Rane anything, ever. He's the biggest freak in the family. Oh, wait, no. I guess Scilla is the biggest."

"Have you heard from her? Did you tell her to look for Olly?"

Althee's affection for the entire va'Everly brood warmed Lelet, even if she didn't understand it. She set down her cup. "Olly, your cousin Olly." She slapped her forehead, "I totally forgot. I don't talk to her much. You're lucky, your family is so normal. Even if they can't do math." She stirred sugar into her coffee and looked out the big front windows. "Know what I wish?"

"That you had big tits," Althee replied promptly.

Lelet snorted a laugh. "What *else* I wish? It'll sound stupid." Althee leaned forward expectantly. "I wish I could have an adventure. A proper one, like in a book. With… pirates."

"You want to be kidnapped by pirates? That's not… no, you're right. That *is* stupid."

"Shut up. A nice one. Clean," Lelet warmed to her subject, "and tall."

"No point in a short pirate," Althee agreed. "He could hardly reach the mizzenmast."

"And smart, with good manners." They paused as the waiter brought their lunch.

"So you want to be carried off by a well-read, polite, neatly dressed pirate with clean fingernails and who knows which fork to use? Sorry, I think he'd be more interested in seamen." Althee laughed at her own joke.

Lelet folded her arms. "Well, ha ha. I'm sorry I told you."

Althee took a sip of her wine and shook her head. "Don't be. You want to have an adventure? What were we just talking about? You're a Fourth. You're free. Run off with whomever you like—who's going to stop you?"

"Come with me," said Lelet, suddenly inspired. "We'll go adventuring."

"Not likely," Althee laughed. "Cecille would drive the business into a ditch, and Luce needs me to help her with eligibles. You know she has no more sense than a spoon. But you should come with us when we go south next summer. There are beautiful boys as far as the eye can see, and they think scrawny northern ladies with pink hair are to die for."

"Hmmm, maybe." But in her mind, she was on a galleon with the wind in her face and a tall stranger at her side.

Chapter 30

Eriis City
20 years after the War of the Door, Eriisai calendar
100 years later, Mistran calendar
Yuenne's family residence

It was turning into the sort of event where everyone showed up early and stayed until the dust rose around the windows.

Ilaan was delighted with the way his father's house looked—every old weapon shone with new polish and was hung with white banners. It was a nicer house than the one he'd grown up in—bigger and in a much more desirable location, close by the royal quarters. The view from his tower was without equal. Plus, the property next door, half vanished by the Weapon, made for a very impressive courtyard. When he had moved the whole family and their retainers to this great house a year earlier, Yuenne had decided on changing the family colors from grey and black to white only—a daring move considering the dust. Ilaan had thought it pretentious at first, but had to admit it did look quite eye catching, all that white. And Yuenne had finally (after much begging) removed his beloved mountain of traveling gear into a back room.

Ilaan had long ribbons of tiny white flowers made, descending from the baskets of glowing stones above the party goer's heads and strung along the rails and. Tables of little bites of fruit, meat, bread, and cheese (cheese was a fairly new addition to Eriis' menu. It was very exciting that his family had managed to serve so much—and in two different colors). And in the center of the great room, an actual water fountain! A stream of real water seemingly coming from nowhere! (He'd hidden the pouring vase behind a screen). And crystal cups for everyone to take home, once you were done holding up your cup and filling it in mid-air. It was quite a trick, if he did say so himself. Rhuun had laughed and asked where he was hiding the river of *sarave*.

"You drink too much," Ilaan told him.

"I liked it better when we weren't telling each other everything," Rhuun replied cheerfully. He had clearly already started on what he referred to as 'liquid invisibility.'

Yes, it all looked quite fine.

And looking most particularly fine was his *shani*, his Niico, who was wearing a white silk tunic heavy with dun embroidery, and dark brown leggings, as his family favored the darker shades. Niico was becoming a bit of a celebrity; his matches and bouts were always fully attended, and he had invented some interesting midair turns and twists. This caused some grumbling among older fans of the sport who were wedded to the traditional air assault, but it made Niico a bit of a hero to the younger set. Now, everyone stopped to congratulate Niico on his string of victories, many taking a moment to surreptitiously touch or tap his shoulder for luck—an old belief that seemed to be gaining some new popularity. Luck draws luck, and Ilaan had noticed a few tugs and pats on his own arm as well. And why not?

Ilaan made his way slowly through the crowd, all drinking, smiling sweetly, plotting, and planning. He listened where he could and made notes on whom to pull aside later. *These will be my tools, and I can find a good use for them.*

Since he'd agreed to join the Conclave Ilaan found himself thinking about the future quite a bit. And with his translation almost done, his best tool was—well, his tool was, drinking too much and arguing with his girlfriend, as Rhuun so often was these days.

The two stood half in, half out of the courtyard. Rhuun liked to be near a shadowed corner and the courtyard was only dimly lit with shallow dishes of softly glowing rocks. Rhuun had a vague half smile and was looking fixedly at the flowers above Aelle's shoulder, hanging on to a glass of *sarave* for dear life. She, for her part, was a beautiful mask with a pretty, dimpled smile. Her hair was coiled and dressed with black and white beads, a daring imitation of the Queen's style which caused more than one party goer to look twice. Their heads were as close together as possible considering how much taller he was. He was definitely at the advantage; if he didn't want to listen all he had to do was straighten up. At the moment they were looking in opposite directions and nearly nose to nose. This was a bad fight. Ilaan waved at them and headed the other way. Neither took any notice.

As usual, Rhuun was the object of many furtive glances and whispered remarks.

Will he ever wed that poor girl? There's only one reason Yuenne even allows that great beast near her. I hear that 'one reason' will actually be here tonight... no love lost between her and Yuenne, no matter how they behave in public. But just look at the two of them over there! Honestly, it hurts the eye. We thought it was funny at first—but little Aelle seems quite serious. Well, they're a serious family, even Ilaan, for all his joking—Ah, Ilaan. What a lovely event. And how lucky we are to share you with the Mages!

In another corner, near the tinkling water fountain, he listened to a group of young ladies he knew from school. He thought they were mostly Aelle's friends.

I saw her last night; she seemed upset so we got a bottle of sarave. And she told me everything. No, she did! Do you want to know? Then stop your mouth, they'll hear us! She says he can't raise a flame at all! Not a spark! Nothing! Shhh! Then she said 'but he makes up for it.' I don't know what that means, but look at him! His best friend calls him the Beast! And what do you suppose our Ilaan means by that? Proportional? Rushta, the mouth on you, Daala, you vulgar thing!

Ilaan didn't blame Rhuun for wanting to disappear sometimes. He knew how difficult this was for his friend, and if he turned to the bottle to get through events like this, well, Ilaan was neither his judge nor his father.

His own father was—as usual—regaling a group of rapt admirers with stories from the Vastness.

"And the wind, it's so loud out there we had to stuff our ears with pebbles wrapped in silk just so we could sleep!"

"It sounds so awful, why do you keep going?" asked a pretty young courtier—one of the Queen's new girls. She gazed up at Yuenne through thick dark lashes, her scarlet eyes shining. Yuenne looked to his wife, who merely smiled and shrugged.

"Tell them, Yu," she said. "I think he must have a collection of *daeeva* mistresses hidden in the rocks out there."

Yuenne moved to her side and touched her fingertips with his own. "You are my only Princess, Siia," he said, "but there's something out there. Every time I go, I can feel it. I will find it, too. This next trip, I will find it. It calls me…."

Ilaan turned away. "Ugh, he's so dramatic!" he whispered to Niico.

"Is that where you get it from?" Niico replied.

The chatter suddenly came to a halt.

The Queen simply appeared at his side. Her black silk tunic, slashed nearly to the waist and piped in cream, was dramatically set off by the white leggings she wore under it, to honor his own family's place at the foundation of her court. Her hair was dressed as usual. She would certainly notice Aelle had beaten her to that particular punch.

There was a low murmur and a general drawing back as she smiled around the room. She didn't believe she needed an introduction to the home of one of her oldest advisers, although Yuenne had very much tried to convince Ilaan they needed what he referred to as 'sufficient warning.' His father was just so peculiar sometimes. Too much time out in the sand.

"Lovely evening," she said warmly. She made a show of laying her hand on his shoulder. "I am very proud of you, Ilaan. Just think of what we'll do next."

'The boy thinks he's being clever'... don't think about that now....

Yuenne handed her a crystal cup of water, which she also made a show of admiring.

"It's a fine thing," said the Councilor, "our families working side by side. And always a pleasure to receive you at my home, Your Grace."

She had a smile for Yuenne as well. "It waters my heart that our children have grown up so close and so well."

She obviously hasn't seen Rhuun lately, Ilaan thought. *I should let him know she's arrived.* He looked back to the courtyard, but only saw Aelle. She was, if anything, looking happier than ever, chatting with some boy swathed in grey—Hollen? *A friend of Niico's*, he thought. They were flanked by the gossips he'd overheard earlier. *In her element.* He nodded at her and she smiled brightly back at him. He was glad she'd come, and resolved to work on fixing their bent if not broken relationship. *I hope you get your time, sister, I hope Rhuun does as well.*

It wouldn't be a bad idea, though, to keep an ear on what she and her friends were talking about. He passed Niico and gave him a sign to go and talk with her. Niico gave a tiny nod, after making sure Rhuun was not to be found, and made his way towards the courtyard, trailing admirers.

What a funny group we make, he thought. *Why can't we all just be friends?* He had decided to tell the Queen about the little misunderstanding with the scrap of paper, a good start on showing her that even if he was now to be called Mage, he still was her trusted confidant.

"May we have a word, Your Grace," asked Ilaan. He steered her, taking care not to touch her, to a quiet corner. The light from the flowers above them gave her a charming glow.

"Is this to do with your father?" she asked. "I can ask him to retire his hiking boots if you're worried about him."

"He is not as young as he was, that is true, Madam, but I think he'd miss the empty sand if we asked him not to go. No, this is something else. An odd thing happened today. With the Zaalmage. No, it was with all the Mages, they all seemed a bit odd. Of course, it's difficult to tell…."

"Odd how? In general or specifically?" She looked less charming and more worried. There was a vertical line between her arched brows he'd never noticed before.

"Well, you know I had my *Naa Kansima*. It was the last step. Something strange happened."

"I assumed it went well, otherwise this would be a funny sort of party!" She was still hanging on to her smile.

"Oh, no, it was fine. I passed, I guess you'd call it. They said I'll start training with them very soon. No, it was after that. It's hard to explain." He began twisting and pulling the cuff of his white tunic.

"Try," she said.

"Well, you get this bag, and you put some important thing in it—" he began.

"I know what *Naa Kansima* is. Was it something you saw?" She looked concerned. *She should,* he thought.

"No, that part was—unpleasant but, no, it wasn't that. The book you gave me. You know. *The* book."

"What about it?" she asked, looking a bit pale. She began scanning the room. *Who is she looking for?*

"Somehow, a scrap of paper—just a corner, really. It got in the bag. I didn't bring it down there on purpose, of course. But they saw it, and they examined it pretty closely. And they said the strangest thing! They said it was in a human's hand this very day. Isn't that odd? I told them that wasn't possible, and that seemed to settle them."

"Did you," she cleared her throat. "Did you tell them who owns that book? Whose hand it was in?"

"Well, of course, there's no harm in telling them it's Rhuun's book, I mean, obviously he's not…."

Her hand shot out and gripped his wrist.

"What have you done?" He tried to withdraw his hand, but she held him tightly. He could feel the length of her nails driving into his skin.

"What? Nothing! They must have known it belonged to the human who gave it to you, because Rhuun isn't…" *Of course he is. You idiot, of course he is.* He saw the man on the cover of the book, a dark haired giant with no power, a great beast who felt pain. A human. *I am a fool.*

It was his turn to settle his face into a blank mask. It was that or scream.

"What have I done?" he whispered. "I mean, what will they do?'"

She dropped his hand. "How close are you to having that charm ready?"

"It is just a matter of a few words."

"Use it. Send him away. Do it now." She looked towards the entranceway. "I imagine the Mages are on their way. The only thing that would ever get them up those stairs is human blood, and now they know where to get some."

A million questions rose to Ilaan's lips, but she held up her hand. "We will talk later, you and I. Oh, we'll have a *very* long talk. Now go get my son through the Door and save his life—if you value your own. I'll deal with the Mages." He stood frozen in front of her for a moment. "Ilaan!"

"I will go," he stammered.

But he had to see Aelle first.

***

"Rhuun left, of course," she said. "More than five people showed up and that was just too much for him." Her smile was brilliant. "I imagine he went back to his dark little cave to sleep it off. You're not leaving, are you? *Rushta,* you're as bad as he is! You can't leave your own party! Father will string you up!"

Ilaan struggled to compose his expression. He took a moment to send a Stand Ready signal to Niico. "I'm really, really sorry, Aelle."

"Light and Wind, Ilaan, whatever is wrong with you?"

"I have to go. I'm sorry." He shimmered away, leaving her, for once, open mouthed and staring. Niico was already making his way towards the entrance, where some sort of commotion had started.

Chapter 31

Eriis City
20 years after the War of the Door, Eriisai calendar
100 years later, Mistran calendar
Royal household

Once in his room, Rhuun stretched out with his back against the bed and his feet up against the far wall. That held him nicely in place. He'd slept on the floor in more or less this position before, as his bed, reassembled to accommodate his height, was fine in theory but never felt quite right.

He decided the floor was a safer bet than the bed, or, Light and Wind forbid, a chair. That was asking for trouble. He didn't exactly completely remember walking home from Ilaan's party, but he'd made the short stroll (no shimmering for him) so often he could have done it with his eyes closed.

He'd thought about taking his boots off but as Ilaan had once pointed out, they were very, very far away. He did manage to close the heavy curtains and shut the door, so, night over. Another party done and finished. He closed his eyes, which turned out to be a bad idea—the room moved rapidly and unpleasantly. Maybe lying on the floor would be wiser? But that was pretty far away as well. He pulled the flask of *sarave* he'd lifted from Ilaan's out of his coat and upended it. Empty. An earlier version of himself had obviously finished it off. But when? He knew there was another bottle stashed in a cabinet, unfortunately out of arm's reach, and resolved to get it. But before he could remind his legs how to get him up off the floor, Ilaan shimmered into the room. There he was. His friend Ilaan was sitting on the floor right next to him. That was nice.

" 'lo. Why are you here?" He could see Ilaan better, as it turned out, through just one eye. "Party over?"

"I have to talk to you. It's really important." Ilaan looked uncharacteristically flustered.

"She wants. Do you know what she wants?"

"I don't have—" Ilaan was almost frantic, but Rhuun continued. He had things he wanted to say.

"She wants me to," he spoke slowly and carefully, "'Request More Official Duties.' 'Be more active in the life of the Court.' 'Work with Mother on a more formal level.' Why don't you understand?" His imitation of Aelle's clipped vowels and dropped inflection would have been funny in any other circumstance. "We'll be so good at Court together, why aren't you happy Rhuuuuuunnn?"

Rhuun tried to close his eyes. He opened them again immediately. "Rather sand swim through the Vastness." He looked at Ilaan. "Oh, hi Ilaan. When'd you get here? 'fraid I had a fight with Yell." He sighed. "She's so pretty. Don't even mind that she has to stand on a chair—"

"Okay, that's enough." Ilaan sighed and rubbed his hands together. "I'm sorry about this. It'll probably hurt." He grabbed Rhuun by the jaw and kissed him hard on the mouth. After a moment he released his head and went to the window. Opening the curtains, he blew a dirty black lungful of air out into the darkness.

Ilaan closed the curtains and turned back to his friend. Rhuun now sat on the edge of the bed with his head in his hands.

"Well, that was terrible." Rhuun said. "Deeply uncomfortable, followed by painful, and now I'm embarrassed." He shook his now-clear head. "Usually it takes half the morning to wake up feeling this bad."

"I have to talk to you and that seemed like the quickest way."

Rhuun looked up. His eyes were entirely red now, not just the iris. That would fade quickly, fortunately. "So am I a good kisser?" he asked.

"Please, listen. This is really important. We don't have much time." Ilaan's serious tone got his attention. "There's trouble. With the Mages. And we need to try the spell. You need to try and go through the Door."

"What, right now? Ilaan, what's going on?"

"I don't think I can tell you—"

"So you know but you won't tell me? Seriously? Then go through yourself. The door is right there." He pointed towards his own door. "Goodnight."

"Rhuun, I'm sorry, but this is really complicated—but I can't leave, you *have* to try the spell—now."

"No," Rhuun folded his long legs under him and leaned against the wall. "No, I don't. You're as bad as they are—you and Aelle and my mother, all full of plans. It's my own fault, I suppose. I've been letting the wind push me through my whole life. Good, bad, whatever, I'll just go along with it, as long as I don't get, y'know, set on fire more than twice a day. And I have plenty of this." He tossed the empty bottle across the room, where it hit the wall, shattered, and turned back to a pile of sand. "I've been a tool, and a toy, and sand knows what else. And I'm tired of it, I'm tired of myself. So tell me why I should try the spell, or go home." He rubbed the back of his head. "And no more kissing until you improve your technique."

"Okay." Ilaan thought for a moment. "Okay. Are you ready? It's like this. Look at me. You're human. Or maybe half a human, that's more likely, but unclear. I think your mother is really your mother but we haven't had that conversation. And the Mages know you have human blood, so they are on their way right now to take it. I don't think it involves your cooperation."

Rhuun was silent and still for a second. Then he burst out laughing.

"That is beautiful. Seriously, lots of strong storytelling elements. Did you run this tale past my mother?"

"Your mother's the one who says you have to go. Now." Ilaan had the paper in his hands and was turning it over and over. It was covered not only with dark bloodstains and ancient inscriptions, but now had a fresh layer of writing—still in the old tongue, but spelled out so anyone could read the words, even if they didn't know what it meant.

Rhuun rubbed the back of his head again. "What if I don't believe you?"

"Then the Mages will probably break in here and take you down to the Raasth."

"Even if this nonsense was true, Mother wouldn't let them actually harm me," he frowned. "Would she?"

"She wrote the law. She implicates herself no matter what happens. The law she wrote gives the Mages whatever they need. And they need you. I think they've suspected for a long time, they needed proof… of your blood—the human part of it. The humans sealed the Door with blood, and yours will blow it right off its hinges. I've seen where they'll do it; it's a big flat table. It has drains in it." Thinking on it, Ilaan felt sick. It'd had stains on it. Grooves that fingernails would leave and places to attach restraints. He'd leaned on it, and they hadn't mentioned it. The Mages had acted like it was just another piece of furniture. *Oh this, it's just where we perform our sacrifices.* And he had been ready—eager to join them. He'd traded Rhuun's life for it.

Rhuun slowly rose to his feet. "If this is a joke, it's not a funny one."

"I am begging you, read the spell. I—I'm not sure it'll work, there are some words missing. It might only get you as far as the Veil. But you won't be here, and you won't be dead."

"I assume Aelle doesn't know about this." Ilaan was silent. "She will kill you. Tell her I said not to, and please extend my apologies." He looked at the flimsy sheet of paper, which Ilaan had put in his hand. "Do I get to come home?"

"I don't know. No, I *do* know. I will figure this out. I won't leave you there, I swear it. And if you find Malloy, the writer, maybe he can help you. If we're lucky, this may even take you to him. Get him to help you. After all, he wrote this, he can certainly write another one."

"I…" There was the sound of many running feet from the far end of the corridor. "So. What now, Ilaan? Fight?"

Ilaan nodded at the paper. "Fly. I won't leave you there," Ilaan said brokenly. "I'll bring you home."

"Take care of my mother," said Rhuun. "Take care of Aelle. Lock the door. And let's get started."

Rhuun read the spell slowly, carefully sounding out the translated words. As he read, the page burned itself above his fingers, line by line. There'd be no using it again.

He got to the end. Nothing happened. He'd been afraid, then excited, and he still didn't know what to make of it—human? Half-human? Blood and the Door and the Mages… it was too much to comprehend.

It doesn't matter, you're going, you're really going. You'll see horses, and find the girl….

There was pounding on the door now, and many voices. Somewhere outside Rhuun thought he heard his mother's voice. She sounded very angry. He was tired. He wished he'd never found the book. He wasn't human, that was absurd. He rubbed his aching eyes and looked up, saying, "I'm sorry, Ilaan. It looks like we have to let them in."

But Ilaan was gone. His room and his door and the people on both sides were gone. Eriis was gone. It was dim and quiet and cool, and completely deserted.

He was in the Veil.

Chapter 32

"I heard voices, my Lord" said Gwennyth.
The Duke turned, trying to block what she already had seen.
Cybelle dos Shaddach lay upon the stairs, her head at a most alarming angle, her face quite blue.

-The Claiming of the Duke, pg 110
Malloy Dos Capeheart, Little Gorda Press (out of print)

Mistra
100 years after the War of the Door, Mistran calendar
20 years later, Eriisai calendar
The Guardhouse

Disaster, my sister.

That was the message Scilla saw when chores were done. She'd returned to her cell and eagerly reached for her notebook. The Voice had been telling her about the seasons. They had been discussing whether snow and ice were more beautiful on Eriis or Mistra and she wanted to continue the conversation.

Disaster, my sister.

But how? What did it mean? She quickly dashed a note—could she help? Was her Voice in danger? She paced through the night.

Finally, near dawn, a message. A most disturbing one.

One of our own has fled into the Veil. This degraded creature thinks to escape its rightful place as our prisoner and wreak havoc among you humans. We cannot reach this monster from Eriis.

Let me help—let me go after it! I know I can do it.

We cannot justify putting you in such a dangerous position. I argued against it myself—even knowing as I do, your cleverness and strength. It is simply too much to ask.

You don't have to ask! I want to do it! Just tell me how. If we work together, I know I can capture this beast.

You would do this for us? For me? I won't forget your bravery when the time comes to stand on the City Wall and receive the thanks of all of us in Eriis. Here is what you must do....

And this, the most important part:

As soon as you sense it, it is vital you bind it. It must not be allowed to escape. Capture it, bind it, and hold it. Bring it back with you thus contained and wait for me. I will explain how to dispose of the creature and our gratitude—my gratitude—will be boundless.

Scilla already had the rare and exotic books she'd need to complete the binding spell. In fact, the best and most valuable parts of the Order's library now resided in her own room. No one ever noticed. The rest of the night was spent racing between her notebook and the piles of books on her bookshelf, shoved under her bed, and stacked in her wardrobe.

Finally, with the sky barely lit with dawn, she was ready to go.

She lit the candle and read the words she'd so painstakingly transcribed and translated. *Maybe this was the first time anyone had ever said them out loud*, she thought. Certainly the first time they'd been read in this place.

I am breaking a window a generation old. I am climbing through the window.

She never stopped to wonder if anyone dedicated to patrolling those windows would notice a broken pane. She never considered she might fail. She said the words, she made the shapes, she created the hole. And last and most importantly, she took a needle and pricked her finger. Just a tiny drop—barely enough to see in the dim candle light. But the blood made it work. Without blood, she and the Voice would do nothing but shout at each other through the locked Door until the moons fell into the sea.

The blood hit the page.

She pulled back the Veil and went through.

Her room was gone, and Scilla knew she was in an in-between place. The light, what there was of it, was dim. It was very quiet and it smelled a bit stuffy—like a long neglected closet. It seemed both limitless and cramped. It felt heavy. She waited. Would the escaped prisoner come to her? It was important that she sense it before it found her. She realized with a thrill, that she was a little bit scared.

A long time later, or maybe just a moment, she decided to look around. She walked for miles—possibly the length of her room. It looked the same. There was no way to tell. It all looked the same. It all was the same, really. She was no longer scared or even particularly excited. She felt as if the strange place was seeping into her brain and pushing her own thoughts to the side. Knowing this, she realized she didn't really care.

"I'm looking for something… What was it? Oh well. I guess I'll know it if it happens to come by."

Despite her strangely languid mood, a tiny flare of anxiety lit in her belly. This place—the Veil—looked like nothing, was made of nothing, and what if she couldn't find her way back? She tried to retrace her steps, but it was all the same—cool, dark, and quiet. She felt a strong desire to sit down. Maybe take a nap. The Voice would just have to wait. Her mission drifted until it was a boring story she'd heard ages ago. Unless she'd dreamed the whole thing. Yes, that was likely. She'd been here in the dark forever. It was so perfectly simple. This was real and it was so wonderfully quiet….

Then she knew she wasn't alone. Nothing changed, but Scilla sensed a ripple in the stillness. Something brushed her cheek and she felt the hairs on her arms rise. She heard a breath. Not her own.

"Don't panic. Panic is for everyone else." She tried to slow her heart and control her terrified panting, but her body wouldn't obey. "Say the words," she told herself. "The binding spell. I know them, I'll say them, I'll go back to the Guardhouse. Lower the Veil." She couldn't remember how the words had started. Despite the cool, her shift stuck to her back.

Out of the dark haze, she saw a hand reaching out, blindly groping for purchase. Without thinking, she reached for it. She pulled. And then she screamed and let it go, because the hand was as hot as the inside of an oven. But she'd already said the words, and the Veil was falling back down around her.

She could hear screaming. She recognized the voice as her own. She was tumbling backwards, and the owner of the hand she'd pulled was tumbling with her. She was shrieking the words over and over. Then the Veil and the darkness collapsed on her and the air rushed out.

Chapter 33

Gweynth looked sadly back over her shoulder at her father's farmstead. She knew she'd never see it, or her brothers again. She opened her little bag and made sure for the hundredth time that it was there—her favorite book of children's stories. If she had nothing else to bring to the household of this Duke, at least she had her stories.

-The Claiming of the Duke, pg 25
Malloy Dos Capeheart, Little Gorda Press (out of print)

Mistra
100 years after the War of the Door, Mistran calendar
20 years later, Eriisai calendar
The Guardhouse

Scilla opened her eyes. Same cell. On the bed. Candle still lit, and predawn light at the window, which was no light at all. But there was one new thing—crouching on the floor was a man. At least, it resembled a man. It seemed to have been recently on fire because wisps and curls of smoke rose from its dark grey skin. It looked soft despite the char. Scilla wanted to touch it but realized that would have been forward of her, even if her guest was a demon. She glanced at her hand. The palm was bright pink with a fresh burn. It smarted. She'd deal with it later. This had to be the escapee her Voice had warned about. And she'd captured it! That meant… well, what did it mean, exactly? Her Voice hadn't said. But the Voice had been abundantly clear on one thing; when you captured a supernatural creature, it was prudent—no, *vital*—to put a binding spell on it. Not only could it not set you on fire, or make you dematerialize, or turn you into some sort of lizard, but if you bound it, it had to obey you. The Voice would be delighted by how carefully she'd carried out her mission.

From the Voice's pained tone, she was certain this was a somehow inferior species. Maybe a lower-natured cousin, far removed from the race of elegant demons who walked the glass skyways over the glittering seas. This thing… this creature on her floor looked up at her now. Its eyes were a bright, clear red-gold and it stared at her appraisingly. Other than the eyes, and the smoke, and the skin, it looked enough like a man to almost be one.

"Are you Malloy?" Scilla wasn't sure she had heard it correctly. It repeated itself. "Are you Malloy Dos Capehart?"

"Who? No!" she replied. That name, it sounded familiar.

It sat back, obviously confused. "Then why did you bring me here?"

"I—" She paused. *It knows I went hunting, but the binding should protect me. Just don't tell it anything. Don't panic now. That's for other people. And demons.* "I simply went fishing in the Veil, and look what I caught! You work for me, now."

"Release me at once," it demanded. "This is highly improper."

"Yes, I'm sure you think so, seeing as you're the one who's been caught." She folded her arms and tried to look imposing, even a little bored by the whole thing. *Who doesn't have a captive demon?*

It leaned forward and she drew back despite herself.

It cocked its smoldering head and asked, "What if I were to kill you right now?"

She dared another quick glance at her burned hand. She had no doubt it could kill her easily. But would it? This had not occurred to her. The binding spell should protect her from any attack, but what if she'd gotten it wrong? She kept her face still and said, "If you killed me, how would you get home? You wouldn't."

It sat quietly for a while. She began to make a little list of jobs in her head.

"There will be repercussions for this," it finally said, running its hands over its head. As it did, ash fell to the floor.

"No doubt. But until they come due, you'll have to do as I say." She had no personal evidence of this, but she had grown up on fairy tales and politics—and in any case the demon hadn't argued. The room was starting to fill with smoke. "And can you not do that? It's getting hard to breathe. Can't you do that thing where you hide your face and look like a regular person?" She'd done a great deal of research, her 'independent studies,' on just this sort of thing.

"Not here." It pointed at her stacks of antique books, which she gathered were keeping it from transforming into something else.

"Who is—what was that name you said?" she asked.

"No one. Someone I wanted to talk to." It shook its head. "This is not what I expected."

Scilla felt the start of something—this was going to be thrilling. "Well, you can just talk to me instead! I have so many questions! Where to begin. Um. So, what were you doing so close to my… ah, net?"

It looked deeply uncomfortable. "I was going to meet someone. I was looking for someone. But the Veil is… it was dark.

And then I saw color over here." It looked around the room, she could swear with some disdain. "Well, not here, so much. But the Veil is thin and I was… curious."

"What's your name?" This seemed to alarm it, as it began to smoke more vigorously. It said something that sounded like 'Mammoth.' "What?" She waved her hand to freshen the air in front of her face. It cleared its throat.

"Moth" it said.

"Well, Moth. Do you know where you are?"

"A place of study, I think. A place where spells can be cast by children. Perhaps a school of some sort?" The demon stood up. "You are very young. Is there a headmaster? A teacher? Would they be pleased to see what their little human person had brought back as a souvenir from their trip to the Veil? Would they like to find me here?"

It stood at the foot of Scilla's little bed. It was tall. It was also naked, although modestly wreathed by smoke. Scilla quickly looked away.

"I… I… you should go! Yes. Go ahead and get out of this building. Go hide. Um, find some clothes. Probably first. But listen for my call. I'll have things for you to do. It won't be long, so don't wander off."

It nodded, then turned and merged with the shadows at her door. Then it was gone.

Scilla realized she'd been holding her breath. She let it out in a great shuddery gasp and put her head on her knees. After a moment she took out her notebook, opened to a fresh page, and began to write.

***

The sun was up and Scilla realized with a start that she'd missed her morning duties. She swore under her breath, set her notebook aside—now filled with lists of chores for her new pet—and hurriedly restacked the rare books under her bed. And now she had to race or there'd be hot water and a scrub brush in her future.

When the knocking came, she opened the door. "Pardons, I overslept, I'll be down to the kitchen…"

The entire library staff and the Elders stood outside her door. Brother Blue filled her doorway. She gazed up at him.

"We'd like to look at your books, my dear. Now." His normally kind and distant brown eyes were now hard and suspicious. She was in for it. She had to do something and fast….

Scilla gave a great sobbing cry and flung herself on the floor of the little room, carefully kicking the rag rug over the scorch marks the creature's feet had burned into the floor. As she did, her notebook leapt from her hand into the fire, which still burned quietly in the grate.

"Please help me! The demons said if I didn't do what they said they'd kill my whole family! They made me steal the books! I love the Order, don't make me leave!" she howled.

"Child, you are to calm down. We know about The Veil…."

"Don't make me go there! I was so scared! I won't go back, I'd rather die."

She shrieked and sobbed so hysterically that finally the elderly gentlemen who staffed the library shrugged and handed her over to Brother Blue.

Every time the old man asked her a question, she provided a fresh round of hysterics. He made it clear he knew she'd somehow lifted The Veil and been in contact with the other side, but until she had a chance to think, it wouldn't do to answer him. Blue finally turned her over to the Guardhouse nurse, the only woman in attendance. The woman made Scilla drink something bitter that made her head feel like it might drift away. As Scilla fell asleep, she was smiling. She could get another notebook. She had a pet demon bound to her, and the Voice was safe.

Chapter 34

"Beesley, I've known your family my whole life," said the Duke. "Why would you try and steal from me now? You know you had only to ask."
The man rattled the chain at his wrist and sneered, "Lookin' in the wrong quarter for your man, Guv. Him what stole from you wouldn't never fink to ask."
The Duke shook his head. The man was spouting nonsense.

-The Claiming of the Duke, pg 82
Malloy Dos Capeheart, Little Gorda Press (out of print)

Mistra
100 years after the War of the Door, Mistran calendar
20 years later, Eriisai calendar
The Guardhouse

Brother Blue watched the tea ball bob gently in his cup, the steam rising from the steeping liquid. He'd awakened hours earlier with Hellne's name on his lips, something that had been beaten out of him nearly a hundred years earlier.

"I am old," he thought, as usual with some measure of surprise. "I had no idea I'd live this long." He had many theories as to how he'd done it; his most recent involved his extended stays on Eriis, where time had always moved more slowly. Once he though his Princess had charmed him into long life, then he thought she'd cursed him with it. He hadn't dreamt of her in ages, but this morning he'd been sure she was in his room. It wasn't the old dream, the vision of fire and blood; she was just sitting there watching him with her lovely scarlet eyes. He was surprised upon awakening that she was not there. What would he say to her, if she'd been there, perched on the edge of his bed smiling at him? What do you say to a woman who nearly destroyed your world?

When he'd returned through the Door (*last one through, that's worth noting)* his elders at the Guardhouse had thanked him for his service in keeping the monster occupied. They seemed genuinely grateful. They heaped upon him the praise he longed for, but for once, didn't think he'd earned. Eventually they realized he had no idea the princess was plotting, along with her odious father and his wicked

Counselors, against Mistra and against them all. When it became apparent he was simply dallying with a pretty girl, he was beaten with a stick and locked in his room to repent. At least, that was how he remembered it. It was all so long ago.

Blue was eventually forgiven of his crime, since it was of ignorance, not collusion, and allowed to remain and learn, and finally teach. He was more than grateful and extremely motivated. He knew there was nothing more important than keeping the Door sealed. If he could be fooled and led astray so easily, what chance did anyone else have against them?

And now, all these years later, they were trying again. He saw every bit of his own foolish behavior in little Scilla. If, upon rising, he hadn't followed the ancient routine—check the 'locks' against charms or tampering—he might never have known. In the long, quiet years since the Weapon, that routine, once urgent, had become an afterthought. They would have to be more vigilant. *She's up to something,* he thought. *She's part of this somehow. They didn't open the Veil by themselves, there's no way. They have no human blood, and without that, my little escape hatch wasn't anything but words on a page. Words on a page. Well, there's nothing for it now but to watch her and see what happens next.*

His thoughts returned to his Princess. *I wonder if she liked my book.*

Chapter 35

The girl was finally too exhausted to sob. She still had to clean the Duke's kitchen and then tend to his dogs. The world of glittering jewels and wavering candlelight, of fine meals and soft beds were close enough to touch, but she knew it would never be for one such as herself. She sank down on the stairs and wondered how it had all gone so wrong.

-The Claiming of the Duke, pg 73
Malloy Dos Capeheart, Little Gorda Press (out of print)

Mistra
100 years after the War of the Door, Mistran calendar
20 years later, Eriisai calendar
Outside the Guardhouse

Rhuun put as much ground between himself and the Guardhouse as he could before he had to throw himself down under a tree and rest.

"Hello, human person. My name is Moth," he said, trying it out. It wasn't bad, as names went, and he certainly wasn't going to tell that girl his real name. He'd heard about mages who could call you through time and between worlds by calling your real name. He doubted the girl was a real mage, but she had some odd sort of power. Why take a chance?

This far from the influence of the books in the child's room, he found he was also able to hide his face. Eyes, though, still a problem. For the first time, right shape but wrong color. He'd have to figure something out to hide them.

Why am I worrying about such silly things, he wondered. *How long was I in the Veil?* He was afraid it was a very long time.

I'm part human. He was strangely relieved. He wasn't the worst demon who ever lived. He wasn't really a demon at all.

For every answer—*this is why I never fledged, this is why I have no fire*—a dozen more questions. He knew he must have some Eriisai blood; he could do a few things. He could disappear, after a fashion. And he had his mother's eyes, everyone said so. His father's too, perhaps.

He wished Ilaan was with him. He'd had plenty of time in the Veil to think about things, and much of that revolved around Ilaan.

When he'd read the spell and left Eriis, he quickly realized he'd only made it halfway. The grey and oppressive space pressed down on him and he knew the other side—the human world—didn't look like a dark cave. He knew less about the mechanics of the Veil than he should, although in retrospect he guessed he knew less about every single *scorping* thing in his life than he should. With that knowledge bitter in his mouth he'd decided to take a walk in what resembled a dimly lit corridor, although he couldn't say how long he'd sat before he rose to go. And he didn't really know how far he'd gone. And really, what did it matter? He'd sat back down—was it where he'd started? Or somewhere else? He tried to put together what Ilaan had told him. Human. The concept flew around his head like a little mouse with wings. Half-human? Had his mother accepted the spark from a human person? It seemed unthinkable. She never once expressed an interest in anything other than the superiority and safe keeping of Eriis. But would she take on the responsibility of raising someone else's crippled human child, and never say a word?

He'd wandered the Veil for what felt like days, or minutes. He'd felt himself drifting….

The questions that followed him around had faded away until his mind was as still as a stone. He'd spent a long time sitting in a dim, quiet space watching a dark spot on the wall. Then he'd realized there was no wall and maybe no spot and he'd been literally staring into space. *Eh, that was fine*. The view had been the same with his eyes opened or closed. Finally he'd closed them and prepared to drift off, maybe for a really long time. Maybe for just a few seconds. Maybe forever.

Then, in the middle of all that nothing, there'd been something. A flash of light at the edge of his field of vision. He'd regretted the interference in his perfect still nothingness, but went to investigate.

He'd followed tiny flashes of light, random sounds—like the sound a candle makes as it burns—and the smell of a library. As he'd become more interested, the flashes grew brighter and stronger. He saw color—real color. As red as a woman's hair and as blue as a scrap of silk. He'd eagerly gone towards the source.

It was a mistake. It had been some sort of snare. The control he maintained over his physical form—his temperature, his True Face—was dragged away. He was freezing. He was burning. Then he'd felt as if someone had thrown a rope around his mind. He'd tried desperately to back away from the glowing colors but someone was pulling on the rope and he was yanked closer. He'd thrown his hands out to keep from falling forward.

Someone had taken his hand. Then they were gone and it was all screaming. Then the strange little girl in the stone room. He'd tried to hide his True Face from the human girl at once, but something in those old books pressed down on him like a fist. He could only try to hide his confusion. Ilaan had been right, as he usually was. Naked as a sand hill. And it had been horrible, not funny at all.

He didn't blame Ilaan. What else could he have done? If you thought about it (which he had done at great length) from Ilaan's perspective it had worked as well as it could—they'd known it wasn't quite complete. How could Ilaan have known there'd be a girl waiting in the Veil to pull him through? And where was Dos Capeheart in all this? He'd expected to be greeted by his author, not some random child, certainly not by a child with some sort of power. Ilaan would be interested to hear that binding spells worked on this side.

They'd have a lot to talk about when he got home.

But for now he was here. He'd made it to the human side. He caught his breath and took a look around. Almost immediately he had to clap his hands over his eyes—he had never seen so many things all in one place.

"Start slowly," he told himself. "Let's start with this tree."

He spent a long time with the bark before moving on to the leaves. He was a little stunned when he realized the tree had always been a tree—it hadn't been transformed from something else. He finally let himself look up at the leaves, and even though the constant motion made him feel a little queasy, he couldn't bring himself to look away from the color and light. The sky (which was the same sky on both sides of The Door, it was said) had a sun that was made of light. Light and blue. His sky, the sky of Eriis, was low and grey brown. It was nothing but clouds and most of the time you couldn't see through them. He knew his mother's Mages worked tirelessly to finally break the clouds apart, but it hadn't happened yet and they made no promises. He'd heard about a clear sky over Eriis from stories about before the War. Had the sky back home ever been this bright? And he realized with a start that there was what you might call a breeze, but no wind. He was very far outside, far from any structure or gate or wall, and there was no need for a scarf. His eyes, now more accustomed to the bright day, weren't stinging from sand or grit or ash.

The book had been true. This place was magical.

Ilaan had sworn he'd find a way to bring him home. Rhuun thought about the way the paper had burned to ash in his hands. He hoped his friend had gotten to work. In the meantime, he had to obey the strange child who had caught him. He laughed grimly to himself. *I guess my big plan of living on my own terms is off the table for a while. The wind that blows me around now comes from a human.* Would she follow the law and release him when she was done with him? She seemed a bit... off. But how could he be sure? Maybe the human persons were all like her, not sweet like Gwyneth, or strong like the Duke, or even sly like Cybelle. That was a concern, but things in their order.

When he could look around and handle the color, light, and motion without getting dizzy, he decided to explore. Why not? None of his people had been on this side of the Door in his lifetime. He wondered what people were saying about him, how Aelle had taken the news, if his mother was in trouble. He realized he might be on this side for a very long time.

He walked until he came to a river (with many interruptions to observe leaves and stones) and that stopped him dead in his tracks. He knew what it was—in *The Claiming of the Duke* the characters were always sailing from one river town to the next—but to see one in person! It was nothing like the vast, moving sand rivers beyond the city walls. He forgot his precarious circumstances and crossed the broad swath of green grass that formed a natural border to the bank. He gingerly walked out onto the muddy shore, sinking just a bit, and spent some time squishing the mud between his toes. It was warm from the sun and not unpleasant, although very strange. It clung to his legs much like the dust back home. He supposed mud and dust were cousins. He looked at the water for a long time, at the way it threw back bits of light and the way it never stopped moving. Water couldn't be that different from air. Air was full of light and never stopped moving. He could see the bottom for a few feet, then it quickly got too deep to follow. He waded out until he was knee deep, to where it dropped off, looked at the sky, and stepped off the edge.

After he'd managed to get himself back to the grassy shore, and had stopped coughing up river water, he lay in the sun and turned his heat up. In a moment he was dry. He laughed weakly. *So that was what they call cold! Also I can't breathe underwater. So—water is not like air. And I don't seem to be able to float very well, either.*

He heard voices and quickly retreated to the dense growth that marked the edge of the forest.

A young man and woman strolled out onto the grass, setting down bags and baskets. The woman, like the lady on the cover of his book, wore her hair unbound—which, he decide, was much to his liking. They quickly shed their clothes and jumped—on purpose—into the water. There was much splashing and laughing. The young man would disappear under the dark water and surface somewhere different, and the girl would shriek with laughter every time. Eventually, she complained of being cold. He watched as they got out of the water. There were sprays and drop of water flying everywhere as they shook out their hair. *So far*, he thought, *water is my favorite part*. They continued to laugh, but now seemed more interested in kissing. *Very much like in my book!* he thought with satisfaction. Those people were always kissing when they weren't arguing or traveling.

When they began to make love on the warm banks of the river he knew he should look away, but it was all so interesting. The boy and girl had completely different colored hair, and the skin of his body was darker than hers. Their bodies were hypnotic flashes of color and shape. He was too far to tell for sure, but they didn't appear to ornament their flesh with ink or gold. And that wasn't the only peculiarity—he was surprised to see how gentle they were, as if afraid the other would break. The young man touched the girl's body in a way that looked correct, but no blows, no slaps. No sparks or flames at all. Were all humans like that? How did they know anything had happened? He had to find Dos Capehart. The end of the book surely would make it clear.

As the couple slept the afternoon away, he stole the boy's clothes and the girl's bag. He hadn't gone far before he went back and took the boy's wide brimmed hat.

The river still captured his attention more than the land, and he found a quiet, secluded spot to watch it rush past. Eventually the moons rose, and he understood why people talked about them so much. As it got darker, it also got quieter, and that made it easier to think.

He slept under a tree with the bag rolled up under his head, totally alone, never noticing that every animal in the wood, when it sensed him, turned and went the other way.

***

Very early the next morning, he heard Scilla call, a tug in his mind. There was just enough light to cast shadows, and that was how he traveled to meet her, practically unseeable. He felt much more at ease and could look around without getting dizzy, so he could both watch where he was going and use his one useful ability. Oddly, it seemed easier to vanish in this strange place. Maybe there were just more shadows. Still, he had to step away from shade here and there and stop and look at some really sparkly rocks. Rocks! But they somehow added to the beauty of the scene. This place was full of wonders.

She met him in a clearing in the woods. Still going unseen, he took a look at her in the daylight. She was very young, he'd been right about that. She had long brown braids that were slightly mussed. She wore a heavy cape which looked well used but expensive over what appeared to be a nightdress. She appeared to be anxious, looking behind her back towards the great stone heap of a building she'd trapped him in the day before. Well, she could just wait. Before he let her see him, he spent some time looking at the tree stumps, draped with velvety moss. The green of the moss was the most beautiful thing he'd ever seen. Except, perhaps, light on water.

Chapter 36

The beast was huge, Gwenyth imagined it weighed nearly as much as she did. She held out her hand, palm up. The breast of capon had been intended for her dinner, but this seemed a more sensible course. The dog sniffed it, then picked it up delicately between its massive jaws. It was gone in one bite. The wolfhound licked her hand, its tail thumping against the floor.

-The Claiming of the Duke, pg 49
Malloy Dos Capeheart, Little Gorda Press (out of print)

Mistra
100 years after the War of the Door, Mistran calendar
20 years later, Eriisai calendar
Outside the Guardhouse

Scilla didn't have to wait very long for her demon to show up, which was a good thing because she did not want to be missed at the Guardhouse. So the creature was punctual, that was good to know. She wasn't sure what to expect; would it still be a frightening vision of grey skin and smoke? She took a jump back when a tall young man appeared out of nowhere in front of her. This was called 'Hiding Its True Face,' she knew that from her studies. She noted that the creature had somehow procured a loosely woven shirt of plain dark brown cloth with large bone buttons. It fit well enough, unlike the trousers, which were a good handspan too short. It was barefoot and had a broad brimmed straw hat jammed over its long dark hair. It now looked like a poor farmer. Then it took off the hat so she could see its eyes, and it looked like nothing she'd ever seen.

"I see you have some clothes," she said by way of greeting.

It said, "I see you have something for me to do, little wench. Will you set me free, then?"

"Demon, I think you ought to look at this as an ambassadorship to our side. Think of everything you'll learn here. And when I feel it's time, off you'll go on your own. So stop asking." It nodded unhappily. Good, so it knew this was not a request. "That thing you did, where you are hard to see? I saw you do it when you left my cell. Can you do it whenever you want?" It nodded again. She blew a breath out. "Excellent. That makes this so much easier."

"What am I doing on my great quest to learn about your world?" it asked, rather rudely, she thought. "I feel certain you have some very specific ideas."

She smiled and held out a twist of paper. "You're going to a party and putting this in the wine."

"What is wine?" it wanted to know.

"Um, you drink it? It's red, I guess, it comes in tall bottles. It makes people act like idiots."

"Oh, like *sarave"*, it said, wincing slightly. "You call it wine?" It squinted suspiciously at the paper cone she'd handed it. "I won't take lives. I am bound to you but I'll take this myself before I take lives for you."

"Oh, don't be so dramatic. It'll just give them headaches." It looked relieved. Would it really take its own life? There was so much to learn! "Then you're going to a house and breaking some glass. You know what mirrors are?" She was shaking with excitement.

"Mirrors and wine. So I'm an ambassador slash petty criminal?"

This creature was as petulant as her sister! Scilla wished she could force it to be more enthusiastic, but she couldn't control its feelings, only its actions. She shrugged. "Think of all the people you'll meet! Just don't look them in the eye."

It glared at her. Even in its human form, it was a little frightening to be on the receiving end of that gaze.

"When you go to this house—" she continued.

"The house with the wine? Or the house with the mirrors?"

Now it was just being difficult, she could tell. She drew a deep breath. "The house with the mirrors, the second one. You might see me there. Maybe not. I don't know for sure. But if you see me, you must never try and talk to me or contact me in any way. In that house, you are always invisible."

The demon considered this. She could see it trying to decide what to ask, and what it thought she would answer.

Finally it said, "Tell me about the house. The mirror house. If I am to bring mischief it might be helpful to know who bears the brunt, no?"

Scilla chewed her lip. "You'll find a family."

"Your family?" it asked.

"My family is the Order," she said with a great deal of conviction. "But they are my brothers and sisters, yes. The eldest two are of no concern to you. They are called Pol and May, leave them alone. The next boy is Rane and the girl is called Lelet. Make trouble between them. It'll be easy, they hate each other."

"Not as much as you hate them, I gather?" it asked in a lofty tone.

This thing was turning out to be more intelligent than she'd planned. She could hear an echo of the Voice when it spoke. She hadn't thought about using it as anything other than a blunt instrument. Would there be other, more elegant uses for it? Suddenly curious, she asked, "Do you have a sister?"

There came a pause. *Why would it have to stop and think about that? Maybe they have nests, like snakes.*

Finally, "No."

Scilla nodded and began to pace. She could feel her face getting warm. "Then you don't know what it's like watching someone get everything. Is she smart? Is she kind? Is she clever? No! None of those things. And she gets everything she wants, all the time. She colors her hair pink like a clown. She's a drunk. She's a fool. She… sees men."

"I see men," the demon smirked. "I see lots of things. I'm seeing you right now."

"Not like that," she hissed. "You know what I'm talking about, I know you do. She'll act all sweet and like she cares, but she doesn't. She only cares about herself. She's the one. Do whatever you want to Rane, he'll be sent to our father out at the farms and it'll probably be good for him. But Lelet? She should bear the brunt. Let her know what it's like to lose something she cares about."

"What did this girl take away from you?" it asked.

Scilla had tears standing in her eyes. Her face was bright red. The Voice had agreed with her, it wasn't fair that Lelet got everything and she was left with nothing at all. And now her cow of a sister would find out what it was like when things didn't go your way.

My dresses, my party, my friends, my fancy shoes, my own room, my own house, she listed the stolen things in her head. *The nice dinner because I'm coming home, which you won't be at because you're going to a party instead. There's something special waiting for you at your little party, Lelet.* "She ruins everything." She wiped her face and took a breath. "That's all you have to know. You are *filled in.*"

"This is a waste of time," declared the demon.

"I have nothing but time. I will be locked up here for the rest of my life." Scilla put on her back-to-work face and said, "What is important to remember?"

The demon sighed, she thought, again rather dramatically. "Timing. The wine. And then two nights later, the mirrors. And don't talk to you. Can I go now?"

"Here," she said, handing the creature a fat white candle. "You'll need this."

It examined the candle. "For a romantic dinner?"

"It's so I can talk to you, *of course.* Unless you can *fly* back and forth from the city to the Guardhouse." She frowned. "Can you?" It crossed its arms and looked at the sky. "I guess not. Light it at second moonrise and I'll be waiting."

"Wine, mirrors, candles, houses. Can I go *now*?"

"This is important, demon. Our people, have they ever worked together like this before?"

"We are not together. And whatever you're doing, it won't work. The boy won't love you, the house won't be saved from the fire, the horse will still break a leg. And even if she throws herself out of a window to the cliffs below, your older sister will always be older. Set me free before you damage yourself."

"The… what? What boy? What are you talking about?"

The demon looked down its nose at her. "Go read a book."

She put on her best at-breakfast smile. "Mmm hmm. See you soon. Timing, remember." She turned and walked back to the Guardhouse. The day was brightening and she had to hurry to get back to her infirmary bed.

It's wrong. It's wrong. He's wrong.

***

At dawn, the elderly nurse came through to check on her only patient. Scilla heard the old lady muttering complaints to herself about 'silly children, it's either falling down the stairs or burning themselves on a candle, or they're complainin' about their tummies' Scilla worked on breathing slowly, so she'd appear to still be asleep. Oldest trick in the book.

"I can see you're awake, Miss. Might as well open your eyes."

Scilla blinked up at the nurse. "Hmm? What time is it?" Scilla yawned and stretched and accepted a mug of chocolate the woman handed her. "Will they send me home today?" she asked, trying to look small and downcast.

"The elders don't generally include me in their planning sessions, dear. Just tell the truth of your tale and hope for the best." The nurse paused and then asked. "What made you take up with the red eyes, anyway?"

Scilla teared up. "They threatened my family. They said terrible things would happen if I didn't do what they said."

"Settle your bones, Miss. Don’t start in with all that wailin’ again, Light preserve us. Let me take a look." She kissed Scilla on her forehead, looked in her eyes, and declared her fever and dullness free, and sent her to her room to wait for the elders’ call.

The call came before lunch, which gave Scilla plenty of time to poke through the remains of her fire, but sadly the only thing left of her precious notebook was the spine. The rest was completely burned away. Too bad, but it was a small sacrifice. If the elders had read it, they'd do far worse than just send her packing. Her hysterics and subsequent trip to the infirmary had been just the thing—when she’d woken up from the sleeping draught in the middle of the night, she'd managed to swipe a twist of lacgma. It cured the kitchen dog of worms but gave people a vicious headache.

And she'd had time to perfect her story, *and* send her demon off on its journey. Funny, it had looked terrifying in its native state, but in human form, it looked like a handsome young man—one with very peculiar eyes, of course. She snickered. Her sister would make short work of it, if she ever met it. That was something else to think about, actually….

She was ushered in to Brother Blue's study, and took the seat across from him at his desk. To her surprise, he was the only one to question her. At first, she was pleased, feeling he'd be the easiest to lead about, but she quickly realized he was no simple old fool. He knew just what to ask, somehow, and her story became more and more elaborate. She knew the first law of the lie is pick a simple story and do not waver, but his probing questions made that nearly impossible.

They talked for what felt like hours. Who contacted whom? What did you promise the creatures? What did you tell them about The Door? Why did you enter the Veil? What did you find there? Why did you never ask for help? Through her sobs, she told Brother Blue they hounded her with voices in her head and never left her in peace until she thought she was going mad. They made her promise not to ask for help or her family would pay the price. She didn't know how the Veil lifted, it just did. She didn’t know how the books got in her room—maybe they had her under a spell? Maybe they were trying to kidnap her? She didn't understand and prayed they were gone for good.

Eventually, she began to believe her own story. Finally, it appeared, so did Brother Blue.

Yes, everything was falling into place. She'd convinced the elders she was blameless and contrite, and she'd promised old Blue that she'd spend at least an hour every evening in contemplation and reflection. An hour, it was agreed, at second moonrise.

Ultimately they agreed to let her remain at the Guardhouse. They'd have to watch her closely for signs of corruption, and there was no question about her being allowed back into the library. Pots and pans were her new friends, and she smiled through her tears and thanked the elders for helping and protecting her.

Properly replacing the notebook turned out to be the most difficult task. She wrote and wrote (and burned the pages every morning—she was being watched like a hawk), but the Voice remained silent.

Chapter 37

"My Lord!" Gwenyth cried in shock. "But how—I saw you die!" Sir Edward laughed. "And I thought performance class at University was a waste of time. It appears not." He advanced on her.

-The Claiming of the Duke, pg 181
Malloy Dos Capeheart, Little Gorda Press (out of print)

Mistra
100 years after the War of the Door, Mistran calendar
20 years later, Eriisai calendar
The Guardhouse

"Come in," said Brother Blue to his young assistant's knock. The boy settled himself in a comfortable chair in the corner of Blue's study—you only sat across from him at the desk if you were in trouble. They shared some warm cider, and after he'd asked after the boy's family and general health, "What did we learn today?"

That was nearly always the first question Blue liked to ask when it was time to talk business.

"She snuck out," said the boy. "Just like you said she would. I followed her to that place, the stumps." In Blue's experience, every lonesome, homesick, angry, displaced child to join the Order eventually found their way to the stumps. "She met someone there."

"Ah, now things grow warmer," said Blue. "How close did you get?"

"Not as close as I would have liked. It's just very quiet out there at that hour—it was just barely sunup. Nothing about, not even a bird." The boy paused, and frowned. "Usually birds are up at dawn. I wonder…."

"Who was this person she spoke with?"

"Not sure. Never seen him before. And me too far away to see his face, even." The boy looked crestfallen. "Next time I'll get there first, climb a tree. That way I can hear them better too."

"Please, Olly—let us focus on the task at hand, hmm? What did you see?"

The boy screwed his face up in concentration. "She waited, I think. Then he just appeared, which struck me odd. I didn't see him walk up the path to her like he was coming from the Guardhouse, and he would have walked past me if he'd come from the road the other way, although he might be stealthy. Maybe he knew about another path."

"And his appearance?" asked Blue. He was prepared for the answer: slender, dark, small.

"Big. Tall man, long black hair. He had a hat so I couldn't get a gander at his face, then he took it off but he had his back to me. Had some sort of bag over his shoulder. No shoes. And his pants were too short, isn't that funny?" Olly added, "Like, odd funny, not joke funny."

"Are you sure? You could tell he was tall? Like as tall as yourself?"

Olly looked confused. "Tall as you, sir. I could see the two of them standing next to each other. That'd be a hard one to get wrong."

Blue frowned. "And her demeanor?"

"Well, I was on the lookout for untoward behavior, of course, but it didn't seem like that at all." Olly was obviously relieved at not bearing that sort of news. "It was more like she was ordering him around, and he was just shaking his head about it. I think she was angry at him. Oh, and she gave him a candle."

Blue's brows shot up. "A candle? That is interesting." *You could do a lot of things with a candle*, he thought. You could keep track of a candle, and the one who lit it as well.

"Finally, she turned around and stomped away." Blue gave the boy a curious look. "Yes, I said stomped and I'm sticking with it. Those two are not friends, whatever else may be going on. And then he put the candle in his bag and he sort of disappeared into the trees."

"And our sister Scilla?"

"She snuck back the way she went out, went straight to the infirmary. And I went to morning chores." He chewed the inside of his cheek. "And then I came here. And after this—"

"That's fine, Olly. Let us keep a sharp eye out for this mysterious hat wearer, shall we? And if you can climb that tree, please do get a closer look. We'll just check on Sister Scilla's predawn antics for the next few days, you don't mind getting up a little early?" The boy agreed that he did not. "Then for now, perhaps you'd go fetch her and bring her here for a chat. I'll bet it's an interesting story."

"va'Everlys," he thought after sending Olly on his way. "Nothing but trouble."

Chapter 38

Eriis
20 years after the War of the Door, Eriisai calendar
100 years later, Mistran calendar
Royal Family Quarters

"Do I get to come home?" Rhuun had asked.

Ilaan was sick with dread; he could hear a crowd coming down the hall, and the Mages with them. "I don't know. No, I *do* know. I will figure this out. I won't leave you there, I swear it."

Rhuun heard them, too. They both looked at the door, and then back at the page. "So. What now, Ilaan? Fight?"

Ilaan nodded at the paper. "Fly. I won't leave you there. I'll bring you home." Although he had no idea how to do it or when it might be safe, at that moment he would have staked his life. *That's exactly what I've done,* he thought. *Not only my life but both of ours.*

"Take care of my mother," said Rhuun. "Take care of Aelle. Lock the door. And let's get started."

And he had started, reading the charm slowly but clearly, properly hitting all the difficult letter combinations. Nothing happened. Ilaan thought *It's not working, I'm going to lose him, it was all for nothing*, and then he saw that the page was on fire, burning away from the top. The smoke smelled like meat, too much smoke for such a small piece of paper. It caught him in the eyes and he blinked once, twice, and Rhuun was gone.

Ilaan realized he'd been holding his breath, and now gave a great gasp and took a hold of the edge of the big wooden dresser to steady himself. The room looked too bright and for a moment he thought he might faint. Then he straightened up and went to the door to listen.

"I don't know where you get your ideas," that was Hellne's voice, no mistaking the cool, amused tone. "But I can assure you my son is… I can't even bring myself to repeat these ridiculous accusations." She gave a little laugh. "Yuenne, surely you don't give any credence to this nonsense? You've known Rhuun since he was a child."

"Yes, a very peculiar child, Your Grace." His father sounded just as cool and twice as bored. Ilaan knew what that meant. It was all true, and Yuenne was about to use it to his own advantage. "I recall a close relationship between you and one of the humans, before disaster struck. What was his name again?"

"I will not be accused in my own home, and I will not listen to gossip that was trash twenty years ago. I suggest you all go back to your homes, or back to the Counselor's lovely party. I believe there was still some water left. Be sure to get one of those lovely crystal cups." Hellne still sounded cool, Ilaan thought, but he could feel fear in her voice. He had to leave. They'd get this door open soon enough, and if they found him here they might be able to make him tell them where Rhuun had gone—who knew what the Mages were capable of? As long as it remained a mystery, Rhuun was safely in the Veil, or through the Door and among the humans. Maybe not safe, but not here. Ilaan looked again around the little room, really more suited to a child than a prince, and shimmered away.

Chapter 39

The Duke extended a hand, and Gwenyth shyly reached out to take it. She'd never seen so many fine people in one room before. He led her to the groaning buffet table—the smells were so enticing but there was so much she'd never seen and she was desperately afraid of embarrassing him again. She finally picked out a sandwich of good fresh bread piled with meat and cheese. At least she knew how to eat a sandwich. He frowned, displeased.

-The Claiming of the Duke, pg 120
Malloy Dos Capeheart, Little Gorda Press (out of print)

Mistra
100 years after the War of the Door, Mistran calendar
20 years later, Eriisai calendar
The road through the Great Forest

When Rhuun realized his goal was a house in the center of Mistra City and not a farmstead in the Great Forest, he was elated. After following the horrible child's instructions on where to go, he'd been doing nothing but looking at trees, bushes, and rocks (and of course, the lovely, wonderful river) for three days. He chased the little creatures which at first he thought were mice in the trees; when they flew away, he understood they were birds. When he was a child, someone had told him stories about birds. He was certain it wasn't his mother, but couldn't quite recall who the storyteller might have been. He liked the noise the birds made, and was disappointed they wouldn't let him get close.

The first evening, he'd found a quiet spot with a nice view of the water, and carefully set out some of the food he'd taken from the couple on the riverbank. The first was an item wrapped in wax paper. It was, he was delighted to recognize, a sandwich. He spent some time pulling it apart and examining the layers—the cheese was rather like back home, and the bread could be nothing else, but the meat parts—they were struck through with white bits and were several shades of pink and red. Finally, he reassembled the thing and took a bite.

Instantly, he spat the mouthful onto the grass. It was overwhelming—oily, sweet, salty—the bread was dry and the cheese was damp. People ate this? He tried again, a much smaller bite. This time, knowing what to expect, he had more success. And by now he was hungry enough to eat the parts he liked—the cheese and bread—along with the meat. Next out of the bag was an apple. The Duke fed Mammoth apples all the time, so he figured they were also good for humans. He gingerly bit into it and was rewarded with sweet, and again, sort of wet. The bag held another few wrapped morsels and another three apples, so he imagined he'd live long enough to get to the city. After that, well, he'd figure it out.

Feeling much restored, he waited for second moonrise. When the smaller Fire moon rose in pursuit of the larger Pearl moon, as instructed, he pulled the white candle out of the bag, and sat and looked at it.

Not as smart as you think you are, little sister, he laughed, and tossed it back in the bag.

He had no way to light it.

***

Several hours later, he awoke in the dark with a strange, sharp pain in his stomach. It felt like something was trying to escape through his midsection. Then the awful sensation moved up towards his throat.

Two unpleasant hours later, he made his way to the river, which flowed into a small and quiet cove no bigger than his childhood bedroom. He eased himself into the water and slowly leaned back. This time he had better luck floating. He felt empty, but in a strangely satisfying way, and looked up at the cold and distant stars.

"I'm here, Ilaan. I really made it. I wish you could hear me. I wish you could see this. I am looking at the sky, and it's our sky, the same sky, and it’s clean. Everything here is green. It's beautiful. It's real."

The water around him gently bubbled and steamed.

***

On the evening of the fourth day, he'd just about run out of new ways to look at plants and was eager to look at some human persons. He knew he'd go unseen, or at least unnoticed, and if he got lost, it was just a street in a city. There would be nothing attacking him from above, or throwing sand in his face, or sweeping him away. He'd simply walk until he wasn't lost anymore.

He did get lost. There were humans everywhere, wearing every color that existed (and some, he suspected, they had invented).

There were also horses and dogs—and they could certainly sense his presence. Where he walked too close, the animals got extremely nervous. He tried to avoid them, but the horse drawn carts and carriages were on every street. When he finally worked out how close he could get without disturbing them, he'd lost the way to go entirely.

He found himself surrounded by buildings that reminded him of the older parts of Eriis City—crumbling brick structures that leaned against each other (he had to stop and rap the bricks to see if they were as soft as they looked—he was sorry to find they were not). Some had ramps and walkways connecting upper floors. It was from one such ramp that a pair of small animals—one white and black, and the other striped in brown and grey—glared down at him. He stared back, thinking about the Duke's dogs. They were described as huge and hairy; Gwenyth was frightened of them until she fed them her own dinner and made friends with them. Perhaps these were tiny, crafty dogs. They looked very annoyed, as if he had somehow insulted them with his presence. Finally, with much stretching and yawning, they glided away, exhibiting so much hauteur he was reminded of his mother.

As he walked, he noticed that the houses became newer looking, and straighter on their beams. They had a bit of light between them, then there were small swaths of grass, then great green lawns fenced with twisted iron. The iron heads were bent into the shapes of animals, plants, and things he couldn't name at all. As the buildings got grander, the sounds got quieter. Back home, there was the constant whine of the wind, the hiss of little fires, the soft voices of the court, and the shushing of hundreds of feet moving over sand and stone. Here, there was a positive assault of sound, from animals of every description to the vehicles they dragged, to the shouting voices of the humans, all trying to be heard above the general din. The sounds were harder to take than the profusion of color.

He did decide the smells were mostly nicer here, although dust and ash wasn't much by way of competition. Even the smell of many humans in close quarters, while sharp, was interesting. He spotted people in a street side stall cooking some sort of meat threaded onto sticks over a charcoal grate. Passers-by would stop, point, pay and stroll off with their meal. The aroma was astonishing, and despite his reaction to the meat he'd eaten earlier, he thought it might be worth another try based on the smell alone. Maybe there were different kinds of meat? He lingered in the shadows behind them until their wares had all been sold. Even the trace of grease on the cooling metal had an interesting note to it.

It was the flowers that finally showed him the way. He spent a long time looking at a trailing evening glory climbing a gas-lit lamppost. The flowers, he noted, were the same blue as the deepest part of the river. He felt clever noticing that. And the soft golden gas flame reminded him of something—he couldn't put his finger on it. The flowers were everywhere. Every house, every gate had piles of the things that looked pretty and smelled better. *This must be what a sweet smell is.* He couldn't wait to tell his friends. Flowers that have a smell, they'd never believe it. He thought of the black and white flowers at Ilaan's party. Pretty and delicate, but not like these. He'd had flowers made for Aelle, once. That was a long time ago.

He watched as the oblivious humans rushed past. *Is it possible that I am like them?* He thought about stepping away from the shadows and just joining the throng. He could do it, just step out of the shadows and try his hand at being human. He couldn't possibly make as much of a hash of it as he'd made of being a demon. Maybe they cared less about being ugly and crippled here, it was possible. He could have a nice new life. Until someone looked him in the eye. He sighed and leaned back into the shadows. His peasant's clothing, he decided, that was to blame. It would make him stand out. He had to find something nicer. *Thief*, he thought, *you can add that to your resume*.

For a while he hung back in a doorway and watched them, so many shapes and sizes. You couldn't say they didn't deserve such a world, could you? Moving along, he stopped to look at a large cluster of white rosalies hanging over a gate. They had tiny red throats. He looked up at the house, which had every door and window flung open and streaming with light. This was his destination.

He kept to the shadows to remain unseen, and he kept his hat low so no one would see his face. He was growing decidedly un-fond of the hat. He had enough faith in his ability to be unnoticed that the hat wasn't strictly necessary, but the 'what ifs' gnawed at him. What if someone should look and see, and what if they saw his eyes? He had concocted a story about a childhood injury, but he fervently hoped he'd never have to use it. So for now, the hat stayed on. The main problem it created was that it made it more difficult to see the human faces—it was enough of a challenge for him to tell them apart as it was. Mostly they looked like smears of color. They were so bright! He practiced focusing on seeing the details—an eye (every color, it seemed, but red), a mouth, and hair (once he got over the shock of women with loose hair, he found he was quite attracted to it. He followed a woman with particularly nice hair for two blocks until they'd turned a corner and he realized he'd been following a man).

He followed the crowd, melting in and out of the shadows along the walls and in the doorways. He was pleased to see that the party was underway. The Duke acted like he hated the parties and balls he had to dress for every few chapters, but Rhuun suspected he secretly enjoyed the attention. He on the other hand, did not. Unlike the chore of the endless rounds of parties back home, at this event he'd merely be an observer, which suited him perfectly. He slid through the door, one foot always in enough of a shadow that the human people, if they noticed him at all, would say, 'I think someone just went that way, I didn't see him though.'

In any case it turned out to be more than enough as the mostly young, very loud humans were well occupied with each other.

If he thought he'd seen a riot of color on the street, he realized he'd only scratched the surface of how they liked to decorate themselves. The boys were as brightly colored as the girls. And he was very surprised to see them striking little flames everywhere. They'd hold their hands together—scratch, flare! He resolved to figure out how they all did so easily what he couldn't do at all.

There were some humans dressed all in black and holding things that made noise in the corner, and a crowd of humans leapt about in front of them. He listened for a while and decided he liked the sounds. It was a bit like the birds but more orderly.

He drifted through the rooms, making sure to sample as many of the little bites of food as he could take. They all tasted as good as they smelled, except for a sweet with a coating of something crunchy and tan that made the inside of his mouth feel furry and his lips itch. Other than that, he found them far more interesting and more deeply flavorful than the stolen food he'd been living on. Something called 'baby lamb chops', no longer than his finger, were the best thing he'd ever eaten. He wondered what the humans meant by 'baby', though. He had reconsidered meat, and found it went very well with the glass of wine he took from a passing tray. The server took no notice, of course, and he was extremely anxious to try it. It was almost clear, a little yellowish tint to it, and it was nothing at all like *sarave.* The only thing they had in common was the warmth he felt in his chest and stomach, and the slight detachment he'd been missing.

As he went, he listened to bits and snatches of conversation.

"Well, she's a silly fool to think you'd ever—"

"D'you like this band? I think they're a bit… over, don't you?"

"Be a love and get me another drink!"

But when he heard, "Did you see someone with a hat just now? Who wears a hat anymore?" he realized he had been distracted and set off in search of the rest of the wine so he could complete his task.

When he took a look at the bar, he realized it was a little more complicated than he had hoped or the girl had anticipated. Did she think all these people were drinking from one bottle?

He realized, *That child, the girl—she's probably never been to a party like this. She didn't know.*

And so he didn't know which bottle or glass or cup he was supposed to poison. On the other hand, since she'd been so vague in her instructions, if he complied at all, his task was done. The law she had bound him with, like all laws of a supernatural variety, was very specific. He'd heard Ilaan often enough reading stories of how some Mage or other had tricked a *daaeva* by the use of a magical loophole.

Well, there was the bar. Where was the girl? He looked over the crowd of mostly dark heads, with a few golden haired people and even a tall young man with red hair, which made him feel nostalgic for the library and Ilaan. Then he noticed a streak of pink moving as quickly and unsteadily as a firewhirl in his direction.

The young woman with bright pink hair—who could only be the dreaded, evil Lelet—brushed past him and pointed to a sparkling red. This was a stroke of luck! He hadn't minded the idea of tracking her down, but here she was, come right to him. The horrible child had noted his target would likely be found near the bar. She also seemed to be the only one in the house sporting quite that shade.

He watched with interest as she tried to order a drink. He wasn't sure she needed one—she seemed a bit drunk already—and looked quite put out when the server said he'd have to take a moment to open it as he didn't want to damage the ancient cork.

"Fine! Always something. But be quick!" She tried to snap her fingers but her lacy gloves got in the way, which she seemed to find extremely funny. She waved towards a huge door which led to a garden lit with many dozens of candles in little jars. The shadows jumped and shivered—he could use that. "Bring it there. It's my fav—" she hiccupped, "just bring it." She pulled herself up and added, "Thank you, sir," and stumbling only a tiny bit, went back to her friends.

Rhuun handed the serving man a wine glass. "Use this one."

The man shrugged without looking up as he teased the old cork from the bottle. "Good as any. Silly bitch. This is an excellent wine and she won't even know."

Rhuun held up another glass and said, "Would you mind?" The man poured a splash and set the bottle on ice, nodded distractedly at the demon and went back to the kitchen.

Rhuun (*Moth, I have to start thinking of myself as Moth*) had to agree that the sparkling red was excellent. He thought about all the *sarave* he'd drunk (which, he realized uncomfortably, was quite a lot) and pronounced fine, and felt a little foolish. Transforming sand into *sarave* was something the Mages had set to with a vengeance, but hadn't quite mastered. This was the best he'd ever tasted. Too bad that after this evening, monstrous, depraved Lelet would probably never want to drink it again. He suspected her friends would agree, once they all recovered. He tipped the rest of the powder into the bottle, loosely corked it, and tucked it under his arm.

He lingered at the shadowy edge of the garden and watched the loud girl, who was now definitely drunk, struggle with lighting a cigarette while still holding her empty wine glass. Her cheeks were quite pink, a prettier and more natural shade by far than her hair. The fire in her hand came from a tiny stick of wood, another Mistran miracle.

I shouldn't be doing this, he thought. *But here I am. So—the Duke is at a party. There is a pretty human person. What would he do?*

He set the bottle on a table barely big enough to hold it, forcing himself not to get drawn in by the exquisitely carved vines on the graceful legs, and stood in the shadows just behind the girl and her companions.

Lelet had her head quite close to that of her friend, whispering about something that appeared important. Her demeanor had changed, too. She seemed clear headed now that no one was looking at her. She laughed less and listened more closely. He had to admit she looked more pretty than evil, but he didn't feel like a competent judge of humans yet. The other woman had the same startling height as everyone else on this side of The Door, and her hair was a glossy dark red. He'd seen eyes that color, but never hair. She was also deliciously round. She looked soft, unlike his pink-haired target, who had barely any curves to speak of. In that, at least, the girl shared something with the women on Eriis.

"… just not working out, Al," she said. Al must be the round girl's name, he gathered. "But I'm not going to tell him tonight after all. We'll have to save the Dumping Gloves for another time. He'll make a scene."

"Hmm, maybe he'll need a shoulder to cry on," her friend answered with a smile.

Lelet laughed. "Are you volunteering? Be warned, he is a crier." She looked between her empty glass and handful of matches and unlit cigarette. "Now I'm going to cry!"

Moth moved to stand just behind her elbow, replaced her empty glass with the full one, and took the matches out of her hand.

He said, "Please, allow me."

She thanked him through a puff of exhaled smoke and immediately started coughing. Her friends laughed at her. With eyes back on her, her behavior changed again.

"I hate these things! Why do you let me smoke them? I quit!" She threw it, still smoldering, into the bushes. Moth circled around behind her, admiring her slight form while ignoring her chatter. She was nearly the correct size, as narrow and neat as the women back home. Tall, of course, but that went for all of them. He was sorry to see that her bright hair was carefully coiffed, and imagined himself taking the pins out. The vividness of the image, his hand touching her hair, surprised him. Her dress was black lace with several sheer panels. The gloves reached her elbow and were also made of black lace, and looked slippery. It wasn't helping her coordination.

He had noticed these humans came in all different sizes—maybe that was how they could tell each other apart? There were not only men, but he'd even spotted a woman who was as tall as he was. And no one stared at anyone else with distaste or pity, at least not that he could tell.

"You say that three times a week," said one of those tall young men. His yellow hair was cut short (most of the men had short hair) and his jacket was quite fine. The blond man was looking at Lelet like she was something good to eat. Was this the crier? "Would've lit it for you if I thought you'd really smoke it." He glared at where the demon had been standing, then frowned vaguely, shrugged and completely forgot what he'd seen.

Lelet gulped the rest of her wine and said, "Well this time I mean it, Billah. May will lop off my head if I keep it up. She thinks it's unladylike." She peered up at the blond boy through her dark lashes. "Billah, *you* don't think I'm unladylike, do you?"

"Oh no, you're sometimes something like a lady," he said.

They all laughed again, although the girl's smile was a bit forced. She shared a glance with the round girl, who shrugged and dramatically wiped away an imaginary tear. Lelet held the empty glass up over her shoulder and said to Moth, "Get me another, won't you, darling?"

She assumes a lot, he thought. *She is used to a lot. She speaks to me to hurt the boy, but she doesn't know I'm even here. Only that someone will get her what she wants.* He leaned forward. "Of course," he whispered in her ear.

The girl shivered and then put a hand to her temple. She frowned. "Who has my matches?"

Moth took the glass, threw it in the fishpond, and vanished into the dark street beyond the garden.

***

Moth found an empty rooftop and practiced the match trick (scratch, flare) until second moonrise. Then he lit the candle.

"WHERE HAVE YOU BEEN?"

"No need to shout. I had some trouble with the candle."

In the little flame, he was pleased to see that see Scilla was nearly purple in the face. She took a series of deep breaths.

"Where are you?" she asked.

"Not sure. On top of a bunch of pushed together houses. There's no one around, it's late. I just went to the nicest party. Too bad you couldn't go yourself."

He could practically hear her teeth grinding. "Did you see my sister? Did she see you?"

"I saw her. She seems like quite a popular girl. Lots of friends. I liked her. She didn't see me. No, that's not it. What happened was, she didn't notice me." He knew the child wanted a full report but there was no reason to help more than he had to. "No one did. And wine. Now, wine is a really nice thing. Do they serve wine where you are?"

She looked as if she might combust. "No. They do not. But you know what they do serve? A big glass of not having to do what your human MASTER tells you to do. Now. Did. You. Do. What. I. Said."

He sat back on his heels. "Yes. Powder in the wine. Are we done here?"

"Mirrors. Two nights from now. And don't have any more 'trouble with the candle'." She leaned forward and blew her own candle out.

He did the same. *Very nice work, provoking a fight with a little girl who quite literally owns you*. He wished Ilaan were there, he'd have loved that party. The noisemakers, he had to find out more about them.

He looked around. Another one of those tiny, angry looking dogs was watching him from the edge of the roofline. This one was black. It made a great show of licking its front paw, then turned and vanished into the darkness.

Like me. There and then not there. Well, I suppose I ought to find a quiet place to sleep. He thought about his comfortable bed back home, the food that appeared at mealtime, clean clothes, and cool water. *I wanted this, and look! Now I've got it. But this is not what I expected.*

He thought about the girl's grey eyes. He hoped her headache wasn't a bad one.

Chapter 40

"You must at least consider our proposal, my Lord."
"Must? Now a peasant from the hills is telling me what I must do! Be gone and go back to your fat cow of a wife and take this slattern with you."
The Duke strode to the window, showing them his broad back. The interview was over.
Gwenyth struggled not to cry in front of the Duke. Her father touched her shoulder and they rose from the table.

-The Claiming of the Duke, pg 19
Malloy Dos Capeheart, Little Gorda Press (out of print)

Mistra
100 years after the War of the Door, Mistran calendar
20 years later, Eriisai calendar
va'Everley family residence

The headache kept Lelet from coming down to breakfast on time. Everyone knew she relied on her coffee and chocolate to start her day, it was absolutely required. So the rest of them ate with one eye on the stairwell and with some trepidation. Except for Rane, who smiled at nothing and ate with his usual enthusiasm. May figured she'd give her sister another 20 minutes and then send up a tray.

She had just started to ring for the maid when Lelet made her entrance. Her dark green velvet dressing gown paired poorly with her bright pink hair, which at the moment stuck out like she'd lost her comb. In fact, she looked like a stale candy.

"Slip something in my wine, Rane? So obvious." She held a shaky hand to her forehead, genuinely fearing it might pop off. "I could *so* use a cigarette."

Rane barely glanced up. "Drinks and smokes. Very elegant, Madame va'Everly. You *are* still drunk, correct?"

Lelet let go of her head long enough to snap at her brother. "That is not true, and even if it were you're still a liar. Do you expect me—"

May broke in, "Yes dear. He's a liar, we all know. You're a silly whore. He's mad. You're fat."

"I am not fat."

May wasn't finished. "We've heard it all before, was my point." She looked around the table. The eldest va'Everly, Pol, was reading the newspaper. The youngest, Scilla, was sipping chocolate with one hand and writing in her little notebook with the other. Of the siblings, Scilla and May looked most similar, both like carved cameos with wide eyes and long, curling dark hair. Pol, Rane and Lelet were all fair and grey eyed, but no one dared to mention how similar Lelet and Rane looked. At the moment, Rane's hair was longer than Lelet's.

Scilla looked up. "What?" She blinked at her siblings as if she'd just woken up. "Lelly. Missed you at dinner last night. You know I leave after breakfast."

Lelet shrugged. "Sorry, Scil. Something came up. We'll have a nice dinner together next time. Or maybe I'll come visit you at school."

"Of course she will. That would be lovely of you. Lelly, maybe you can take a writing class with that teacher Scil's been talking about. You know the one," said May. It would get Lelet out of the house and give her a hobby that didn't require a team of workmen and a lot of money. "The one who wrote that book." Scilla looked dubious, but said nothing. May continued, "Lelet, get your coffee and take some powder for your head, it's at your plate."

May ran the meals—and the household—with precision and economy. Or at least she liked to think she did. Sometimes she wondered if anyone would notice if she simply drifted down to breakfast and expected the coffee to be hot and the table set. Last night, now that was a failure of economy, in that the meal had been rather more lavish than a midweek dinner might normally be. But Scilla was so excited to share her last meal at home with her family. No. Her last meal with Lelet, the unlikely and unknowing object of Scilla's worship. Lelet, who so casually dropped hints and tidbits of the life Scilla herself would never get to experience. Lelet, who barely noticed anything that didn't result in a new dress on her back or a new boy on her arm. Lelet, who never showed up for dinner. And here she was, grey faced and smelling like cigarette smoke, but still ready to jump back into the fray with her brother.

The fighting between her two siblings was no longer acceptable. It was unbecoming. In fact, she had resolved to Do Something. What, exactly, she wasn't sure. What would Mother do? May would ask herself, although she didn't like to think about the answer. What would Father do was more tempting because the answer was to leave and just not come home.

May watched the unfolding breakfast skirmish as Lelet slid into her seat at the long table. She contemplated eggs but paused with her fork in midair as if it were all too much. Rane helpfully passed her a plate of duck sausage, bursting with garlic. She gave him a withering glare and pushed them as far from her plate as she could reach. He quickly replaced the plate with a platter of creamed herring. She defiantly speared a bite of fish with her fork and made a great show of eating it. He nodded appreciatively and conceded the battlefield of the breakfast table.

With Lelet sorted out for the moment, May turned to Scilla, lost as usual in her journal.

"Scilla, are you nearly ready? I'll call Per to bring the trap around. Here, I've packed some lunch for your trip. You're to stay at these two inns, the keepers are expecting you and it's all settled, just do try and write when you get back to the Guardhouse."

Poor Scilla, May thought. She hoped her little sister was making nice new friends and learning… whatever it was they taught out there. She certainly spent enough time taking notes, she must be studying something special.

Scilla looked up with a smile as she closed her little book. "I'm ready, all packed. Thank you, May. This has been the best trip ever."

***

After they had seen Scilla off, May and Lelet set off on their morning walk around the garden. It was a lovely, warm day. There wouldn't be many more before the Sugar-Be-Gones would go to seed and they'd find frost on the last few roses.

"Your head?" inquired May, snipping a bunch of mint. She handed it over. She knew Lelet loved the bright aroma.

"Better, thank you." She held the herbs to her face, crushing the leaves and inhaling deeply and with pleasure. "But I know it was Rane—"

"Yes, let's talk about you and Rane. It's time for this to stop." May closed her gardening scissors and put them in her basket. She knew Lelet would have a laundry list of reasons why her fight with Rane was good and true, and how no one understood her torment. This was a conversation she'd been working up to for some time. She didn't like a scene. And true to form, Lelet had begun her defense.

"But I didn't do anything!" She dropped the crushed stems. The fragrance clung to her hands and rose around them both.

A lovely aroma, thought May, *for an unlovely chat. Well, no putting it off now.*

"Hmm. You will, though. Of course you'll retaliate. What happened when he snapped the heels off all your shoes?" May asked.

"I put spiders in *his* shoes," Lelet nodded.

"And what about that thing… he told Billah? About you and the groom?" May made a face.

"Hmm? What thing?" Lelet gave her sister an innocent smile.

"You know… the *thing.*" May's eyes got wide and she pinched Lelet on the arm.

"Thing… thing….Oh, you mean the thing where he said I was F-U-C-K-ing the groom?"

May flung up a hand. She hated that kind of talk.

"I know," Lelet said, "I 'm sorry. You're right, that's crass. He said we were doing *the thing.* We were disturbing the horses, we were—"

"I know you think this is funny, Lelly. But please remind me what you did in return."

"I poured his precious whiskey into his wardrobe, as you know. Rane ruined everything, *again.* What if I wanted to marry Billah?"

"Really? Marry Billah. Really."

Lelet blushed but held her ground.

"You will not be marrying that boy. He believed Rane, for one thing. That's an indication of a mind, shall we say, a bit too wide open. Beyond that, I have had to have too many conversations with the Families regarding your… special relationship with your brother."

"I didn't start it." Lelet folded her arms.

"By the Veil, Lel, are you five years old? It's tiresome to me and embarrassing to the Family. You know it's my responsibility to wed, and soon. And do you know what everyone asks? They want to know how it stands with you two. It was one thing when you were in the nursery, but now it's the next thing to brawling in the streets. I don't like having to explain another round of 'high spiritedness' to my callers." Her callers, who before they even sat down for tea or wine looked cautiously around the dining room for signs of incipient warfare. It was like living with zoo animals, with someone always ready to pounce.

Lelet curled up next to her sister on a little stone bench. May shook her head at Lelly's foolishness and stroked her vivid pink hair. *This color,* she thought, *has got to go.*

"Why do you have to marry some rich Family boy? I won't like him. I want things to stay like they are."

"Lelet, you are not a child. You know perfectly well that the eldest runs the business and the next makes a good marriage. You know it's my job, just as Scilla has a job."

"I don't. Rane doesn't. There's never anything to do. It's so boring. What if I wanted to study at the Guardhouse, or do what Pol does?"

May covered a smile with her hand. "If you can tell me what Pol does, I will talk to him about letting you help."

"He… he…he pays the bills. He does things with paper. He writes letters to Father. Shit."

"Exactly. And as far as you at the Guardhouse, I will forget you ever said it. You do have a job, my little love. Your job is to attend functions, be charming, and not embarrass the rest of us. Take classes, if you wish. Go to lectures with Althee. Read a book. Paint. If you behave like the lovely young lady you are, you might marry a First or Second yourself, so think of that. Your own home, maybe in the Upper Garden. The Families consolidate and protect. Now. Rane." For the first time, May thought she was making headway.

"He poisoned me, I know it."

May took her sister's hands. "Think, Lelly—if he's actually tried to poison you, which I frankly doubt, what will he do next? He won't back down, you know how he is. There is—and I say this with all the love I have for him in my heart—there is a piece missing from our brother. You know what I'm talking about."

"You mean like Mother." May knew she was getting her sister's attention. To mention their mother, that meant there was no more joking. That meant she was deadly serious.

"I'm afraid he'll hurt you, maybe even without meaning to."

Lelet was quiet for a while. "If we are no longer at war, he'll need a new hobby. What does Father say?"

"He's been at the farms so long, I don't think he really knows how it is with you two." The silkworm farms were the major source of the family's income and had been for many generations. May rose to her feet, brushing stray mint leaves from her long morning skirts. "Leave Rane to me and to Pol. Just promise me, Lel, I can't stand the thought of this getting any worse."

To May's relief, Lelet nodded and gripped her hands. "I will, May, for you. But what happens when he loses a scarf or breaks a lace?"

And in fact, that was exactly what happened. But instead of a missing cufflink, it was only two days before Rane discovered his mirror smashed and jagged shards strewn across the floor of his room.

Despite Lelet's nearly hysterical protestations of innocence, no one really believed her.

May was furious.

"Why do you lie? Who else would have done this?"

"I've told you a million times! I don't know! It wasn't me!" Lelet was nearly as angry at someone else daring to try and injure one of her siblings as she was at being falsely accused.

May rubbed her forehead so hard it left red marks. "Well, I've tried. I give up. Just please do two things for me."

"May, I would do anything-"

"Don't see this spread around town. And Lelet? Watch your back."

Chapter 41

"She never loved me!" cried Sir Edward, perched precariously on the windowsill, "And so she had to die! And without my only love, why should I trouble to live in this world either?"
With that, he looked once more at Gwenyth, who tried so hard to save him, and with tears in his eyes stepped out to meet his fate on the sea-torn crags below.

-The Claiming of the Duke, pg 155
Malloy Dos Capeheart, Little Gorda Press (out of print)

Mistra
100 years after the War of the Door, Mistran calendar
20 years later, Eriisai calendar
va'Everly family residence

Moth (for he now thought of himself that way) had found the perfect place for himself. It was dry, safe, hidden, and gave him access to the horrible child's family. It was Lelet's balcony. It was a small space with a roof overhead, a sturdy trellis leading to the ground (and the roof, where he contacted Scilla), and it had a row of tall potted bushes cutting it nearly in half. At first, he couldn't understand why she'd diminish her outdoor space, but he quickly discovered the plants served as a cover for evening activities she didn't want observed by the neighbors, or her family. The row of plants made a perfect privacy screen for both of them. And even in full daylight, it was all shadows.

At the moment it was full of blankets, cast off clothing he'd picked up and found wanting (usually too small), silver he'd taken from the kitchen (he enjoyed having whatever the family ate for dinner), and a scattering of items from Rane and from Lelet herself. He returned the silver every morning, and when this was finally over, he'd give the two back their pins and cuffs and shoes.

After watching them for nearly three months, he'd gotten to know the family fairly well, and with no excuse not to contact her, learned more than he cared to about Scilla. Sometimes she treated him like a barely civilized convict, like a criminal. Other times, he was her confidant.

"Wait," she'd said, as he was about to blow his candle out that evening.

"Well?" he asked.

"Umm, what did you do today?"

"What did I do?" he repeated. "What did I do? Well, I spent a while waiting for Lelet and Rane to go off to whatever they do all day, which I'm sure was more entertaining than what I did after that, which was tipping over all of your sister's pictures and whatnot in her room. As you required. It was another big day for me, and I can't wait until tomorrow when I get to—what was it?—ah! Go into Rane's room and hang his shirts so the hangers are facing the wrong way. Can't wait. But I think the real centerpiece of tomorrow is going to be over-salting the soup. I honestly, really wish you could be here to witness it for yourself."

"Well, there's no reason to be so mean about it. It can't all be throwing fireballs or whatever you did back on Eriis."

He looked at her coldly. "What I did on Eriis is not part of this conversation. Are we done?"

"I just thought you might want to talk about it! Sorr-rry! Contact me again day after tomorrow." She blew out her candle.

He thought perhaps she was lonely. He knew he was. He had no one to talk to, no one who even knew he existed except the horrible child. Well, her, and one of those angry little dogs. This one sometimes sat on the railing of the balcony and watched him. He named it Mouse and tried tempting it with food from the kitchen. It never let him get close enough to touch it, but when he awoke, or returned from an errand, the food would be gone.

The worst part of being on his own, he decided, was finding wonders in this world and having no one to share them with.

One afternoon, while still getting his bearings on the house and its scattered outbuildings, he was almost caught near the stables. He knew the family had two horses living there and very much wanted to visit them, but there were also lots of loud voiced humans in and out, day and night. At least one appeared to live there in the building with the horses. He was watching them come and go when one of the big animals must have noticed he was nearby. It tried to run in the other direction, so the men figured there was some sort of predator in the bushes. As one of them calmed the spooked beast, two others strode with staves and sticks in hand in his direction. As much as he craved contact, he didn't want to find it at the end of a shovel, so he found the shadows under the trees and under the stable's peaked roofline. They wouldn't be able to see him now even if they looked right at him, but the horse wasn't fooled. It still stamped and snorted and refused to be soothed. He slipped around the side of the building, and then through an unlocked glass door. He heard the two with the makeshift weapons go by, agreeing that the horse was startled by the wind, or a squirrel, or its own nose.

He was in a jungle.

The little room was made of glass, but so full of greenery that no one could see in. It was small, he could go from one end to the other in four steps, and it was warmed by the sun and the brick wall it was built against. He stood and breathed for a few minutes, the green smell filling his head, feeling his skin relax. The air was full of moisture and fanned by a gentle breeze. He found a metal chain with a big glass pull, and discovered he could lever the upper panes open and closed, and spent some time making it warmer and cooler.

The plants, though, were in a bad way. They appeared thirsty and neglected, the pots were dusty and the floor was littered with debris. He picked a rake out of the jumble of supplies in the corner and began to clean.

***

As evening fell, Moth watched the family wander back from their daily activities. He listened to them discuss their days. Pol had spent the day arguing with a ship's captain who swore his holds had somehow gotten both smaller and more expensive. May, as she often did, spent her day with her best friend Stelle, poring over lists of eligible First and Second sons. Rane wasn't seen to leave his rooms, but simply materialized at the front gate when dinner was called.

Lelet had spent the morning praying for a quick death, and the afternoon having only small, sensible cocktails. Clearly, she had a plan for later that night that required a clear head.

Moth slipped from shadow to shadow and watched all of them with great interest. He had grown particularly fond of May, who had the nicest voice. He was more cautious around Rane, who out of all of them seemed most likely to see him standing nearby. The horrible child had told him to focus his attention on her pink haired sister, and he had done so. He didn't enjoy that his actions were making Lelet nervous and testy, drinking more, smoking more, and sleeping less, but he had no choice. He hoped before he went home he might apologize to her, or simply explain.

Scilla had called Lelet a vain, shallow, profligate (he liked that word), and this evening he was to steal something she loved. He knew her possessions fairly well by now and he had his eye on her hairbrush.

It was silver and had the form of the body of a human woman. He felt like she'd miss it and he'd be a step closer to his freedom.

By the end of dinner, everyone was in a tense mood. He had whispered to the cook that the soup needed a great deal more salt; surely you have more than that? And recommended to the maid that she might try setting the knives where the forks normally went. Spoons? No one uses spoons anymore.

He knew the household staff almost as well as the family, and he knew where all the shadows in the kitchen fell.

"Oh, and Rane?" said Lelet. "I can't believe I even have to say this, seeing as how neither of us are seven, but please do stay out of my room."

Rane barely looked up from his soup, which for once had enough salt in it. "Why would I go in there? It smells like the Gorda at low tide."

She was instantly furious. "You knocked all my pictures over! Every one of them is on its back!"

He opened his mouth—it was almost too easy—but stopped when he saw twin murder in the eyes of his older siblings.

"Just one. One peaceful dinner after a day of actually working," said Pol.

Lelet saw her opportunity and threw down her napkin. "You always take his side—both of you! I'm going up." She stomped up the stairs for all she was worth. Moth lingered at the doorway, watching the rest of them. He wanted to follow her, but thought he'd wait until they wrapped things up down here.

"Was that taking a side?" asked Pol. "May, would you please talk to her?"

"Yes May," echoed Rane. "Please talk to her."

"Rane," said Pol, "Not helping. But I am glad we have a moment to talk."

Rane was on his feet in an instant. "Dinner was lovely! I am expected—"

"Sit."

Rane sat.

Pol cleared his throat. Took a sip of coffee. Stirred in a bit more sugar. Took another sip. Templed his fingers. Sighed. Finally he said, "This is going to sound a bit unorthodox, but I think you'll agree that you feel yourself to be above convention."

"I am the man this family made me," Rane smirked.

"Yes. Well. I have wonderful news," Pol said.

"Yes," agreed May, "you are going to love this."

Rane's smirk faltered. "Are you increasing my allowance and sending Lelet to live in the stables?"

"Ha. No." Pol glanced at May, who nodded encouragingly. "We have talked with Father and his duties increase daily. You know how you're always looking for new things to do? Going to work with Father at the farms—won't that be exciting? A turn in the fresh air?"

"Work? Me, work? On a farm?" He had turned a bit pale.

"Well," said Pol, "of course the choice is yours. As a Third, no one *expects* you to join Father out on the farms. So as long as a certain equilibrium is maintained here at home, things can remain as tradition demands. If, however, you two cannot behave like the proper children of the Fifty Families instead of dogs in the street, we both think—we *all* think—working with Father will be the best course of action."

Rane was white with rage. "And what does *she* have to do? What is her unorthodox remedy?"

May said, "I have already spoken with her and she is more than willing to behave herself."

Rane looked from Pol to May with sheer disbelief. "And you believe her?"

May said, "After the poisoned wine incident, she's ready to wave a white flag. Really, Rane, you could have killed her."

Rane looked wounded. "I had nothing to do with that. And I don't think anyone ever died from a hangover. But if my choices are working on the farm or accepting victory, I'll be delighted to leave her alone. She said it herself. We aren't seven years old anymore. Now if you'll excuse me…."

After he'd left, Pol and May sat with their coffee.

"Do you believe him?" asked Pol.

"Do you believe her?" replied May.

"Can we send them both to the farms?"

May sighed and sat back in her chair. "What a beautiful dream."

Moth left them at the table and followed Rane down the street until he hailed a cab. The horse sensed him and snorted and shook its head until he backed away, so he turned and headed for Lelet's little terrace. He would spend the night watching the stars through the trees. Watching the slow rotation of the sky had turned into his favorite thing (except water—that was still the best). This world was almost unbearably busy during the day, but night was better. He could focus on one thing at a time.

Tonight Lelet had lit a few candles and taken care to pick up her clothing. The room looked almost neat. That was new. He found himself nearly stepped on as a young man climbed over the low rail and knocked on the glass door.

He recognized the boy as his rival in match lighting from the party. He was pleased with himself—he could tell them apart after all.

"Billah! Shhhh, you shouldn't be here!" She grabbed him by the elbow and hauled him through the door. He followed her happily enough, looking perhaps a bit confused.

"But you invited me! Here, I brought you this." He thrust a bottle of wine into her hands. She handed it right back to him, laughing and shushing as she rummaged for some glasses.

As they drank and teased, Moth made himself comfortable outside on the balcony. This was much closer than he'd gotten to the couple on the riverbank. With the doors shut he couldn't hear them, but he didn't care, he had yet to hear a human person say anything interesting. The boy—Billah—blew out all but one of the candles. Now, that was annoying. Still, in the wavering candle light he got a fairly good look as they threw their clothes on the floor. He squinted through the glass at their bodies. He'd been correct. No ink. Not a single piercing. He thought of Aelle's jet beads piercing her skin, his own golden ornamentations. What was wrong with these people? Billah, having fortified himself with half the bottle of wine, eventually followed the girl from the floor to the bed, climbed on top of her, and they rubbed against each other for a few minutes. He seemed to be doing most of the work. Moth waited for cries, marks, smoke—any sign that they'd even accomplished anything. After a while, the boy threw his head back. Then he slumped down on top of her and—could it be? The boy was asleep.

For the thousandth time, Moth considered his book. This nonsense with the horrible child had prevented, or at least postponed, his search for dos Capeheart. But he absolutely *had* to find a new copy in a human library—one that had an intact final chapter. If he thought all human joining ended in snores and dissatisfaction—and even he at this distance could tell the girl had not found her pleasure—what then? He thought about Gwenyth and the Duke—all those charged glances, the sparks (not the actual burning kind, the sweetly thrilling kind) that jumped from one hand to another when they were close, all those fast heartbeats and various overheated body parts. The thought that joining among the humans was even less satisfying than back on Eriis was inconceivable. In his heart, he knew that finding out how it was with the humans in bed was what started him on this journey. If it turned out to be a scant few moments of rubs followed by snores… no. There had to be more to it. While his people felt less, these humans did less. So far it had been the one thing—really, the only thing—he'd found horribly disappointing.

Research beyond reading and spying had not occurred to him.

***

The moons rose, the small Demon moon chasing the bigger orb of the Order (as the humans called them, he came to learn), and the girl woke her sleeping friend. She appeared to be apologizing for something, her hands held up in a way he knew meant 'sorry.' The young man wasn't pleased, and Moth could hear snatches of their conversation as their voices rose.

"…when were you going to tell me? …using me for all these months?"

"…had to be sure… just not working… please don't…" and finally, "you should go."

The young man didn't look like he was ready to leave and shook his finger quite close to Lelet's nose. "…no one else…."

Moth opened the big glass door by just a fraction, in case things escalated. The young man was of a decent size and appeared fit, but Moth was bigger and if it came to it, he was stronger as well.

But the young blond man quickly dressed, his handsome coat unbuttoned, his elegant tie hanging loose, and brushed past Moth without seeing him. He smelled like old wine and sweat. Billah paused on the balcony, one hand on the trellis. "You're making a mistake. You'll see." He swung over the low rail and out of sight.

Lelet shrugged on a cream silk robe decorated with a beautiful pattern of pink and red roses, her hem barely missing the candles she'd set on the floor. She watched Billah creep across the lawn and out to the street. As Moth watched her, the robe fell open. Her breasts were small but to him they appeared perfect. It almost looked like the roses were blooming on her pale skin. It was the longest he'd seen her awake without hearing her speak. She lit a cigarette and stood in the open doorway. He could see her eyes reflecting the tiny spark. She stood there for a long time before closing the door and going back to her bed.

Once he could see the gentle rise and fall of the bed covers, Moth slipped through Lelet's room and lifted her hairbrush from her vanity. He coiled himself back in his corner of the terrace. He felt it unseemly to watch her sleep—it seemed somehow more intimate than watching her with her young man—but he was comforted by her presence nearby.

He watched the sky and presently he also slept.

He hoped she wouldn't be too sad about the hairbrush.

***

"It's Rane's turn," said Scilla. She had a new notebook out and was consulting what she'd written. "We need the blame to fall on Lelet next."

Moth was so bored with the whole thing he didn't even respond. Here he was, in the human place, surrounded by the magical, mysterious creatures he'd spent much of his life wondering about, and he was trapped in one house at the whim of one child.

"Can I take a day off and visit the art museum? It's near the student's district and the university and I want to go there as well," he finally asked. "I have to get out of this house."

She smiled thinly. "You should have thought of that before I caught you. Maybe packed a book."

"The study in this house is nothing but ledgers and the biology of the silkworm. Not a single thing to read. How is that even possible? How about you let me go to Mistra's big library for a day or two, and then I'll get back to breaking dishes and whatever else you have written there."

"I'll think about it. For tomorrow, though, I want to you go through Rane's things and find me something interesting." Scilla had gotten less and less specific in her assignments, having also almost run out of ways for Moth to make trouble.

"How should I know what you think is interesting? No, never mind. I'll show you something tomorrow. I'm sincerely hoping you'll let me out of here when I do."

He blew out his candle and climbed the trellis down to his little balcony, his temporary home. Out of all the things he expected—anticipated—from his perilous trip through the Veil and The Door, all the amazing things he'd learn, he never in his wildest imagining expected boredom to be one of them. He'd mentioned to Scilla that he'd followed Rane to one of his evening haunts, and she'd promptly put the brakes on it, she wanted Moth in the house, where he could do the most damage. Stick with the property, she'd said.

He knew every member of the family almost better than his own. Pol ran the business, but secretly dreamed of a life on the stage, collecting scripts and underlining the roles he longed to play, although the moons would fall into the sand before he'd abandon his responsibilities. Even now he was in the planning stages of leaving for the silk farms where he could keep his responsibilities and follow his dreams. The rest of them didn't even know that, yet. He'd contacted a repertory company in the small farming community and had high hopes for the next season. He favored serious, dramatic male leads, but Moth felt he'd be better served in character roles. May (still his favorite) was dragging her heels on her inevitable marriage. She was finding this and that wrong with each young man who came to call: Rynne was too abrasive, Hollis had short teeth, and so on. She preferred to spend her days with her best friend Stelle. He liked Stelle—she had nice hair, long and black, it reminded him of Aelle. Although, unlike Aelle this Stelle spoke in such a soft voice he could barely ever understand what she was saying. He could understand the way she looked at May well enough, though, although as far he knew it had gone no further than a little hand holding and heated glances. Would May respond in kind? He rather hoped so, he liked a happy ending, even if there was none in sight for him.

Rane made him slightly uncomfortable. He did a lot of nothing, seemingly living by day inside his own head and spending his nights doing Moth didn't know what. He went through a lot of wine, though. He retired late and rose later. Once or twice Moth thought he spent a beat too long looking in his direction. And Lelet? She seemed as bored as he felt, picking up new hobbies like painting or fencing or raising her flowers and putting them down again, anything that required a large outlay of cash and a lot of equipment. Once they were no longer new and interesting, they were pushed to the side. (After discovering the greenhouse, he continued to care for her orchids, he hated to see such pretty things ignored to death. They reminded him of home, being carefully bred, exquisitely artificial, and without scent.) And despite what Scilla claimed, Lelet didn't have that many gentlemen in and out of her room at night. It was just Billah, although since she'd thrown the boy over he'd seen the groom climbing down the trellis once or twice. She smoked a lot, drank too much, and went to parties, and to his mind she seemed the unhappiest of the va'Everlys. She was currently wild about riding, spending most days out with her horse, and the rest of the time modeling her new riding clothing for the other siblings, who were enthusiastic (May), vaguely supportive (Pol), or utterly contemptuous (obviously Rane).

Her hair was still pink, which was a source of much heated discussion when she was out of the room.

He'd done Lelet the most damage and wished he could make it up to her, but of course she couldn't see him. She'd never find out it wasn't Rane who rummaged through her clothing, it wasn't her brother who broke her candles and hid one shoe (and occasionally left an orchid on her pillow). Moth did as he was instructed, bided his time, and had faith (diminishing, but still held dear) that Scilla would do as the law required and release him when she was done playing with him.

He also listened for Ilaan calling him home, a call that so far hadn't come. He didn't know at this point which he would prefer—the freedom to wander Mistra alone, or a trip back home to an uncertain fate.

He was stuck.

It was late afternoon and he wandered through Rane's suite of rooms, looking for something that would satisfy the horrible child's demands, sliding from the shadowed back of a door to the fold of a curtain. At first he'd been careful to never go into one of the family's rooms when they were there, but as the days and weeks went by, he gained confidence in his invisibility. And an occupied room at least had the potential of something interesting happening. And it was easy enough to keep track of them—since being bound to Scilla and tied to her house, he'd noticed he could see them all as tiny sparks in his head, and could even close his eyes and follow their progress from room to room and on their various errands through the city. He couldn't see Scilla, though. Maybe she was too far away? *One day*, he thought, *Ilaan is going to spell this whole thing out for me, and I'll probably realize there was an easy way out, and I'll be angry.*

At the moment, Rane was nodding off in his favorite chair—dark blood-colored leather edged with tiny brass studs, and a matching footrest (one of the seams had sprung from years of lazy feet). He had a magazine open on his lap which was making its slow, but sure, way towards the floor. Moth paid him no more mind than another piece of furniture.

He looked at Rane's bureau. The mirror that had hung over it was missing, and he could see its dark outline in the pattern of the wallpaper. The frame rested against the wall, shoved partway behind the large dresser. He noticed a brass letter opener in the shape of a long fish sitting on top, and stepping into a shaft of sunlight, reaching for it.

"I'm actually rather fond of that thing, it was a gift from my grandmother."

Moth froze. This wasn't possible.

"I mean," continued Rane, "it is attractive, and I know you have a thing for jewelry and silverware. Shiny, nice things. I am guessing you were poor before you died and now in the afterlife you go around collecting them. Can you speak?"

Moth turned. "You can see me?" *That was a stupid question.* He ran his hands through his hair. *Now what?*

"Yes, of course," Rane agreed. "I've been watching you on and off for a few weeks. I wasn't sure at first. I have a long history of seeing things that aren't there. Ask my father, he'll tell you. The family thought I was following our proud family tradition of being completely birds and bats when I was younger. Saw faces in the trees and the dogs used to talk to me. Dogs make excellent conversation, by the way. Always trust a dog. I may be birds and bats, for all I know. But even if I am, I also know no one else can see you. At first I thought you were a sympathy hire for the kitchen, maybe you were simple or something—you never said anything and everyone ignored you. Then I saw you disappear a couple of times and I figured it out."

Moth thought Rane looked very calm for someone communing with the spirits. Visitations by ghosts, or *daeeva* as they were called on Eriis, were considered very bad luck and always came with some message of disaster. He'd never seen one, and didn't really believe they existed. Demons were difficult to kill, and lived generally long lives, but dead was dead. The recipient of such a visitor was always someone rather prone to drama anyway.

He asked, "Well, how would you know? If you were, um, birds and bats, I mean. I may not really be here."

"Oh, I'm pretty sure you're really there. If I'd invented you in my head, I would have made you a naked woman. And if it was just my things going missing, I'd have kept you to myself—that's the best way to make people think you're not starkers, just keep your mouth shut—but it's not just my things, is it? I think you're the ghost of someone, maybe who died in this very house, and for some reason you're attached to my sister." He laughed. "Poor bastard, you must be paying off a shit ton of spiritual penance."

Moth decided this was perhaps not the time or place to defend Lelet. He said, "Well let's assume you are correct and I am a ghost, and not the symptom of a brain tumor. Will you try and get the house… ah… unhaunted?"

Rane shrugged and toyed absently with a thick bandage wrapped around his left hand. "Don't know. Will you keep stealing my things?"

Moth picked the letter opener off the desk. "What if I just borrow them? I'll return this tomorrow. And then you won't have to explain to your family that you're seeing things. Again."

"That would be an awkward conversation. They're just looking for a reason to ship me out of here, anyway. And I want *all* my things back. You can keep Lel's crap." Moth nodded. Rane looked interested for the first time since they'd started talking. "What's it like? Where you are?"

Boring. "You'll understand that, sadly, I am not at liberty to talk about the conditions of this particular haunting or why I'm here or where exactly I came from. Rules, you understand."

Rane reached under his chair and pulled out a bottle. "Are you corporeal enough to have a drink?"

"O Light and Wind, yes."

Rane handed him a glass of something amber colored and foul tasting. It was fantastic.

***

"Now, Scilla," Rane was saying about halfway through the bottle, "if there were any justice in this world, she'd be running the family farm and Pol could take a day off. She's the smart one, even if her head's in the clouds half the time. But sweet as pie—you know, I don't think I've ever heard Scilla raise her voice. It would do her good to be less timid, maybe they would have thought twice about locking her away in that stupid school. Can you believe it? Forever! Like she's a criminal!" He tended to gesture with his glass to the point that he was wearing a good deal of his drink. His handsome light blue shirt was speckled with dark blue flecks.

Moth wondered if Rane would be proud of his little sister's emotional development. He also wondered briefly what pie was. He asked, "What kind of a place is it, anyway?" There was an old expression on Eriis about knowing the mind of your master. "Why do they have her locked away?"

"It's supposed to be a great honor—oh, thank you, I will take a splash more… more… more… that's fine—for the family. Fifth child goes to the Order. Stupid thing to do with some crazy old story about demons."

Moth froze, the glass halfway to his lips. "But you don't believe in that."

"No one does, I mean really! Demons!" Rane shook his head and continued with some real anger. "That's like the whole point of the school, they train the Fifths to keep some imaginary Door portal thing shut so the demons can't get in to invade the fair and innocent city of Mistra. Which, if you ask me, could use a good invasion. So the Families endow the Guardhouse, and it's just a big scam. So yeah, that's where she lives. And from what she says, she loves it there! Spending her life keeping us safe from imaginary demons. If that isn't the stupidest thing you ever heard in your life. Er, afterlife. Apologies."

"So no demons, but you believe in ghosts?" *Tread lightly*, he thought.

"Well, obviously I've never drunk a bottle of very nice…" Rane peered at the bottle "… '87 Reserve with a demon, now have I? I guess if I wake up in the morning and there's only one glass the jokes on me and my brain tumor. Why? Do you have some sort of post-viability inside information?"

"No," said Moth, "I think I know less than you. I was… away for a long time before I came here." He wished he could say more, although he could tell Rane was not one to trust with a secret. He'd been on this side long enough to know perfectly well that dogs couldn't talk. "Tell me why you fight with your other sister. She seems nice enough to me." At Rane's look he added, "It's possible I'm wrong, of course. I could be a poor judge of character, being a ghost. Which I am."

Rane laughed again and poured them both another healthy shot. "I could tell you stories that would make your hair fall out about that girl. Do you know, she put spiders in my shoes! Real spiders! But honestly, it's just something we do. I can't remember a time when we didn't have some sort of grudge death-match going on." He looked slightly confused. "But it wasn't her that's been getting into my things recently, is it? So we really haven't been fighting for a while." He looked at Moth suspiciously. "It's you that's doing it." Rane stared down at his bandaged hand and back at Moth, who began to look around the room for a good, deep shadow.

Rane lost color and set his drink down with a bang. "I may have done something bad," he said. "I may have made a mistake." He stood and began to pace. "I wasn't sure it was you, after all. It might still have been her. Birds and bats. I had my suspicions, but the mirror pieces in my bed, well, look!" He shoved his bandaged hand under Moth's nose. "I was angry. There was blood—my blood. What was I supposed to do? Nothing?"

"It was me," said Moth, keeping an eye on a dark place behind the door, "and I am sorry about that, but I had my reasons. What did you do?"

"It isn't my fault!" Rane's voice rose alarmingly. "I didn't know it wasn't her, and even if I did, she had it coming." He looked out the window, at the floor, anywhere but at Moth. "Whatever happens, it's her fault."

Moth took Rane by the arm. He knew these humans liked to touch each other and found comfort in it. "Tell me what happened." He pitched his voice quiet and low, the voice he used with Aelle when she was trying to have a fight. "Just tell me and we can figure it out and fix it. Its fine, you'll see. Here, sit down. Here's your drink." Rane took another swallow of the liquor and a deep breath. When he looked up, Moth thought his eyes looked like that of a bird in the trees – shiny and blank.

"I paid a boy to cut the girth on her tack."

Moth knew what 'cut' was but the rest meant nothing to him. "I don't… why is that bad?"

"You don't know what I'm talking about, do you? City ghost." He gave Moth a scorching look of disgust and spoke slowly. "The saddle. On the horse. It holds the whole thing together. And I had it cut almost through. So your little friend is probably lying in a ditch somewhere, and now that I think about it, it's really all your fault. You did it."

Moth still wasn't completely clear about what Rane had done, but he understood 'lying in a ditch'. "I'm going to find her. You're right, this is my fault." In a way, it was. Also, he figured it was best to just agree with everything Rane came out with. If Scilla had looked a bit off, Rane looked exactly like someone who had conversations with dogs. "Just stay here. Have another glass. I'm going to go make sure she's fine, and then we can talk some more."

"You'd do that for me?" Rane looked so nakedly hopeful it made Moth afraid he'd never get out of the room if he didn't agree.

"I owe it to you, don't I? Isn't this my fault?"

"I'm feeling a little tired. Let me know she's fine, won't you?" Rane turned his back on Moth and looked out the front window, down towards the street and the horses and flowers and humans and dogs. "Goodbye. It was nice meeting you."

Chapter 42

The Duke slapped Mammoth on his shining neck. "You and me, my lad, that's all the company I could ever want or need."
The horse rolled its great eye back at its master as if to say, "That's kind of you to say but not completely true."

-The Claiming of the Duke, pg 71
Malloy Dos Capeheart, Little Gorda Press (out of print)

Mistra
100 years after the War of the Door, Mistran calendar
20 years later, Eriisai calendar
Rosemont Park

Mistra, as it turned out, hadn't satisfied itself with its network of bridges, neighborhoods of huge houses, cramped apartment buildings, theaters, universities, museums, and libraries. It also took into account that someone, one day, might like to go riding. So a long series of interconnected parks ran practically through the center of the city, perfect for a day out with your horse.

Moth thought about Eriis—the Quarter he'd once found so enticing and dangerous, the Market where you'd meet everyone you knew. His family's quarters—which despite its grand size had only ever housed himself and his mother. His library. The school and the play yard. Burning plains outside the city wall. And all of it seen through a dim haze of ash.

He wondered if he'd ever see it again. Every now and then he would ask himself if he still wanted to go home. And he did. But sometimes he couldn't remember exactly why, other than that it was his.

Following a footpath to a pedestrian bridge to an ornamental roundabout and past a stable and restaurant (he kept well clear but even so, the horses could tell he was nearby) he found himself at the edge of a huge, velvety green, manicured lawn. *How do they get the grass so perfect?* He'd have to worry about that later. He could see buildings rising in the distance, on the other side of the parkland. He thought that was where he'd attended the party with the wine, but he couldn't be sure.

Right now he was following the tiny spark which he recognized as Lelet. He thought again how much he didn't know. Why could he see them? He'd never seen such things back home, and it wasn't likely this was some new skill he'd suddenly manifested. Was it because he was bound to the household? Like the mystery of the perfect lawn, it would have to wait.

He'd stuck his head through the kitchen door and asked a maid, elbow deep in hot soapy water, if she'd seen Lelet. 'Riding, as usual', the woman responded without looking over her shoulder. He'd waited for the pull, the mental leash that kept him from leaving the house, or speaking Scilla's name, or the hundred other rules she'd made him follow. But this time, he'd felt nothing. He could go and look for Lelet.

He'd retrieved his stupid hat from his pile of possessions on Lelet's balcony and left the house, reverting back to carefully slipping through shadows. He was surprised to find the ability felt easier and more natural than it ever had back home. *I'm good for something after all.* And then he thought, *My blood likes it here.* And then, *Don't think about that now. Everything in its order.*

He'd been strenuously avoiding that line of thought since he'd arrived in Mistra.

What if she's lying with a twisted ankle in the middle of a field? What if I have to carry her back to the house? He wanted to throttle Scilla for putting him in the middle of this family of screamers, clowns, drunks, and outright lunatics. *I fit right in. An occasionally invisible half demon who may also be either a ghost or a brain tumor.*

He followed a little stream, taking a moment to admire the rills and tiny falls it made over the rocks—water was still his favorite part, although the green smell of the park was a new and intense pleasure, huge and sweet, similar to his glass house (which was more intimate and a little bitter) and as he continued he could feel Lelet's spark growing brighter. He was close. If he kept on this particular path, at least he'd be close to the cover of the trees. He looked at the sky, noting it would be getting dark soon, and that was good news for being invisible, but bad news for finding one small woman in an unlit forest, or field, or up a tree, or wherever she was.

From behind, he heard a series of muffled thumps, a sort of loud snort, and something that might have been a grunt. He turned to find himself eye to eye with the object of so much of his fascination. The horse, however, didn't seem so happy to see him, it made the angry little dogs look like stuffed mice. Its face, startling in its size, was dark brown with a big white stripe between the eyes, and it had huge yellow teeth. He was sure it was going to bite him, and quickly took a step back. It took a step forward. He backed up again, this time tripping and landing on the grass. It stood over him, giving him a good look at its teeth, but at least it did not seem like it would take his head off.

Despite its general appearance of ferociousness, its nose looked so soft, he was touching it before he could stop himself. It blew into his hand and nodded with such enthusiasm he had to duck out of the way. Maybe it wasn't terribly angry after all?

"It's very nice to make your acquaintance," he told the horse as he stroked its nose, braving a tentative pat between the animal's enormous brown eyes. "Are you Lelet's horse? Is that why you're upset? Because you have to deal with these crazy humans also? And why are you not nervous that I'm near you? This is one of Pol's shirts. Maybe you think I'm him." (It was tight through the shoulders, but Pol enjoyed his meals, so in other respects it was roomy enough.) The horse had no answer, but moved so fast that he had to roll out of the way to avoid getting stepped on. Its feet were huge and appeared to be made of bone. He noted the part you sit on—some sort of elaborate leather contraption—was twisted underneath. It looked uncomfortable. He gathered that was the reason it was in a bad mood. "I don't suppose you'll be leading me to her? Because that would be extremely useful."

It snorted again and wandered back the way he'd come.

"Well, it was nice to meet you," he called after it.

He got to his feet and followed Lelet's spark deeper into the parkland. He thought it was possible that the horse was the most sensible creature he'd met so far. The Duke's enormous affection for his Mammoth became even more understandable.

Well, Malloy, you got that part right. And if there's a Mammoth, maybe there's also a Gwenyth. In any event, I very much look forward to our sitting down for a talk.

He continued to follow the little stream and follow the tiny light that led him towards the girl. Finally, he thought he saw something on the far side of the water, very close to the bank, breaking up the unending vivid green—although long shadows were starting to turn the meadow and the forest black. A bit of red, he thought, could that be her? He paled. *Blood? What if she was dead? Rane was right, I've as good as killed her myself.*

He put on some speed, flowing invisibly along the darkening treeline. He got closer.

He was too late.

Chapter 43

Eriis
20 years after the War of the Door, Eriisai calendar
100 years later, Mistran calendar
Dzhura Square

If it was the purpose of a party to fill the mouths of every gossip at Court and in the market square, then Yuenne's fete to celebrate his son's ascension to the Mages was the one to which all others would aspire, until the moons fell into the sand.

'The Queen shimmering in as if it were her dry room and not the home of the Counselor, that was interesting, don't you think? She takes liberties, if you ask me.'

'The Prince staggering off during an argument with poor Aelle, well, that was common enough, but still worth mentioning. And didn't that nice young Hollen pay her some proper attention? That would be a match that made sense to look at, too bad Hollen's family came from nowhere. Does he even have prospects at Court? Oh well. Yuenne would never allow it, he's already invested too much in the Prince.'

'But hadn't you heard? That was the best part. The Mages came bursting through the door—Yes, I know, but there they were.'

'Half a human? Things are starting to make sense regarding that unfortunate young man. And now he's nowhere to be found. I heard he went through the Door.'

'I heard he's fled to the Edge, and his mother close behind.'

'I heard young Ilaan had something to do with it. He may never get that Zaalmage robe, after all.'

'And poor Aelle, no Seat for her. Yuenne is beside himself.'

'Wouldn't have expected it of our Queen.'

'You didn't know her in the old days. Before the War. Everything was different, then.'

'Everything is different, now.'

***

Standing in front of her son's door, Hellne put on her best smile, the one she saved for emergencies, and thanked everyone for their concern, but insisted the Mages were mistaken, and even to consider such a thing was preposterous. But she watched as Yuenne and the Zaal whispered together and knew it was only a matter of time.

You are recorded, Princess. Payment due.

She heard nothing from behind the door. Was Rhuun safely away or simply passed out? She wanted to kill him. She wanted to hide him.

She couldn't hold them off forever; the Mages, Yuenne, and a handful of curious partygoers were pressing in. She made a note of which of them tagged along to Rhuun's door, and she wasn't going to forget their names. But finally she had to agree to let them 'just talk to him.'

The room, she was relieved to see, was empty. The Mages made a show of looking under the bed and in the dryroom, and Yuenne stood in the doorway, sadly shaking his head.

"Hellne, you should have told someone. You could have prevented this… ugliness. You should have confided in me."

She barely glanced at him and said, "Can we reconvene this little carnival tomorrow before the High Seat?" She had to find Ilaan and make sure Rhuun was through the Door, and that meant she needed all these people gone.

The Mages were loath to leave the room. The Zaal was in a blind rage, "You swore. You wrote it into law. The first and the best. Can you say you gave it to us?" He squeezed the bridge of nose. "The blood was here all along. I can still smell it." He pulled the coverlet from the bed and held it to his face. "It's in everything."

Hellne yanked it out of his hands and snapped, "We are talking about the prince, not a bucket. Take your leave. All of you. Now." The Zaal, furious to be denied his prize, led his Mages back down the stairs, where they would no doubt open a special *sarave* of their own vintage in honor of being right all along. The partygoers wandered off, looking for places to spread this new, astonishing story.

Hellne pressed the heel of her hand to her forehead. Was her debt cancelled with the death of the old Mage? Was Malloy still alive, and would Rhuun be able to find him? She needed to sit and think, she needed this night to be over. But like sand in your sheets, Yuenne was hard to get rid of. Yuenne colluding with the Mages. She should have seen it.

"This isn't like hiding a torn dress from your father, Hellne. A human man? What in the world made you think it would never come to light?" Yuenne moved closer to her and made to touch her shoulder. "Let me help you now. Just tell me where he is and we can deal with the Mages after that."

She drew back from him. "'We can? Really? And how do you intend to do that? Give Rhuun up to the Mages? All at once or in pieces?" She narrowed her eyes. "How quickly can we get our children wed, do you think? And how long will he live afterwards?" She laughed bitterly. "I always wondered why you pushed her on him, all those years ago. I knew you disapproved of him, now I see what you were up to, you and your friends in the Raasth. Well, I guess the wedding's off."

He shrugged. "Maybe not. Plans change. Perhaps we can salvage something from this after all. But you have to let me help you. Where is he?"

She smiled, "The last place you'd look."

Yuenne stopped smiling. "What do you mean?"

"You're not the only one making plans. Well. Places to go. I suggest you go home and see to your party."

Yuenne took another look around the room before leaving, "Human trash on the walls, well, aren't you the permissive parent?" He let his little smile slip. "If Ilaan is mixed up in this, they'll both find themselves in the Crosswinds with their mouths full of sand. And where will you be, Madam?"

Hellne waited until he was gone before shimmering away, leaving a bright spot in the air of the dark little room.

Chapter 44

Gwyneth gave a little scream of laughter as he kicked Mammoth into a canter, and she let go of the pommel and clutched at his legs. "I've never felt anything so powerful. It's so big!" She twisted in the saddle to look up at him, and as their eyes met he....

-The Claiming of the Duke, pg 131 (fragment)
Malloy Dos Capeheart, Little Gorda Press (out of print)

Mistra
100 years after the War of the Door, Mistran calendar
20 years later, Eriisai calendar
Rosemont Park

Since her conversation with May, Lelet had been as good as her word. Despite her hairbrush vanishing off her nightstand, and the pictures mysteriously toppling themselves over, she'd done nothing in return. More peculiarly, there would appear every so often an orchid on her bed. She hadn't thought of the pretty glass house in ages, and had forgotten all about the plants, but it looked to her like Rane—or someone in his employ—was keeping them alive.

When the second dainty blossom appeared, she became curious enough to go through the garden to the greenhouse, which was tucked against the sunny wall of the stable. To her astonishment, it looked as neat and well maintained as the day she'd abandoned it. It was a pocket of a building, only one wall and three shelves of orchids, but as she went from one to the next, she could see someone was misting them, trimming dead leaves, and even staking blooming stalks so they wouldn't droop or rot. The leaves were as shiny and leathery as the day she'd had them brought in, the pots were in good order—either glossy or painted or made of some exotic stone or wood, and of course the flowers—long sprays everywhere of purple and white and orange. It didn't look real! How had this mystery person gotten them to all bloom at once? She didn't even know that was possible, but of course she hadn't made a thorough study of orchid propagation. All she knew was the one word she'd memorized: *phalaenopsis*, also known as the Moth Orchid, the prettiest ones, and those most invulnerable to death by neglect. After all, her good intentions were just that: intentions. And sure enough, she'd forgotten to mist for several days in a row, and then forgotten she'd forgotten, and after that? She dreaded seeing a room full of dead plants, so she put the whole project aside. Clearly, someone else had taken it on, even the red clay on the floor was swept and clean, and she could see more evidence that someone had been here—large footprints, back and forth. One of the gardeners, she decided. She hoped they enjoyed it. They certainly earned it.

As for herself, she had been enjoying two things lately—going riding, and being a martyr. The latter was a new experience for her, but she threw herself into it. Her friends spent much time and a lot of wine trying to get her to confess what she had planned for Rane. All she'd do was sigh and say, "That's behind me now. I've... moved on." They'd howl with laughter and insist whatever plan she was cooking up had to be world class.

In fact, she had no plan, and was enjoying the results of doing the right thing almost as much as the thrill of doing the wrong thing. It must be driving Rane crazy, he was still accusing her of taking and breaking, when she knew for a fact that couldn't be the case—unless the house had a ghost!

So if Rane wanted to carry on stealing her toiletries and leaving her flowers, well, that was strange, but that was her brother in a nutshell.

She'd had plenty of time to think about how strange he was and how far he'd be willing to go to force her hand, having spent the last several hours in a ditch.

The afternoon had started promisingly enough, she'd even given one of the grooms little helpers an extra coin to help her get the horse ready to ride. What a sweet child! She'd been wearing her favorite red coat, trimmed in black satin, with her second favorite boots (the best ones were at the cobbler) and turning heads as she rode was often enough to seal a good mood.

Then, a tiny jump, not even a jump, really more of a lunge over a trickle of water, and the saddle had come completely apart. That little boy seemed like an old hat, but he clearly didn't know what he was doing. And here she was, her horse, Petrel, long since wandered off, and she at least not in the water and in a shady spot. She thought her wrist might be broken—she was afraid to look at it, much less move it around—and there was something unpleasant going on inside her boot at the ankle, but she wasn't about to hop up and try to limp home. She knew eventually someone would spot Pete with his gear in tangles and someone would come and find her.

She made herself as comfortable as possible and looked at the sky. She hoped they'd find her before it got dark. With much hissing and gritting of teeth, she managed to get her coat off, so someone coming by could see it, but she was afraid it would be too dark to see even the bright scarlet wool pretty soon. Also, her boot was getting extremely tight and she didn't want to think about what her father would say if they had to cut it off. At one point she thought she heard a horse but no one came along. For the first time she began to worry.

"Miss Lelet? Are you alright?" A tall figure stood in the last bit of sun, and she had to shield her eyes.

"Oh, Per—am I happy to see you! Had a tumble. I think I've done something to my ankle, and my wrists gone all funny too. Did you find Pete?"

"No," said Per, kneeling next to her and gently examining her wrist, "but we will. Not to worry. Horses know." He tried to rotate her foot and she yelped. "This boot, I'm afraid it's a goner. We'll cut it off back at home. You stay put and I'll bring the cart around, we'll have you home in a flash."

***

Moth watched from the treeline a few feet away.

I wanted to rescue her, he realized. *Too late.*

For her part, Lelet seemed more upset about her boots than anything else. Did she know what Rane had done? He imagined he'd find out soon enough. He watched the groom (not the one who he'd seen on her trellis, he decided) lift her off the damp grass and help her into the little cart and then drape her red coat around her shoulders.

Dinner should be interesting.

Chapter 45

The door opened and the Duke strode in. Gwenyth spun to face him with a sharp gasp; she thought he was out riding Mammoth.
"Why are you wearing that?" he asked. He does not sound angry, she thought. Do not provoke him.
"I'm sorry," she said, "I'll take it off and hang it away at once."
"Do no such thing, Gwenyth. You were born to wear silk."
Her heart pounded in her breast and she felt warm all over. He had never called her by her name before.

-The Claiming of the Duke, pg 142
Malloy Dos Capeheart, Little Gorda Press (out of print)

Mistra
100 years after the War of the Door, Mistran calendar
20 years later, Eriisai calendar
The Guardhouse

Three months.

Scilla had the days and weeks checked off in one of her notebooks. She kept one for important events: when she got a letter from home she put a circle around the date. When she was particularly clever in class, she marked it with a check. When she spoke to the demon, that was an X, when she got him to do something he didn't want to do, a double X. When she heard from the Voice, she planned a star, but three months had gone by, and there were no stars to be found.

Three long months, and finally, the Voice came back to her. When Scilla opened her notebook (a special one, just for this purpose) and saw:

...await word, as ever.

She had fallen back on her little bed and sobbed in relief. Not only had she dearly missed the conversation of an equal, but she was growing desperate to send the increasingly surly demon back where he came from. She didn't know why or how, but here was her Voice, returned to her. They had a lot to catch up on. She decided there was no reason to tell the Voice what she'd been doing with her pet for the last few months. And if Moth tried to accuse her, well, who were her friends on Eriis going to believe?

Where have you been? she wrote. **I've been so worried!**

We have been prevented from contacting you somehow, but you have never been far from our thoughts. Thank Light and Wind you are well—and you captured the beast? You were successful in your trip to the Veil?

I do have the creature; I've held him all along. He is safe—we both came through the Veil unharmed—and no one but me knows he is here.

You are clever and strong beyond our imagining. I sincerely hope you have not spent too much time with him, he is a well-known corrupting influence. We couldn't bear it if anything had happened to you.

I've spoken to him, and you're right, he's nothing like you at all. It's hard to believe you are from the same place. (This wasn't really true, but Scilla felt flattery was called for. What if the Voice changed its mind and left the beast here for her to deal with? She'd be stuck with his nasty remarks and condescending attitude forever!) **He's definitely some sort of criminal. But what must I do with him now? And what happens next?**

Why, you send him home where he'll be dealt with. You've done enough, as far as this creature is concerned. And you—well, you will step through The Door to my city. Eriis awaits—if you still want to come.

It is all I want. I can have him back to you in a matter of a few days. I am ready to come to you right now.

And I would love to receive you, but there are preparations that must be made. For this to be done properly, what you must do is have someone take your place. This will be different than a short trip to the Veil, and you know how difficult that was. There must be someone there for you, someone you trust to make sure your passage is smooth, and someone to close The Door behind you. Someone who can help you ensure the creature does not somehow escape, when he is so close to being where he belongs. I believe you might know someone like that.

Scilla ran through the list of her fellow novices and immediately discounted them. They'd run to Brother Blue like their robes were on fire. *Someone fairly smart,* she thought. *Someone who'll wind up holding the bag, taking the blame, explaining where I've gone. Someone who deserves a good scare. Someone who has a big party coming up soon....*

You're right. I know just the person. It will take a little more time, though. We will be ready in ten days.

***

Scilla couldn't help but notice that the demon had begun behaving differently.

He was contacting her from indoors. That was new, although she couldn't tell where and he was a master of evasion. He would appear in the candle flame with a glass in his hand, looking quite relaxed. And, she was afraid, he was starting to get a little too close to Lelet. A silly whore and a criminal—she shouldn't be surprised. He might be making a home for himself in this world, however temporarily, but all she could see was a creature who didn't belong here, poking and rubbing against the edges of what was real. She was glad their association was almost over.

"Did you do as I told you?" she asked.

He shrugged and looked off into the distance. "I didn't have to. A horrible tragedy occurred without my help. Imagine that. The girl is incapacitated and will remain indoors—I believe the human doctor said for another week. And the boy—your brother—they've sent him to your father, wherever he is."

Scilla wasn't sure if the demon had a hand in the accident or not. He could be painfully literal minded. If he hadn't physically pushed Lelet off the horse, he could easily say he hadn't caused the fall. And she'd long believed Rane would benefit from a trip to the country. He was better off.

"I am glad," the creature continued, "that she is not dead."

Scilla was not surprised to hear it. *Better cut this off at the root*, she thought.

"Why do you care? You aren't growing fond of her, are you? That would be a mistake, because she's a terrible, terrible person. As I've told you, she is the enemy. She deserves everything and worse. You think she'd be your friend? Or something more? You? She'd take one look at you and run screaming. She only likes rich, pretty boys. She's stupid, vain and—that hair! Pink was stupid, and now it's white! It's even worse. Like a dead animal! Like she lives in a cave like a…a lizard!"

The demon had heard this line of reasoning before and cut Scilla off. "If this underground reptile is your enemy why not let me kill her and have done with it? Why the petty attacks?" They both knew he'd never kill anyone, but he liked to needle Scilla.

"You are asking a lot of questions, demon. It's *still* none of your business. I have one more job for you."

He rolled his eyes. "Another mirror? Or would you like me to pour her perfume on the floor this time?"

"Demon, do not speak," Scilla snapped. She was satisfied to see he could not, although he clearly wanted to. "You have enjoyed your time here. You'll have lots of stories to tell the others, the ones that are all better than you." Seeing the rage building in his eyes, she quickly added, "And of course no matter what happens, you may not ever harm me." She decided baiting him may have been unwise, particularly since she was already in control. *Why does he make me want to be awful? It must be because he is awful himself.*

"Here it is," she told him. "It's simple. Get a horse and cart. Go to my house, use the back gate. Lure her to you and bring her to me. And then you go home."

He raised his brow and waited.

"Oh, you may speak," she added.

"Thank you, kind and benevolent child," he sneered.

"No need to be sarcastic."

"As you say."

She still didn't like the way he was looking at her. "Remember what I said about not harming me."

He sighed rather dramatically. "Our rules are not suggestions. I cannot physically harm you. You don't have to keep repeating it. Where am I supposed to get a horse? And what will prevent your evil, corrupt, not harmless at all sister enemy from running off?"

"Steal the cart and horse. Lelet has never been outside the city—she goes to parties and friend's houses. And whoring at the docks, probably. Get her off the main road and she won't dare run off. It should take you about three days. I will be waiting for you here. Don't be late and don't be seen. And definitely don't let anyone see your True Face."

"And if they do? Should I direct them to you for further inquiries?"

She'd had about enough. She hadn't caught a demon—which *no one else* was smart enough to do—to have it be rude to her. "Show my sister if you have to scare her. Anyone else, I guess you'll have to just kill them."

Now he looked concerned. "You would try to force me to murder a human person? Is that what you want your mark on this world to be?"

"No, demon, I'm not forcing you to do anything. Keep the face you're wearing now and no one has to get hurt. If not, it's not my fault."

He raked his hands through his long hair. "Fine. Whatever happens, I won't be going around killing humans. I told you before, even you can't make me do that. I'll bring you your sister and this ridiculous enterprise will be over. But tell me this. If she's so popular—

in grim contrast to you may I add—won't she be missed? A search party would be inconvenient."

Scilla nodded, deciding to overlook the insult. "Someone should overhear someone else saying they heard her talking about visiting friends on the coast. Start with the downstairs maid, she loves to gossip. Now, the Quarter Moons party is in a week. She never misses it. That's when you should take her."

He frowned. "She will no doubt want to know where I am taking her and for what purpose."

Scilla shrugged. "Tell her whatever you want. Just don't mention me."

"Why?"

"Because I said don't mention me! Don't mention me, or the Guardhouse. Other than that, I don't care. Oh, and don't look for me in the candle. When she sees me I want it to be a surprise."

"Is she to be harmed? Three days travel with a human person—I assume the rest of them like to talk as much as you do. If she thinks she is in danger she may try to run away despite what you say."

Scilla laughed. "If you think I talk a lot, you may long for the days of breaking glass and stealing shoes. I think you should just tell her you will deliver her safely to someone for a reason you haven't been told. Simple. And it has the benefit of being true." Scilla thought about the Voice. It *had* seemed simple. Lelet would take her place, take the blame, and she—Scilla—would finally be in Eriis where she belonged. And once she handed this low criminal back to the Voice, her real life with her new friends would begin.

"Ten more days, demon. Can you entertain yourself for that length of time?"

"I think you would have made a very fine demon. All this plotting is wasted on a young human. What will you do with your time when I am gone?"

Scilla leaned towards the flame and said, "I wouldn't be in such a hurry to get home if I were you. They have big plans for you, back on Eriis." She knew she shouldn't tip her hand, but it felt glorious to get in the final word.

"They?" the demon repeated, frowning suspiciously. It set down its drink. "Who exactly is ‘they’?"

"Ten days. And then it’s over." She blew the candle out.

Chapter 46

"Why must you be so cruel?" Gwenyth asked, dry eyed for once. She held the torn book of children's tales to her breast. "This is all I had and now it's ruined."
The Duke gently took the pages out of her hand. "I thought this was a gift from Edward. I would never have... I'll make this right, Gwenyth, please don't cry."
She looked away. "I'm done crying."

-The Claiming of the Duke, pg 157
Malloy Dos Capeheart, Little Gorda Press (out of print)

Mistra
100 years after the War of the Door, Mistran calendar
20 years later, Eriisai calendar
va'Everly family residence

In the late afternoon, May liked to take her tea and knitting into the front room, and open the heavy silk curtains. They were silk, the couch cushions were silk, the rugs beneath her feet, the balls and skeins of yarn were all silk, all sent back from the farm and from Father. Right now she was working on a blue and copper scarf Rane would need when it turned cold in the countryside. She worried more about him than her other siblings—Scilla seemed happy enough, although May couldn't imagine why—it was like being in a prison, but at least Scil felt useful, that was something, surely. And Pol, well, he thought his impending move to the farms was a big secret. She knew he was afraid she'd fall to pieces without him at home, but in fact it was a feeling of relief she could barely put into words. She ran the house, of course, but only because it was a job no one else wanted. Pol would follow Rane to work with their father, and they'd both be off her hands, Scilla was firmly in place at the Guardhouse—and that left Lelet. Well, Lelly was always looking around for an adventure or something to do, maybe next it would be her turn to run a household, and she'd find out wine bottles don't magically disappear when you've finished them, and they don't appear out of thin air, either. She'd seemed to have finally tired of sneaking Billah in and out of her window, which was good news. No, Billah simply wouldn't do, and Lelet was smart enough at least to figure that out, her next project would be finding Lelly someone suitable. Once Lel got back from whatever jaunt she was off to on the coast, they'd talk about her future. And once she no longer had to organize a household, she thought she might let some of the help go, as well, and close up some of this big house.

Something flickered in the corner of her eye. She held still and was rewarded by the appearance of the ghost. She'd seen it several times over the last few weeks, but only a hand or a shoulder and the back of a head with long dark hair, or a foot disappearing into a corner. It seemed to like the shadows. This was the first time she'd gotten a good look at it—at him. He glanced at her (she carefully looked down at her knitting) and returned a candlestick to the mantle. She looked up and said, "You must have been an extraordinarily good looking young man, when you were alive."

The ghost turned and realized she was talking to him, and to her surprise, he went absolutely pale. She hadn't thought the dead could react in such a human way, but she'd never startled a spirit before. She had obviously upset him, the poor thing looked ready to bolt.

"Please forgive me, that was rude. Perhaps you don't like to talk about your former existence. And here I am mentioning it again! I'm not normally such a dolt. Please, you look positively rattled. Do come over here and sit down."

The ghost of the young man said, "You can see me? Of course you can, you just said so." He put her basket of brightly colored yarn on the floor and sat on the ottoman, the worn leather creaking under his weight. He was surprisingly solid, for a visitation. "These are beautiful," he said. He picked out a ball of bright red silk and held it up to the light.

"It matches your eyes," said May. "Do all ghosts have red eyes? No, there I am again. Ignore me. Would you like some tea? Do ghosts eat or drink at all? Oh, another foolish question. I'm full of them today."

"No tea, thank you. I don't need to eat or drink, of course. Being a ghost. As you said."

"No tea, well, something stronger? I fear I gave you a start."

He hesitated, "I wouldn't say no, honestly."

She poured him a thimble sized glass of some deep brown liquid, one of an assortment on the little cart in the corner. "Some port, I think," she told him, "Pol likes it. Personally I find it too sweet." She watched his face, moving from suspicion to pleasure as he took a sip. "I'm sorry I made you uncomfortable. I've never met a ghost before."

"It's fine," he said, looking at the rainbow in the basket of yarn. "It's just difficult for me to think about what came before this."

She nodded. That seemed reasonable for someone in his condition. Perhaps he had died tragically, after all, who would want to dwell on that? "I'm glad I saw you today. I've been meaning to talk to you."

He surprised her again by laughing. He had a nice laugh. She wondered if he'd laughed a lot, when he was alive. He tossed the ball of yarn back into the basket. "Of course. Is there anyone in this house who *hasn't* seen me?"

May thought for a moment. "Well, I don't believe Lelly has, I'm pretty sure you're dramatic enough for a fit of hysterics out of her, at least. And Rane, well, who knows what he sees?"

"He saw me as well. I… I think sending him to your father was perhaps a wise idea."

She frowned. "You know us rather well. How long have you been haunting this house? And what were you doing with that candlestick?" He stood and went to the window, quite close to the shadows thrown by the curtains, and she realized she could see through him. He'd be gone in a moment. "Please, don't leave. I'm sure you have your reasons. I won't pry. And… and you haven't finished your port." He rematerialized so quickly she thought it was possible he hadn't wanted to leave at all. "I imagine we're a difficult bunch to haunt. We're all a bit haunted ourselves. Will you tell me your name? You don't have to."

"My name is Moth," he said. He really did have the most striking eyes.

"That's a nice name. Are you attracted to the light?" He looked at her blankly. "Moths, they fly into flames and lights and things."

"I'm attracted to shadows, then." *My goodness*, she thought. *A depressed ghost*. She decided to change the subject.

"I've been wanting to ask you for a favor," she said, and was pleased to see his gloom replaced with a look of genuine curiosity. "One can't help but notice when one has a ghost—things move around, sometimes there are no spoons—no, I'm not angry, but here's the thing. My friend Stelle—well, you've probably seen her."

"She's pretty," he said. "I like her."

"Yes, I think she's pretty too, and I like her very much. In fact, with Rane and next Pol off to work with Father, I've decided there's too much room in this house for just Lelly and me. I've asked Stelle to come and stay with us. With me."

"I'm glad. This is a big house for just two people. And she reminds me of someone…."

"From when you were alive?" She bit her lip, hoping she hadn't said the wrong thing, but the ghost nodded.

"Someone who was very important to me. Funny, they are nothing alike, except that they both want us to be…."

"Exceptional?" she guessed.

"Exactly! I'm afraid I let her down, this friend of mine, but I'm sure you won't bring Stelle anything but happiness." *How nice*, she thought, *not to have to explain myself, or how this affects my being a Second. Whoever he was in life, he's a kind man in death.* She wondered whom he had let down and what the lady's role in her own disappointment might have been. He continued, "You mentioned a favor?"

May nodded. "Please don't scare her, if you can help it. She's a bit shy. I don't want to have her regret coming to live with me, getting upset and dashing off into the night. If you must do… ghost things? Do them to me and Lel, and leave her be. Just until she gets acclimated."

"Acclimated," he said. He looked to her as if his whole mortal life was unspooling in his mind. Finally he said, "It was never my intention to hurt or frighten any of you. I wish… well. Of course I won't harm your friend. I'm going to be leaving very soon."

"Oh. Ghost mission completed?"

He shrugged. "Something like that. All your spoons and shoes will be back in place before I go."

"Keep the spoons, we have more than we need of all that sort of stuff."

From another room, there came a shout. "May!"

The ghost—Moth—tensed but May smiled in what she hoped was a comforting way and held her hand up. "It's Pol. Let me see what he wants."

"Yes?" she called.

"May?"

"What is it, Pol?"

"MAY?"

"WHAT?"

He stuck his head around the corner and saw her sitting with her basket of knitting on the floor and her needles jabbed into the ball of yarn, and one of his port glasses sitting on the end table.

"Early in the day, isn't it? Anyway, if you see the ghost, please tell it I want my cufflinks back." He disappeared down the hall, and Moth stepped out from behind the door. She was working on stifling her giggles, feeling as if her guest wouldn't find the humor, but he had his hand clapped over his mouth and finally both of them dissolved into laughter.

When he caught his breath, he asked, "Do you have a spare room? Maybe I should just have moved in."

"Now, don't be like that. We talked, Pol and I, and he's never seen you. I think he's a little jealous. Every time something goes missing or anything odd happens, he blames you. I gather Rane was borrowing Pol's cufflinks? I notice nothing of mine, or Pol's, has been moved or taken."

"You are exactly right. I'll return them, of course. Before I go."

"Must you leave?" He nodded. "Will it be someplace better?"

He gave her a sudden, dazzling smile. *He's not my type,* she reminded herself*, and he's also a ghost. Too bad.*

"I guess I'll find out. Good luck with Stelle. I think she'll turn out to be brave after all."

"I've enjoyed talking with you," she said, hoping he might linger.

He took her hand, and another surprise—he was quite warm. He said, "This is the nicest conversation I've had with anyone for… I'm sorry we didn't meet sooner. And about your candlestick."

"Are you certain you're a ghost?" she asked.

"May, what else could I possibly be?"

She let go of his hand. "I hope whatever's next makes you very happy."

He nodded at her and, stepping into the lengthening shadows at the window, he vanished.

A ghost, well now I can say I've seen everything. And a sweet one with excellent manners, at that. I'd say that's a successful haunting. She thought about introducing him to Lelet, and laughed at the absurdity. *Someone alive, sister, he's got to be out there. We'll find him for you. But those eyes….*

Chapter 47

"Allow me," he said, and stepped behind Gwenyth to fasten the strand of diamonds and sapphires around her slender throat. He was so much taller that from behind he could see the rise and fall of her creamy bosom barely concealed by her deep indigo silk gown. "What a fool I've been," he thought to himself.

-The Claiming of the Duke, pg 190
Malloy Dos Capeheart, Little Gorda Press (out of print)

Mistra
100 years after the War of the Door, Mistran calendar
20 years later, Eriisai calendar
va'Everly family residence

Moth immediately made his way to the rooftop to sort it out.

So everyone (except perhaps Lelet) had seen him, or knew about him, or talked about his activities. If he'd done something contrary to the horrible child's dictate, the leash in his mind would have yanked him back. So his talk with May wasn't against the rules. And what a strange thing to say—what had she called him? Extraordinarily good looking? Him? He could count the times he'd been complimented on his looks on no fingers. Of course, Aelle had told him his *yala* was the nicest she'd seen (but how many had she seen?), but that was nothing like this. It was a terrible thing to say—and here he'd thought May was the nice one! Maybe insults and compliments operated under a system he hadn't worked out. Or maybe May was more like Cybelle, sly and up to her own errands. He decided to forgive May for her insult because in every other way, she was the kindest person he'd met since arriving on this side of The Door. He hadn't realized how much he missed simple conversation.

Returning to his little balcony he retrieved the old leather bag from under a pile of blankets. He poked through the household things he'd accumulated, selecting a silver pitcher (in case they needed water), as many matches as he could find, and of course the little sewing kit he'd found in with a pile of laundry. Already he'd managed to alter his stolen clothing so that everything fit him—they still looked stolen, but at least stolen from someone his own size. He also tossed in an old blanket, a heavy dress he'd taken from one of the kitchen girl's cast-off pile, and the dreaded hat. He'd have to do his best to keep Lelet from seeing his face—there'd be no convincing her he was a ghost once they were on the road. And he took care not to pack anything she would recognize—he put the pitcher back, but kept the blanket.

Then it was just a matter of going from room to room. Pol's cufflinks he left conspicuously on Rane's (now abandoned) dresser. He looked around the boy's room sadly. He wondered if fresh air and hard work would really clear his mind of the talking dogs and fits of rage. Before he left he fished the remainder of the bottle of whiskey out from under the chair. Glasses were a luxury he supposed he could do without.

Lelet was home, enjoying the last day of her convalescence before she'd return to society at the Quarter Moon Party the following night. He arranged a few sprays of orchids in the silver pitcher and left it outside her door. The rest of her things he left in a neat pile on the floor in Rane's room.

He'd begun with the downstairs maid, as the child had suggested, and told her—through a partially closed door—that Lelet was leaving with friends directly from the party to head for a few days on the coast. As far as the household knew, this was her plan. Everyone, in fact, but Lelet herself. So when her maid asked her about packing a bag, she was first confused, then irritated.

"I'll have everything I need, I won't be gone that long. I assume they have a washroom and a kitchen, after all!" The maid, relieved that she didn't have to endure the ritual of selecting and rejecting every garment in Lelet's closet, dropped the subject and went on her way.

The only thing left was to procure a horse and a cart. Moth decided to start with Lelet's own horse, Petrel. He managed to get into the stables and found himself once again face to face with the terrifying animal.

"Remember me?" he asked it. The animal obviously did, because it threw itself at the half door of its enclosure. Unlike last time, this time it looked quite willing to bite his face off. And even if he'd managed to get it out of the box, what then?

He backed out, apologizing for alarming the huge beast.

He slipped around the corner into his glass house. He didn't suppose he'd see it again, although he already had plans to recreate it, should he ever get home to Eriis. He closed the window panes, hoping the heat and moisture would last a little longer, that the flowers would survive without him, and that someone else would come along and take care of them.

There was something going on at the front door, and making absolutely certain he was hidden in the shadows, he went to investigate.

"Billah, we've been over this," May was saying to the yellow haired young man. "She is still resting after her fall, and she is not receiving. I'm sure you'll see her at the party tomorrow night."

"She won't," said Billah angrily. "She says not to call on her, and I want to know why and who."

May looked completely different from the kind-eyed woman he'd shared a drink with earlier. "I don't appreciate your tone, Billah. I am not your errand boy. Now if you will excuse me, we are all quite busy." May closed the door—not quite a slam—but Moth could still hear Billah muttering under his breath. "I should go look for her at the back gate," he was saying, "along with the trash carts and the dock boys. Won't see me? She's seeing someone. I'm going to find out who."

Trash carts, thought Moth. *A cart and a horse.*

The next evening, Lelet got a message from a very apologetic maid letting her know that Per would be collecting her at the back of the house, at the Green Leaf Gate.

Chapter 48

Eriis
20 years after the War of the Door, Eriisai calendar
100 years later, Mistran calendar
Yuenne's family residence

Aelle sat in the now-empty courtyard of her father's house, sitting and thinking and sipping a glass of *sarave.* The glow from the stones still shed a lovely light on the little white flowers and the water fountain, but in their haste to learn a new bit of gossip, the guests had left their half-drunk glasses and plates everywhere. Her father had gripped her hard by the arm and told her to stay here, so she had, even when her mother had followed him out the door along with most of the guests. The Mages had gone first, with the Queen on their heels. Well, she supposed what really happened was Rhuun had gone first, and Ilaan after him, as usual. Those two.

The Mages had gathered around the queen and accused her of hiding a human, and Hellne laughed in their faces. Hiding a human.

"Where is the prince?" her father asked the queen. Why would he ask that? He knew perfectly well Rhuun went home before Hellne even arrived. And what did it have to do with hiding a human?

"Are you all right?" Ilaan had appeared from somewhere and he was sitting next to her. He took the glass of *sarave* out of her hand and replaced it with a cup of cool water. "Aelle? Are you all right?"

"Why wouldn't I be?" she answered. "Father is going to be furious, his party got ruined. Look at this mess."

"Aelle, do you know why the Mages were here?" He was talking to her slowly, like she was simple or drunk. She hated that.

"Don't talk to me like I'm an idiot. The Mages were looking for a hidden human. And they wanted the queen to turn it over. Why they decided to come out of the Raasth tonight I don't know." She leapt to her feet and began gathering empty cups and plates. "Father won't like to see this when he gets back."

Ilaan took her by the wrist and turned her to face him. "You know why they came here. You know who they were looking for."

"I don't know what you mean, it has nothing to do with me, and I don't care." She jerked her arm away. "And you could help me for once instead of just adding to the mess."

"Rhuun is gone," he said. She didn't respond. "He's worried about you, he told me to take care of you."

"Gone where?" she asked. "And worried why?" She used a leftover *serviette* to try and scrub a water ring from an end table. Real wood, and this would ruin it. It would take the rest of the night to clean up, and if Ilaan wouldn't help, he could just leave.

"Aelle, put that stuff down and come and sit. We need to talk. Rhuun is gone—"

"You keep saying that. Where could he go with the drink he put away tonight? He could barely see to walk home. He's the one you should be worried about." Such a lot of trash left over. She balanced cups and plates atop each other.

"I sent him away, to protect him from the Mages. You know why."

It was all too much to carry at once, and the reasonable thing seemed to be to throw it all on the floor, so she did. "Where is he?"

"We couldn't tell you—"

"Where is he?" Her voice rose to a near shriek. A part of her observed from somewhere far away. *That's not like me, screaming like a back country hill wife,* she thought.

Ilaan sighed and said. "The Mages would have taken him away because they have plans for his human blood, so I sent him through The Door."

She stared at him. "That's the stupidest thing I've ever heard in my life. Why are you making up an awful story like that? Is it because you're jealous? You can't even let me have a part of him? Does he have to belong to you only?" She could hear the blood singing in her head. *What a terrible thing to say,* she thought. And in fact she'd never seen her beautiful, perfect, impossible brother look so sad.

"Aelle. I know you don't mean that. You know I'm telling the truth. You know that's why the Mages came here. They found out about Rhuun—that his father was a human man, and they came for him, so I sent him somewhere safe."

"Father is going to kill you. I don't know what you did but when he finds out, he'll fill your mouth with sand." Her eyes blurred with tears. "Why didn't you tell me?"

"You would have run right to your father. Isn't that true, *shan*?" Siia picked her way through the party debris and joined them in the courtyard. "He's the one who makes it rain for you, doesn't he?" She tucked a stray curl back into Aelle's coiled hair. "Everyone else is a distant second."

Aelle glared at her mother, shaking her hand away. "You all treat me like I'm simple."

"The truth is I didn't know any of this until today," said Ilaan. "But Mother is right, I wouldn't have told you anyway." He turned to Siia. "How bad is it?"

She said, "Gather your things and leave." He looked stunned. "I will do what I can to pour water on your father's heart, but I make no promises. You've put a foot through some of his dearest plans. You and Rhuun." She shook her head. "I knew there was something strange about that boy. Well, it all makes sense now. Shame. You would have made such a lovely queen, Aelle." She turned back to Ilaan. "I don't know when your father will return, but I can't recommend he find you here. Go up to your room and take what you need. We will talk again soon, when he's cooled down. Best to let me contact you."

Ilaan moved to embrace Aelle. "I was supposed to take care of you."

She stepped back. "I can take care of myself. And if I can't, Father can." She lifted her chin, daring him to disagree.

He nodded, his face remade by grief. Then he was gone, a smudge of light in the air where he'd been standing.

"Well, that's done," said Siia after a moment. She looked around the courtyard. "Your father will be home soon. We might as well clean up."

Chapter 49

...second moonset, and as he'd been instructed, McVeigh waited at the front gate with a hot towel and a brandy.
"Where would I be without you?" the Duke asked as his valet helped him out of the rough wooden cart.
"Ours is not to know, although I'm feeling a ditch might be involved," the older man replied, passing the driver a stack of bills.
A familiar woman's voice came from the back of the little cart. "Are we there yet? I'll never get this smell out of my hair!"
"I'll draw a bath for Miss Cybelle, then," said McVeigh, handing over a few more bills.

-The Claiming of the Duke, pg 91
Malloy Dos Capeheart, Little Gorda Press (out of print)

Mistra
100 years after the War of the Door, Mistran calendar
20 years later, Eriisai calendar
Night of the Quarter Moons party

Where to get a horse and cart? He didn't have a choice, he had to follow that miserable child's decree, and finally it had been Billah, with some assistance from The Duke, who'd given him the idea. A trash cart, and the back of the house. The night of the Quarter Moons party, well, all the regular cabs would be taken, and anyone with a vehicle might earn some extra coin transporting the good citizens of Mistra to and from events. He made his way to the Green Leaf Gate and said, "I have to leave the property." His head did not respond with a painful yank, and he took a step, and then another, until he was around the corner and out of sight of the house.

He took a deep breath of the damp, cool air. Not as pleasant as the horse riding park, or even the forest, but at least he was outside. It was getting dark, and the muddy road alongside the canal was rich with shadows. He passed several human persons on their own errands, but no one looked his way. The road turned away from the canal and the paving became more regular, although it was still mean and dank compared to the neighborhood they called the Upper Garden. This place was called Fool's Hill, which didn't make sense since it was as flat as a floor. As to the mental character of the residents, most humans seemed fairly foolish to him anyway.

He smelled the stable before he came in sight of it, and slipped into a shadowy corner to watch how it worked. There was a line of ragged men (no women looked for work here tonight) who signed their names or made a mark on a board and drove off with a horse and cart, presumably looking for late night revelers to ferry home. He pulled his hat down and got in line.

When it was his turn, he wrote his name under everyone else's—M. Moth—and followed the example of climbing up into the driver's seat.

"Oi, Mister…Math?" the man passed him two leather ropes. "You new around here?"

"Aye," he replied, hoping his voice did not betray him as one of what they called the Fancy Fifty down here. He knew he sounded foreign and hoped it would work in his favor. "Beesley sent me."

The man frowned. "Beeseley?"

"Oh, aye. Billy Beesley. He woulda come but his wife was dead set on a party tonight or he'd be sleeping with the horse himself. Said I oughta try and rake in some coin." He gave the leads an experimental shake, and to his relief, the horse started moving. "Well, see you in the morning. Heiresses to kidnap and all, right?"

The man scratched his head and was about to reply, but the horse, uncomfortable with what was now behind it, began to move at a fair pace out of the stableyard and up the street. The man shrugged and turned to his next driver.

Moth didn't look back or dare to breathe until they were out of sight of the other workers. "I did it," he told the horse. His hands were shaking, he couldn't recall ever being so excited. "I did it; they thought I was a human." The horse ignored him. It was on the skinny side, white with big black spots, and not as big or as shiny and well groomed as Lelet's Petrel, but on the other hand it didn't appear to be as nervous and high strung.

He pulled the strap in his right hand, the horse stopped moving.

"No," he said, "I need you to keep going." He pulled the other leather rope, then slapped them together on the animal's back. It gave a disgusted snort and began walking again—to the left. "No, I—fine. We'll do it your way."

The horse seemed to prefer left turns, and finally they had completed a circle of boarded up storefronts, businesses closed for the night, and dimly lit taverns and come out where they'd started. They were now pointed in the right direction. There was enough light from the moons and from gas lamps to throw back an oily sheen from the canal. "Never thought I'd be happy to see something so ugly," Moth told the horse. The animal seemed content to amble down the canal-side road, and when they had come nearly in sight of the Green Leaf Gate, he pulled on the leads until, with a whining moan, the cart came to a halt.

It was dark on the path, the gas lamp above their heads was unlit—either broken or abandoned, and the dank reek of the canal combined with the garbage smell of the cart nearly made Moth's eyes water. "Stay here," he told the horse, who found something to nibble on between its feet. "I'm already late, she should be there." He could only imagine what her mood would be like. Well, he had a plan for that, too. The Duke would serve as his model. She would understand he was to be respected. Keeping close to the stone wall and out of sight, he edged towards the back gate of the house.

"Per?" It was Lelet, and she was coming his way fast.

Rushta, he hissed, and stepped into her path. In the dark, she slammed into him, and without thinking, he scooped her up.

"Don't scream, wench, or it'll go worse for you," he told her.

Instead of being quiet and obeying his order, Lelet screamed so loud the rats ran away. She punched him the small of the back and wriggled like a jumpmouse. They reached the cart and he set her on her feet.

"Please," she said quietly. "My family has money. You must know that. Whatever you've been paid, they will pay more. Just set me down and I'll walk away. No one will know. Let me go."

He wanted to tell her he was sorry, that he would take care of her, that he thought she was pretty and clever, but of course he couldn't do any of those things. He lifted her and dropped her over the side of the cart. Too late, he realized he'd misjudged how deep it was, because she bounced off the bottom and lay still.

He scrambled in next to her. *If I've damaged her, I'm throwing myself straight into the canal.* But she muttered something and rolled onto her side. A curl of white hair had come loose from a jeweled pin, and he brushed it back from her brow. Sitting back, he noticed she was barefoot.

"She'll be looking for her shoes," he told the horse. He retrieved them, along with her muddy wrap and her little clutch. It held only a slim cigarette holder and a few folded bills. He put all her things in the big leather bag, then covered her with the blanket. She opened her eyes and tried to sit up.

"Where…."

"Shh, Lady, you must rest." He pitched his voice low and gentle.

"Where am I?" she whispered.

"Why, surely you are dreaming, Lady. Close your eyes and sleep again."

He'd chosen the words that Sir Edward had used to placate Lady Cybelle—of course, Sir Edward first poisoned poor Cybelle and planned to murder as soon as she closed her eyes, but the little speech had the same effect on Lelet. She appeared to be not injured but merely asleep. He was relieved that he could fall back on his book after all, since he'd have to talk to the girl eventually. There were hours until dawn and he hoped she would sleep quietly and wake peacefully. Perhaps he'd start with the speech the Duke made to Gwenyth when they met? He'd come across as stern, not to be trifled with, but ultimately fair and reasonable. He was sure she would respond in kind.

Chapter 50

Cybelle awoke with a great start into darkness. Where was she? Why was she outside? She groped for her clutch, hoping the tiny dagger was still inside.
"Shh, Lady, you must rest." Cybelle frowned. The voice was familiar, she couldn't place it, but she felt strangely comforted.
"Where am I?" The last thing she remembered was a goblet of sweet wine.
"Why, surely you are dreaming, Lady. Close your eyes and sleep again."
As soon as he was sure Cybelle slept, Sir Edward crept towards her, the knotted silk cord wrapped in his fist.

-The Claiming of the Duke, pg 95
Malloy Dos Capeheart, Little Gorda Press (out of print)

Mistra
100 years after the War of the Door, Mistran calendar
20 years later, Eriisai calendar
Road through the Great Forest

It was daytime, that much was clear, and there were tall trees bending towards each other overhead. Lelet sat up and took a look around.

The road was wide enough for two carts to pass without the drivers being able to touch hands, although at the moment they were the only ones traveling. It was indifferently maintained and the cart bumped over the occasional branch and into a few ruts. There were many ways to get out of Mistra, but this particular road ran from the city straight to the Green Sea, snaking through the deep and dark Great Forest. There were better routes to visit one of the nice resorts on the coast, so unless you were in a great hurry, there was no real reason to travel this way. Who left Mistra City to visit a farm or a tavern? The big farms (including those held by the va'Everly family) were in the other direction, in the valleys and lowlands between Mistra and the mountains.

Lelet frowned, trying to remember—she'd had the strangest dream—someone talking to her in a sweet whisper… but it was gone.

She touched the back of her head, fearing the worst, but found only a small bump and no blood. Nothing seemed to be broken and her vision was clear. She wriggled her hands, her wrist was fine. The person who had taken her was sitting up on a bench at the front of the cart, wrapped in a cloak of some sort, with a hat pulled low. He was talking to the horse.

"Well, it's true that you aren't as big as I was expecting, but I feel that if we work together we can get this over with-"

"Are you insane?" she asked. He glanced over his shoulder.

"I am glad you aren't dead. Or impaired. I apologize for hurting your head." He pulled awkwardly on the reins until the horse gave up trying to figure out what the man wanted and began walking in a large, slow circle. She watched, her initial terror draining away, until he finally got the animal to stop. His accent was faint and strangely familiar, but she couldn't place it. He sounded young, but who used words like 'impaired'?

"I have some things for you," he said.

He jumped down and handed her a large leather bag. He was tall enough that he didn't have to reach up at all to pass it to her over the wooden plank which gated the back of the cart.

She looked at the empty road behind him. On the one hand she wasn't tied up or secured in any way. On the other, she was barefoot, her beautiful white dress was damaged beyond repair, and she had no idea where she was. The trees were so tall that when she looked back to where they'd come from, she couldn't find the city skyline at all. She decided to look in the bag, which she snatched away from him and pulled to the far side of the cart. He kept his head down, the hat hid most of his face. He had unfashionably long dark hair, was tall, possibly insane, and couldn't drive a cart. Beyond that she had no idea.

She looked in the bag and her heart sank. She pulled out her white shoes.

"I thought you'd probably not want to lose those," he said, as if that was an explanation.

She pulled out her white satin purse.

"Don't worry," he said with a smirk. "I checked it for weapons."

"You think I carry weapons in my purse?" She pulled out a slim cigarette case—yes! Matches! She had a brief moment of ecstasy as she took a long drag.

"Why are you doing that?" he asked, waving his hand at the curl of smoke.

"I know, it's disgusting, I mostly quit. But I think I earned it." She stubbed out the cigarette and narrowed her eyes at him. "So, you grab me, knock me unconscious, and then go back and fetch my bag?"

"Your wrap thing is in there also. I tried to clean it off but it got pretty muddy."

She threw the stub away and edged towards him. "How much did Rane pay you?" She swung herself over the back of the cart, climbed down and advanced on him. "Or was it Althee? That bitch, is this her idea? Are you supposed to be the pirate? Or was it the two of them together?"

To her surprise he took a step back as if she were his size and a threat and not a small and barefoot girl in need of a bath and a change of clothes. "Rane takes advantage of people. He figured you were simple and he got you involved, am I right? I bet it was Rane, Althee has more sense than this. So, what are you supposed to do with me now?" She took another step forward and he continued his retreat.

"I am not simple. Why does everyone…" He shook his head and said in a louder voice, "That's enough, wench! Get back in the cart or I'll leave you here to starve in the woods." He nodded approvingly to himself. She stared at him with disbelief.

"Wench? Are you from a hundred years ago? What is going on?" He didn't answer. "Well, there's absolutely no way I'm going anywhere with you." She turned and began walking the way they'd come. He walked behind her.

"There are bears lurking in the woods, you know," he told her. "Bears and, um, what else lurks? …Brigands! Bears and brigands. You're much safer with me than out here alone."

After stepping on the fifth or sixth sharp stone, she swore under her breath, turned and stomped past him. "Fine. Take me on your little cart to Rane and he and I will have it out once and for all. He's going to pay for this. My dress is ruined, I missed the party, and my feet are crippled. And stop calling me wench, it sounds ridiculous."

"There is a warmer dress in that bag. Put it on and if you give me this one," he pointed at her white gown, "I'll fix it for you. I won't look."

He held his hand out to help her back into the cart. She glared at him and hoisted herself back over the rail. Peering in the leather bag, she found an enormously ugly dark brown dress. She looked over at the man, who already had turned away—polite, at least. He had crossed his arms and was looking at the sky. She wished he'd take off the hat, she wanted to get a better look at him. One thing at a time, though. She wiggled out of the white dress and into the brown one in a flash, and threw the white silk at his back. The new one came to mid-calf and felt like carpeting but it was certainly warmer than the silk.

"I don't know what you mean by fixing it, but knock yourself out." She continued to root through the bag, next finding several apples, a lump of cheese wrapped in paper, and a loaf of bread. "How rustic," she sneered. "Well, I won't starve, I guess. So. Instead of a pirate, I get you. Rane is supposed to be out with my father at our farm. How did he pull this off? You might as well tell me." She began working on the apple.

"I am to deliver you to someone. I won't hurt you. That's all you need to know." He took his seat on the driver's bench and began tugging—randomly, it looked like—on the reins.

She glared at his back. "Try keeping them the same length," she said, "and we might go in a straight line."

"It doesn't become a woman to give orders," he informed her.

When she had recovered her composure she said, "All right then. We're not going to talk anymore right now. Good luck with your new friend."

Chapter 51

Cybelle dos Shaddach peered into her tiny hand mirror and applied more color to her already perfect coral lips. She laid a slim hand on the Duke's arm. "For you, my Lord, the great wide world is your arsenal. You may pluck your weapons from wherever you chose. But we women, we must keep our weapons close at hand."

-The Claiming of the Duke, pg 53
Malloy Dos Capeheart, Little Gorda Press (out of print)

Mistra
100 years after the War of the Door, Mistran calendar
20 years later, Eriisai calendar
Road through the Great Forest

The day wore on and the landscape didn't change much.

Lelet couldn't remember the last time she'd been out of the city. There was nothing out here but trees anyway. She'd never been able to understand the way Billah went on and on about how wonderful the outdoor life was. This was proof, as far as she was concerned, that fresh air and green things were better in theory than in practice. She wondered if Billah had missed her at the party last night, and if he'd wondered where she was. Did he have it in him to look for her? Was anyone looking for her?

She ate another apple and wondered for a second if she should offer her peculiar abductor anything to eat. She decided not to. She might have to run for it after all and would need her strength. She thought about simply slipping off the back of the cart and hiding in the woods until someone heading back to the city came along, but they hadn't seen another soul all day. And besides, the man—whoever he was—was correct about brigands, even if no one had called the thieves and robbers one heard about by that name in a hundred years. The open road was a dangerous place, and without even a pair of decent shoes, she doubted she'd have much luck on her own. No, best to go and find out what Rane thought he was doing, then have a story to tell when she got home.

Once she decided to allow herself to be kidnapped, she tried talking to the strange man again. Wench, brigand—maybe he was an actor? Or a scholar who needed Rane's money?

"What's your name?" she asked. He had hardly said a word since he'd given her the bag.

"Moth," he said.

She snickered. "Moth? That's your name? Really? Were your parents angry with you?" He slumped even further down on the bench. "My name is Lelet." Nothing. Then she said, "Let me go home," not for the first time.

The dark figure at the front of the cart sighed. *He's a perfect picture of depression, whoever he is*, she thought.

"I've said I can't do that."

"Of course you can. Just stop—right now and let me out. I'll make my way home and you can tell your 'employer' I escaped. Or better yet, turn around and drive me home. You can drop me off at the back gate again and sneak away. It's a perfect plan. I can better whatever Rane is paying you. We can do this right now." This was such a perfect plan it had practically already happened. She was already planning her story. Althee had probably gone for a drink with her brother before he got exiled, and said something about her pirate idea. And when he got sent away, it was the perfect time for him to strike—he had a foolproof alibi. Her friends wouldn't believe her. She'd have to whip out the ugly brown dress for a climactic reveal.

"It's not about money. And women shouldn't talk about money, anyway. It's demeaning," he replied. "One might say it's even vulgar."

"Well. That's... interestingly... crazy. But honestly? It's always about money," she said, thinking, *If he's an actor, maybe these are lines from a play? Because otherwise Rane has hired a lunatic.*

"Well, not this time," he said.

"Just let me go home. I can tell you're not really like this. You're not bad. This isn't you." Just in case, she hid one of her satin shoes behind her back. It had a sharp heel and was the closest thing she had to weapon.

"What isn't me?" he asked, although it sounded like he really didn't want to know.

"You don't want to be doing this. Someone is making you. I can help you!" She had a sudden image of herself—beautifully backlit—being congratulated by someone—the Mayor? Her father?—for rehabilitating a poor, simple criminal.

The man sighed again and flicked the reins over the horses back. She noted that he'd listened to her and was holding them evenly, but the animal was clearly a good judge of character and slowed its pace, ignoring his commands.

"I'm not like this," he said. "The only thing I've ever stolen is *sarave* from my mother's kitchen." *Sarave*? she thought, *What in the world was that?* "And I sincerely doubt you or anyone can help me." He shook his head and sat straighter and taller. "Mind your mouth and behave, wench. Your voice is an assault." She gasped. It was like he was two people—one was a lunatic but at least polite, and the other was arrogant and rude in addition to the lunacy. Rane needed to check references more carefully the next time he hired a felon.

"How do you even know you have the right victim?" she asked.

"I was told that the slattern had white hair and white skin, like a dead animal," he told her.

"A *what*? Who said that?" Her voice rose to a near shriek.

"I believe you were also described as looking like a cave creature. A lizard, I think it was, who never sees the sun." She gasped again and he turned, saying, "Forgive me. That was unkind. And untrue. I shouldn't have—" and caught one of her satin pumps in the ear. It knocked his hat off. He rose to his feet.

"You get one blow and this is how you waste it?" he roared. "On vanity?"

"Vanity?" she replied. "You call me a cave lizard and I'm supposed to…" Her mouth snapped shut. She stared up at him.

He looked at her anxiously. "I'm sorry I scared you. I was about to say you don't look like a cave lizard. I'm sorry I yelled, but you shouldn't have thrown your shoe at me." He rubbed his ear where she'd clipped him. "I *did* scare you, didn't I? Some?"

Lelet, for her part, had played enough lawnball that her aim was more than fair, and had simply aimed for his head. Knocking off his hat was a bonus, because now she could see his face.

He's young, maybe only a bit older than I am. And he's handsome enough to be an actor, she thought, *but how strange....*

His eyes were bright red. Red eyes… *they got red eyes….*

She finally said, "You're from the other side of The Door."

"What are you saying? No I'm not. That's madness." She thought he looked a little sick. "*Rushta*," he muttered.

"Your eyes. You're a demon. I'm right." She stood on her knees in the back of the cart, swaying slightly, her hand stretched out as if it still held the shoe.

"You're wrong," he told her. "I was kicked in the head. By a horse. And it's rude of you to stare at me."

She gaped at him and then laughed. "I'm certain you were kicked in the head, but that has nothing to do with the fact that you're a demon. My sister is practically an expert and she told me you can hide your… what's it called? Oh, True Face! Some burny thing! But not your eyes." She paused and shook her head. "Rane got a demon to kidnap me, that's pretty impressive. I can't wait to find out how he did it." She rearranged herself in the cart, tucking her long brown skirt around her knees.

"There's no such thing as demons. They are mythological." He picked the hat up and made to put it back on, then sighed and tossed it into the cart near where she sat. She grabbed it and shoved it in the bag.

"Show me," she said.

"Show you what?" She thought he knew.

The horse, sensing a moment, had come to a halt. The forest was silent. Even the birds were watching.

He sighed, "You didn't know until just now, when you saw my eyes?" She nodded. "Good. I didn't know if I was doing it right."

"Doing…?"

"Being a human person, as you said. I've been here a while, and no one seems to have noticed me at all. I haven't really had anyone to talk to. Until now. You."

She wondered which one he really was: the polite one or the jackass. He seemed to be leaning towards the former. She hoped so. She drew a long breath. "This is just amazing. You really are from the other side? How did you get here? How long have you been here? Are you by yourself? Do you miss it? What is it like?"

He gazed at her for a moment and she wondered how anyone could have looked in those eyes and thought to recognize a fellow human. And look at him and not notice him? Impossible.

"Show me," she repeated softly. He looked at the ground, his golden skin reddening to his ears. *So he can blush*, she thought. It suddenly felt much warmer.

He finally said, "No. No. You'll just have to take my word for it."

"Why don't you want to show me? Is it frightening? Is it dreadful? Are you ugly?" This was all just so interesting!

He looked shocked. "Ugly? Am I… Do you have eyes?" He straightened up. "Yes, ugly and terrifying. One might say a beast, in fact. I hope you never have to see it, because if you see my True Face, it means someone is going to die."

She bit her lip, then burst out laughing. "That is the single most dramatic thing anyone has ever said to me." She bounced a little in the cart, wide-eyed. "What happens next?" She wondered if Rane had told him what to say, or if he was a writer along with a player. In any case, he was very good. Playing the part of a demon—he was very convincing! She couldn't wait to tell this story to her friends, even if she had to miss the party to do it. For his part, he seemed at a loss for words—not that he had that many to begin with. He glared down at her, but she felt sure there was also something like shame in his expression.

He turned back to the horse. "No more questions."

The cart rolled forward.

Chapter 52

The Duke looked Gwenyth up and down. She could feel the heat of his gaze. She shivered in her thin bodice, despite the warmth of the great room. What could he want with her?
"Can you cook?"

-The Claiming of the Duke, pg 60
Malloy Dos Capeheart, Little Gorda Press (out of print)

Mistra
100 years after the War of the Door, Mistran calendar
20 years later, Eriisai calendar
Road through the Great Forest

Moth—now hatless—squinted through the trees. "It's getting dark. We'll stop here." He climbed down from the front of the cart, warily approaching the horse.

She folded her arms and glared at the back of his head. She was hungry, and while having an adventure seemed like an exciting idea, being carted through an empty forest in a dirty cart—there was a distinct smell of garbage—was both boring and a little scary. The only way to get her captor, whatever he was, to talk to her was to provoke him. He was certainly good looking enough to be interesting, but he sat there like a stone, he didn't pay her any attention at all. And this whole being a demon thing, the thing with his eyes, well, there had to be some trick to it she wasn't seeing. Rane was going to have to come up with the explanation of a lifetime. She'd deal with Rane in due course, but right now she was in a mood—a Low Snit. And this person—Moth of all things, honestly, what sort of a name was that?—wanted to stop.

"What's the difference?" she said. "You're just going to slit my throat and eat my flesh."

"You might as well be rested when I do."

"Was that a joke? Are we joking about murdering me now?" Low Snit was quickly escalating.

"I am not going to murder you," he replied. "I am also not going to eat your flesh, skin you, cut off your hair, cut off your feet… what else was it you said before? Oh, I'm not going to make a necklace of your eyeballs. You are very imaginative, though. You should write a book."

Did he actually think this was funny? He was doing something with the horse, which turned into a slow motion ballet of him trying to tie the leads to a tree and the horse pulling just ever so slightly far enough away to prevent it. She stalked up behind him and grabbed the leads away and secured the animal, which calmed down when he moved away from it.

"I am so glad you can see the humor in dragging me off in the night and throwing me in a filthy wagon. Or did you not do that, either?" she snapped.

He looked up from fiddling with a collection of rocks. He was making a pile, like a small pyramid, with bigger stones at the bottom. "I am to deliver you. That's all."

She knew he wouldn't say where or to whom, having asked more than twice. "What are you doing? With those rocks?" she asked, more out of frustration with his behavior than actual curiosity. After all, how many different things could you do with rocks?

"It will be cold tonight. I'm going to light them," he told her. Unsatisfied with their formation, he carefully rearranged several near the top. As he did, the form collapsed. He again said something that sounded like rush toe or rich tea, and started over.

She barked a laugh. "Light them? Do you think they're made of wood?"

"There isn't much wood where I come from." This time the pile seemed to be the right size and shape, and he sat back on his heels and brushed the dirt off his hands.

"On the other side of The Door," she said, hoping to catch him in a lie. But he was sticking with the demon thing and said, "Well, obviously we don't call it that."

She put her fists on her hips. "What do you call it?"

He looked back at the rocks, did something with his hands, and they began to glow. "It's called Eriis. We call it home."

***

They sat across from each other with their scant dinner of water, cheese and bread. The pile of rocks was warm and nearly bright as a small campfire. She could almost forget her situation—cut off feet and eyeball necklaces and so on—she was so entranced by the sight.

"Is it magic? How does it work? Can I do it?" She leaned forward, seeing how close she could get her fingers to the stones without singeing them.

"It's called magic here, but I can't make a fire with wood so I guess it works both ways." He went back to building tiny sandwiches out of bits of bread and cheese. She watched his profile, he sat half in and half out of the wavering light, which occasionally tricked her eye into thinking he had entirely vanished.

She toyed with a stick, tossing it onto the pile of stones. It instantly turned to ash. "Why is there no wood?" she asked. "Where you're from. You said there wasn't any."

He turned to face her and looked puzzled. "Certainly you know what happened during the War?" She returned his confused stare. "It was only about 20 years ago. I know most of you human persons don't know much about us, but you knew about The Door, you recognized me—don't you know about—"

"I'm sure if there was a war I would have heard of it. Was it a real war? With soldiers and fighting?" What was he talking about? Why make up something so obviously untrue? Probably he was just a red-eyed lunatic hired by her brother after all, despite the magic trick with the rocks. That was a frankly disappointing thought. Kidnapped by a genuine demon was a much better story than kidnapped by an (admittedly) good looking crazy person. She sighed. Not a pirate.

He took a long time to answer. "I don't know why you don't know this. The War was very—"

Suddenly she remembered a story, a legend from the past. She could picture herself part of a semi-circle of children sitting on the floor in a classroom. But it hadn't been a history class. "You don't mean the locking of the Demon Door thing, do you?" she asked. "But that was supposed to have been at least a hundred years ago. And it's just a story, no one even knows if it's really true."

He stared at the stones. She could see the light reflected in his strange eyes. They were nearly the same color. Finally he said, "It happened, all right. A hundred years on this side? And now a story for children?"

"Then tell me the story." She folded her legs under her and settled down to listen. *Convince me.*

He considered it, then nodded. "I'll tell you the way it was told to me. I think parts of it are even true. It began many lifetimes ago, long before the War—"

"The locking of The Door? Before that?"

He nodded. "Yes, because there was no Door," he said. "A long time ago, there was just a place of passage, and anyone could go through. Your world was described to me in sight and color and smell as I see it now. Of course, one reads about these things, but seeing them… The people here, the human persons, they are unexpected, but this place looks as I think it must have always looked."

"Not on your side, I gather," she said. It had never occurred to her that a place could change.

"My home—Eriis—was not always what it is today. But I'm jumping ahead. In those long past times, our people traded knowledge and your people traded goods, back and forth. But it was never a friendly border.

"The humans never trusted their demon neighbors, those elegant and slightly contemptuous distant cousins, not even when you could walk out of Eriis and back home to Mistra in the space of a drawn breath. The demons coveted the ease and bounty of the human's home, and the humans were disinclined to share with the lithe, slender men and women who all looked stamped from the same mold. They could snap their fingers and create a flame! They could stretch their arms and wings would sprout. And worst of all, they could show what they called their True Faces, and become a living weapon. An Order was formed, originally to keep order at the boundary. Would it not be wise, they asked each other, would it not be prudent to put up some sort of barrier? These creatures are decadent savages. They are unlike us. We do not know their minds. Perhaps we ought to build a door.

"And they did. And for many years, it was possible—though only by permission of the Order—to lift the Veil of darkness and confusion that surrounded The Door, open it, and travel to the other side. At this time, Eriis was a great stone city surrounded by fields and ringed by mountains. Three times a year storms would sweep in and water the gardens. The King, though old, was well advised, his son was clever and quick, his daughter was fair, and the people were at peace, enjoying the slow trickle of luxuries from the other side. The few humans that visited were treated as guests. Requests to visit Mistra from Eriis were generally politely declined. Emissaries, ambassadors, and spies traveled back and forth in those days.

"Then," continued Moth, "there was a war. I don't know why the Order attacked us, but when it was over, the gardens and the fields were all gone. So were most of the people and half the buildings. And The Door was sealed. That's when I was born, right after that, and I was… not a joy to my family." She wondered how that could be, and why, and what he had done, but it could wait. "But there were so few of us, all were cared for. It's better now, there are many more of us, and we've learned to do things like keep ourselves cool, because it's gotten very hot there. It doesn't rain anymore, it's really nothing but sand."

"What do you eat?" asked Lelet, thinking of burning orchards.

"Well, we can transform things, and as I said, we have plenty of sand."

She was aghast. "You eat sand?"

"No, by the time we eat it, its bread or meat or water." He paused and looked at the forest around them, cool and quiet. "It was normal to me. It was just what we did." He threw a twig at the stones. "Well, that's not really true. I always wanted something else. It never seemed like enough."

"So our world attacked yours somehow and you've been locked away over there eating sand and broiling for a hundred years." She frowned. "Why don't you hate me? Aren't I your enemy?"

Again, he was slow to answer.

"From what I am told, the human persons, most of them, had never seen one of us and didn't know much about The Door, or that there was a war at all. And that certainly seems to be true. You think we are mythological. You still don't think I'm real, not completely." She shrugged uncomfortably, having been thinking exactly that. "Our enemies were those who built the Weapon." Then he looked to her as if he wanted to say something, but couldn't get the words out. With a dark look, he gave up. Instead of whatever he'd been trying to say, he continued with, "If I was to hate something it would be The Door itself, keeping me—us—locked away, as you said. It's the locked away part, most of all. I knew there was something else. I always knew." He ran his hands through his hair. "I just didn't think it would be so difficult."

She spoke suddenly, half singing.

"*The Quarter Moons for us to see*
Keep us safe and keep us free
So lock your Door and hide the key
Lest evil come to you and me

"That's the song; that's the song we sing at the Quarter Moons party. It's about you, isn't it? I never knew what it meant, I never even thought about it. That was the party I was going to, when you, um, when we met. It's our biggest party of the year. We celebrate our safety. And I think when the song says 'evil', I think I remember when I was little, it originally said, 'lest demons come.'" She looked at him as if seeing him for the first time. "This is a true story, isn't it?" she asked. "You really are from somewhere else and you really are seeing this all for the first time." Despite his strangeness and his odd eyes, she had just in that moment really considered the fact that he might be telling the truth, and this wasn't some elaborate joke. Maybe the trick with the rocks wasn't a trick at all.

"Yes," he nodded, "it's really true. I wanted to come here. I've wanted it for a very long time. But nothing is like I thought it would be.

It's so loud, here. And everything is a different color. It's not that I'm sorry I came, I just...."

"Have you been by yourself the whole time?" She could scarcely think of a worse fate.

Again his mouth worked but nothing came out. He sighed and finally said, "Yes."

"Well," said Lelet, "maybe you just need a tour guide."

He smiled—or at least it might have been a smile. "Are you volunteering? Aren't you worried I'll, um, cut off your feet?"

Lelet had decided the demon wasn't going to hurt her, and after accepting Moth was probably—hopefully—what he claimed to be, she was forced to upgrade the whole thing from elaborate joke to bizarre prank, still most likely engineered by Rane. How he'd procured someone as exotic as a demon was a mystery, but he'd be too proud of himself not to tell her. This was going to be an adventure after all. She should thank her mad brother—an adventure was just what she'd wanted. This was going to be better than pirates.

"No," she said, "I've changed my mind. I think if you were going to do something awful it would have happened already. Now, that... is... a... tree." She spoke the last part very slowly and pointed up.

"Lelet," he said with a genuine smile, "I do know what a tree is."

"Well fine, we'll start tomorrow when it's light with bushes and shrubs—possibly a squirrel." She threw a pebble into the stones, wanting to see if it would catch. It didn't. "Until then, tell me what your home is like. Is it nice? Do you miss it?"

"It's the same." She looked puzzled. "Not the same as here. I mean, it's the same as itself. It's not confusing or sharp or bright. There are so many things to look at here, it's hard to see. I've never seen so many colors. It's so hard to know what to do when everything is always changing."

"Why are you here? If The Door is sealed, how did you even get here?" She watched him struggle to answer.

"It's a long story. There was a book..." he shook his head. "I made a mistake. I thought I was answering someone's call, but someone else was calling me. I got caught on this side. And then I made a promise."

"I am the promise," Lelet said.

He looked at the ground. "I just want to go home. This is not what I thought it was going to be. I don't belong here. I won't hurt you, you know that now? I will keep you safe but I have to deliver you."

There was a pause. "I can try and show you how to light the rocks, if you'd like."

"Oh, fun. It can be my last act before I'm sliced open like a trout. My executioners will laugh and clap."

He stood and walked into the dark forest. She watched him leave.

You didn't have to say that. She was annoyed with herself and could clearly hear May's voice in her head. *You don't always have to be clever. Be nice to him when he comes back.*

That he might not come back never occurred to her.

Just when she was starting to wonder if she ought to call after him, she heard the tinkle of glass, as if someone had thrown a bottle against a tree, and he stepped out of the shadowed woods and rejoined her at the glowing rocks.

"I would like to learn about the rocks," she said politely, "If you think you can teach me. I suppose there's a chance I won't be strung up or filleted."

"Well, fine. How much Basic Principle do you know?" She looked blank. "The Order of Sameness? Transformation? It's the basis for all magic."

"There is no magic here," she said. Then she looked at the warm stones and his eyes, and wondered.

"Everything is the same. That's all you really need to know. These rocks are the same as the trees, and both of them are the same as light and warmth. The magic part is reminding the rocks that they're made of light. I think… I'm sorry, I don't think I'm a very good teacher. I'm not very good at these things to begin with."

"You did this," she said, holding her hands over the warm stones. "You must be good at it."

"Well, anyone can do this. Every child can do this. Making heat is the simplest thing of all, maybe because we already have so much of it. We all have some abilities we just start out with. And some are better than others. I'm really not good at it at all. Actually, a bit the opposite." For a moment he seemed not to remember she was there, he was seeing someone else. He shook his head and the moment passed. He brightened and said, "Like, with your people. Some of you are good at that thing where you move your hands and it makes a nice noise." He made a vague strumming motion. "What is that thing called? That they use?"

"A dog," she said, pressing her lips together.

He frowned. "No, I don't think that's it. It sits on your lap and noise comes out. It's brown."

"I am certain it's a dog," she said.

He looked up at her, his eyes brighter than the glowing stones. "You are making fun of me."

"Your eyes are so beautiful." She gasped and clapped her hand over her mouth.

He walked back into the woods without a word.

May's voice asked, *Was that your idea of being nice? Mocking him? Look where that foolishness got you with Rane. And then giving him a compliment, as if that should make it all better.*

And in her head, she answered. *Oh, come on. That just slipped out, about his eyes. And the other thing—that was just a joke. And the way he acted like he didn't know what music was!*

May said, *What if he is telling the truth? He can't be this exotic creature and also be another version of Billah you just met at a party. Pick one, Lelet. And you might as well give up on flirting. That was tragic.*

She had to admit, this hadn't gone the way conversations with men usually went. In her experience, they flattered and laughed and flirted back, they didn't barely glance at you and then take offense at everything you said. She'd been nice to him, albeit accidentally—why had he looked so hurt?

Eventually she wiped her eyes with the hem of the blanket and lit her last cigarette with a shaking hand. She whispered, "It's a harp, Moth. It's called a harp."

This time he didn't come back until morning.

Chapter 53

Billy Beesley wrung his now shapeless hat between his hands. "I don't know nuffink about no jewels, Guv'nor." He pointed at his sister, who was mirroring his actions with her spotless apron. "I was wif' Betty an' the family all night. You can't pin this one on me."

-The Claiming of the Duke, pg 75
Malloy Dos Capeheart, Little Gorda Press (out of print)

Mistra
100 years after the War of the Door, Mistran calendar
20 years later, Eriisai calendar
Road through the Great Forest

They settled into an uncomfortable silence after a short breakfast.

Lelet handed Moth the last of the bread and took the apple for herself. They split the rind of the cheese.

"There's no more," she said. "What should we do?"

He shrugged. "Get where we are going faster, would be a suggestion." He was determined to not engage in any more witless chatter with her. Dogs, eyes: maybe the horrible child was right about her sister. In fact, maybe all the humans were petty and mean. Even May had said something insulting. He had yet to meet one that wasn't deficient in some way.

Quietly (for once) she did things with the leather horse straps and the cart, and handed him the leads. Instead of climbing into the back, she sat up front, next to him. She looked away into the forest pretending to watch the birds. Other than the horse itself, they saw nothing bigger than a squirrel. And why couldn't he stop looking at her? The back of her neck was long and very pretty, so what? The back of the horse was also pretty. In a different way. He trained his eyes on the animal's rump.

Finally she said, "Harps." What was she going on about now? Well, it didn't matter. He wasn't going to be drawn into some new and ultimately insulting conversation. She could just sit there.

"And what are harps?" he asked. *I must have lost my wits along with my real name.*

"What we were talking about. Last night. The people who make the nice noise… Well, that noise is called music. And the things you were describing are harps. They do make a very nice noise, you're right. Um, so you liked the music?" She had turned to face him. Her eyes were grey, not properly red, but other than that *She looks like me. In a way. Is that what I look like?* It made him feel very strange, like he was shifting inside, like he was gazing into a warped mirror, and he looked away.

He said, "We don't have anything like that back home. The closest thing I can think of is the noise a sandstorm makes when it moves through the city. It almost sounds as if it's alive. It can be beautiful—but it's wild. It belongs to itself. This… music?" She nodded. "Music. It belongs to the people making it."

She watched him intently. "Not the people listening? Or the person who wrote it?"

"No. The ones who create the sounds are the ones who control it." He had been thinking a lot recently about having—and losing—control.

"I never thought of music like that before," she said. "I guess I thought it was sort of there for the taking."

"Well," he said, "it's nice that you have that luxury. Things 'just sort of there' for you to take." When she didn't answer, he was at first satisfied that he'd made a point. For a moment it was wonderfully quiet. Then he heard a tiny sniffle.

"Oh, *rushta*, please don't do that. I'm sorry. I shouldn't comment, I don't know what your life is like. Really, please stop that."

She turned her back and used the sleeve of her dress to dab her eyes. "I don't know why you're being so awful. I tried to apologize. After all, I'm the one who had to sleep in the woods last night. By myself! With the… bears." She turned to face him again. Tears glittered in her lashes. "I promise I won't make any more comments about your eyes or any other part of you being attractive."

I used to be able to have a conversation without feeling like I was falling down a hill, he thought. "I won't leave you alone with the bears," he promised. "I'll take care of you until we get… where we are going." He decided to abandon his efforts to emulate the Duke, since she responded not with wide-eyed admiration or even respectful silence, but something closer to contempt. Maybe arrogance wasn't as easy to slip into as a pair of boots. He was beginning to wonder what else his book had gotten wrong.

She was looking over his shoulder, her tears and their argument forgotten. "Stop the cart," she said. "And look at that. Oh, let me." She took the leads and they pulled to a halt at the foot of a dirt road that ran a quarter mile or so up to a little house. Plowed fields rose into the low hills behind it. It was the first intact structure they'd seen. She wondered why anyone would put their house in such an isolated place.

"I don't think anyone's home," she said. "There are no animals about, and there's no smoke from the chimney. Want to go look at it?"

"Absolutely not." She jumped down, yipping as she tried to avoid stepping on sharp stones, and set off up the road.

Rushta. Again. Where's my hat?

"What if the horse wanders off?" he called in what he hoped was something like a whisper.

She loud-whispered back over her shoulder. "Tie it to a tree, of course. And keep your voice down! We have the element of surprise! And get the bag out of the back!"

"Wait!" He hurried after her.

"Ow—what?" She stood on one foot, using his arm to balance, as she brushed pebbles out from between her toes.

"Um, are you trying to escape?" He handed her the bag.

She laughed. "No, I am not out to ruin your and Rane's grand plan. You'd get into a world of trouble if I ran off, I bet." He agreed that would be the case. "I don't want to escape. I want lunch." She eyed the property. "Come on, let's go around the side and sneak up. The grass is better to walk on, anyway."

He decided he liked adventurous Lelet better than sarcastic, or—Light and Wind forbid—crying Lelet, so he followed her off the road to a cluster of gnarled old trees and shaggy bushes. They could see into one large main room. The windows were small and the glass was hazy but it appeared she was right, there was no one home.

"I'm going first," he told her. "No, there is no argument. Stay here. If there's really no one there, you can burgle to your heart's content." She grudgingly agreed and he set off across the lawn, feeling very exposed. When he reached the rear of the house, he looked back.

"Watch this," he said, and stepping onto the shadowed back porch, disappeared. He was gratified to hear her gasp and see the delight on her face. Hanging on a hook from the rafters was some sort of small animal, skinned and on a stick, probably waiting for the evening's stew. *Not too different from taking shoes and hairbrushes*. He grabbed it and stepped into the sunlight, watching her face as he reappeared. He made his way back to where she still knelt in the bushes.

"Can we eat this, do you think?" he asked, trying to sound casual.

"You vanished! That was brilliant! How does it work?"

"I can use shadows to be invisible. I told you, my people have different abilities, and even then some are much more gifted than others. My best friend, he has the real talent. He's a Mage now, and they only take the smartest." At her confused look, he added, "Mages work the talents of the word. That did not clear anything up. Sorry. Let's just say he's really clever. And my other… someone else I know, you should see him fly. He's so good, people line up to see his matches. And then another friend, well, she can barely lift herself across the street. But she can change her face, it's amazing to see. Me, well, you've seen just about everything I can do."

He knew she probably had no idea what he was talking about, but it felt good to talk about his friends. It felt good to talk to anyone at all. And she did catch one thing. "Wait, fly? Your friends have wings? How gorgeous!"

"No, you can't see them most of the time. They just sort of jump straight up, and their wings open. And you fly away. But I don't have wings. But my friend—the talented one—he doesn't need wings anyway. He can just appear anywhere he likes. He'd have just popped himself into the house and out again while we were standing here talking. And he'd have made friends with the neighbors and gotten us all invited to dinner, which he would have cooked himself."

"You miss him."

"I miss a lot of things," he agreed. She nodded and played with the leather thong holding the bag shut.

"I don't know how Rane's keeping you here or what sort of bargain you've made, but I won't keep you from going home, if that's what you want to do." Before he could respond, (and how could he respond? She had so many things right, and so many things wrong) she set off for the front of the little house. "I can't vanish, so I hope no one's here!"

He watched her rooting around in a box on the porch and stuffing things in the bag. He hoped she found something good, maybe baby lamb chops? Then she did vanish—the front door was open. He began to feel uncomfortable and finally decided to get her out of there when something moved in the forest behind him. It wasn't a squirrel. A bear? He figured it was a good time to get back on the road and followed her to the front door. He leaned in and was about to hiss for her to follow him back to the cart, but almost crashed into her on her way out.

He didn't want to scare her so he didn't run back to the cart, but didn't linger at the little house, either. She hurried to match his long strides, but once on the stone path, she told him to slow down because her feet were being massacred. He picked her up and carried her back to the cart. She closed her eyes and said she was pretending she was flying.

"I heard something," he told her when they got the horse moving again. "In the woods."

"You are a very nervous person—I mean demon. Are all of you so jumpy?"

"I told you not an hour ago I would protect you. When something jumps out of the trees and eats you, it means I am not protecting you."

She frowned. "I have to tell you something. The house—it was a mess. Someone left in a hurry. Or they just threw everything on the floor." Then she shrugged. "But no one was there, and now we aren't there." She grinned at him. "That was so exciting! You disappeared and I flew—sort of—and we broke into a house! And we got away clean!"

"Technically, we just walked in, since it was open. That is to say, you did. I believe I waited outside. They can't pin this one on me."

"Here." She handed him a pastry, potatoes mashed with carrots and ground meat baked into a sweet crust, that she'd taken from the house. "Now you're a co-conspirator. Welcome to your life of crime."

Chapter 54

Eriis City
20 years after the War of the Door, Eriisai calendar
100 years later, Mistran calendar
Outside the Arch

When Hellne appeared in Diia's small walled courtyard, she found her relaxing with two visiting clan sisters and their children, enjoying the cooling evening. The young ones screamed and ran in the house.

"They're scared of you," Diia joked, "you should visit more often." She handed Hellne a cup of water, which they passed quickly back and forth.

"I apologize for the intrusion. I need your help." They both noted the water in the cup, which shook and quaked in the Queen's hand. "Something has happened. I need your strongest clan sibs. Ones who can block and guard. I need them in the palace, outside Rhuun's room."

"Whatever you need, I'll contact them at once." The gate slammed as one of her sisters was already on her way down the alley.

Hellne set the cup down and took Diia's hands in her own. "I am in your debt." She paused. "Before the war, I was a very foolish girl. I did some things I can't even regret, because the things—the thing I did gave me my son. But I thought I could keep it a secret. I was wrong."

Instead of the expected frown or shake of her head, Diia nodded sympathetically. "His father, he must have brought you much pleasure, before he went back through The Door."

Hellne stared past her. "I seem to recall that he did. But do you know, I can barely remember his face? But it's all come out. The Mages want Rhuun for whatever awful blood games they play. I think… I think he's safe. I sent him after his father. He may be there now. He may be in the Veil. He may never come home. But if he does, we must make sure he comes home to us, to me, and not to the knife."

"So you want my clan brothers and sisters to guard his door? The Mages have come up into the light—people must hear about this." Diia's second sister slipped out the gate. "The Mages out of their Raasth, and a half human prince." She shook her head. "Jaa was right about that boy. Ah, but everyone had something to say, back then."

"Maybe I should have paid more attention." Hellne thought she'd have time for regret, but it would have to wait.

Diia stroked the Queen's hand soothingly. "The young people, they don't remember what the humans looked like, most of them never saw one. There are not so many of us left from the time before the Weapon, but I saw plenty of those people with my own eyes, and your boy, well, he wears a human face." She paused. "What people said… they are still saying."

"Yes, I can't stop Court gossip any more than I can shut off the wind. 'Ugly, crippled.' I know."

"This is not what I mean. I mean our people. Those who thought he would bring back the rain. That he is different and special. They still think so."

I can use this, Hellne thought at once, and flushed with shame.

Diia said, "Things will be changing, I think. And we will help you now."

"Your people helped guard the way when he came into this world. I would trust no others."

"What about you?" asked Diia. "The Mages will try and take the Seat away from you. And that Counselor friend of yours…."

"Is no friend. I see his hand behind the Mages. If it comes to it, may I count on your clan for one more favor?"

"The Edge is a big place. It would be hard to find one woman in all that sand." Diia rose to her feet. "Now, let us decide what to pack, and what to leave behind for when we are ready. When the day comes, we will want to leave behind only our footprints in the dust."

***

It was late and Hellne was exhausted by the time she shimmered back to her own quarters. She threw her heavy brocaded gown on the floor and poured herself some water. She hadn't found Ilaan, and that was a problem. Had he gone with Rhuun into the Veil? Or had neither of them managed to escape? They both could be out on the sand right now. She threw back the silk drape which opened onto her courtyard to let some air in, and looked out at the same low clouds she'd watched every night since the Weapon.

They're turning him into something he's not, those people in the Quarter. But if they think he'll lead them to the rain, I can use them to hold the Seat. She sighed. *For how long? And to what end?*

For the first time, she tried to picture Rhuun on the Seat. People would be looking at him all day long, staring. He'd hate that.

Well, he ought to be used to it be now. And he's not lacking in wits, certainly, at least when he's not in the bottle.

She heard a noise, a rustle and soft thump from the courtyard. Had Yuenne already sent someone after her in the night? They'd find her ready.

She decided not to shimmer the few feet into the open, it left her vulnerable for the second it took to reform. She slipped through the open door and went towards the sound, against the far wall and behind a big stone urn which had once held a water garden. A familiar figure stepped into the low light.

"Ilaan, thank Light and Wind. Tell me it worked."

Ilaan was pale and his handsome white tunic was smeared and grimed, but he straightened and said, "It was as successful as it could be. He's gone. To where and what fate, I don't know. But he's gone."

For the first time since the party, she took a deep breath. "Thank you." He'd been sitting on a box and she saw several other bundles against the stone wall. "What's this?"

"After he went through, I went back home. It was an uproar. My father was gone, and so were the Mages."

"I know, I was with them."

He frowned. "Then you know my father was—"

"Working with them. Yes. For as long as you and I, it would appear." She thought of Yuenne's tight little smile. "He was trying to get the proof he lacked about Rhuun for the Mages. I know he's always suspected. But I wonder what he got in return? He didn't know what you were up to, though, did he?"

"He knows now." Ilaan ran his hands through his long, dusty hair. *He picked that up from Rhuun*, she thought, and her heart twisted. He was gone, really gone. "I took as many of my books, and some other things; I just grabbed whatever I could. My mother didn't think it was wise for me to wait and see my father. She said she'd try and sort it out. I didn't know where else to go." He looked near tears. "Why didn't you tell him what he was? Why did we have to find out like this?"

"I had my reasons. I was trying to keep him safe."

"From the Mages. Well, that one is on me." He barked a laugh, "I let it out of the bag, didn't I?" His fists clenched and unclenched. "You should have told me; together we would have had a chance to protect him. Why didn't you tell me? Did you think I'd love him less?"

"Yes," she answered. "Because I loved him less." She took in the shock on his face, the distaste. *I earned that*, she thought. "It’s not a pretty thing, is it? But there it is. You saw your friend. I saw every mistake I ever made. I saw a weapon."

"A weapon? You looked at Rhuun and saw a weapon? Turned against whom?"

"Do you know what the people in the Old City are saying? They think he's going to lead them one day. He has a destiny, it is said." She paused. *Don't say any more,* she thought. *Let him be clever.*

"Everyone has a destiny, Hellne. Even Rhuun. What if they're right? That didn't occur to you. He's just a weapon, your weapon. Tell me, once your weapon is spent, who sits on the High Seat after you?"

"There was a time I thought it might be you," she said.

"Oh, you are good. Very good." He glared at her. "A few drops of water in my path, that's all it ever takes. You still think I'm your boy? You think I'll just go live down there and make sure all the right things are said? What should we call him? The Chosen One, that's a bit of a cliché, don't you think? *Rushta*, you already have this figured out, don't you?"

"Do you really want to stay here? You can't go home, Yuenne has some sand set aside for your mouth. I suppose you can throw yourself on the mercy of the Zaal…" *I do have this figured out*, she thought. *And I am not ashamed.*

"There are conditions," he said. She nodded. "I want the whole story. Where that stupid book came from. What really happened?"

"The author was Rhuun's father," she said. "A human from a religious order who had a hand in the Weapon."

Ilaan was horrified. "But you—that's where we sent him. He's gone to look for that man. The human—does he know he has a son?"

"No." She smiled. "Imagine his surprise when he finds out. I've been waiting for that meeting for a long time. I wish I could be there for it."

"That man. He's the target." He looked sick. "That was what you wanted, for Rhuun to bring the man back here, so you *could* be there for it."

"Yes, I planned on making sure he lived long enough to answer a few questions. Something for the Mages, and something for me. But that little scrap of paper at your ceremony, well, that put a hole in my plan, didn't it? They'll take anything with human blood in it, bad luck for Rhuun. Oh, don't give me that face. I know I'm not living up to your high standards of integrity, but just exactly how many times did you say 'no' to anything I asked of you? You were so proud of yourself, running my errands. You might not have had the whole picture, but you were in it, Ilaan. I wasn't the only one who lied."

Ilaan gathered his bags and bundles around him. "I'm leaving. I'm going down to the Old City. But I'm not doing it for you. Don't send for me again." With a shimmer, he was gone.

She sighed deeply and went back inside. She poured herself a full glass of *sarave*.

Well, that's done. He's his own man now, and he'll do whatever he can for Rhuun down in the city. Untied from me, they will believe what he says. He'll be the Prince's lifelong friend and companion, not the Queen's errand boy. She took a sip. *I will miss him.* She looked around her high ceilinged room, the colored tile inlay on the floor, tan and white against the black stone, her closets set aside for gowns and silks, her airy and comfortable dry room, her wide bed. *I'll miss this place too, and soon.*

Chapter 55

The Duke woke from the same nightmare as always—burning and falling.
The girl—Gwenyth—was holding his hand. He was gripping it hard enough to hurt, but she made no mention.
"You cried out, my Lord! I was afraid for you."

-The Claiming of the Duke, pg 125
Malloy Dos Capeheart, Little Gorda Press (out of print)

Mistra
100 years after the War of the Door, Mistran calendar
20 years later, Eriisai calendar
Road through the Great Forest

"I think it's going to rain." Lelet shaded her eyes at the clouds that were both bright and leaden.

"Hmm. Rain. Right." Moth shook his head.

"What, do you think I'm joking? This moving palace of yours doesn't have a roof. I saw another house, we passed it a while ago. Well, not much of a house. It looked sort of collapsed. Probably there was no one there. I think it burned down, maybe? But we should definitely turn around and go there. Right away."

He glanced at her. "We should? Really?"

"Moth. I seriously felt a drop. Please? I am not teasing you or making fun in any way. I don't want to get wet, it'll be too cold." Why was he being difficult? They had done crimes together—didn't that count for anything?

He hauled on the reins until the horse stopped. They sat for a moment. Finally he sighed and asked, "How do you turn this thing around?"

It turned out to be not easy and not quick. The horse seemed prepared to stand motionless in the road until the moons fell in the sea until Lelet took the leads and got them pointed in the right direction.

There was barely enough roof left of the one room stone structure for it to be rightfully called a building at all. One entire side had caved in or fallen away, and she drove the horse inside, cart and all. It looked as if the kurdza vines were all that was holding it together. But it had a flat stone floor and there weren't too many places for vermin to come out and attack her while her back was turned. It was her new favorite place.

She spread her increasingly dirty blanket on the floor and sat, trying not to touch anything. The rough stones that still showed white plaster in places were too damp to lean against, and anything resembling furniture was long gone. There were scorch marks on the floor and the walls. It appeared they weren't the first to shelter here. She hoped they wouldn't have company today.

Why wouldn't you want that? she wondered. *Don't you want a band of human persons to come along and rescue you? What if the kindly farmer had been home in that house this morning?* She eyed Moth, who was contemplating tying the ends of the horse's reins to something—he apparently hadn't decided to what, how, or if it was even necessary. He looked between the leads in his hands and the horse, as if waiting for the animal to give him some instruction. She wasn't certain she needed rescuing. In fact, he was a terrible villain. He acted as if he had never met a woman before (maybe he hadn't), or as if he were afraid of her, which, if her novels were to serve as a clue, was not the usual order of things in a proper kidnapping.

If he was warty or fat or had bad teeth, would I have tried to run away? Or if he seemed violent? Shoes or no shoes, I'm not sitting around waiting to be violated. She wondered what was going on under his shirt. When he'd picked her up, he'd felt like a warm stone wall. *Oh, that's nice work, Lel. Imagine yourself in a little scenario with your kidnapper. Like that's not written in a textbook at a university somewhere.*

But, seriously, look at him.

After a long moment, *Okay, if he doesn't stop messing with those reins one of us will die here today.*

She got up and took the lead out of his hands and looped it loosely around a half burnt beam, all that remained of the missing wall.

"Thank you," he said, although he didn't sound particularly grateful. They sat on their respective blankets (he had thrown his down in a spot where there was no roof, proving that demons were capable of spite) and looked at the darkening sky. There was a low growl of thunder.

"Did you hear that? What was that?" He looked quite alarmed.

"It's just thunder. I believe I mentioned rain. You'll want to move over here if you can stand the proximity. I couldn't provide anything larger than birds and stolen lunch for the Grand Tour today, but it looks like we'll have our weather for you to observe in a minute."

With a great show of scowling and huffing, he moved next to her under the shelter of the roof. As usual, he sat half-turned away, so, she gathered, he didn't have to look at her.

The rain came in a torrent almost at once, and she was glad to be out of it. It was nearly the end of the long dry summer months and this storm looked to want to make up for it. She went and stood at the ragged remains of a window, watching the rain sheeting down, and turned back with a smile.

"The flowers will thank—"

He was crouching on the floor with his hands clapped over his ears saying something she couldn't make out, the rain and thunder were making too much noise.

Now what?

Unsure of what to do, she leaned down next to him.

"Loud! It's so loud!" he said.

"It's just rain. It's loud but it's just… rain." She awkwardly patted his shoulder. "Is it hurting you? Are you hurt?" He flinched at the thunder, or perhaps at her touch.

As a tiny child, Lelet had decided she was afraid of the dog next door. Her family wasn't even allowed to talk about dogs while Lelet was in the room without her having a screaming, crying fit. The whole thing lasted less than a year, and then one day the dog was just a dog again. May had always made her feel like there was a guardian at her door keeping the awful beast away. Even though May knew the dog was just a dog and didn't really have knives and forks in its mouth, she understood the fear was real enough.

Lelet gently stroked the demon's hair. "Moth, listen to me. It's fine. I promise." His hair was as soft as a kittens—not like any human hair she'd ever felt. "It won't hurt you. It's just a lot of noise."

He slowly lowered his hands and sat up. There was another roar of thunder and he ducked as if it was coming at his head.

"I know what it is. I'm fine." *Are you, now*? She wondered. He looked past her, out the door at one more new thing.

"I'm sorry if I startled you," he continued. He stood up a bit too quickly, looking embarrassed. "I've never… we don't have rain. I didn't know what it was. I mean, I know what it is, I've read about it. But so much noise…" He went to look out what had once been a door. "Will it last a long time?"

"I think it might. I'm glad you brought us here."

He turned to face her. "I didn't believe you," he said. "I thought you just wanted to make me go in circles. I'm sorry."

She nodded. He sat next to her and they watched as the rain beat down the leaves. The thunder got further away.

"When we were talking last night," she said, "you told me you were looking for someone. And something about a book? Will you tell me about that?"

He got the tense look on his face she was starting to recognize, and as she had seen before, opened his mouth to speak. As before, he couldn't bring himself to say whatever was on his mind. He finally sighed and said, "I had a book, growing up. It was about a human man and his friends. It made me want to come here. It was written by a man named Malloy Dos Capeheart. Do you know that name?"

She was frowning as she struggled to place it. Who had just been talking about him? "It sounds really familiar… I think it must be from a long time ago, though. What was the book called?"

"*The Claiming of the Duke*," he said. "It is a great book."

Do not laugh, do not laugh, do not laugh, she warned herself. "I, ah, I actually know that book. My mother had it, I think."

He looked as if he might faint. "Can you tell me what happens at the end? My copy had pages missing. The end, the whole last part is missing. It's very important. Please."

"Well," she said, "let me see if I remember. Um, the evil one—Phillip something?"

"Sir Edward? I think you mean Edward." He was wide-eyed.

"He dies, for real. He faked it the first time, so he could steal the jewels that Cybelle wanted to give that silly sap Gwyneth."

"Wait. What? You must have the wrong book after all." Now he looked offended. "Gwyneth was—"

"No," she continued, "That's the book. My girlfriends and I stole it from my mother and passed it around. It ends with a wedding, of course, all those books do. I remember loving Cybelle, she was a better choice for that Duke character, not that he was any prize. Gwyneth, she was like a wet rag. Couldn't stand her." Moth looked as if she'd insulted his sister. Or his girlfriend. "You liked her, of course." She shook her head. "Typical. Not a thought in her head and a big pair of heaving bosoms."

He turned a bit pink, and avoided looking at Lelet. He said, "Gwyneth, if I stop and think about it, she's the reason I'm here. She was a lovely girl and not—a sap? Not a sap. Tell me about the end. Please."

"Well, the Duke finally shows up—I'm sorry, I can't remember why he was late to the wedding, and of course your girl Gwyn is all sobbing into her lace, no self-esteem on that one, she couldn't imagine he was just running late after all the other nonsense they put each other through. Finally he rides up and leaps off the horse—I remember that part! It was very romantic. He lifts her to her feet and in front of all their friends—well, his friends, really—in front of the whole town and with the crashing sea as the backdrop, they become man and wife. And that's the end."

"That's all?" He looked disappointed. "They don't… that's really the end?"

"What did you think was going to happen? This book is way older than we are. It's bound to be old fashioned." A light went on in her head. "That's the reason. That's why you say such strange things. You called me a wench!" Now she did laugh. "Just like that idiotic Duke! Oh no, did you think we were like those people? In that old book?" He was getting another look she recognized, the one before he marched off. She swallowed her laughter and said, "And you came here by yourself. There was no way to know what we would be like, other than what you read. I hope it hasn't been too disappointing."

"This world has been a series of surprises," he said quietly. "Not one thing is what I expected." He looked at her again. "But not all disappointing, no." He took a breath and said, "Well, what about the author? I… I would very much like to speak with him. It's extremely important."

"I suppose he *might* still be alive. I'm sorry, it's a really old book." She watched his face, he looked like a man who'd just burnt his last match. She wondered what was really going on. Again she found herself filled with the desire to touch him. *Not a very Gwyneth thing to do*, she decided.

The rain continued. He'd stopped flinching every time there was thunder, but he still looked so sad. Finally she came up with something she thought might cheer him up.

"You know, you could go outside if you wanted to. There's no reason not to. You'd get soaked but you'd have a story to tell your friend back home—the smart one—how you did something he'll never get to do."

The look on his face made her feel like she'd won a prize. He clearly thought this was the best idea anyone had ever had. He stepped through the door, dead authors and old books forgotten. He was soaked in an instant. She watched as he turned his hands and face to the storm.

And that, thought Lelet, *is something my friends won't ever get to see. I know I should be scared, I don't know what's going to happen next, but Rane, I'll have to thank you for sending this extremely strange, interesting and wet person—demon—whatever—my way.*

***

After a while he'd had enough and as he walked back through the doorway, a cloud of steam engulfed him. When it had cleared, he was almost completely dry. He sat down next to her with a thud.

"That was amazing. I am never going back to Eriis," he said.

She laughed and patted his cheek. "Welcome to Mistra, sweetie." She pointed at his face. "And you're getting a little scratchy."

He rubbed his chin. "Why does this keep happening?" he muttered.

"Um, because you're alive? You should keep it, it suits you."

"Hmm, yes. I suppose it covers up some of the ugly." He turned away from her.

"Ha! Right. Ugly. Sure. You're prettier than me," she said with a laugh.

He rose and walked to the door and it took her a moment to realize he wasn't amused and he hadn't been kidding.

Oh, for the love of—

She joined him at the place where the door had once been. "Moth, you are worse than my sister on her monthlies. You absolutely cannot keep walking off when something offends you." He shook her hand off his arm. He was positively vibrating with—what? "What did I say," she asked, "this time?"

"I know what I look like," he answered. She could barely hear him over the rain. "I've been reminded every day of my life. I am deformed. I am an aberration. A mistake."

She tried to pull out all her hair for a second, then said, "I am not making fun of you. I don't know why anyone would tell you those horrible things. I don't know what other demons look like, but I do know what other human persons look like, and you look perfectly fine to me."

"All the same," he said. "That's how we look. All slight and quick and narrow. All small. All the same, except for me."

"All your people look the same? That sounds—no offense—kind of boring."

He gave up his spot at the doorway and sat back down. He looked tired. "We value uniformity. And it's not boring, it reassuring. At first I couldn't tell you humans apart, I didn't know what part of you to look at." He paused. "You think I look normal?"

And then there was the time I had to convince a demon he was pretty. She took a breath. Someone, somewhere had taken this poor creature apart. *Why?* She realized she was worried about sending him back to wherever he came from. She said, "Let me ask you a question. You don't think I'm ugly, do you?"

"No, that is not what immediately springs to mind."

"Yes, well, thank you. But I don't look like everyone back home on… ahh…."

"Eriis," he reminded her.

"I don't look like all your friends back on Eriis, do I?"

He admitted that she did not.

"So isn't it possible for you also?"

"No."

She gritted her teeth. He'd made it clear that if she told him he had the kind of beauty that stopped her breath in her throat and made her foggy in her wits, he'd think she was lying. And anyway, he hadn't done or said anything that made her think he was even interested in her. The only thing he'd called her was a 'cave lizard.'

She thought again of his friend, his good friend who was so clever and handsome and capable. Maybe the kind of friend who liked to remind you that you didn't quite measure up? That you were lucky they were around? She'd had her share of friends like that. She looked at the way he sat, his long legs folded under him and turned mostly away from her. He sat like that all the time, she realized. Not so he wouldn't have to look at her, as she had originally suspected. He sat like that so she wouldn't have to look at him. *To spare me. What good manners. If he's so ugly, what in the world do the rest of them look like*? She frowned. Something back on Eriis wasn't adding up, beginning with the reason he'd given for coming here in the first place. You go to see an author read at a bookshop in your neighborhood, you don't leave your home and risk your life.

The book thing, that's a lie, or at least partly a lie. He says he has no magic, and he obviously does. He thinks he's some sort of hideous beast, and well, I have eyes. She knew she'd get the story out of him eventually. It was just another part of the adventure.

For the moment, it was all she could do not to cross the space between them and see again if his hair was really so soft, and if his mouth was soft, and if his body was hard. She gave her head a shake to clear it. No, if she were to follow her instincts and do the kind of convincing that never failed to work on any other man—any human man—he'd take it for a joke or worse, pity. Perhaps start with 'normal' and work up? She figured it was worth a try. She took a deep breath.

"Okay. You may be a very unattractive demon, since you are not—what did you say? Small? Slight? But as a human person you look completely normal. Trust me, on a crowded street no one would even look at you. It'd be like you were invisible." *That is the biggest lie I've told today*, she thought.

He frowned. She could see she'd made an impression.

"I am going to go out and be in the rain for a while. I am not marching off and I do not have my monthlies."

When she was done laughing she thought, *I am either going to have to kill him or introduce him to the family. One or the other. I guess I'll just wait and see.*

Chapter 56

Gwenyth could hear her heart hammering in her breast.
She could feel the heat of the Duke's body, now pressed against
<page missing>

-The Claiming of the Duke, pg 210 (fragment)
Malloy Dos Capeheart, Little Gorda Press (out of print)

Mistra
100 years after the War of the Door, Mistran calendar
20 years later, Eriisai calendar
Road through the Great Forest

"Does it seem colder to you?" She pulled the coarse blanket closer. "It feels colder to me." After the sun came back out they'd moved on for another hour or so, but it was getting dark earlier. They had decided to stop for the evening and she stood looking around the little glade.

"No, not really," he answered. "I think my people are set a little warmer than yours."

Then why bother with a fire at all? she was about to snap. Then she realized. *For me.*

"Well, I'm tired of glowing rocks. I think I'll show you how to make a fire. I don't know how to cook rabbit *a la* rock." She picked up a handful of twigs. "Bring me a bunch of these, and then a bunch of bigger ones. Brown ones, not green. And some leaves. Try to get dry ones."

"How do you know how to do this? Isn't it a farm thing? Or a servant thing?"

She looked at him curiously. "A servant thing? Making a fire? Did you get that idea from your book?" She supposed he had—the Duke always had a battalion of valets, chefs, butlers and maids, most nameless, lighting fires and gas lamps and cigars for him. "No, when we were children we would make a camp out on the back lawn. May and Rane, and even Scilla when she was old enough. Pol was already too much of a grownup and he was always off balancing the books or something. But the rest of us would be out there all night. We'd bring out food and hot drinks and pretend we were lost in the Great Old

Forest. And we took turns and had contests to see who could build the best fire; we took great pride in them. Rane usually won, he had the best eye for balance back then. It was such fun! We called it Running Away from the Dem…" She turned pink and tossed her branch on the ground. "I can't ever be kind to you, it seems."

"That game sounds nice," he said slowly. "Your family sounds nice."

"Well, what sort of things did you play, growing up?" she asked. "Do you have many brothers and sisters?"

"No," he answered.

"No, you don't have a lot of siblings, or no, you didn't play games like that?" It was like unknotting a necklace, with this one.

"No to both, actually. We are small and then we are expected to be what we are. Not so many games like that."

She chewed her fingernail for a moment and came to a decision. "I'm going to do something, and I don't want you to get angry or upset. Just stand still."

As she approached him, she could see the effort it took for him not to draw back. She reached up and put her arms around his neck, and after a moment she felt the tension drain from his shoulders. He closed his eyes and rested his cheek against her smooth, cool hair. She heard him sigh softly as he leaned against her.

"Now," she said, stepping back, "let's build a fire."

***

Hours later, the moons were up, and—as Lelet had predicted—it had gotten quite cold. Her fire had come together nicely, even if the rabbit had been burned in places and almost raw in others. He was fascinated by her pack of matches, and remarked, "My whole life could have been different if I'd had these." But as usual he wouldn't explain what he meant.

She was making a mental checklist called Things They Don't Have On Eriis:

Matches
Rain/water
Music
HORSES
~~*Humor*~~

They ate the raw/burned rabbit with stolen bread and another pastry and called it "perfect, lovely, just fine." She figured that while she would have preferred their meal prepared braised with a nice mustard sauce, it was probably still a lot better than sand. She reached into the leather bag. "Look what else I got today," she said gleefully. She held out a pair of worn slippers. They were a faded blue and brown fabric, padded on top and looked only slightly too big. "They were on the porch. I *stole* them."

"Now you can run away," he observed.

She shrugged. "Maybe in the morning. Too cold for a proper escape right now. And look at this." She held out something lumpy and green. "While you were being invisible at the house, I got this off the tree."

"Too bad," he said. "You couldn't find any good ones?"

Her eyes narrowed and she tossed the ugly fruit back and forth between her hands. "Moth, what do you think this is?"

"It's an apple," he answered, frowning uncertainly. "But it's gone bad. It's the wrong color and the wrong shape." She grinned and he shrugged. "Not an apple, then."

She held her hand out. "Try it."

"This isn't going to turn out to be another dog incident, is it?" he asked suspiciously.

She laughed and bit into the fruit herself. Then she held it out again. He took her by the wrist and took a bite of the fruit as she held it.

He looked up at her, astonished. "You have to tell me what this is." Without thinking, he took another bite, licking the juice off her fingers. Instantly he went scarlet and stammered, "Please forgive me, I don't know why I… That was… um, what is that?"

She cleared her throat and said, "This is called a pear. Please, take the rest of it." She carefully set it in front of him.

He forced himself to finish it slowly. "Rain," he said. "Music—harps?" She nodded. "Pears. I like it here."

He's making his own list. I wonder if he knows about chocolate, she thought. *He'll never leave.*

***

He watched her trying to get comfortable in her oversized blanket. Finally he said, "I'm going to do something and I don't want you to get angry."

She laughed. "I promise I will not get angry." He carried his own blanket to her side and stretched himself out a decent foot or so away from her. Her eyes widened. "Did you just do that? Make it warmer?" He nodded. "Thank you." She reached out and pulled on his shoulder until he was facing her. "You know, I'll probably feel differently tomorrow, but right now? I'm not sorry."

"What could you possibly have to be sorry for?" he wondered.

"I'm not sorry that I'm here. Nothing like this has ever happened to me before." She leaned on her elbow and nodded. "Magic. Stealing. Going invisible. It's all very exciting."

The smile fled his eyes. "I am an adventure to you."

"Oh no! No, this—" she indicated the fire, the horse and the cart, the moons, "this is an adventure. You? You are… I'm not sure what you are. Maybe I'll find out tomorrow." She leaned forward and kissed him lightly. "Good night." Then she turned back to the fire and pulled the blanket up so only a few pale curls were showing.

Chapter 57

The Duke stood on the cliffs as the sea below him boomed and called. The huge dark bulk of Gardenhour rose at his back, at once a blessing of family and security, and a prison and curse of loneliness and lies. Somewhere in the great manor the girl lay sleeping. "Another beating heart," the Duke pondered. "Think on that." He turned away from the sea. A single candle burned in an upper window.

-The Claiming of the Duke, pg 168
Malloy Dos Capeheart, Little Gorda Press (out of print)

Mistra
100 years after the War of the Door, Mistran calendar
20 years later, Eriisai calendar
Road through the Great Forest

Licking her fingers? Have you gone simple in your wits? Moth tried to tear his eyes from the silhouette of Lelet as she relaxed into sleep. *She should have slapped you, or gotten up and left.* But she didn't do those things. She didn't even seem upset.

As he did every evening, he performed what he thought of as his exercise in futility. He tried to say 'sister' or 'Scilla' or 'Guardhouse' or 'it's all the fault of your sister Scilla at the Guardhouse'. But even when he could convince his jaw to move, nothing came out of his mouth, not even a whisper.

She wanted to know about his family. The horrible child has asked him as well. There wasn't any reason not to tell Lelet, at least, about his life on Eriis, other than that he didn't want to. How could he explain the Court, the play-yard—his Mother, by Light and Wind? What would she think of him then? Not even a proper demon, and never anything but a target.

He leaned back and watched the moons and the stars wheel through the trees and thought about the taste of pear on his lips.

Moth slept, and as he so often did he visited his nursery crèche in his dreams. He felt the same old mixture of humiliation and anger with a deep desire to protect the small demon he'd once been. The dream took him to his clan cousin's daily games, where every day was the same. In his dreams, he never got any older, never learned about reaching up, never grabbed a wing. Sometimes he was banished to the Crosswinds. Sometimes he was caught in a firewhirl.

Now his mother was leaning down and saying, "You're special. You're different. You'll see. It's like a game." He enthusiastically told her circle of friends at Court that he was "different, special" until she slapped him and told him to never say anything like that ever again. He waited for his magic to manifest. It never did. He waited to grow his wings, so he could fly away. That never happened either. And then he found out about his blood—he was different and special after all. But it was the worst game ever.

He woke with a start, not knowing where he was, and threw up a hand to keep the fireball out of his face. When he understood that it had been a dream he shook his head and laid back down. The fire was almost out and Lelet was curled into a shivery ball under her smelly blanket.

I should tell her everything. When exactly is a good time to tell someone you've spied on them? Stolen from them? Lied to them?

The least he could do was keep her from freezing. Moving carefully so not to wake her, he rearranged himself close at her side. Eventually he slept and this time it was the other dream, the good one about water. In his dream he reached out and let it run through his hands.

***

Hours later, Lelet woke in the dark. She was deliciously warm. The distance between them had closed, he was lying right behind her with an arm thrown over her, both of their faces towards what remained of the fire. His hand gently cupped her breast. She was about to carefully move it away when he sighed, shifted, and pulled her closer.

She watched the fading embers and listened to him breathing and wondered how it was possible to feel so safe in such strange company.

Chapter 58

"Don't you see?" asked Gwenyth, pressing the glittering rope back into Sir Edward's hand, "I'd rather wash his pots than wear your jewels. Because that is what love is." She laughed, although she felt nothing but fear. "Why, you mean no more to me than... this windowsill!"

-The Claiming of the Duke, pg 150
Malloy Dos Capeheart, Little Gorda Press (out of print)

Mistra
100 years after the War of the Door, Mistran calendar
20 years later, Eriisai calendar
Road through the Great Forest

The next day turned fine, with a blue sky and warm sun, and Lelet found her disposition much improved. She knew plenty of things about herself—she could be a horror without a proper meal or a decent night's sleep—but there were things that she didn't know. Stealing had been so much fun it made her a little worried. And how she'd essentially run off with this strange man—because if she was being honest, she knew she could have taken the horse and left a dozen times over. Why hadn't she? He'd get in trouble with her brother, but what was that to her? There was a time not long ago when that would have been all the reason she needed, the idea of ruining one of Rane's little games. She wondered again what her brother was up to. Unless something vile was planned for the end of this trip it didn't feel like he was taking revenge for being sent away. And she didn't think Moth would allow anything to happen to her, anyway. *What are you playing at, Rane? Did you think I'd magically fall in love with someone utterly unsuitable? Is that your idea of revenge? That's a long game, even for you.*

It was an interesting idea, though.

To her own surprise, she was even getting used to sleeping outside. She was, however, not surprised at how much she wanted Moth's arms around her when she woke up, and how disappointed she'd been to open her eyes and see him bothering the horse. It was funny, really, they hadn't seen anything other than birds, and she knew the woods were full of deer from listening to tales of Billah's frequent hunting excursions (his stories usually involved a lot of beer and someone falling out of a tree).

She wondered if all animals didn't like Moth. It was too bad, he was absolutely determined to make friends with the horse, who even now was slowly backing away from him. Maybe he was coming on too strong?

"They have feelings, you know, they can tell things." She stood between the demon and the horse, whispering to it and rubbing its ears until it calmed down.

"Such as?" He looked offended, but was trying to hide it. When the horse made any move, from flicking its tail to shaking its head, he jumped, at the same time trying not to jump.

"He knows you're afraid of him, and I think he knows you're not a regular person. Oh, don't look like that, plenty of people don't get along with horses. And he's right, you aren't regular. Give me your hand."

"No. He'll bite it off." She took his hand and together they stroked the animal's nose. Then she moved to its side and they ran their hands, fingers entwined, along its long neck. As long as she was between them, the animal relaxed. Eventually, so did Moth.

She felt a sudden warmth, as if they'd been plunged into high summer. For a moment she wondered if she had come down with a fever, then she realized Moth was simply radiating heat, much as he had done last night. She looked up at him, wondering if she should be concerned, but he looked fine—in fact, better than fine. He looked happy.

"You see?" she said to both of them. "You just have to trust that everything is fine, and nothing is going to hurt you."

He folded his hand around hers. "Thank you," he said.

***

She leaned against his shoulder and dozed on and off. He stole a glance at her, face tipped up to catch the warm sunlight. She caught him looking.

"You look different," she told him. And he did—he'd found a piece of string and tied back his long hair, and that plus the scant beard which caught the light and gave his fine features a slightly rougher appearance. He grabbed at the end of the tail which hung just past his shoulder.

"What do you mean? Different how?"

"Different as in with your hair like that I can see your face." She put her finger to his lips before he could start in. "I like your face.

If May was here she would say something about how everyone looks better with their hair out of their eyes."

"I think I am learning how to see things here."

"What do you mean? Can't you see normally? Do eyes work differently back… where you are from? Wait… I know this… Eriis!" she finished triumphantly.

"Eriis, that's right. Very good. No, when I first got here there was so much to see I didn't know what to look at. I'd have to stop and look at every tree, all the rocks, I didn't know what was important." He looked her in the eye, and she realized how infrequently he'd done that. "I think I'm learning."

She smiled and looked away, not wanting to draw attention to his gaze and embarrass him. "I think you mean background and foreground. Like in a painting."

"I know what paintings are. It's from art, isn't it?" he asked.

"I take it you don't have artists?" she replied.

"Oh, we do, but making a design or a mark on something isn't considered very special. Our artists are more… performance? They create an emotion, or an experience. I'm not sure I'm explaining it. We have excellent and brilliant artists. They create themselves for us at Court."

She laughed. "At Court? What are you, a Prince?"

"Yes."

It was almost a full minute before she could manage a reply. "A Prince. You're a Prince? Prince Moth?"

He laughed, but there seemed to be no humor behind it. "No, not Prince Moth."

"So Moth isn't your real name."

"It's my name while I am here." He paused. "Lelet, please don't be impressed. I am not gifted. Even if I had properly manifested, I have almost no abilities—no more than a child. My being a prince doesn't mean anything. It's like being a building's best windowsill."

Lelet had known men who liked to feel sorry for themselves and she guessed 'can't do magic' wasn't much different from 'can't ride a horse', or 'can't throw a ball.' Men hated the *can't* part. Demons couldn't be all that different—particularly this one. She took his hand and laced his fingers between her own. He looked down at their joined hands and back up at her curiously.

"Well it means a great deal to me. I've never met a prince before, much less been kidnapped by one! When this is over, you will be positively immortalized when I tell the story. My friends will froth at the mouth and die from jealousy." She figured this was the right thing to say, and he was at least that much like other men, because he draped his arm around her waist. "If you're a prince you must have a great Lady waiting for you back home."

He dropped his arm. "I… ah… well…."

"Are you married?"

"No! No. No. Definitely no. No."

"Hmm, whoever she is she must be a peach. *Definitely* no. So tell me about her. She's beautiful of course." He didn't answer. "She's probably tall." Lelet bore a grudge against tall women, having conveniently forgotten his repeatedly describing his people as small. "We've established that she's a bitch, your Madam Definitely No, so I'll venture that she's insanely good in bed."

"Lelet!"

"I'm right, obviously. What is it like, between your people?" She thought of what he'd told her—flame and flight. "I'll bet there's fire involved. Do you literally set each other on fire? And you can put your arm back, I'm not going to tear it off."

"Well, it's funny you should say that. About arms." He paused and she wondered if he was about to do that 'can't get the words out' thing. His arm remained at his side.

Lelet, idiot, do not tease this one. She was afraid she'd ruined it, but to her relief he continued. "If we are going to have this conversation, you should know that my people aren't as sensitive as human persons. Hot and cold, for instance. That doesn't bother us. Pain. Pleasure. We don't really differentiate between the two. It feels—I am told it feels almost the same. And we heal extremely quickly. So our joinings tend to be… aggressive. Extremely. So, yes, there is literal fire."

"You hurt each other," she said. She wondered what he meant by, "*I am told.*"

"Sometimes quite a lot. Although it's not supposed to feel like pain." He was quiet for a moment. "I told you I'm different… I don't have the same kind of abilities as the rest of my people. I just can't do it."

Lelet considered this. *He can't do it? Why would he tell me that? That's horrible!*

Finally she couldn't stand it and had to ask. "Are you telling me you can't do the joining part?"

"No," he looked surprised. "No, I didn't mean that at all. I mean if I am hurt, I feel it. Pain feels like pain to me—although not as much as it would to one of you. And it takes me longer to mend. No one else is like me, as far as I know."

"Oh! Well." She felt quite relieved to hear it. And that explained the 'I am told.' "You feel pain. You probably don't inflict as much either." He shrugged uncomfortably. "You can't do all that magical stuff. Moth, I have news for you." He looked down at her serious face.

"Moth, you're a human."

His laugh was strained. "No. Ha. No. My mother would have. No. That's funny though. Human. Hilari—Ow!"

She had pinched the tender skin on the inside of his elbow.

"Human."

He pulled the offending hand away and held it up as she laughed. He pulled her close and looked into her pale eyes. She stopped laughing and waited to see what he would do.

Why does he look so sad? He held quite still, he was waiting for her. She wound her arms around his neck and her mouth found his. For a long moment, he held perfectly still, not breathing, just waiting. She could feel the heat slowly rise as he relaxed into her arms. His lips were as soft as she'd hoped, he felt like silk and fire. She wanted more of him, and pushed his stolen shirt off his shoulders.

She knew he was tall and now she could see he was lean and beautifully formed. But she looked again and gasped.

"Oh, Moth."

"What? Oh, those are just rings. I know your people don't ornament themselves-"

"No! No. Oh, your skin." His body was a patchwork of pale scars and silvery lines, stark against his golden skin. He looked like a badly mended porcelain cup. She was sure she could see the faint outline of a hand in the middle of his chest. It had been a fine boned, delicate hand.

"Moth, who did this to you?"

He thought for a moment, gave up and said, "Everyone."

She gently traced a finger along a scar which snaked across his collarbone. He shivered.

Why, she wondered, *do I want to care for him? Why do I want him at all? Is it only because he is beautiful and sad?* He looked at her again with such longing and such despair, and she wondered *What does he think is going to happen*? Just ask quickly she answered her own question. *He is waiting for this to feel like pain. 'I am told', he said. He doesn't know any other way.*

"I will *never* hurt you," she told him.

"Yes," he replied, "I think you will. I think before this is over, we both will."

There was only one response to that, and because she knew the moons would fall into the sea before he did it himself, she unlaced her dress and shrugged out of it. He reached for her and that was answer enough for both of them.

She buried her hands in his silky hair and kissed him fiercely. He held her like he was afraid she would fly away. She felt, as much as heard, his groan as she reached up and twisted the gold ring that pierced his nipple, figuring correctly that that was what it was there for. And there was the familiar rush of heat rising from him, surrounding her. In his soft hair, she caught the faint, sweet aroma of wood smoke. She could feel him, too, hard against her stomach, and slid herself along up against his warm, flawed skin. She could feel the golden rings against her own body. They were cool but he was so warm… and then he wasn't. He pushed her away.

"Lelet, move." She felt the sudden sting of angry tears. "Do as I say, move away from me right now." He actually shoved her back onto the seat. She scrambled to retrieve her dress as he practically leapt over her to get out of the cart and create more distance between them.

Her face burned with humiliation and she was about to tell him she had only kissed him because she felt sorry for him, when she realized they were being watched by two men. One had a club. The other held a dented sword.

Chapter 59

Eriis
20 years after the War of the Door, Eriisai calendar
100 years later, Mistran calendar
Before the High Seat

"You cannot say your behavior was acceptable. You cannot say you performed your duties with honor and dignity." Yuenne had made more or less the same speech in front the High Seat every day for the three weeks since his disastrous party. And for three weeks, Hellne had sat on the Seat and smiled politely and thanked him for his advice. She examined the cuff of her gown until he was done.

"Your comments are always welcome at Court, Counselor. I will consider them."

He allowed the tiniest sneer. "You should have considered them while you were entertaining the enemy. It is not as if you weren't warned. I myself—"

"Again, we welcome everyone to speak freely at this Court. As long as they do not overstep." She had no intention of admitting to any impropriety, despite the truth of the accusations. Her original intent had been to simply wait and let the exciting story of the prince's parentage burn itself out. But that looked less likely to happen, as Yuenne continued his attack. It was a bit of a relief to have his enmity out in the open, not whispered behind a hand. No, she had to do something and soon, because every day, more friendly eyes turned away, and more friends failed to appear to show her support. Even now, she felt the disapproval in the room falling on her skin like dust at dawn.

"Do you intend that as a threat?" Yuenne asked.

"Just an observation. Are there any other matters to address this afternoon?" Yuenne, dismissed, stepped back, and no one else stepped forward to face the Seat. "If that is all, let us thank Light and Wind for the gift of this day." She rose and nodded to Diia, who gathered her silver cup and papers and followed her out. The courtiers followed the Queen and Yuenne followed behind them. He caught up to her in the Great Hall.

"Hellne," he said, "be reasonable. I'm not doing this to harm or insult you." At her laugh, he said, "Truly, I am not. But Eriis needs stability and reassurance that their leaders are united. I think… and please forgive my bluntness, but I think the people no longer have faith in their Queen."

She stopped and turned to face him. "It was my hope that this ridiculous uproar would blow over when the next scandal came along, but you have made that impossible."

"Ridiculous? You would have put a human's son on the High Seat. That's not ridiculous. It's treasonous."

He has been waiting to say that to me, thought Hellne. *He has been practicing in the mirror. At least he spoke in private.* "He is my son, raised here, by me. And I strongly advise you to consider your words."

"You don't know what harm you've caused by sending him away." Yuenne leaned closer to her ear. "We will have him back, the Mages and I. What can you do against us? You and your friends from the hills."

She smiled calmly. "I am still the Queen."

He smiled back. "The day is not over." He gave a polite bow and left them.

Once safely inside her own chambers Hellne dropped her smile and sat heavily on a carved wooden bench. She held her arms out as Diia took off the heavy robe of office and hung it neatly away. She handed Hellne a lightweight black silk tunic trimmed in cream. The cream piping was a bit faded, but it was Hellne's favorite. "He's right," she told Diia as she tied it at her hip. "I am short of friends and he'll move against me soon. But I can't leave yet. What if Rhuun should come back? With no one here to protect him, he doesn't have a chance."

Diia poured Hellne some water. "He has friends he doesn't know about, many friends."

Hellne sighed. Gossip and rumors were easy to repeat, but if it came to it, how many ‘friends’ would it take to stand against both Yuenne and the Mages? "Perhaps it would be best if he made his way to the human world and stayed there."

"His place is here," Diia said. "He must come back." She spoke rather more loudly than usual, and Hellne cocked her head curiously.

"You've been listening to talk in the Quarter," she said. *Control the message*, Yuenne had once told her. She had to admit, he’d been right. "It sounds like you believe it."

"There's been talk in the Quarter for a long time," Diia replied. "Talk about bringing back the rain. Young Ilaan only repeats what's been said since the Weapon. Since before Jaa and I bore your tales to town. The prince must come back, and he must follow you to the High Seat."

Hellne kept the phrase 'superstitious nonsense' to herself. Right now, being the mother of the prince was a more valuable weapon than being the queen. She would have to rewrite her plans accordingly.

***

It was second moonrise and Hellne was about to send for her dinner when Diia brought her a message.

"The Zaal wishes to see you."

"By all means, send him in. I'll receive him on the balcony. Have him wait the usual amount of time." That gave her half an hour to arrange her heavy quilted robe, this one in cream and in better condition than the black, and neatly recoil and ornament her hair. The Zaal found her admiring the burning plains. If he was annoyed at being made to wait he didn't show it.

"Zaal, this is a surprise, to say the least. Please do sit." She poured him water and they passed the cup. She found she didn't want to follow him in sipping, but it would be unspeakably rude not to drink. The Zaal remained as blank faced as the most experienced courtier, deftly not noticing when she turned the cup away from where his mouth had been.

"I know this has been a trying time for you, Madam, so I will not trouble you long."

"I suppose you'd like me to tell you where Rhuun has gone and that I ought to listen to my Counselor."

The Zaal shook his head. "No, Madam. We know where he is. And I come to you on my own errands."

She gave a gasp before catching herself. "You know where Rhuun is now?"

"Why yes, certainly." The Zaal paused. "Don't you?"

"Of course," she snapped. "Of course I know. But if you know, what brings you out of the Raasth?" She had to bite her tongue to keep from begging the Zaal to tell her where Rhuun was.

"I wish to give you a gift." He waited, and she nodded. "Yuenne will formally petition for your removal from the High Seat within days. Perhaps tomorrow. He will further petition for your immediate exile to a transform farm at the Edge and call for the breaking of the regency. He will arrange elections, and he will win."

She waved her hand. "I saw this on the horizon. I have enough followers to stall the petition, if not dismiss it outright."

"You do not," the Zaal said. "He has been busy, the Counsellor. We think he will have his way."

Hellne frowned. "Why would you tell me? Why do you give this to me?"

The Zaal smiled blandly. "I have something else. One I think will be of great interest to you. In fact, I believe you've been waiting many years for it." He pulled a stack of dirty paper out of his sleeve. There was a smell of age and dust. "Many of us went missing because of The Weapon. Including your brother."

She stiffened. "I know you have a good reason to mention Araan, rest him now."

"Perhaps he is not resting. Perhaps he is somewhere nearby, just out of reach."

"Not this rubbish again? The Hidden Cities theory has been disproven utterly."

"They are not hidden, Madam. They are behind another Door."

She couldn't keep the startled look off her face. "Did you say another Door? You're certain?" *Not dead*, she thought, *just gone. What if this is true? It changes everything.* "Show me."

He was certain, and once he showed her what the Mages had found, what long years of work had yielded, what the maps meant, she was convinced as well. She wanted to snatch the maps away from him and examine them more closely, but he pushed them aside.

"This brings us to the matter of your debt," he said.

Finally. Well, let us see what he wants, and what I'm willing to give. She composed her face, showing him nothing. "What is the price, Zaal? I swore I would pay your old master, so I suppose now it falls to you. How convenient."

"I give you a chance to leave here under your own power, and a way to find not only your brother but the others we thought lost forever. Find them and bring them home. How fortunate for you that my Mages and I are otherwise occupied, or else this task would fall to us. But as it happens, this will cancel your debt, paid in full." *That*, she thought, *is no price at all*. The Zaal wasn't finished. "But in addition, I have a request."

"I won't give you my son. You understand, even if I could, I would not." She gave him a hard look. "If the price of the charm did not involve him, he's not a part of this."

He nodded. "You hid him from our sight his whole life. You broke your own law and sealed your own fate. It would be not only within my right, but my obligation to have you deliver him. But that is not what I ask. Only that you remove the guard from his door and allow my brother Mages access to his belongings."

She frowned. "That's it? Why bother with me at all? If Yuenne has his way, the guards will be following me to exile anyway."

The Zaal sniffed. "The Counsellor and the Mages do not always speak with one voice."

"He doesn't know you're here, does he?" She smiled. This was interesting.

"Once he moves against you, Madam, all our efforts will thenceforth be on his behalf, you will no longer be 'on the board', as your friends the humans might say. We think it better to keep all pieces on the playing field. If you return with those we lost, all eyes will turn to you, they will want to return you to your rightful place on the High Seat. And you will remember your good friends in the Raasth."

"Access to his room?" Hellne said. The Zaal nodded. "You'll get nothing else from me."

The Zaal smiled politely. "Eventually the prince will return to us. He will tire of the world of humans, or more likely, we will retrieve him. And we will have him with or without your consent. You should have given him over to us when he was an infant. You perhaps would have been less attached." He frowned. "Although it is true we'd have had less of the blood to work with."

"What an utterly repulsive thing to say." Hellne stood and turned her back on the Zaal, leaning against the stone retaining wall. She watched a firewhirl burn itself out in the distance and forced herself to breath normally. "Leave the maps. I'll remove the guard. But don't expect me to sit on my hands when my son comes home."

"Two gifts after all," the Zaal said as he rose to leave. "The prince's room, and a warning."

So, thought Hellne, *my boy made it to Mistra after all. Thank you, Zaal, for your third gift.*

***

Once the Zaal was gone, Hellne called for Diia. "It's time to go," she said.

Diia looked relieved. "Past time. We'll go to the tents first?"

Hellne nodded. "First the tents, and then…" She made a neat stack of the papers and maps the Zaal had left behind. "Please find something to put these in."

Diia peered at the scribbled over old pages. "What are they?"

"If that nasty creature is right, and I think he is, they are the key to a Door no one else knows exists. Our enemies don't trust each other, and that gives us an opportunity. Diia, release your kin from my service. Tell no one where we're going."

Diia paused in pulling garments from the queen's wardrobe. "Then you no longer fear for the prince when he returns?"

"You say he has friends? Let's make sure they are ready to help him on his way when he needs them." She folded her arms. "Not the heavy one, leave it behind. I won't be needing it for a while. I'll have to contact Ilaan, but we'd best be on our way first." She smiled. "And make sure to find the boots, they'd be in the back, I think. No more sandals for me, but at least I don't have to face Yuenne at the Seat anymore."

Now that she was ready to go, she felt a strange exhilaration. Might she be the one to bring her people home? It felt appropriate, since she'd allowed the humans into her home—and her bed—to be the one to set things right. The people in the Quarter would rise to help Rhuun, and he'd have Ilaan to whisper in his ear while he held the Seat. And when she returned with an army of those thought lost forever at her back, they'd beg her to reclaim it. She'd be the queen of a real kingdom, and Araan and his family would have children of their own to follow her. Her stain would be cleansed and her legacy would be of honor and pride, not betrayal and lies.

And if her son somehow managed to bring Malloy back to Eriis with him, that reunion would be short and sweet. Very short for Malloy, but what a nice gift for the Mages. And as for Rhuun, she'd find something for him to do. Maybe he could write a book.

Chapter 60

Lady Cybelle took the girl in at a glance—her flawless skin, wide blue eyes, her long blonde curls.
"We have much work to do if you are to be presentable," she said, picking up a pot of rouge.
"Are these your weapons?" Gwenyth asked.
Cybelle chuckled. "These are merely the foot soldiers. That," she said, pointing at Gwenyth's creamy bosom, "that is your real weapon."

-The Claiming of the Duke, pg 80
Malloy Dos Capeheart, Little Gorda Press (out of print)

Mistra
100 years after the War of the Door, Mistran calendar
20 years later, Eriisai calendar
Road through the Great Forest

Moth swam up through a river of pleasure and opened his eyes. He wanted to see the look on her face, but what he saw instead was two large men, armed, watching them. Lelet was still wrapped around him, arms and legs both, and hadn't seen them. He got out from under her as quickly as he could without hurting her and leapt to the ground to meet them.

He took stock. He was in luck for once. The sun was behind him, so they couldn't see his face clearly, or his eyes—most likely—at all. They no doubt would mistake him for a farmhand with his flame lit. Plus, there were only two. He figured neither one could fly or shower him with fireballs. He could protect Lelet and this would be fine.

The smaller of the two held the sword. He said, "By the Veil boy, did you roll around in baling wire?"

The other, the one with the club, was as tall as Moth and twice as fat. In fact, he was the biggest person, besides himself, Moth had ever seen.

The fat man said, "Maybe his girl's got sharp teeth. He's got some pretty jewelry through his titties, though. Don't see that every day."

"Well," said the swordsman, "I'm not going to take them out."

The man with the club rolled his eyes and pointed to the knife in his belt. "Fine. I'll do it. Bet they come out the same way they went in."

While they were chatting about dismembering him, the two were edging to the right and left.

That's what I would do, if I were them. "Gentlemen," he said. "Nice afternoon. You've interrupted us, but I don't hold a grudge. Why not move along now?"

They stared at him—shirtless, unarmed, and both burst out laughing. The club man continued to move oh so slowly to his right.

The fat man said, "Well, we're certainly sorry, and we can see we busted in you for fair. But, the problem is this is our bit of forest. Ever since you two conducted that stunning farmhouse raid, we've been following you. See, we had our eye on that place ourselves. Especially since the previous owners were called away."

The sword man snickered. "A sort of permanent vacation, they're on."

"As my friend says, pressing business, and our little house empty. Us returned from a pleasant evening with friends to find our new home sweet home violated. So strike one, theft." He shook his head, still slowly moving to the right. "Very serious. And add to that, you've unfortunately violated our… ah… anti nudity ordinance. Shame. It's new, so you might not have heard about it. You're in luck, though, because the penalty is one girl and one cart."

Several things happened at once.

Moth heard Lelet scream his name and without turning he fell into a low crouch. The sword whistled over his head. The man had elected to try and lop his head off rather than skewer him, which was good news.

Ilaan would be proud, he thought. *All those hours, paying off. Never thought I'd be using any of that stuff here*. And for the thousandth time*: This place is not what I thought it would be.*

The club man had decided to make his move and rushed towards him, swinging the stave. He sidestepped the man and managed to grab the business end of the club, gaining a palm full of nails but also knocking the fat man down with a hard elbow to the gut. He seemed in no hurry to get up so Moth turned back to the cart.

Stay down, fat man, he thought. *Can I possibly do this without killing anyone?*

The man with the sword was reaching across the driver's bench, and had managed to catch the sleeve of Lelet's dress. He yanked her off the cart and held her up by one arm. She was shrieking and pointing at Moth with her free hand, for some reason not paying any attention to her captor.

Moth hefted the club. *More pain to put away, just put it with the rest.* The thing was heavy and had nails poking out of it, some of which had been driven through his hand when he'd grabbed for it. He couldn't help but notice that along with his own new blood, the nails were crusted and brown, and there was even a little bit of hair stuck here and there. He felt more revolted than injured.

These people are disgusting. I'll be doing the human world a favor.

Pulling the nails out of his palm, he ignored the squelching, wet sound the meat of his hand made. He swung the club around so he was holding it properly, and started to line up his blow at the sword man, feeling relieved at not having to change his form. It was too dangerous to show himself that way, no one should see that. And once they'd seen his True Face, they'd have to die.

He took a quick glance back and saw the fat man still on the ground. He had gone quite purple in the face and was giving his prodigious gut an exploratory feel with one hand. Moth turned his attention to the sword man, who was trying to get a better grip on Lelet, who was still screaming and struggling madly. It sounded like she was saying 'Behind you', but the fat man was still down and looked to remain that way.

He just had to get in one good strike. He figured he was fast enough to knock the sword and possibly the man's whole arm off before he could use his weapon and hurt her. He'd certainly have to kill the man for laying hands on her but at least he'd spare Lelet the horror of watching him put them to death by cooking them from the inside out.

I'm going to kill human persons. This is not what I came here for. But he has his hands on her....

Even if he couldn't raise a flame, he was not without resources.

They'd be just like the rocks. Remind them of their very great heat. If I have to, I hope I don't have to. But I can do it, I think. I hope.

Anyway, the sword man. Well, that was odd. He was simply pinning Lelet's arms behind her back, he wasn't even holding his sword anymore. She was still screaming but it no longer sounded like words.

This would be over soon. He took a step forward.

The Duke would dispatch them quickly, then say something clever so the lady won't cry.

Something shoved him hard in the side of his head. It was hard to breathe. It got very bright and then dark.

Chapter 61

Gwneyth wiped away her tears and crept to her door. She turned the lock, and the 'click' sounded as loud as a whip crack. She pulled her old bag out from under the bed—the lovely soft bed, the lonely bed she'd never sleep in again, and began to toss her clothes in. Only the ones she'd brought with her. At the bottom of the bag she caught a gleam of light. It was the stolen jeweled necklace.

-The Claiming of the Duke, pg 160
Malloy Dos Capeheart, Little Gorda Press (out of print)

Mistra
100 years after the War of the Door, Mistran calendar
20 years later, Eriisai calendar
Road through the Great Forest

Once she had caught her breath and gotten her dress back in place, she tucked her bare feet under herself and waited for Moth to incinerate the armed men.

What do they want? wondered Lelet. *Why is he talking to them? He should just show his true face or whatever it's called and burn them up! What is he waiting for?*

Instead of making the pair burst into flame, he was talking to them as they all maneuvered around each other. The two villains were trying to place themselves on either side of Moth, who was trying to keep her behind him while keeping both of them in front of him. She realized with a sick feeling that she was the pivot around which they all moved. She looked around wildly. She had no weapons and there were two of them. Run away? Could she leave Moth to fight and escape on an ill-fitting pair of shoes? No, and probably not since the leather slippers were in her bag in the back.

She did have one thing she could use, and when the sword man, who was the furthest from Moth's eyeshot, began to raise his weapon, she screamed his name for all she was worth.

It was enough. He dropped to the ground and the man missed him completely, the sword passing over his head. But instead of trying again, the man raced to the cart, reached across the driver's bench and began to grab for her dress. She made for the far side, intending to jump down and run after all, but he snagged her sleeve and hauled her back, pulling her down next to him and holding her fast. Her feet barely touched the ground and she was afraid he might break her arm.

Moth was doing something with the club man—now the man was on the ground and he had the club! Moth's hands were covered in blood, and she realized with horror that it was his own. The end of the club had nails sticking out of it, but he'd grabbed it like it was nothing.

"He'll kill you both," she shrieked at the man who held her.

"He can try," said the sword man mildly.

That was when the third man stepped from behind a tree. He was holding a good sized rock. She screamed again, pointing at the man and struggling to get away from the sword man's grasp. *Why won't he look behind?* Her captor had tossed aside his sword and now had both her arms pinned behind her back.

The third man came up behind Moth and knocked him in the head with the rock. He fell instantly.

The fat man and the third man stood over him.

"Put up a bit of a fight, this one," said the fat man. "Oh well." He kneeled down, pulling out his knife, and slit Moth's throat.

You will not faint, thought Lelet, although the world had gone grey. *Maybe he's still alive and he'll need your help....*

"Wake up," she whispered. "Moth, wake up." Her legs were gone. Her lips were numb.

The sword man said, not unkindly, "He'll wake up in the next world, sister. If you believe in that sort of thing."

The third man pointed at Moth's chest and said, "Get those."

The fat man laughed. "Said I would, didn't I?" He hesitated, pointing his knife at Moth's tracery of silvery scars. "Look at this boy. Must have used him for bait at dog fights."

The third man snickered. "Maybe he won those things for beating the dogs."

The fat man considered the corpse. "Strong, though. Got me right in the gut. Took on the both of us, and him without a weapon. Brave, your man was," he said over his shoulder to Lelet. She started to scream again, although now without much volume behind it.

The fat man said. "Yes, well, you ought to scream, dearie. That's what the dead like to hear as they leave us. Sends 'em on their way. Get that noise out of your system now, though. We can all sing proper songs of respect for your fallen hero later. We ought to be on our way."

The third man, who had dropped the gore-splashed rock, scratched his head. "What are we going to do with the girl?"

The fat man looked up at him. "What do we usually do with 'em?" He nodded at the sword man. "Phee, tie her hands and toss her in the back. No, don't toss her—place her." He bowed towards her dramatically. "My lady."

She tried to scream but could only whisper *No, no no.*

He looked back down and thumbed one of Moth's eyes open. "Look at that—full of blood. Must've had a soft head."

"I've seen it before. Startling, isn't it? They'll do that, if you hit 'em in the right spot. No one's head's harder than a rock, Beb, except maybe yours."

They all three laughed at that one.

The fat man—Beb—poked at Moth's torn and bloody hand with his knife.

"Never saw anyone grab the end of Barbara like that before, either. Like he didn't even feel it."

The third man frowned. "I thought that thing's name was Nancy."

"Nah. Nancy and me had a falling out. Can you believe it—she told me she thought I was getting too fat. Me, too fat! Have you seen the ass on that girl? I tell you, it hurt my feelings. So yes, it's Barbara now. Aren't you, my darling?" He picked the club off the ground and looked at it admiringly before setting it close by his side. "Barbara appreciates me just as I am. Maybe I'll make her a present of these. Just don't none of you tell her where they came from. She's got delicate sensibilities."

He lifted a gold ring with the tip of his knife.

"How'd he get 'em in there? It's a mystery of the age, why people do what they do to themselves."

He leaned over with his knife laid flat. There was a great deal of blood.

That was when Lelet fainted.

Chapter 62

"What is this trash?" exclaimed the Duke. "Who has turned her into such a slattern? Cybelle, I see your hand in this." The Duke swept the dainty pots of paint onto the floor. "Now wash your face and stop that infernal noise!" Gwenyth stifled her sobs as best she could.

-The Claiming of the Duke, pg 89
Malloy Dos Capeheart, Little Gorda Press (out of print)

Mistra
100 years after the War of the Door, Mistran calendar
20 years later, Eriisai calendar
Road through the Great Forest

"Wake up, sweetheart." Moth was whispering in her ear. "Wake up, now." She smiled. He had such pretty eyes. She'd tell him that, right away.

"Time to wake up, Missy." She opened her eyes.

Three dirty men looked down at her.

Moth was still dead.

They tied her hands behind her back and one of them—the sword man, Phee—lifted her into the back of the cart.

"My family has money," she whispered, but they didn't hear her. They were moving.

Beb climbed into the back of the cart with her. He laid his club by his side. She wondered if she could throw herself on it in such a way that it would kill her quickly.

He noticed her gaze and said, "Plenty of time for that, sweetheart. We'll get to camp and then have a nice evening together. You, me, and Barbara."

"Please," she whispered, hating herself for the begging whine of her voice, "please don't hurt me."

"Leave her alone," said Phee over his shoulder. "She's had a bad day." They all laughed.

"One might say!" said Beb. "Bad luck, wrong place wrong time, all that. Good luck for us, though. Can you cook, girl? Wash a pot? Keep three gentlemen of the road warm at night?"

"Not all at once, though," pointed out the third man, "We're not animals."

"My family has money," Lelet said again. "They'll pay you to bring me home." The three laughed again, taking in the leaves in her hair, her torn dress and her dirty, bare feet.

"What'll they do, trade us a cow for you? Give us a loaf of bread?"

"No," she said, trying to keep her voice even, "I live in Mistra, in the city. Big house. Money."

Beb shook his head, chuckling. "And I'm Loquacia, King of the Fairy People. Pleasure to make your acquaintance!"

"Check her hands," advised Phee. "That'll tell where she was raised."

"Smart boy," said Beb. "That's why I love you like a brother." He reached out a huge hand and swatted Lelet to one side. With no way to brace herself, she fell on her face. Beb took his time rooting around, getting big handfuls of her legs and thighs before looking at her hands.

"Funny," he mused. "She's as skinny as a fence post, no more ass than an old chicken, and hasn't got a rough spot anywhere. Despite her outwardly slattern appearance and overall loose demeanor, this girl hasn't scrubbed a floor in her life. I may have to go back and check the front—just to be on the safe side."

She turned so she could see his knobby shaved head outlined against the sky.

"My family will pay if I'm unharmed." He pulled her upright, helping himself to a generous squeeze of her breasts.

"Well, there's unharmed and then there's unharmed." He pinched her leg—the tender part just above the knee, and she screamed through her teeth. "See? You're still 100% intact, arm and leg-wise."

The third man said, "Find out about the money, Beb."

"Ah! Excellent. Important to focus, keep one eye always on our objective. Not be distracted by a yard or so of very nice looking girl meat." She shrank back, trying to pull away from his huge hand, which still rested lightly on her knee. "So, dearie, where is this magical family estate that turns into a bank?"

"In the city. I don't know how far from here. Please, don't hurt me."

"Well, there's plenty of time over a nice dinner to talk about the future. Maybe we'll find out why a nice city girl like you was out humping a recently deceased farm boy in the middle of nowhere. Maybe you'll tell us where your pretty clothes vanished off to. Or why you're vacationing in the woods with no shoes. All sorts of interesting things may come to light." He turned to the third man, who'd taken the reins. "Pull over, I have to respond to nature's call."

As he relieved himself against a tree, Beb sang:

"Oh the Demon Queen
Loved mortal peen
And that was her undoing
She picked the lock
And licked—"

"Beb, there is a lady present!" said Phee. Lelet huddled in the back of the cart. She missed her family with a pain that surprised her. She wished she was sitting in the garden with May, or even arguing with Rane. She didn't want to even think about Moth. Time for that later.

If I can convince them I am worth something maybe they won't rape me to death. The big one—Beb—he'd do it for fun. Maybe the other two wouldn't? I don't want to die in the dirt. I want to go home.

She was sitting on something that was jabbing her in the rear. She shifted slightly and looked down dully at one of her white satin pumps. The heel had broken off and it was more grey than white, but the sight of it filled her with rage. Less than a week ago her biggest worry was getting these shoes dirty. There were no such things as demons. She'd never been hungry or cold a moment in her life, and she'd never seen a dead body, much less witnessed a murder. Or given someone his very first taste of pear.

This is your fault, Moth, she thought, *How could you leave me?* She hid her face in her shoulder so no one would see her cry.

Beb climbed back in and picked up the wrecked shoe.

"One mystery solved! You do have shoes! Or at least, you did. You won't be running away on this thing." He tossed the shoe out and they were on their way.

Please don't hurt me.

***

Hours later the three decided to make a temporary camp for the night. Killing Moth had taken a bite out of their schedule and they hadn't made it back to their base after all.

"We should leave her in the cart," said the third man. "I don't want to listen to her crying for her boyfriend all night."

"She won't cry, will you sweetheart?" asked Beb. "She's a good girl. She's got new boyfriends now. And I like to look at her. Tie her to that tree. No tears, am I right?"

Realizing he expected an answer, she stammered, "No, I won't cry. I'll be good. Just—"

"Yes, I know, 'please don't hurt me.'" His imitation of her voice was a simpering whine. "I won't hurt you, dearie. I think we'll get along just fine. After all, you like 'em big, that man of yours was good sized."

"Went down fast enough, though," observed the third man. She began to cry. Beb cuffed her head.

"I thought we agreed there'd be none of that."

She bit her lips hard to stop crying. Her head swam and she thought she might vomit.

He'll kill you just like he did Moth if you get sick on him. She took a deep breath and forced her face into something like a normal expression.

"Can I have some water?" she asked. "I promise I won't cry." Beb shrugged and Phee held a cup while she drank. Then he tied her to a young pine, taking a little care not cut off the blood to her arms.

"Help me," she whispered. He laughed.

"Not a chance, sister. Don't worry, I expect it'll all be over by morning. Tell you what. I'll make sure it's quick."

"You two making friends over there?" Beb called. "Get back over here and let's get a fire started. Dinner won't cook itself. Although this little white rabbit certainly jumped into our pot." He laughed at his own cleverness and the other two chimed in from long practice.

***

"Time for a serious discussion, lads," said Beb.

They had eaten their stew and drunk up their beer, and Phee had even held the spoon while Lelet ate a few bites. She found it vile and her throat tried to clamp shut but she forced herself to swallow the shreds of meat and bits of onions. *If I eat,* she thought, *I can run. If I can run I can grab a rock.*

"Now," continued Beb, "Miss… uh, what's your name, sweetheart?"

"May," she replied. It made her feel closer to home somehow.

"Ah, now, our Miss May Morning, she says she owns a big pile of gold in the middle of Mistra City. All we have to do is deliver her to the doorstep."

"Sounds like a reasonable plan," said the third man. "Mum and Da will be happy to see us. Open the vault for us, most likely."

"See, but there's only one small hitch in this otherwise foolproof endeavor." Beb screwed his face into a dramatic version of a sobbing mother. "'Our darling girl,' Mum will say. 'Our darling girl restored to us—but where's her kit? Her fancy capes and hats and jewels what we sent her off with? Where's her luggage? Where's her chaperone?' And who'll take the hit?"

"Might be us," nodded Phee. "We should end this quick and forget about her."

"They won't blame you," said Lelet, "I'll tell them you were… you took me in when I was lost in the woods. I was robbed, and um, I was left for dead, but you showed kindness and fed me and brought me home. For a reward." She hoped she sounded more enthusiastic than she felt.

"Who was that fella? He was no city man," said Phee.

"No one," said Lelet.

"That was a lot of screaming and crying and carrying on for no one," said Beb, "I say that he turned your head and you run off with him, leaving a life of comfort for one of adventure and uncertainty. Well, you got yourself a bucketful of that! These mythical parents of yours, would they still pay for a runaway dragged home after leaving with… honestly, Miss May, that wasn't your garden variety lothario. What was he? And how did he lure you from your cushions?"

"What's the difference?" she snapped. "He's dead."

"Care to explain this to the assembled?" Beb put out his hand. The gold rings lay on his palm.

"I put them in," she hissed. "Myself. With a needle."

All three men winced. Then they laughed and Beb put the rings back in the little leather pouch.

"Well, there's no accounting for taste. Anyways, they're Nancy's now."

Phee tentatively put his hand up. "I thought you and Nancy was on the outs."

"I am having second thoughts. Barbara, recall, let me down at a most critical juncture. I tend to follow my gut in matters of the heart. If the namesake fails me at just the wrong time, might not the lady follow suit? Thoughts, gentlemen. Thoughts that are best sorted out in the embrace of slumber. Gentlemen, I propose we table the ultimate fate of our May Morning here until the actual dawn. My brains are tired after a long day of rescuing wayward maids from roving bands of… of… whatever your friend there was." He paused and frowned. "Something about that boy was… Well, it's behind us now. Miss May,

I bid you a pleasant night, and tomorrow we'll get to know each other better. I've got a friend I'd like you to meet!"

He roared with laughter, which the others, on cue, joined in.

Finally, the third man and Phee both wrapped themselves in blankets and turned away from the fire. Beb yawned hugely and threw the last bottle he'd emptied into the darkness.

"Nature's call," he told her. "Back presently."

He wandered off towards a tree yet again. She thought, *How can one man piss so much? He's got to have something wrong with him. Maybe he'll die soon.* She listened to him sing again.

"Keep the Door well locked, boys
Keep the Door tight shut.
For if ye don't—"

There was a soft cough and a rustling.

Maybe he peed himself to death she thought. *Has that ever happened?*

That was when the fire exploded.

Chapter 63

"You will pay for what you've done," snarled Sir Edward.
"With my life?" asked the Duke.
Sir Edward replied, "You have nothing else of value."

-The Claiming of the Duke, pg 172
Malloy Dos Capeheart, Little Gorda Press (out of print)

Mistra
100 years after the War of the Door, Mistran calendar
20 years later, Eriisai calendar
Road through the Great Forest

Moth came awake with a great start and leapt to his feet, and his knees immediately buckled. He sat back down. He was covered with blood. Dried blood. How long had he been lying there? His throat ached horribly and he leaned over and spat out a mouthful of thick black fluid. Almost immediately, his stomach heaved and he retched great gouts of half congealed gore. The smell and taste of it burned his nose and made his innards twist, but finally there was nothing left. When he could raise his head, he touched his neck, afraid of what he'd find, but there was nothing but the slightly raised band of a new scar where the knife had cut him. His hand bore a constellation of pink circles, each no bigger than a nail, and there was also a knot on the back of his head.

As soon as he'd lifted his hand to feel the back of his head, he felt a horrible, tearing pain in his chest. He looked down.

"Awww, *rushta*," he muttered. He took a moment to be grateful they hadn't stripped off his trousers—that would have been even more unpleasant.

He found a chunk of rock with a splash of blood on it on the ground next to him.

"Well, I've solved this crime."

He looked around but the cart, the two—no, there must have been three men, and of course Lelet, were all gone. He couldn't even see her tiny light in his mind, but that didn't mean anything, did it? He could barely see what was right in front of him. The late afternoon sun gave everything shimmering halos and there were shadows everywhere.

He stumbled to his feet.

He tried to remember what direction the horse had been facing, and began to walk that way. He couldn't think of what else to do—he couldn't sprout a pair of wings and fly over the trees, or somehow hear them talking across the miles....

This had to be the right way.

He tried to make his legs move faster, although the big muscles in his thighs burned and he saw black spots in front of his eyes. He could barely swallow for the pain in his throat.

Ilaan was walking next to him. He was happy to see his friend of course, but it was strange how Ilaan was wearing the handsome blue silk coat from the party where he'd learned about music. Wasn't that a human's coat?

Before he could ask, Ilaan said, "You should have killed those human creatures when you had the chance. I had no idea you were so squeamish, Beast. I am seriously disappointed."

Aelle was on his other side. She was wearing Lelet's ugly brown dress. She wore it like her robe of office. Her hair was decorated with shards of broken glass. "It was a mistake for you to come here at all, of course. You can't say I didn't try to warn you." She wrinkled her nose. "You smell terrible, by the way."

"Shut up, Aelle," said Ilaan.

"Shut up Aelle," he whispered.

Ilaan continued. "Boy, talk about a lost opportunity! I think you were getting somewhere with that human girl. Another couple of minutes and you would have had the boring human joining you've always wanted. You had the advantage and didn't use it! One little change, a little smoke—bam, those men are dead and you're a hero. Why didn't you show your True Face? Is it that much worse than the one you're walking around with?"

"You like that silly girl, don't you?" said Aelle. She sounded annoyed. "Someone even softer than you are. Why didn't you just ever tell me to stop? 'Aelle, please don't leave a mark.' Was that so difficult? I know what pain means even if I've never felt it personally," she paused. "When did you make up your mind to leave me?"

"He didn't want to hurt your feelings," said Ilaan. "So he left our world entirely instead." Ilaan gave a whinnying laugh that Moth had never heard before.

"Please, stop," he said in a rasping whisper. "Why did you even stay with me, Aelle? I never understood why...."

Aelle smirked and answered, "One becomes acclimated."

Then they were standing in front of him, blocking him, and he had to go off the path into the shadowy forest to get around them, he fell, he was falling… then he was back on the road and they were each holding an elbow, dragging him along.

"Did you remember to tell him he's never coming home?" asked Aelle.

"Oh right! You know how I said I wouldn't leave you here? I'm leaving you here. You were never really one of us, anyway. Everyone was right about you! You're going to die here. Maybe really soon! And that girl of yours is already dead. You're too late."

Moth shook his head. "This isn't real. I know it's not real."

Ilaan barked, "Why didn't you show your True Face? Tell us. Were you afraid of showing that girl what you really are?"

He staggered to a stop, the dark world spun. He said, "I've never killed anyone and I didn't want to start now, today, in front of her."

"That's *a* reason, but it's not *the* reason. Is it, Beast?" asked Ilaan. "Is it more to do with the way she'd look at you when it was done? Maybe not so eager after all. Maybe she'd see you were ugly inside and out. Well, it doesn't matter anymore because SHE'S DEAD SHE'S DEAD AND SO ARE YOU YOU'RE NEVER GOING HOME IT'S TOO LATE YOU'RE TOO LATE"

He did fall, finally, and clapped his hands over his ears.

Lelet's white shoe, or what was left of it, lay on the ground in front of him. He picked it up and asked, "Is this real? Am I seeing this?"

Ilaan and Aelle were gone.

He got up and kept walking.

***

Several times he thought he smelled human urine. Once he gave himself a few minutes to rest, but when he closed his eyes, all he could see was that fat man and her fear. He pulled himself upright and kept walking. It got darker and he kept going, although he sometimes couldn't tell if his eyes were open or not.

I'm going to find her, he told himself. *Because the Duke would find her, and she'll be safe and so happy to see him... see me...* he awoke leaning his forehead against a tree. He sighed and tried to remember which way he'd come. It was completely dark and he had no idea. At this rate he'd be walking in circles and they'd carve her into pieces and he'd be too late….

There was a noise. Someone was… singing? That was singing, wasn't it? And it was real this time, wasn't it?

He crept towards the sound and nearly fainted with relief when he spotted her pale hair in the faint firelight. She was sitting next to a tree with her arms behind her, he gathered they were tied. Her head was slumped over her chest. He hoped she was just sleeping.

The fat man was carrying on about something or other. The other two men were his audience. They were all drinking from bottles and then tossing them into the dark forest. The remains of their meal, some sort of meat stew, still clung to the bottom of an old iron pot. It had an unpleasantly gamey, almost metallic smell, but his stomach made such a rumble he was afraid he'd be heard. He tried to remember the last time he'd eaten and could only think of the taste of a pear. It was a better thing to think of than the burning in his head and in his throat.

He found a spot where he could see them all and settled in.

Finally the man with the sword grunted and rolled himself up in a blanket to sleep. He patted his weapon lovingly before turning away from the fire. The other man soon did the same, although Moth couldn't spot a weapon. *You must be the one who killed me*, Moth realized. *I hope I can return the favor.*

The fat man said something to Lelet—he couldn't make it out—and got up to piss against a nearby tree. Moth rose to his feet, pain and exhaustion forgotten, and he changed.

Chapter 64

... and with one final great shove, the Duke heaved Sir Edward through the window. It was a long fall to the crags below, and Sir Edward screamed the whole way. The Duke and Gwyneth held themselves silent and still until they heard no more screams, then a thump. Then, as if a string had been cut, they fell into each other's arms.

-The Claiming of the Duke, pg 183
Malloy Dos Capeheart, Little Gorda Press (out of print)

Mistra
100 years after the War of the Door, Mistran calendar
20 years later, Eriisai calendar
Road through the Great Forest

Moth saw Lelet straining against the ropes. Had she seen him? He couldn't worry about her now. He held up his hands, roiling with ash and smoke, dark smudges against the smolder of the fire pit. The flame crawled up his legs. He didn't feel it.

Phee was first on his feet, but hadn't even lifted his blade when Moth stepped out of the fire and fell on him in an embrace that blotted him out. He didn't get a chance to scream, he just made a whistling noise and sank to the ground.

There was a distinct smell of cooked meat in the air.

The third man shouted, "Beb! Where are you? Phee?" He'd found the fat man's club and was swinging it in a wide arc. It had gotten quiet except for the hiss and crackle of the newly stoked fire. "Beb?"

There was no answer. The third man made a dash for the cart, meaning to take the horse and escape, but a lump of darkness tripped him and he went sprawling into the dirt. The man swore and got to his feet, holding the club in front of him like a shield.

Still nearly invisible, Moth said, "Now, are you the one that hit me with the rock? Or are you the one with the knife?"

The man let the club fall to his side. "You're dead," he said.

"No, as it turns out, I'm not," Moth said amiably, "but you are."

"What are you?"

"I'm a… I am the Beast."

By the unstable flickering firelight, Moth watched as if from a distant place as his hands close around the third man's throat. He, like Phee, made a shrieking, whistling noise before he fell. The cooked meat smell was overpowering.

Moth quickly hid his True Face, and rested on his knees for a moment. He'd never been so tired. An injury as extensive as the one he'd gotten required more than a quick nap, and he still wasn't sure how he'd made it through the forest. Later on, he'd be unable to remember most of it at all. Had there been others walking with him? It didn't seem likely. At least Lelet appeared to be unhurt, although the blank look on her face made him worry about her mind.

"Lelet? It's me. Look at me. You're safe now," he said as he untied her hands. She jerked her head away. He thought she'd be happy to see him, or at least relieved, but she took no notice. She stood up with some difficulty but as soon as she was on her feet she walked right past him, heading for where Beb had fallen. The fat man was slowly moving his hands in the dirt, and Moth cursed himself for not searing his throat completely, and prolonging this for Lelet. She pulled a leather pouch from his belt and laid it aside. Then she found his knife. She held it up, looking at the firelight glitter on the blade.

Beb suddenly gave a heaving gasp and tried to sit up. He fell back, hands at his neck. He stank of charred meat. She looked back and forth between him and the knife. He tried to talk through a seared throat.

"What's that, Beb old friend?" she said. "Can't quite make it out. Say again, but take your time. We've got all night. Maybe you'd like to sing a song for us!"

He kept up the whispering and pawed weakly at the air above his face.

"What? Hmmm? Please, don't hurt me?" she said. "Is that it? Please don't hurt me, please don't hurt me…" she repeated in a singsong voice that sounded nothing like her own.

"Lelet…" Moth stood behind her. He'd have to take the knife away from her in a moment.

"Shut up," she hissed at him. "You shut up. You're dead and you left me alone with them." She turned back to Beb, and put the knife against his burned neck. "Say it again, Beb. Please don't hurt me…" Beb's whispers had stopped. "Say it!" she shrieked.

"Lelet, he's dead. Put the knife down."

She threw it away and rose to her feet. Breathing hard, she took the three steps between them. He could see she was fighting to stay on her feet. She took another staggering step and fell against him. He could barely hold himself up and struggled not to fall.

"You died," she said in that strange grating voice, "and you left me alone with them." She looked up at him. "Am I dead too?"

"No, *shani.* No, and I didn't die either. At least, not for long. I told you how it is with me, that I can heal quickly. They hurt me but I didn't die. And even if they had killed me, I'd still come for you. Don't you know that?" She covered her face with her hands. "I'm sorry I left you alonc. I got here as fast as I could." He blinked a few times and found he was sitting at her feet. "I'm sorry," he said again, "I've had a hard day."

She sat next to him and peered at the dark purple line on his throat. "I imagine you have," she said. "I'm sorry I yelled."

"It's all right. I didn't mind. This is yours." He handed her the remains of her white shoe.

Then everything was sideways and he closed his eyes.

***

It was barely light when he awoke. She had gotten a blanket and thrown it over him. She'd also set a cup of water next to him, and his clothing, retrieved from his hiding place among the trees, sat in a neatly folded stack. He gulped the water, then shook out his trousers and climbed back into them.

She was sitting cross legged some distance from him, staring into the now dead embers of the firepit with that strange vague expression still on her face.

"Did they hurt you?" he asked.

"You mean did they rape me? No. But look!" she said in a bright, brittle voice, "Now we match. I have some marks now too!" She pulled up her sleeve and showed him a bracelet of finger-shaped bruises on her upper arm. He looked away.

"They talked about it a bit, who was going to go first and so on, and that fat bastard got a couple of feels in, but I told them my family had money. Ha, just like I told you, remember?" His face burned. "They decided to put any major life choices off until the morning. I'm pretty sure they'd have gone for a bit of fun and then thrown me in the river. They didn't seem like long term planners." She picked up the knife. "Beb kept saying he had something for me, something I was going to like. A friend for me to meet. Do you suppose this is what he meant?" She laughed but it sounded like a scream. She tossed the knife aside and stared at the ashes. He couldn't think of a thing to say other than that he was sorry.

She shook her head. "I know you are. I know." She started to cry and he reached for her, but she put up her hand.

Finally she looked up. Her eyes were red and her face was puffy, but her voice was her own when she said, "It looks better. Your neck, I mean. Does it hurt?"

He touched the new scar. "Not so much, any more. They also took my rings. Now, *that* hurt."

"Oh!" she said. "Here." She handed him the little leather bag she'd taken from Beb.

"Thank you," he said, "for getting them back for me."

"Thank you," she replied, "for not being dead. And rescuing me. I don't know why I was so angry with you." She sighed. "I was going to kill that man. I wanted to. Why did you stop me?"

She remembers it differently than I do, he thought. *She stopped herself.*

"But they're dead and I'm alive," she continued. "And somehow you're alive, too." She touched his throat. Her touch was cool and he leaned against her hand. "Please never do that again." Her hand lingered on his cheek. He kissed the inside of her wrist. She made a soft sound. He kissed her palm. She sat back and pulled her hand away.

"Soon," she said with a small smile. "Really soon. But not here—with them, and the smell."

"Of course." He felt foolish. "I am thoughtless."

"No, you're very brave. And you saved my life. It's just, I need to think about some things. Everything's been happening so fast. Almost killing that man. I would have done it. What does that make me? I don't think my family would recognize me. What happens when I get home? And—" she looked him in the eye. "I've met a man who shouldn't exist. A beautiful mythological creature. And I've developed… intense feelings for this person."

"Oh, do you mean me?" he said with a smile.

"You are the most interesting thing that's ever happened to me. But I have to figure out why I should have to be kidnapped—twice—and meet someone who isn't strictly human for things to finally strike me as 'interesting'. Shouldn't it take less drama to get my attention?"

"I had to leave my home, my family—such as they are—and someone who would almost certainly have spent her life with me had I allowed it, everything I ever knew. I knew there was something else. And I thought I might find it here. So I imagine either you weren't paying attention, which is possible, or more likely, you weren't as content as you supposed."

She considered this.

"You are very clever."

"Well, if I'm adding correctly, I'm almost a hundred years older than you. I've had time to think."

They scattered the ashes of the fire, and together they carried the sword and Barbara (she had to explain the name) to the river and threw them in. She insisted on keeping Beb's knife and had found its sheath, which she wore low on her waist over the brown dress.

"You might die again," she said, "and beside, this awful thing needs a belt."

They watched the weapons vanish into the water. She said she wanted to jump in as well, but it was too cold.

"It's unfair, the way you're perfectly clean," she said. "And your beard, that's gone, and yet somehow your hair is still there. There are plenty of women, and not a few men who'd like to know your secret." It wasn't only his scant beard that got burnt off when he changed form, the stink of blood and gore had been scorched away as well. It was like nothing had ever happened.

While she worked on getting only her head wet—she said the smell in her hair was making her feel ill—he dragged the three bodies well downstream and pushed them in. He was only sorry he couldn't kill them again. He thought perhaps Aelle would approve, but couldn't say for sure why.

***

They sat quietly together on the driver's bench of the cart. The campsite disappeared behind them and the road rolled forward. Moth finally said, "Intense feelings?"

She blushed and said, "It was your well-honed sense of outrage that finally tipped the scales."

"For me I believe it was the constant questions. All the questions. All the same questions, over and over."

"I got better answers from the horse," she laughed.

"Do you want to drive?" he asked, pretending to take offense. *I've never* pretended *to take offense before*, he marveled.

"No, no," she said. "You and this horse have forged a relationship so beautiful, I couldn't think of coming between you."

"Fine, then." He thought about the dead, the scattered ashes, and the river, washing it all clean. It seemed like a bad dream and a long time ago. "Let's finally get you to your sister."

She gave him a curious look.

"My what?"

Chapter 65

"Ach, she'll be the sweetest bride this parish has ever seen," smiled Mrs. Beedle.

"And high time the Duke was wed, there was talk he'd be a life-long bachelor, and him with his sparkling eyes and white teeth..." sighed the cook.

"Have you been in the brandy?" Mrs. Beedle asked suspiciously.

-The Claiming of the Duke, pg 203
Malloy Dos Capeheart, Little Gorda Press (out of print)

Mistra
100 years after the War of the Door, Mistran calendar
20 years later, Eriisai calendar
Road through the Great Forest

"My what?" Lelet repeated. Moth was staring at her with his eyes wide and hadn't appeared to have heard her. Then he dropped the leads and grabbed her by the arms.

"Your sister! It's your sister!"

"You said that," she said. She wriggled away and reached over him to pick up the leads. "Which one?" She cocked her head at him. "How do you know I have… did we talk about…?"

He shook his head, the string holding his hair back came loose and the dark mass flew in his face. He raked it back and repeated, "It's your sister! I can't believe it. How did this happen?"

"Moth." She pulled the horse to a stop and tucked his hair behind his ear. "Calm down and tell me. What about my sister?" Rather than calm down, he pulled her into an embrace and kissed her, then jumped down from the cart and began walking back and forth alongside it. She touched her lips. He'd been uncomfortably hot.

"I don't know how but it's gone." He looked up at her, perched on the edge of the driver's bench. "You must think I've gone simple in my wits all of a sudden." He broke out in a grin. "But it's gone. The rope, in my head, it's just gone. I'm free." He resumed pacing. "It must have been… of course, it must have been when they killed me. So they really did kill me. Strange." He glanced over at her, his eyes gleaming. "Being dead, I can’t recommend it. But I suppose I should be grateful…."

She watched his monologue with her arms folded. It had been amusing to watch right up until the ‘killed me’ part. "Whenever you’re ready."

"Oh, sorry. Of course." He reached up to help her to the ground, but as soon as he touched her, she snatched her arm away.

"Ow! Moth, you’re burning!" She pointed at him. His shirt was smoking.

His exuberance faded as quickly as it had begun. His smile vanished and she felt the air turn cool between them. "Did I hurt you? Let me see."

"No, it’s fine. Look, it’s not even pink."

He lifted her to the ground. "I’m so sorry, I didn’t realize."

He looks like someone hit him in the head with a shoe, she thought. "Take a breath. Everything is fine. Tell me what happened. Why are you grateful that you were dead?"

"Um. Let me see." He started pacing again. "When they killed me, it must have broken the binding spell. So now I can say it."

"Say what?"

He stopped pacing and faced her. "The binding spell was put on me by your sister Scilla at the Guardhouse, when she brought me here from the Veil. This was all her idea. To kidnap you. I’m to take you to see her."

Lelet stared at him for a moment. Tears were building behind her eyes. "You’re mad. Oh no, you’re a lunatic after all." She punched her fist against her palm. "Dammit! Why are all the pretty ones crazy?"

"You know perfectly well I am not a lunatic. Please don’t do that." She took a hitching breath. "There have been times you’ve asked me things and I couldn’t tell you."

"Yes," she said, "and I thought you were just being difficult and evasive." But she did recall the times he looked as if he was struggling to speak. Could this be true? "What in the world is a binding spell, and what does it have to do with my sister?"

He was silent for a long moment. They leaned against the cart. She was sorry she’d ruined his joyous mood, and hoped he had an answer that she could believe.

Finally he said, "I have a great deal to tell you, and you aren't going to like any of it."

***

"Tell me again. From the beginning," she said. Before he could try and figure out exactly where the beginning was, she continued. "Are you one hundred percent sure we're talking about Scilla? Because she isn't anything at all like you're telling me."

"I am sure. And she's very angry at you. I think she feels as if you've neglected her. And she thinks you're spoiled. And selfish. And, um, loose?"

"Oh, come on!" She glared up at him. "I think I know my own sister better than you. And I'm trying to imagine her somehow dragging another person through this Door you keep talking about, and basically making them her servant. She's barely more than a little girl, it's not possible."

"It's not 'another person' and it's not 'them', it was me." She looked away. "Why do you think I took you from that alley? Did you think it was my own idea?"

"No, it was Rane's. We talked about this. You said he was the one that got you to do this." Hadn't he? She struggled to recall. It seemed a long time ago, that night.

"No," he said. "No, you talked about it, you decided it was his doing, and I couldn't say anything at all. There's more, I'm afraid." He looked at the ground, his face grim. "Scilla made me go to your house."

"Well, obviously, that's where you threw me in this stupid cart." She looked at him, willing it not to get any worse.

"Before that. A long time before that. She had me create trouble between you and your brother."

She turned even paler. "You were in my house?" She took a step back. He said nothing, and didn't look as if he ever wanted to speak again. "It was you, wasn't it? The mirror. My things. Oh…" She put one hand over her mouth and thought for a moment. Then she looked down at her wrist, the one he'd burned, the one she'd broken. "My horse? Please, please, Moth, tell me you didn't."

"No, I didn't have anything to do with that. I was there, though. If your groom hadn't shown up, I would have carried you home myself. I'm sorry, but that really was Rane."

"At least he didn't get sent away for something you did." She pulled at her hair and walked back and forth. "Do you know, I was starting to think we had ghosts? So many strange things, and Rane swore it wasn't him, and I knew it wasn't me…" She stopped pacing and said, "The orchids. Of course." She shook her head and smiled, although she was the farthest thing from happy. "You have a way with them. Moth orchids, I really should have known."

"Why do you say that? Why did you call them that?"

"This is just one big learning experience for you, isn't it?" She sighed. "That's the name of the flowers in the glass house—moth orchids. You didn't know that, did you? Okay, well. Let's see. You read a book, came from Eriis to visit, and on the way my sister—who apparently now is a big time sorceress, put a spell on you and forced you to steal my stuff and break our things. And in your spare time you cultivate flowers. And then she made you kidnap me and bring me to see her at the Guardhouse. Why?"

"I'm not sure. She's said some things which make me think she is in contact with someone from my home. That's the other half of the story."

She snorted a laugh. "There's *more*?"

"I left home in a hurry. Because. Because I… It's not important." He turned away. "I just left. Forget it."

"I knew it, it wasn't that stupid book." She took his arm. "Tell me, Moth. How can it be worse than what's happened over the last few days? You *died*. What happened to you back there? Why did you really leave home? I know it wasn't because of some old book."

He shook her hand off. "*Rushta*, Lelet, leave it. Please, I don't want to talk about this." He tried to walk away but she followed him. "You know everything important. You are *filled in,* isn't that what humans call it?"

"*Rushta*, I know what that means by now. What was so bad?" She had to nearly run to catch up and get in front of him. She put her hands on his chest, "Would you stop walking away from me?"

He looked down at her hands, then back up at her. "You are a perfect person, you won't understand this."

Her heart twisted and she dropped her hands. "Try me, Moth. Please, make me understand."

"You were right and you didn't even know it. You were making a joke, and that's what my life is—a joke." He laughed bitterly. "I only had half a life, I was only half of everyone else, even though I was twice as big."

"You were different. You were special. Why?"

"Because I am half human. You see? Even you could tell there was something wrong with me. My father was a human person. I don't even know his name. That's why my mother can't stand to look at me. Oh, and a cripple, let's not forget that. And a drunk. I'm a famous drunk. The only reason I'm not drunk right now is because I finished the whiskey four days ago. So that's your prince, Lelet. A drunk, a cripple and a *scorping* shame."

He thinks I am going to laugh at him, or set him on fire, or walk away, she thought. She reached for his hand and traced a scar that ran the length of his thumb. "I figured. Everything you've told me about your home and your friends and how hard it was for you, it was pretty obvious something was different about you. But different doesn't have to mean worse, I think. And you're no joke to me. Far from it. Different and special, well, that's true enough." She paused. "Have you always known? About your father?"

He shook his head. "I found out literally just before I left home. I ran because my human blood has a value far beyond that of my own life. My friend—the smart one—saved me by sending me here. I can't go back until he tells me that it's safe."

"How long has it been since you've heard from him?"

He sighed. "It's been more than 3 months, and I haven't heard anything at all. Not one word. And I don't know how long it's been back home, time runs differently and I can't work it out. But the Mages—the ones who want me—if they are somehow working with your sister, I need to stay far away from there. I don't know what part she intends you to play in all this. Honestly, I don't know what she's got in mind at all." He moved a bit closer to her. "I know you must be very angry with me. But I hope you believe I would never intentionally hurt you. And now, it just feels so good to have this… rope… it felt like, untied from my mind."

"And you really couldn't tell me any of this? Until now?"

"There's only one way to break most spells, if you are without power yourself. It's usually a more permanent solution, though."

She chewed on her ragged fingernail. "You want me to think none of this is your fault. I think there are things you still aren't telling me." The way he looked at the ground and not at her told her she was correct. But she knew she'd find out eventually. And after what he'd confessed, how bad could it be? She had a feeling it had to do with the lady he'd left in the other world. She decided to let it go—for now. "But losing a pair of earrings or a hairbrush is nothing compared to what you've been through. I may be the selfish, spoiled monster my sister says I am, but I've never made anyone a slave. I still can't believe she did that to you. And when someone threatened my life, you were there. You came for me." She moved a little closer. "Are you really a prince?"

"Oh yes. In fact, not *a* prince, but *the*. Just me."

"Prince Moth," she smiled.

"Not exactly. But let's stay with it, if you don't mind. I like the way it sounds when you say it. But when it comes time for me to take the High Seat, I don't know what will happen."

"Because of the human thing?" she asked. "Or the drinking thing?"

"Because of a lot of things. I wasn't… I haven't been exactly leadership material. I spent most of my life trying to disappear. Still working on that one." He paused and looked down at her and she wondered what he saw; a dirty face, stupid hair, a perfect person. "In fact, I can only think of one thing in my whole life that I've wanted, that I got on my own without someone else whispering behind the scenes or working behind my back."

She smiled. "What did you want?"

He smiled back at her. He was free. "Don't you know?" And when he pulled her close and kissed her, this time there was no one to interrupt them.

It got quite warm.

Chapter 66

Gwenyth peered through her fine white lace at the chapel. Everyone was there, all waiting, looking back through the doors. She could still feel his touch like a burning brand against her breast. Would he bring her so close to her heart's true desire only to leave her here alone? The smell of the flowers was overwhelming, and she felt faint.
<remaining pages missing>

-The Claiming of the Duke, pg 218 (fragment)
Malloy Dos Capeheart, Little Gorda Press (out of print)

Mistra
100 years after the War of the Door, Mistran calendar
20 years later, Eriisai calendar
Road through the Great Forest

Eventually she laid her hand on his sleeve, and nodded towards back of the cart at her neatly folded blanket.

"Take that," she said. Then she looked again at the scrubby forest floor. "Better take both of them."

She led him through the trees towards the river, because she knew he liked the sound of the water and the sparkle of the light. Perhaps it would help to settle him, because she thought she could see nerves running alongside his anticipation. She felt he tended towards jumpiness.

Then she thought of his hands wreathed with smoke as he stepped out of the flames. He hadn't seemed nervous then.

She found a spot that was less rocky and grassier and had him lay the blankets down. He was watching her carefully and waiting for her cues. She nodded and he sat. She hiked her dress up around her knees and curled up in his lap. It was like sitting on the hearth of the fireplace in the front room back home, but warm and inviting, not dangerously hot as he'd been earlier.

"I have to tell you something," she said. "I lied to you. No, don't look like that. It's not like that. Listen. You remember how I told you that you were utterly average?"

"When it was raining. That wasn't true?"

"Not in the least bit." She took him by the shoulders as he tried to twist his face away from her. "I said you were perfectly ordinary looking, no one would look at you twice, that you might as well be invisible. That's a lie." She put her hand on his chest. Her hand was far larger and less delicate than the shadowy print underneath it. "You're beautiful. I can't *stop* looking at you. And you deserve to know. And if you weren't so fine to look at on the outside, it wouldn't matter at all because you're just as lovely on the inside. Every bit of you is beautiful. And this? Right now? This is where I have wanted to be since I met you, and I realized you weren't going to…."

"Cut off your toes?"

She raised a brow. "I was going to say since I understood that I was safe with you. Which was practically the whole time. You're not very menacing." And she thought again of the smell of cooked meat, and tried to put it aside.

"And how do I know you're not lying now?" he asked. But he was half-smiling and had his arms looped around her waist. She slid her hands under his shirt.

"I think you know I'm not. I wanted to touch you so much I practically had to sit on my hands. So that was me lying. You're so, so…" whatever he was, she never got around to telling him because she decided to kiss him instead.

He looked at her uncomfortably. "It occurs to me that I haven't exactly gotten around to telling you how pretty I think you are. And now it seems a bit late."

She laughed. "You can tell me now." She helped him unlace her dress and it fell to her waist.

"These, for instance, are exceptionally pretty." His hands looked even bigger against her small breasts, and they were wonderfully warm on her bare skin. His lips were just as warm. "They're so delicious, they're like… baby lamb chops."

She pressed her lips together hard. Finally she cleared her throat and said, "Baby lamb chops. What a lovely thing to say."

"Because baby lamb chops are practically the nicest things there are," he added.

"Yes, I know," she agreed. "They certainly are. And now I want to see you." She kissed him slowly. "You don't mind? If I look at you?" He did not. *He likes to look at me, too.* He watched as she unhooked the knife from the rough leather belt around her waist and laid it well aside. She had his shirt off in a moment, and swallowed her pain at seeing those scars again, but he didn't turn his face away or try to hide from her gaze. She let her hand fall between his legs and gave a gentle squeeze—it was far more than a handful and couldn't be very comfortable pressed up inside his clothing. She brushed her lips against his chest, and across his nipples, which had either grown back or somehow otherwise repaired themselves. Either way they were tender and new, and she held back her usual inclination, which was to use her teeth. Most men liked that, a little nip, but she feared hurting him and was mindful and gentle.

He likes this, she thought, based on the soft noise he made and how he moved under her mouth, *well, mostly they all do.* Then she paused. She looked up again at his molten eyes, his dark-golden skin, the great length of him. She thought briefly of the others, the Billahs and the grooms and barmen, the first name no last name, sometimes not even a first name, flirtations and flings and drunken nights and dirty mornings. She knew that was over. *'They.' There is no 'they.' There's no one like him, not on this world or any other.* She kissed him again, marveling at the softness of his skin, and leaned against him until he was on his back.

"Lift up," she said, and took his trousers by the waist and gave them a careful pull. "That must feel better, doesn't it?" And that was when she shrieked.

It wasn't much of a shriek, and it was muffled by her hand, but it got him bolt upright. "What!? What?" Then he saw what she was pointing at. He sank back onto his elbows.

"Please," he said. "Do not tell me you've never seen one of those before."

She was saucer eyed, and pushed her hair behind her ears as she leaned forward. "Not like that. It's got... you've got... did that *hurt*?"

He reached down and gave his *yala* a companionable tap, after which it continued its efforts to poke him in the stomach. "It didn't feel so good the first day, but after that? Works perfectly."

It was studded all around, from the crown down the length of the shaft, with small golden beads, at least a dozen. As it increased in girth and width, the pattern they formed changed.

"Is that for me?" she asked, fervently thanking the unseen forces that guided her days.

"I would prefer to say it's for both of us," he replied.

She put her chin in her hand. "Huh. Can I touch it?"

"Well, yes, obviously!"

At first she gave him a series of tentative pats, and poked at the beads, unsure of what exactly to do with them. But then she found some strength in her hand and he sighed with pleasure and leaned back and closed his eyes. Then she got an even better idea. He looked up to see her at work with her mouth and little pink tongue.

She glanced up. "I had better not chip a tooth." *Worth it.*

"*Shani*, this is better than pears, even, but better stop," he pleaded. "Or I'll finish before we've even begun." He sat up and pulled her towards him, and her dress fell from her waist to the ground. He paused and looked at her curiously, holding her at arm's length.

"Huh," he said.

"What's wrong?" She had a horrible thought involving demon women and what their privates might look like. Flowers? What if they *all* had penises, men and women both? What if her lack of jewelry below the waist was ugly to him?

"Nothing," he said, "it's just..." He cocked his head, looking more amused than alarmed.

She took another look at his body, and then back at her own. "You've never seen a person with hair on their body before, have you?"

"I... actually, no."

"Does it look weird? It does, it looks weird. I'm sorry." She bent to gather her dress, her face crimson, but he took her by the wrist and raised her back up.

"Don't do that," he said. "I imagine even Gwyneth probably had... whatever you call that." She laughed and nodded in agreement. "I just wasn't expecting it. Stand up. Let me see. There, it's fine. It's... I like it." He brushed her light brown curls with the back of his hand, and again, more slowly with his fingertips. "It's soft." He looked up at her, eyes bright. "What else do you have that's different? Can I look?"

Looking involved his mouth and his hands, and when she couldn't hold herself up with her hands on his shoulders any longer, he lowered her onto the blanket and continued his exploration. His long hair brushed her stomach and her thighs, and his mouth was so soft—but that wasn't it, she realized his face was just as smooth, not the slightest bit of a beard. That must be why men like this, she thought, it all feels like silk, all cool and hot together. Then he did something with his hand—was it inside her? Or outside? She couldn't tell, and she didn't care, it was enough to push her over to what he called finding her pleasure. When she could put a thought together again, she decided that was a very good name for it.

She sat up. "Now you. Please." She reached down to help guide him, and for once the heat of her body was greater than his. As he entered her, he said something, a word she didn't recognize, although maybe it wasn't a word at all. She began to understand what the golden beads were for and felt herself moving towards her pleasure again, and then realized he'd stopped.

He was looking down at her, utterly confused.

"Something is different," he said. "Something is missing."

He's a clever man, I know he is, and I hope I'm there to see it when he begins to understand his own mind. "What is it?" she asked gently. "What do you feel?"

"Nothing," he answered. The way he trembled in her arms told her that wasn't true. She twisted her hips and drew him deeper inside her. He groaned and rested his head on her shoulder.

"Really? You're feeling nothing?" she asked.

"Nothing," he said again. "Nothing… bad." He looked at her again with something like awe, and began to move against her. *I'll think about this later, and I might cry*, she told herself. *But not now*. She pulled him down on top of her. "No," he said, "I'm too heavy."

"You're not," she said. He was still holding back, he was still pulling away from her hands, not moving into them. "Darling, if you were ever to hurt me, I'd tell you at once." She wrapped her legs around his waist and arched her back. "And you're not." She smiled wickedly. "But you can try."

He finished with his mouth against her bright hair, his hands pinning hers to the blanket behind their heads, with the echo of her second wave still racing through both of their bodies. She felt as if fire was flowing between them, she could see it behind her eyes.

The sun in the trees created a pattern of light and dark that shifted and dappled across their skin.

"Can I ask you something?" she said after a while. He made a small sound of assent. "The thing that was missing… did you miss it?"

The pause before he answered was longer than she had anticipated. "It was different," he said. "It was like something else. Like the difference between walking and running."

"Were you walking, just now? Or were you running?"

She watched the sunlight moving across his closed eyelids. "I was flying."

Then she did cry, but only a little bit, and he didn't see it.

***

When they awoke, the shadows had already started to lengthen. The afternoon had come and gone, and she was talking about food. "Roasted game hen," she said, "with new potatoes in cream with dill. And fresh radishes on black bread with butter and salt. And ice cream for dessert."

"I got 'new' and 'salt' and 'ice'," he said. "The rest you'll have to show me."

"Leek and chestnut soup," she added. "And then coffee and brandy for after."

"Would you like me to go get the bag from the cart?" he asked.

"What a wonderful idea! I'm starving." He didn't bother with his clothing for the short walk, and she got to try and decide whether the view was better leaving or returning. Since he had their meal in his hands, returning ultimately got the vote, although it was an extremely close decision.

They'd found several links of sausage, both hard and greasy, along with some bread and a handful of dried fruit in the sword man's bag, and as they ate she promised him, "a real sit down meal," as she called it, "and as soon as possible. I'll even cook." She paused to gnaw on the fruit. "Maybe I'd better not."

"Where are we going to have this 'sit down' of… um, salt and… ice… things?" he asked.

She frowned and thought. "We could go back to Mistra, our cook will feed you until you can't move. Or my friend Althee is a brilliant cook, she'll love you. Or we could head the other way and visit our farms, out towards the mountains. Or just go until we see an inn, that's the easiest." Then she smiled. "You decide."

"I… don't know. Do I have to pick right now?" He had a look of stunned happiness about him and she knew it wasn't only from their lovemaking. "Lelet, you know I can't stay here forever. Eventually Ilaan will contact me. And I'll have to decide whether or not to answer him. There are people at home, I'm worried. Things may have changed a great deal. I don't know exactly how much time has gone by, or what I'll find when I get there."

She nodded. "And we have to deal with my sister."

"But not right now." He looked at her cautiously. "If that's all right."

She nodded. "I am a bit of an expert at putting off decisions. I think you'll enjoy it."

He tried to replace his sweetly dazed smile with a serious expression. "There is one thing I'd like you to show me, and I want to do that first."

"Oh, of course." She waited. What could it be? Dragons? Sailing ships? More horses?

"I want chocolate." She burst out laughing. "It's in my book—which by the way is not stupid—and it seems to be magical. Can you find it for me?"

"It is my new life's work." She wiped her fingers on the hem of the ugly dress and stretched and rose to her feet. She took his hand.

"Chocolate it shall be. And a dress that doesn't make me want to cry. And a shirt that fits you, too."

"What? I like this shirt."

"And shoes that I can walk in, and a hot bath—you'll like that in particular, I think…."

"Chocolate first," he reminded her.

"Absolutely!" she agreed. "One inn with a hot bath and chocolate, coming up."

They rolled up the blankets and threw the rinds of the bread—too hard even for the horse to bother with—into the trees. As they walked away from the little clearing, neither of them noticed a single slender curl of smoke rising from the brush only a few feet from where they'd lain. If it had been kindled even two days earlier it might have taken half the forest down with it, but after the rain, much of the underbrush was damp, and the bright spark soon sputtered and finally, with no hand to tend it, it went out.

Epilogue

Eriis
20 years after the War of the Door, Eriisai calendar
100 years later, Mistran calendar
Yuenne's family residence

Aelle let herself into Ilaan's tower room. Well, she reminded herself, it wasn't his room anymore. She looked around at the mess of books and clothing. He'd taken what he could carry away with him the night he left—the night everyone left—and Yuenne had made it clear he wasn't welcome to come back around for the rest. Siia had forbidden the maids from entering. *She still thinks she can mend this*, Aelle thought. *She can't.*

Ilaan working for the Queen. And Rhuun half a human. And the two of them conspiring together to open The Door. How did she not see it? What did she think they were doing all this time? She shook her head, she was just so stupid. Stupid and blind. She stood on a chair to look at the top of the bookcase, of course the book was gone. Something so precious to the Queen and to Rhuun—Ilaan wouldn't have left that prize behind. If she'd found it she would have torn it up, burned the pages, and tossed the ashes out the window. If she'd done that the day they'd found it, maybe Rhuun wouldn't have left. She took her favorite spot at the window and looked down at the city beyond the arch and wall. If she was quiet enough, she thought she could still hear people talking.

Daala had come for a visit and shown a sweet face to Siia, and her mother had let the woman practically drag her out to dinner.

"It's been over a week," Daala had said. "Starving yourself and hiding is helping no one. We'll have a nice dinner and talk about nice things."

"I am not hiding," she'd replied, but finally agreed to go out. She'd suspected Daala was just trying to get new tales to take away, but perhaps she was wrong. Her judgment was seriously in question, after all. As she'd taken her scarf from the hook by the door, her mother had been so relieved as to be comical. But it had been just as she feared. Hiding was better.

As she'd walked with Daala through the Old City she'd noticed the stares, and once they were seated it was even worse. As she ate (or tried to eat) she'd heard whispers. 'Human', she'd heard. '…behind her back…' and, 'Poor thing', she'd heard that, too.

Daala had stopped chattering about 'nice things' long enough to make a face. She'd loudly remarked, "A shame that some people have such dull lives." Then she'd leaned forward, unable to resist. "You knew, though, didn't you? I mean, you had to know."

"About what," Aelle had replied. "Which part? What would make a better story? That I knew, or that I didn't." She'd sipped her drink and pitched her voice louder. "What's the story people are telling? I must have known about Rhuun. I mean, look at him. Oh, you can't, he's gone through The Door to be with his beloved humans."

Daala had widened her eyes. "Aelle, be calm."

"Why? Don't you want to know? Don't you all?" She'd looked around the café. "Anyone have any questions?" Then she'd lifted her glass in Daala's direction. "I know you do. Anything to do with Rhuun, you're right there asking."

Daala gripped her *serviette* in both hands hard enough to show white at her knuckles. "You are making a scene," she'd whispered. "I was just trying to cheer you up."

"Oh, apologies, mustn't make a scene." She'd lifted her glass in a cheery salute to another diner, who quickly looked away.

Daala had made a sad face. "I don't know why you're angry at me, but if it makes you feel better, say what you like." She'd glanced at the other diners who were following their conversation with thinly veiled glee. "Shame on yourselves. Leave this poor girl alone. Light and Wind know she's been through enough."

It was funny, really, watching Daala twist herself in knots. She was desperate for Aelle to confide in her, but didn't want to appear too eager. Watching her admonish the other people in the café had been the first thing that cheered Aelle up since the night of Ilaan's party. She hadn't let Aelle leave until she'd sworn a solemn vow—if she needed anyone to talk to, ever, about anything (but about Rhuun especially and in particular) Daala would always be there for her.

Well, at least I was right about that one, Aelle consoled herself. *Wrong about everyone else, though.*

The worst part of it, the part she'd never confess to anyone, was that beyond her anger and humiliation, was relief. He wanted to leave, anyone with eyes could see that. He wanted to leave, and now he was gone. She could stop waiting.

She leaned against the window frame. The lights of the Quarter below her flickered as dust blew up and down the streets. She wondered if she was looking down on Ilaan, and if he was looking up at his old room. She wondered which one of the two of them would come home first.

The door to the tower room opened. "Niico," she said, and waved him over.

He sat next to her at the window. "Your father said you were up here." He peered at her. "You look terrible."

"Well, I haven't flung myself out of anything." She returned his gaze. "Did you know?"

He shook his head. "A lot of late nights and quiet conversations. I rather thought they were joining, but then I've thought that since school." He frowned. "It would have been better, maybe. Then we could just have a fight and get over it." At her expression, he laughed and added, "You're right, that's not better."

"Have you been to see him?" she asked. "I thought he might have sent you to check up on me."

He picked up a left-behind notebook, the pages full of scribbles in at least four languages. He flipped through it and set it aside. "I am capable of worrying about you without prompting, you know. Anyway, I wanted to talk to you about this new club I'm forming. We get together and share *rushta* about our terrible taste in partners."

That made her laugh. "I'm in." But then she turned serious. "You could see him, though, if you wanted to. He's down there." She pointed out at the city. "You don't need magic or books or blood to see Ilaan. Will you?"

Niico sighed. "He made his choice. I think he would have followed Rhuun through The Door if he could. You know how it is with them. We all follow behind."

That's not really an answer, she thought. *Magic and books. Love and blood.* Was any of it real? She could ask Niico, she could go down there and find her brother, or follow Rhuun through The Door. And her father, surely he'd have something to say. Everyone had something to say.

But she didn't want to hear any more lies, at least not tonight, and so she let it alone.

Acknowledgments

So many people. So many patient, kind, thoughtful people who read this book (and reread and reread it) and helped make it better. I owe you all a drink!

My team at Booktrope - Jennifer who gave me my first 'yes', Jesse, and Kellie--the Boss of Me.

My magical editor, Crimedog Carly.

My fellow Fictionistas, Cait, Daphne, Kenya, Sami-Jo and Genevieve.

Shari Ryan, who designed this beautiful cover.

My first editor, Debra Ginsberg who pointed me in the right direction.

My early reader Nazila Fatah, who taught me how to unpack.

Mike and Tony, Vanda, Kitten, Jacques, Lynda, Barbara and Dennis, Mira, Jasper and Sarah, who made sure I had pizza and bourbon.

From Sirius XM - My partner and sister Maggie, and Mindy, Kenny and Don

My Scones - Mark Says Hi, Dave Z, Jason S, Anabella, John, Chris, Quint and Paul

Fabulous inspirations - JT Ellison, Tasha Alexander, Kristy Claiborne Graves, David Baldacci, Karen Kondazian, Katherine Neville, Zac Brewer, Alma Katsu, Leslie Rossman, Rosanne Romanello, Scott Allie, Aub Driver and the gang at Dark Horse

Brothers and sisters - Michael Kennedy and

Matthew Roberts, and the Roberts clan who lent me their couch at Lake Rosemound when I really needed to get my mind right.

Eryc, the angel on one shoulder and Jaysen, the almost always nearly perfectly correct devil on the other.

Antigone Barton, it's been a pleasure.

My husband Dyon, for everything.

Rhuun and Lelet will return with more adventures in Mistra and Eriis in 2016. Until then, here's a peek at what's coming up:

"I want to talk to Ilaan," Rhuun said again. The great hall was full of people, a shifting sea of greys, whites, and tans, pausing in their errands to turn and watch. He recognized many of them. None would meet his eye, but he could feel their gazes following him. At least Lelet was safe. He'd think about that later. Right now he spotted a familiar face, and gave a sigh of relief.

"Aelle. Thank Light and Wind." She stopped on her way to wherever she was going and looked him up and down, taking in his dusty human clothing and tied back hair. Her white silk tunic was freshly pressed, her hair tightly coiled and intricately woven with white beads, brilliant against the black gloss. He could see a filigree of new tattoos in black and gold peeking out from under the cuffs of her wide sleeves and reaching towards her fingers. She had lined her eyes with green and gold, which made her look older and mysterious. Her hand was lightly resting on Niico's arm. "Aelle, I have so much to tell you ...."

She tipped her pretty head forward and spat on the ground at his feet, then turned towards Yuenne. "Father, I will see you at dinner." She glanced up at Niico, who was looking studiously at his nails, and they continued down the corridor.

"Burned that bridge, as the humans say," murmured Yuenne.

About the Author

Kim Alexander lives in Washington DC with a houseful of books, two cats, an angry fish, and a very patient husband. Find her online at kimalexanderonline.com, on Facebook at Kim Alexander Author, and on Twitter @KimAlexander80.

Made in the USA
Charleston, SC
08 August 2016